THE ONE GOOD THING

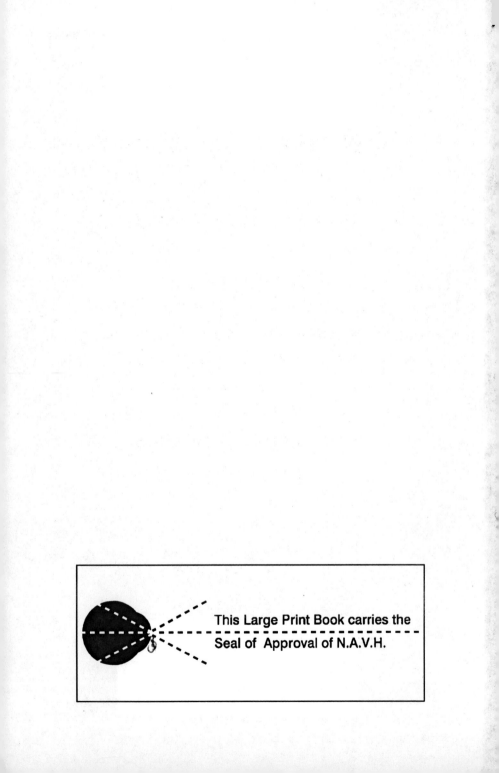

This Large Print Book carries the
Seal of Approval of N.A.V.H.

THE ONE GOOD THING

KEVIN ALAN MILNE

KENNEBEC LARGE PRINT
A part of Gale, Cengage Learning

GALE
CENGAGE Learning®

Detroit • New York • San Francisco • New Haven, Conn • Waterville, Maine • London

GALE
CENGAGE Learning

LIBRARY OF CONGRESS CATALOGING-IN-PUBLICATION DATA

Milne, Kevin Alan.
  The one good thing / by Kevin Alan Milne. — Large print edition.
    pages ; cm. — (Kennebec Large Print superior collection)
  ISBN-13: 978-1-4104-6191-9 (softcover)
  ISBN-10: 1-4104-6191-2 (softcover)
  1. Traffic accident victims—Fiction. 2. Family—Fiction. 3. Texas—Fiction. 4.
Domestic fiction. 5. Large type books. I. Title.
PS3613.I5919O54 2013b
813'.6—dc23   2013020195

Published in 2013 by arrangement with Center Street, a division of
Hachette Book Group, Inc.

Printed in the United States of America
1 2 3 4 5   17 16 15 14 13

*To my wife Rebecca, for
too many good things to count.*

"And, behold, one came and said
unto him, Good Master, what
good thing shall I do . . . ?"

— MATTHEW 19:16

PROLOGUE

Nathan

Is there a difference between being secretive and keeping a secret? I've always thought so. The former smacks of deception and deceit, while the latter is more about trust and confidences. Still, I doubt my wife would appreciate such semantics if she knew who I received an e-mail from today.

They say everything's big here in Texas. If my secret were the measuring stick, I guess I'd have to agree.

"Did you use all your pebbles today, dear?" Halley asks from the other side of our bedroom.

To anyone's ears but mine and my kids', that question would be nonsensical. "Yeah," I tell her as I undo my tie and the top button on my dress shirt. "But nothing really worth mentioning. Just a few small things here and there, but I did at least manage to get all of them from one pocket to the other, unlike yesterday."

I reach into my right pants pocket and pull out six tiny stones, each of them a slightly different shade of red. I cup them in the palm of my hand and shake them gently as I mentally rehearse the events of the day, then I drop them in a small dish on the dresser and continue getting ready for bed.

"Oh, c'mon," Halley prods. "Don't be so modest. You know I love to hear."

Yes, I know. And you know I love to tease. "What's it worth to you? A kiss?"

She gives a mocking laugh. "How about no kiss if you don't at least share the highlights."

"Fine," I say with a chuckle. "Let's see . . . I took Martin out to lunch and had a good talk with him. Did I tell you he lost his job last month? His wife is out of work too, so he's been pretty down. If nothing else, I think he really appreciated getting out of the house. I also gave him a couple of job leads, so hopefully something will pan out soon." I pause to pull my pajama top over my head.

Halley is putting on her pajamas too. "Keep going," she urges.

"Okay, umm . . . I gave the waitress a very healthy tip — probably too healthy, come to think of it. Her service wasn't all that great,

10

but she looked like she could use the money. Then there were some very minor things at work. An intern who failed the bar exam and needed some cheering up, a legal secretary who was having fits with her computer and needed assistance, little things like that. And lastly, I dropped off takeout at Dave and Theresa's on the way home."

"Oh, and here I thought you volunteered to get Chinese tonight just so I wouldn't have to cook."

"That can be number seven," I say, winking at her. "I really feel bad for Theresa, though. With her health being the way it is, I wish they'd let us do more."

I take a quick peek at my profile in the mirror. *Am I getting a gut?* I try to suck it in, but it won't go all the way. Probably too many hours sitting in the courtroom, too few hours in the gym. Oh well, there are more important things in life than one's physique. Halley approaches from behind and wraps her arms around my expanding waistline. "You're a good man, Nathan Steen. You and your funny little stones. The world needs more men like you."

"The world needs funny men with little stones?"

She lets go and pokes me in the side.

"That's not what I said."

With a quick tug I pull her back and give her a peck on the cheek. "Enough about me. How was your day? You were quiet at dinner."

"Was I? Well, maybe the kids had so much to tell you that I didn't want to interrupt."

"No, it was more than that. I can tell when something's on your mind. Did something happen at the store today?"

She lets out a long sigh and flops backward on the bed. "Am I that transparent?"

"After all these years, you're an open book to me. Let's hear it." She probably thinks I'm an open book too, and I guess I am. Only my book is missing some chapters that she doesn't know about.

"Well . . . there was this customer —"

"Oh, wait," I interrupt, "let me guess. Someone died and needed flowers for the funeral, and you became emotionally involved. Am I right?"

Halley picks up a small pillow near her head and hurls it at me, hitting me in the knee. "Not just anyone died. He was young and had kids. *Younger than you.* He had a heart attack, completely out of the blue. His poor wife doesn't have anyone to help her make the funeral arrangements, so she came in all by herself over lunch. Can you imag ine? She had to leave the kids at a baby-sitter just so she could come see me about a casket arrangement."

I pick up the pillow, walk it to the bed, and hand it back to Halley, then I lay down next to her on top of the comforter. For a second or two I don't say a word. I just stare at her in admiration. "Dare I ask if you gave her a discount?"

With a little giggle she says, "Fifty percent. She basically got everything below cost."

"Such a bleeding heart." Before she can object I add, "Which is what makes you so incredible. Probably too tender-hearted to be a successful florist, but I love you all the more for it." I bend down and give her another quick kiss.

"Isn't it sad, though? That poor family. All I could think of when she told me her story was that life is so fragile. What if you or I die, Nathan? What then? It makes me queasy just thinking about it. Speaking of which, when was the last time you had your blood pressure checked? Or a physical exam of any kind?"

"Are you calling me fat?"

She pokes me in the side again. "No, I'm calling you perfect, but I'd like a second opinion. Preferably from a doctor. I'm go-ing to call first thing tomorrow and make an appointment for you. I can't have you dying on me."

"Oh please, I'm as healthy as an ox. Anyway, when God says my time is up, my time is up."

"All the same, you're going in for a checkup. *Soon.* Whatever it takes to keep you around."

"For you, fine. But I promise, I'm not going anywhere."

Halley interlocks her hand with mine and squeezes it hard. "Good. Because without you, I'm not much of anything."

"That's not true, and you know it. But imagine me without you. I'd just be some crazy guy with a pocketful of rocks."

She closes her eyes and whispers, "You're a crazy guy with a pocketful of rocks with or without me, dear."

I laugh, but don't say anything in response. It's getting late and I'm tired. It's been a long day, and now it's time for the conversation to give way to a good night's sleep. She's right, though: I've been carrying the pebbles in my pockets since long before I met Halley, and if anything ever happens to her, I'll be carrying them long after she's gone.

Until the stones are smooth or the day I die. That's the promise I made, and sooner or later, I'm bound to make good on it.

Thinking about that promise, my thoughts rewind thirty-two years, pausing finally on a gangly, disheveled, and sometimes smelly outcast who was as smart as she was awkward: *Maddy McFadden,* the least-liked person in middle school.

Long ago, when we were still dating, I told Halley the basic story of why I'd been carrying those little rocks in my pockets every day since seventh grade. I'd feared that she wouldn't understand, or that she'd think me nuttier than a jar of cashews. Instead, thankfully, she found it endearing, in a quirky sort of way. I didn't tell her everything, though. I omitted some details that probably don't matter in the grand scheme of things, along with other details that probably matter a lot.

It's true what they say — *the devil is in the details.*

But if I told Halley about Maddy now? If she knew that Maddy still keeps in contact? If I told her what she e-mailed me about today? No, that wouldn't go over well. Anyway, there are things I can never tell. A promise is a promise.

Halley rolls over and drapes an arm over my chest, which jolts me back to the present. "You're staring at the ceiling, hon," she says. "What's on your mind?"

"Nothing," I reply. "Just thinking about how busy my day is tomorrow." I lean over and give her a final kiss good night, then I turn off the light on the nightstand and close my eyes.

There is a familiar sensation in the pit of my stomach as I start to drift off. It's the same feeling I always get when I pause to think about my past. As the feeling grows, I can almost hear my father — the pastor — preaching to me as a kid. "Honesty isn't just the best policy, Nathan, it's the *only* policy."

Is it? Is there no other policy? Is everything black-and-white like that, or are there sometimes instances where nobler motives justify certain shades of gray? I honestly don't know. Maybe my dad was right. Maybe that's why I never told him what happened. And maybe that's why my stomach still aches when I think about it, because the truth literally hurts. And the truth is that the best thing I ever did — the one good thing that really mattered — was a lie.

■ ■ ■ ■

PART I
STICKS AND
STONES . . .
AND STEENS

■ ■ ■ ■

CHAPTER ONE

Alice

Remember who you are.

Long before I crawl into the front seat of my dad's car, I know that he won't drop me off at school without also dropping that age-old advice. It's part of his fatherly routine — his *thing,* so to speak. He's offered those same parting words every single day before school for as long as I've been attending. If you're counting, which I am, that's precisely seven years, two months, and nineteen days.

Dad is a classic creature of habit. I love that about him — love that he is predictable; love that I can guess what he will do from one moment to the next; love that he has his little mantras that he lives by and that he won't let you forget, like "remember who you are," or "don't sweat the small stuff," or "we're all just rolling stones," and his personal favorite, "one good thing leads to another." That predictability fosters trust

— trust that I can depend on him when I'm sweating the small stuff, because talking through the small stuff helps me know that I can turn to him when I need help sorting through the *big stuff.*

Lately, my life has been nothing but big stuff. Or at least big to me, but then, I'm not that big of a girl, so maybe it's just a matter of perspective.

Size-wise, I'm thirteen going on nine, maybe ten. I'm easily the smallest girl in my class. I say "girl," because there's a boy in my grade who is smaller, but he and both of his parents are little people. I don't like to use the word "midget," because that's not PC, but because that's what he is, being small for him is apparently cool. For me? It makes me a target.

As Dad's car pulls into the school parking lot, I tilt my forehead against the cool glass of the window, staring at a group of kids with trench coats, nose rings, and their hair dyed the same jet black. Seeing them makes me wonder what new thrills seventh grade will present me with today. Every day there seems to be something. Drama, mostly, and cutting remarks. I already know which people I should avoid, but it won't matter because they'll probably find me anyway. They always do.

I still remember my first day of kindergarten. The giant yellow school bus rolled to a stop in front of our home as Mom made a final adjustment to my ponytail.

"There. You're a princess," she said. "And you're going to act like a princess at school, right?"

"Yes."

"Good. I'll be right here waiting when the bus comes home, okay?"

I nodded and gave her leg a pint-sized hug.

Then Dad stepped closer, all smiles, and said the magic words. "Alice, you're going to do great things, I can tell. Just remember who you are." He paused, then asked, "Who are you?"

"I'm Alice, silly," I told him with a giggle.

He smiled all the more, then bent and gave me a kiss on the forehead. "Yes, sweet thing. You're Alice. But you're also much more than that."

"Alice *Steen*?"

"Even more than that, pumpkin. But the bus driver is waiting, so we'll talk about it later. Now you go have fun at school and be the best Alice Steen you can be."

We did talk later. Multiple times in fact, but it was several years before we had a conversation that finally stuck. We were running late that day on account of my older brother, Ty, not being able to find a clean pair of underwear, so Dad offered to drop us off at school on his way to work.

"Hey Ty," Dad said as he prepared to get out of the car in front of the middle school.

"I know," Ty droned. *"Remember who you are."*

"Exactly. Remember who you are."

I half expected my brother to come up with one of his usual flippant, teenage remarks, but instead he just smiled and said, "I will, Dad."

Once Ty was gone I scrambled over the seat to sit up front the rest of the way to the elementary school. "Dad? Tell me again what you mean when you say that."

Dad's mind was already on something else. "When I say what, hon?"

" 'Remember who you are.' "

"Ah. Well . . . who are you?"

"You know who I am."

"I know I do. But do you?"

"Yes."

He glanced down at me while we sat waiting for a group of kids to cross an intersection. "Then tell me."

"Well . . ." I replied thoughtfully. "I'm Alice. I'm a third-grader. I like to dance and draw. I'm your only daughter. And I'm your smartest and *favoritest* child."

He let out a little chuckle. "You're on the right track, Al. Anything else?"

"I dunno . . . I'm pretty?"

"Of course you are. But this is about much more than that. You see, it's not just a matter of who you are right now, but how knowing who you are can help you become who you want to be later on."

"I wanna be rich," I stated matter-of-factly.

He rolled his eyes at me, but they were still twinkling. His eyes always have a little twinkle in them when he talks to me, like he's happy about what he's looking at. "Waaaay off target, sweetie. Listen, you said it yourself, you're my only daughter, right? Mine and Mommy's. What does that mean?"

"That you guys should have another baby."

"Not even close. Try again."

"Uh . . . I dunno. That I kinda look like you guys?"

"More like your mom, I hope. But you're getting warmer. Not only do you *kinda look* like us, you *are* like us, in more ways than you know. There is a part of us inside of you. You are our daughter, which means you have . . . ?"

"Cold sores? Mom says if I get them when

I'm older, it's because of you."

Dad shook his head and laughed. "Maybe you really are my smartest and *favoritest* child. But I meant *potential,* Al. Not that you're not great already, but if you try real hard, you can be even better. And I don't mean you should try to be just like me. That'd be aiming low. Inside you is an infinite ability to do good, so when I say 'remember who you are,' what I mean is to not forget how much potential you have, and then do your very best to live up to that each and every day." He paused briefly, then added, "Does that make any sense to you?"

By then we were nearly at the elementary school. "Yeah, I think so," I told him. "Thanks, Dad."

Thirty seconds later we pulled to a complete stop along the curb in the drop-off area, but I wasn't quite ready to get out. "Dad? Did you want to be like your dad when you were younger?"

The smile on his face faded a little. "I did." He hesitated just a second, like he was thinking of something long forgotten. "Did you know he used to tell me the very same thing before school? *'Remember who you are, Nathan. And make us proud.'* "

"And?"

"What?"

"Did you? Make him proud?"

He sighed through his nose. "Most of the time, sweetie."

"How come we hardly ever get to see him?" Me and Ty, and sometimes even my mom, had been asking that question for years.

"Grandpa Steen is a busy man."

"That's what you always say."

"And it's always the truth. A pastor's job is twenty-four-seven. Now, it's time for you to get going. Have a great day, pumpkin."

"And?" I coaxed.

He smiled again and ruffled my hair. "And remember who you are."

"I will, Daddy. Love you."

"You okay?" Dad asks as the car pulls up in front of the middle school.

I pull my head out of third-grade memories and look at him. "I'm fine. Just looking forward to another day in my glamorous seventh-grade life."

"Anything I can do to help?"

"Homeschool me?"

"Anything besides that?"

"Nah. I'll survive. I always do."

His mouth curls into a little frown. "Should I talk to the principal again? There's got to be something he can do."

25

"No!" I snap. "The last time you talked to him, kids who got in trouble found out what you said, and it only made things worse for me. I just need to get through this on my own."

For several seconds he stares at me, then his frown slowly bends upward. "Do you know how proud I am of you?"

I roll my eyes, just a little. "I gotta go. The bell is gonna ring."

"All right. I'll see you tonight, after Ty's game. Love you, Al."

"I love you, too." I climb out of the car and start walking away. But something doesn't feel right. I pause after a few steps and turn around.

Dad is already rolling down his window. "Alice . . ."

"I know, Dad."

He yells it anyway. "Remember who you are!"

What a goofball. Some eighth-graders are watching, and I'm sure I'm turning red, but I can't help but smile. "I will."

When Dad is gone, my smile dissolves. It's been forever since I've wanted to smile at school. Okay, so it's only been a little over a year, but it feels like a stinking eternity. Last year, near the start of sixth grade, Ashley Simmons — my next-door neighbor, former best friend, and the girl every boy dreams of kissing — decided I wasn't good for her image. You know how it is. I'm short and smart, she's tall and pretty, and I think she finally concluded that she couldn't float in the cool crowd with me as an anchor. I mean, she didn't come right out and say it or anything, that's just my hypothesis. Rather than just saying she didn't like me anymore or didn't want to hang out, she started ignoring me, which, in my opinion, is way worse. That, alone, would have been fine. But during PE one day, when we were changing into our gym clothes, she took it a step further.

"Oh! My! Gosh!" Ashley shouted. "Alice, isn't that the training bra you picked out in fifth grade?"

I froze. "What . . . ? Oh . . . no. I mean . . . I don't think so."

"Yes, don't you remember? I was with you when your mom helped you pick it out." She let out a cackle that reminded me of a witch. "You thought the ladybugs were so cool." Without looking down, I knew that there were ladybugs on my chest. I tried to ignore her as I pulled my school-issue T-shirt over my head, but Ashley wasn't done. "What size are you anyway, A negative?"

"She belongs in grade school," one of her new friends said.

"Yeah," said another, "until she grows up."

"Maybe she needs a magic cookie to help her grow," Ashley said with a giggle. "Like Alice in Wonderland." When she realized what she'd just said, she started laughing her brains out. "Alice in Wonderland! We've got our very own little Alice in Wonderland!"

The other girls started repeating it, between fits of giddy hysteria.

I didn't think it was all that funny, or even clever, but it didn't matter. The cool kids were laughing themselves silly, which meant I was in trouble. Sure enough, by lunchtime I had a new nickname. People I'd never even spoken to before were stopping me in the halls saying things like, "You must be Alice in Wonderland — I can tell because you look lost." And of course, "Hey little girl, where's your Cheshire cat?" One boy even asked if he could see my little ladybugs.

The next day I was standing at my locker, waiting for the morning bell to ring, when I saw Ashley coming down the hallway, tailed closely by a pack of her new gal-pals. "Here, Alice," she said sweetly. "I made this for you." She was holding a small paper plate covered with tinfoil. When I peeled back the aluminum, there was a single cookie in the center of the plate, with frosting letters that spelled *Eat Me!*

Since then I've become a perpetual joke. It's amazing the things kids will say when teachers aren't listening. Oh, and of course I get a magic Eat Me cookie about once a month from some new bully who wants to keep the laughs going.

But I still have to go to school. So, with a long breath, I square my shoulders and push through the front doors to face another day. Thankfully, it's Friday. If I can just bear the next eight hours, then I'll have all weekend to lick my wounds, cry on my parents' shoulders, and prepare for next week.

"Hey, looking for the White Rabbit?" someone calls as I'm walking down the hall. Then, "Are you lost, little girl? The elementary school is down the street."

Just remember who you are, I tell myself as I continue walking, *and everything will be okay.*

I have a knack for being right about things. I'm just smart that way. But this time, I'm wrong. Everything will *not* be okay. By the end of the day the social injustices of seventh grade will be nothing more than a tiny blip on the radar of my concerns.

Dad is right: I shouldn't sweat the small

stuff. Heck, I shouldn't even sweat the big stuff. I should save all my sweat to form tears when the gigantic stuff comes and shatters the world.

CHAPTER TWO

Ty

The senior table, as it's called, sits in a spot that's elevated slightly above the rest of the tables in the cafeteria. Not a lot higher — only three feet or so — but high enough that we who have earned the right to sit there can easily see everything going on at the underclassmen tables.

"Dude, I think that group of freshman chicks is checking us out," says Dillon.

Dillon always thinks girls are looking at him. They rarely are. I don't even know which girls he's talking about, but it doesn't matter. "Maybe you should go get their numbers," I deadpan.

"Ya think?"

"No, Dill. They're *freshmen.*" Dillon doesn't let many people call him Dill, because it's too easy a jump from there to Dill-weed, his unofficial moniker back in eighth grade. But he lets me, because I've always called him that, and we've been friends forever.

"Yeah, but they're hot."

I finally bother following his gaze. Okay, so he has a point — a couple of them are cute. And they do seem to be watching us. When they see they've got my attention, they start to giggle. Then one of them waves.

"Dude, she waved at me!"

I don't have the heart to tell Dillon she wasn't waving at him. I don't remember the girl's name — Angie? Angela? Agnes? — but I recognize her, and I can tell she recognizes me. Earlier this week she tripped going up the stairs between classes, so I stopped to help her pick up her things.

Once she got over the embarrassment of tripping, she asked, "You're the quarterback, right? Ty Steen."

"That's me."

Yeah, that's me. That's what people know me for — being the quarterback. Not for getting good grades. Not for being a good guy. Just for being a good quarterback, and even then they're only happy when I win.

Once she was sure who she was talking to, she got embarrassed all over again, even more than she'd been from tripping in front of everybody. "Thanks for helping." She paused, glanced at me. "Why did you?"

Angelica. Yeah, that's her name. Angelica's question was interesting to me, and not in a good way. Well, not the question so much as not having a decent answer. The only thing I could think of was, "because it's what my dad would do," which would have sounded totally lame, so instead I simply said, "Why not?" Then I handed her the stack of papers I'd gathered and walked off.

But since then I keep thinking about that question. *Why did I stop to help?*

"You should wave back," I tell Dillon.

"Ya think?"

"No, Dill. They're still freshmen." I pause to look around at the crowded cafeteria. It's kind of like looking at my mom's patch of wildflowers behind the house — if you just gloss over it from a distance, everything is picture-perfect. But if you focus on the details, you soon start to notice weeds cropping up here and there, or flowers that appear broken or out of place.

I narrow my gaze.

At a table to my right a kid is sitting all alone; his demeanor is almost like he doesn't want to be noticed by anybody. At the table next to him, a boy named Marshal, whom I happen to know because he's one of only two sophomores who starts on the varsity football team, is teasing a much smaller boy about his cowboy hat. Marshal finally swipes the hat right off the kid's head and tosses it to a girl a few seats down, who quickly tosses it to another boy who puts it on his own head and runs off and stuffs it in a garbage can. The hat's owner looks like he wants to cry. All the way on the other side of the cafeteria I see a girl with pink hair flipping the bird to a small collection of cheerleaders who have obviously said something to get her riled. And in the middle of the lunchtime gathering I spot a boy from my Physics class — Mark something or other — harmlessly punching numbers into his calculator, until some jerk in a Che Guevara T-shirt walks by and fists him in the back of the head for no apparent reason. Mark pretends nothing happened until the assailant is gone, then he rubs the back of his head and winces in pain.

Weeds and broken flowers. The cafeteria is crawling with them.

"Why so quiet all of a sudden?" Dillon asks.

"Just thinking."

" 'Bout what?"

Good question. I'm not even sure I know what I'm thinking, and even if I do, there's no good way to explain it to Dill, because he has no idea what it's like to be Nathan

Steen's son. So I ask a question instead. "You think that if I loaded my fries up with ketchup and launched them at someone, it would start a food fight?"

"Dude, don't even think about it."

"Why not?"

"Because you could get suspended! And we need you at the game tonight."

"So. We have a backup. Jim's been on fire in practice lately."

"But he's not you, Ty."

"But maybe he —. Forget it."

"No. What?"

Now I wish I hadn't opened my big mouth.

"C'mon," he prods. "Spill."

I can tell Dillon's not going to give up until I give him a satisfactory answer, so I toss him something to chew on. Not the whole skeleton, just a bone. "Well, I was just thinking, what if Jim wants to be the starting quarterback more than me? What if my heart's not really in it?"

"Shut up, dude. You're scaring me."

"I'm serious, Dill. Maybe the team would be better off without me."

"Get out of here. I don't care what anyone says, you're the only reason we're in the hunt for a league title. Not to dis the rest of us, but without you our post season is hosed."

Dillon doesn't know it, but he's just hit the nail on the head. Somehow he managed to articulate the very thing that's been eating at me since my stupid little conversation with — what's her name again? Angelica. I know high school football and helping a random girl in the hallway are completely unrelated, but in a strange way they're totally the same. If I fall short of perfection on the gridiron, the team loses and I'll know I've let everyone down. Helping the girl is more complicated, but no less stressful, on account of my dad, who just happens to be the world's nicest guy. No, seriously, he's like the Mother Teresa of Mesquite, Texas — or like Father Teresa, I guess. It's his life mission or something to help everyone he possibly can. Friends, neighbors, acquaintances, strangers on the street, people who don't even like him — he helps them all every chance he gets. And the older I get, the more I realize that he wants me to carry the torch.

But I don't think I can.

I can't live up to his perfection, because I know if I fall short — which I will — that I'm somehow letting him down. Sure, I helped one clumsy freshman on the stairs, but did I do it because I really wanted to, or because I was afraid of letting down my dad if I didn't?

Am I making sense?

So what if I stopped to help this one time? Does it really matter? Nope. It doesn't change the fact that everywhere I look around the cafeteria there are more kids than I can count that could use a hand — like the boy who's fishing his crumpled cowboy hat from the trash, or Mark, who's still smarting from being punched in the head. But there's no way I can help them all, so why should I help any of them?

"Maybe," I mumble to myself, "instead of worrying about all the broken flowers, it would be easier to be a weed."

All Dillon hears is the final word. "Weed!" he says sharply. "Ty . . . dude . . . don't even think about it. That'll get you kicked off the team for sure."

His comment makes me laugh, and somehow pulls me temporarily out of my self-reflection. "Not that kind of weed."

Right then the phone in my pocket starts to vibrate. It's a lengthy text message from none other than Father Teresa. *Hey Ty. I probably won't see you before kickoff, so I just wanted to wish you good luck tonight. I know it's a big game. You're going to do great!*

Score one for me, okay? But win or lose, you make me so proud. — Dad.

"Is that from a girl?" Dillon asks.

"Yeah," I say as I stand up and head off to put my lunch tray away. "A really hot one. And she's asking about you."

He quickly grabs his things and follows. "Seriously?"

"No, Dill."

"Dang. Who was it, then?"

"Just my dad."

Yeah. Just my dad. Just my thoughtful, caring, helpful dad, being his perfect self.

Seriously, I don't mean to sound ungrateful. I know I'm lucky to have a dad like him. Dillon doesn't even know who his dad is.

Then again, Dillon doesn't have anyone to be compared to. No expectations. No shoes to fill. No giant shadows of perfection dimming everything he does.

CHAPTER THREE

Halley

They say, in life, you should stop to smell the roses. For me, that's never a problem, because my life is all about the roses — buying them, cutting them, arranging them, and selling them. Ask yourself: Is there any place in the world that smells better than a flower shop? Maybe a Laundromat, on a good day, but who dreams of owning one of those?

I take a deep breath of the fragrance that surrounds me for the hundredth time today and then remember that I'm actually in a hurry. It's Friday, which means I need to close up Velvet Petals right at five thirty so I can make my evening deliveries and still get to Ty's game.

I run through a mental checklist of things that absolutely must be done every Friday before I close up shop.

Turn off neon Open sign? Check.

Take cut stems to the outside trash? Check.

Fax in an order to my supplier for the next week's fresh deliveries? Check.

Lock up cash register? Check.

Thank God above for a husband who put a down payment on my dream business rather than buying himself a new car? Check, check, and triple check. *I love that man!*

I actually turned off the neon Open sign fifteen minutes ahead of time to dissuade would-be patrons from stopping by. If not for one of my regulars — Mary Lou, an old woman who buys a single carnation every single week — I might have turned it off even earlier. Unfortunately, customers who order by phone can't see my neon sign. So of course, at 5:28 p.m., with everything else in the store prepped for the weekend, the phone rings.

And rings.

And rings.

And at 5:29 I make the mistake of answering. "Velvet Petals," I say politely. "This is Halley. Can I help you?"

"Are you still open?" asks a somber voice on the other end.

"Technically, yes. But we close in about sixty seconds."

There is no immediate response. Then a very languished, "I see."

I hesitate, checking my watch. At this hour I should know better than to stick my nose into other people's lives, but I can't help myself. "You sound a little down. Is everything okay?"

It's no secret that I enjoy probing customers for details. Sometimes their responses make me laugh, other times they make me cry, but they almost always remind me of how important my work is in other people's lives. In the three years since opening the store I've heard everything from "I need seventy roses that are as radiant and lovely as my wife of seventy years," to "If you can't deliver something — anything — in the next thirty minutes, I might as well write up the divorce papers myself." The fact that my floral creations play some small part in conveying love from one person to another is what keeps me coming back each day.

"It's . . . nothing. If you're closed, you're closed."

I'd love to let him hang up, but something in his voice says this man needs my floral help. "Well, hold on there just a second," I tell him before he puts down the phone. "Yes, we're almost closed, but my store hours are kind of like spandex shorts on a fat rear — if there's a genuine need, they can probably be stretched to fit."

The man's voice perks up a bit. "Um, okay. Thank you, ma'am. Then, is there any chance you have calla lilies in stock? Everyone else seems to be out. My daughter's name is Lily, so naturally they're her favorite. She's . . . well, she's over there at the children's hospital — been there a few weeks, actually — and we just found out they aren't going to be able to operate again." There is another long pause. It's a pause I'm all too familiar with: the blaring silence of someone struggling to keep their composure. "They're sending her home . . . so she can be in her own surroundings when she passes."

Sometimes I could kick myself for being so nosey.

Then again, sometimes people need to talk, you know? So maybe my nosiness isn't such a bad thing. In my line of work, maybe people even expect a little nosiness. It's not always easy, but I'm learning to accept that good and bad things happen to people every day. It's unavoidable. Each time I pick up the phone, I know that instead of budding, passionate, or lifelong love, which I absolutely love hearing about, the floral need might very well be tragic in nature — sickness, sorrow, and even death. I don't enjoy hearing about those last ones, but it comes with the territory. "How old?" I ask gently.

"Ten."

Now I want to cry. Nathan's right, I'm a bleeding heart. "How many do you need? I have a few other deliveries anyway, so it won't be a problem. I can get them to you in half an hour anywhere in the city, depending on traffic."

After a moment of reflection, the man settles on eleven, hoping there's enough magic in that number to see his daughter through to her next birthday.

I lock the front door of the store and begin assembling a tall bouquet of fresh white lilies, offset with tufts of bright purple lavender. He's not paying for the lavender, but I don't care; it looks good, and his daughter deserves it. When I'm done, I hold it out in front of me to admire my handiwork, then pull it close to breathe in the aroma.

That's when the phone rings again.

On the off chance that it's the father calling back about Lily's lilies, I pick up.

It's not him. I have to ask, "This is who?" after a few seconds, just to be sure I heard correctly.

"Ma'am, this is RayLynn Harper, from

Metro Police. Am I speaking to Holly Steen?"

"Halley," I reply.

"Oh, I do apologize, Halley."

"I'm in a bit of a hurry actually. Are you calling for donations, because I'm sure my husband already gave to the Bureau this year."

"No, ma'am, I'm not." There's something in her voice that has me suddenly on edge. There is an extended pause — too long for a telemarketing pitch. Then, "Actually, it's about your husband that I'm calling." She pauses again. "There was an accident this afternoon out on the highway."

Have you ever felt your own heart skip a beat? Me neither, until now. "And?"

"And . . . well, I don't have a lot of details yet. But I'm afraid Mr. Steen was involved. We're going to need you to come down to the hospital as soon as you're able."

I don't remember dropping the vase, but after not breathing for several seconds I look down and find that I'm standing in the middle of broken glass, water, white lilies, and lavender. "Is he okay?"

She doesn't say anything. Did I just ask a question? I mean, that wasn't in my head, was it? I actually said the words into the phone. So why isn't this woman answering?!

Finally, in a drawl that seems to be laid on extra thick — maybe to soften the blow — the woman says, "Ma'am, I am *truly* sorry 'bout this, but I'm afraid your husband didn't survive the accident. He was just in the wrong place at the wrong time. An officer will meet you there. There are things we need to go over with you . . ."

Miss RayLynn Harper is still saying something, of that I'm sure. But I can't make out the words. Can't focus. My head is swimming, my thoughts drowning.

Wrong place, wrong time? Nathan's gone? Didn't survive?

I slump down on the floor, vaguely recollecting that there are shards of glass everywhere, but not really caring. Cut me, make me bleed, doesn't matter. My life, like the vase, just shattered.

I don't really remember getting in the car or driving. The last place I wanted to be is at the hospital, but those were my instructions. I should have been delivering flowers to some ten-year-old girl whose chances of living are dwindling, not staring over the broken body of my already-dead husband.

"You can confirm this is Nathan Steen?" asks a man who works with the coroner's office.

I can't take my eyes off Nathan's face. His chest, arms, and legs are in terrible shape, but his face seems so perfect, like he's sleeping peacefully. *Of course it's him,* I think. *Who else could this be? And why did they have to bring me in here to confirm it anyway? Wasn't it his car at the scene? Couldn't they run the plates? Didn't they pull his driver's license from his wallet and look at the photo?*

I give a little nod. "Yes," I say, choking on the word. "It's him."

A social worker at the hospital has some paperwork for me after they wheel Nathan's body away. During our discussion she explains that identifying the body is as much for the family of the deceased as it is for the coroner's records — helps start the process of closure, she says.

Closure?

Does she not understand who was lying on that gurney? That was Nathan Steen! That was my husband! My best friend! The world can't lose someone like that and ever expect there to be closure.

"Mrs. Steen," she says as I sign the last of her forms. "I know this has been an awful day for you. Are you able to get home okay, or should I arrange a ride?"

"I'm fine," I say. "Yes . . . I think I can make it home."

Chapter Four

Alice

I used to pretend that I enjoyed football. Maybe I did enjoy watching Ty make great plays, and hearing everyone cheer for him, and seeing how excited Mom and Dad got every time he threw a touchdown or evaded a tackle, but the rest of it bored me to death. I guess I'm not really a sports person. Mentally, it's just not all that stimulating. Plus, there are people at those games. People who I don't especially like. Seventh-graders, specifically.

I used to go to the games all the time. Now, Friday nights are "me time." Me, myself, and I, alone at the house. Free to watch, read, or do whatever I please. Last Friday I reread *Anne of Green Gables* for the fourth time. The week before that I memorized the first eighty-two elements of the periodic table, including all of the lanthanides. The Friday before that I put on one of my mom's bras and tried to calculate how many decades it would be before I fit into something like that.

Anyway, if it weren't for mean people, I'd probably still be going to the games with my parents. The last one I attended was the season opener, at the end of August. After our team won, rather than leaving with my parents I hung around the stadium to hitch a ride home with Ty. I figured, hey, if I'm spotted with the star of the team, maybe people will treat me differently.

What a mistake that turned out to be.

While I was waiting for him to change out of his uniform, Ashley saw me standing there and sent Bridgette, one of her poufy-haired friends, to dump a soggy hot-dog bun — loaded with ketchup, mustard, and relish — in my hoodie when I wasn't look-ing. But that wasn't the worst of it. What really hurt was when I turned around to see who'd done it, Ty was walking toward me, just twenty paces away. I knew he'd seen what happened, but he didn't do anything to stop it! A bunch of kids were laughing off to the side, and my own brother acted like it was no big deal. When he got to where I was, he was so embarrassed by me that he didn't bother stopping to help me clean up; he just kept walking without even slowing down. When he passed by, he mumbled, "Sucks to be you."

Sucks to be me? *No kidding!*

The stains on my sweatshirt eventually came out. The marks on my self-esteem, however, along with the utter disappointment in my brother for allowing such a thing to happen, won't fade so easily.

So rather than watching my jerk of a brother getting cheered by thousands of adoring fans, I'm glued to a show on the History Channel about ancient Mayan civilizations. The narrator is explaining why the Mesoamericans sacrificed humans to their gods, when I hear a car in the driveway. I don't look up when Mom walks into the room. There's a gruesome-looking stone altar on the screen, but I'm not so into it that I don't realize she's home really early. While still staring at the screen, I ask her why she isn't watching Ty's game.

"Alice," she says. "We need to talk."

"Later? They're about to reenact cutting out a woman's heart."

"Let me tell you how that feels."

It's a weird thing for her to say, and her voice sounds strange. I look up to find Mom is fighting back tears. "Mom? Are you okay?"

She shakes her head, then falls into the

cushions of the couch next to me and wraps me up tightly in her arms.

I'm shaking. I don't know if it's coming from my body or hers, but I'm definitely shaking. I think it's mine, because all of a sudden I feel this overwhelming anxiety. This is *not* the way that Friday nights are supposed to go down.

What's going on? Mom doesn't miss Ty's games. She's not known to cry for nothing. And it's certainly not her norm to flop on the couch and hug me like she's holding on for dear life.

"Alice, honey . . . I have some very sad news to share." I take a long breath. Mom's dad, out in Ohio, has had poor health for a couple of years now. I prepare myself to hear that his aged body has finally failed. Only she starts again with, "Your dad . . ."

Instantly the shakes are gone — my body is now rigid. This isn't about Grandpa Giles? *"Dad!"* I spit out. "What about Dad?"

"Al," she continues, wiping at the river of water flowing down her face, "your father passed away today in a car accident. There's no way to sugarcoat it, honey, so I won't even try. He's gone."

I want to scream, to lash out at somebody, but Mom has me wrapped up too tight to do much of anything. Instead, I melt into a puddle in her arms and we both cry until all the tears are gone.

CHAPTER FIVE

Ty

If someone were dumb enough to stare up at the stadium lights for more than a couple of blinks, would that be enough to blind them? This is the largest high school stadium in Texas . . . there's got to be enough watts up there to do some damage, right? I don't even need permanent loss of vision. Just a minute or two of impairment would suffice.

That's what I'm thinking as I'm marching down the field, trying to salvage the game. I wish the defense would just look up at the lights for a second or two to blur their sight. Aren't linebackers dumb enough for that?

The newspapers say I'm the heart and soul of the mighty Mesquite football team, but I'm not so sure. All of the guys out here give everything they've got every time we suit up. I just happen to be the senior captain and starting quarterback, so I'm an easy story for local journalists — the unflappable hero when we win, the inglorious scapegoat when we lose.

Unfortunately, tonight we are. Losing, that is. On our home field no less, against North Mesquite, our biggest rival. You name an appendage and I'd gladly give it up for a come-from-behind win. Not so much for myself, but for my team. And for the fans who showed up tonight expecting me to deliver. And for my dad. I know his text said he's proud either way, but I've seen the twinkle in his eye when I do well.

I take a quick peek to the corner of the end zone where he likes to sit with my mom. Usually I can pick him out in a crowd, but tonight I haven't been able to spot him.

There's only a minute to go in the fourth quarter. We're trailing by three, but we've scored fourteen unanswered points, and with the ball on the eighteen-yard line, we're quickly closing in on the go-ahead touchdown.

"This game is ours!" I shout at my teammates in the huddle. "We own them! Let's keep 'em guessing with another play-action fake. Their safety is overprotecting the middle, so I want you receivers to go straight at 'em like you're running a post route, then cut hard to the corners. That's where I'll find you. Everyone else run the same play we just ran, but option left on three." I zero in on the linemen, hoping they understand how important they are to what we are about to do. "You guys hold your blocks long enough for me to get the pass off and we'll have six points. Got it?"

Dillon, who plays tight end, clears his throat to speak. I usually don't like a lot of extra chatter in the huddle, but he's a co-captain, so he's earned it. Still, I cross my fingers that he has something more inspiring to say than he did last week, when he railed on the guys to "man up, 'cuz the ladies are watchin'." "Uh . . . dude," he says. "Why is your mom talking to Rawlins?"

I follow his gaze to the sideline, hoping that Dillon's eyes have deceived him. But there she is, standing in the drizzle without a coat, chatting up the head coach at the most critical point in my entire football career. She's never talked to him or any other coach during a game before, so why now?

As much as my mother's interruption ticks me off, I scowl at Dillon as if the whole thing is his fault. "Who knows? Probably thinks the other team shouldn't be allowed to hit me so hard." Before any of the linemen can chuckle, I turn on them again and bark, "Which they wouldn't be able to do if y'all would just hold your stinkin' blocks! Now, are we gonna win this game or not?"

The huddle erupts in a deep chorus of cheers and grunts, then everyone disbands and takes their places on the line of scrimmage. The mental image of my mom and my coach is hard to push aside, but I am reminded of what my dad taught me about handling pressure way back when I was throwing bullets in Pop Warner football: *Your greatest strength on the field, as well as in life, isn't your arm, it's your mind. You've got to keep your head in the game to win. Lose focus, and it's all over.*

With one calming breath, I call out a cadence to start the play.

The snap of the ball in my hands brings me back to full attention. Like I've done a thousand times before, I turn to my left and fake a hand-off to the halfback, then drop three steps and check downfield for an open receiver. But instead of a receiver, all I see is the white jersey of an opposing linebacker blowing through the line like a tank.

What the . . . !

Instinctively, I bolt to the right, heading for open space a little closer to the sideline where I might still be able to make a clean pass, or at least scramble for positive yardage.

That's when I see my mom again.

Only now she isn't just talking to the coach, she is hugging him. Right there in front of God and everyone in the stands.

Holy crap!

I slow just a step, distracted, but that's enough.

The blind hit is so fierce that my head is spinning. The would-be assassin is a blitzing cornerback I hadn't accounted for, though I swear I could have avoided him had it not been for the Mother-Coach sideshow. As I'm flying backward toward the artificial turf, tangled in a web of arms and football pads, I'm still trying to wrap my head around whatever is going on with my parents. Why is my mom hugging my coach rather than watching the game? And where the heck is my dad? None of this makes any sense.

To seal our fate, the football slips out of my hands just before I hit the ground. During the ensuing melee, the linebacker who'd pounded his way through my offensive line picks up the fumbled ball and runs it eighty-two yards in the opposite direction for a touchdown that puts the game out of reach.

The rest of the offense is walking slowly to the sideline, their heads hanging down. I don't move a muscle. I could, but I don't want to. I just lie there on my back, unwilling to pull myself off the damp field. I don't want to see the disappointed looks of my teammates who were counting on me to lead them to victory. Nor do I want to see the crowd, whose once-raucous cheers have devolved into morbid silence. But mostly, I don't want to see if my mom still has her arms draped around Coach Rawlins.

Dillon finally comes and yanks me to my feet, swatting the back of my helmet like he always does. "Don't sweat it, dude. Anybody would have coughed up the ball with a hit like that. You got rocked."

"Yeah, well, I'm guessing most of the fifteen thousand people watching don't see it that way. Wait; make that fourteen thousand nine hundred and ninety-eight people. I don't think my mom or Rawlins saw any of it."

Dillon smirks awkwardly. "I don't know about that. Coach looks like he's been kicked in the crotch. Better hurry over. He wants to talk to you."

CHAPTER SIX

Halley

It's drizzling outside, and I'm freezing. Should have put on a coat . . . and brought an umbrella . . . or not come at all.

What was I thinking?

I should have just waited for Ty to come home on his own so we could break the news in private. But somehow in our commiserating, Alice and I decided we needed to get to the football game. "Dad would want someone there for Ty," Al pointed out. I knew she was right, so we hopped in the car and drove over. Only when we finally found a parking spot, several blocks away from the school, Alice wouldn't get out, saying she couldn't risk "the seventh-grade snots" seeing her cry.

"Fine," I said. "But promise me you'll stay in the car until I get back. There are too many people here to go looking for you in the crowd. I'll be back with your brother as soon as I can."

As the scoreboard comes into view, it's clear that Alice won't have long to wait. There are only a few minutes left in the fourth quarter. If I'm on the sideline when it ends, I should be able to grab Ty and go.

I snake through the crowd, trying to go unnoticed, until I find a clearing right behind the team bench. The area is roped off from visitors, but I don't figure anyone will mind.

It's not hard to pick Coach Rawlins out from among the players. He's the one with a shaved head who stands at least a head taller than anyone else and is barking orders to the offense.

My eyes dart over to Ty, who is on the field. He takes a snap, drops back, and fires a pass to the near side. The crowd goes wild.

Almost instantly, the announcer is heard over the PA system. "Pass complete from number seven, Ty Steen, to number fifty-six, Chad Hastings. That'll be good enough for another Yellow Jacket first down!"

As the announcer's voice dies down, someone says, "Mrs. Steen?" It's one of the trainers standing behind the bench. I recognize him from a team party we hosted last year, but I can't remember his name. "Is everything okay?"

I don't want to lie, but I don't really want to talk about it either, so I just shake my head.

"Well, come on over here," he says.

Rather than make a big scene by protesting, I join him at the trainer's table.

"Don't take this wrong," he continues, "but you don't look so hot. What seems to be the trouble?"

"I just . . . need to talk to my son."

The man looks out at the field, then up at the game clock. "It's kind of a bad time, you might say. But follow me." He leads me through a group of players, all of them wet with sweat and rain, toward Coach Rawlins. When we're standing right next to the towering man, the trainer says, "You just stay put right here, ma'am, and as soon as the game is over, Coach Rawlins will take care of you."

Upon hearing his name, the coach glances down. At first there's no recognition, then a lightbulb seems to go on. "You're Nathan's wife, right? Ty's mom?"

"Halley," I say. I don't expect him to remember my name. We've only met informally at football functions.

He looks me up and down. "Right. Halley. I'm Randy." He pauses to watch Ty hand the ball off to a tailback, who gains

60

five or six yards. As the team goes into a huddle, he turns back to me. "Halley . . . I can't help but notice you got makeup all down your face. Everything all right?"

I shake my head, just as I did for the trainer. "No. Not so much." I can feel tears trying to squeeze their way out of my tear ducts. I don't want them to, but at the moment they are stronger than my will to fight them off. Coach Rawlins is really looking concerned. I can tell my brief, weepy answer is not going to satisfy him, so I ask, "You knew Nathan, didn't you?"

"Back in high school. Yeah."

"Friends?"

He nods. "Something like that. For a while."

"Well, if it's okay with you, I really need to talk to my son as soon as the game is over. I need . . . to be with him."

The coach crosses his arms. "Mrs. Steen, what's going on? This is terrible timing, but if something's wrong, just say the word and I'll do what I can to help."

When I hear his offer, it occurs to me that having his head coach around when Ty hears the news might not be such a bad idea. He'll need his support. "Well," I venture, "the truth is . . ." I hear another roar from the crowd, but Coach Rawlins and I both ignore it. "I mean . . . there's been an accident. I hate to burden you with this, but I know Ty looks up to you, so maybe you can help him through it."

"Is it Nathan?" he asks slowly.

"Yes," I say through another gush of tears. "He died today. Unexpectedly." I can't say any more. The words won't come.

For a moment Randy's face hardens into something completely unreadable. Then he purses his lips tightly as he opens his arms, and suddenly I'm hugging this giant man. I don't know how long we're standing there like that. Thirty seconds? A minute? It eventually registers that the game is over, and I look up to see we've lost. The other team is celebrating another touchdown in their end zone.

As he finally pulls away, Randy barks at Dillon to go get Ty, who is lying on his back on the grass about thirty yards away.

Even under the pads and helmet I can tell by Ty's body language as he's walking toward us that he senses something is wrong. As soon as he's within reach, Randy wraps an arm around him and mutters, "Great game, kid. You did good out there."

"What's going on?" Ty asks his coach, motioning at me with his head.

Randy suggests we find someplace drier

to talk. He leads us to a private room under the stadium where he keeps some of the equipment. Dillon watches us go, clearly unsure whether to follow. I wave at him to join us — not only to be there for Ty, but Nathan was about the closest thing Dillon ever had to a father, so he needs to hear this from me.

When the musty room's single bulb flickers to life, Ty finally removes his helmet. Most people say he looks more like me than Nathan, but right here, at this moment, I see every last part of my husband reflected in my son's face. Just watching him looking at me breaks my heart, because I know he's waiting for me to say something, but he has no clue that I'm about to break his heart too.

"So," he says, "is someone gonna tell me what's going on?"

As I'm looking at him, my eyes begin to lose focus, and I realize they're filling with water. I wipe it away, then cross to him in two strides and wrap him up. Ty is much easier to hug than Randy Rawlins.

"Mom," he says as he hugs me back, "just say it. Whatever it is."

I squeeze harder, then whisper — or whimper — in his ear, "There was an accident, Ty. He's gone."

He pulls back nervously so he can see my face. "Who?"

I can't do anything but stare at him and sob. It doesn't matter. After a few seconds it's obvious that the bad news has registered. I can read the sorrow in his eyes and in his quivering mouth. He knows who I'm talking about without me having to verbalize it.

"No!" he says defiantly. Then, more as a groan, *"How?"*

Before I can answer, I hear Dillon ask, "Did someone die?"

"Ty's father was in an accident today," says Randy soberly. "He didn't make it." Now Dillon lets out a little moan too, and in the next moment he has his arms around Ty and me. Then Coach Rawlins joins us as well.

As I'm standing there, huddled with my son, his friend, and a grown man I hardly know in a dimly lit utility room, the day's events flash through my mind. This wasn't how today was supposed to end. Nathan and I were supposed to meet right before the game. Then we'd share a hot dog and soda as we watched our son play the game he loves. His team would win. We'd go out for dessert afterward. Nathan would make me laugh. I'd tell him about how much care I put into Lily's lilies, and he'd tell me about

the simple acts of kindness he did throughout the day to pass his stones from one
pocket to the other. Then we'd go home,
spend some time with the kids, and he'd
give me a kiss before going to bed.

Everything would be right in the world.

But everything is wrong, and I fear it will
never be right again.

CHAPTER SEVEN

Madeline

The knock on the door makes me jump in my seat. I sit straight up and plant a quick smile on my face, hoping it looks natural for whoever is about to enter.

It doesn't feel natural on my face. It feels . . . *guilty.*

I know I shouldn't have sent that e-mail to Nathan. But I did, and I need his answer. It's hard to plan a trip for two when I'm not sure if the other one is going.

A girl with a brunette bob pokes her head in the door. "Professor Zuckerman?"

"Yes," I say coolly. "What can I do for you?"

"Hi, I'm Amy, the new admin. I thought I'd bring the mail around in person today so I can meet everyone." She crosses the room to my desk and hands me a small pile of junk magazines that I somehow got signed up for through the university. "If there's anything I can help you with, just give me a holler. I sit in Cindy's old spot. Same phone and all."

"Thanks, Amy. I'll be sure to do that. It's a pleasure to meet you."

We seem to go through a lot of administrative assistants around here, but I don't mind. Most of them are undergrads trying to get to know the staff in their field of study. It's a win-win really. They get a small paycheck and some good experience, and we get to know them a little better before considering them for the graduate program.

As soon as she leaves, my attention turns back to the phone on my desk. I've already spent too long staring at it, debating whether or not to call him. "Stop acting like a schoolgirl," I tell myself as I finally pick it up and dial his cell.

It goes to voice mail. "Hi, Nathan," I say after the beep, "this is Maddy, following up about my little proposition. I promise, if you just spend one weekend with me in California, we'll finally be able to put an end to all the secrecy. Don't you want that? This is really important, so call me back. I'll try your work number, too. Love ya."

Nathan's told me before that it's probably better if I don't call him at work — and definitely not at home — but I *really* need to speak to him. It's been three days since I sent my e-mail, and I've got to know what he's thinking.

After a quick breath, I pick up and dial a different number.

It rings half a dozen times, then a woman's voice answers. "Whitaker, Steen, and Brennerman," she says. "How may I help you?"

"Can I speak to Mr. Steen, please?"

There is an inordinately long pause. Then, "I'm sorry, that won't be possible."

"Oh, is he not in today?"

The voice on the other end of the line wavers slightly. "Is this . . . a client of his?"

Should I say that I am? No, then she might look me up in her records. "Just a friend." That's perhaps the biggest understatement ever, but still the truth.

"Well," she continues pensively, "regrettably, I've been asked to inform anyone calling for Mr. Steen that he . . . er, passed away suddenly."

Did she just say what I thought she said?

"You're . . . serious?"

"Yes, ma'am. It's very tragic. The whole firm here is taking it very hard." She stops talking, like she's waiting for me to speak, but I don't know what to say, so she starts back up again. "You said you're his friend, but if you do happen to have any legal issues that Mr. Steen was helping you with, his partners are happy to assist in any way they can. Whatever compensation they receive on his behalf for existing clients will go directly to the Steen family."

"This isn't a joke?" I say numbly, almost too shocked to speak.

"No, ma'am. I imagine I'd be fired for joking about something like that."

So Nathan is . . . *dead*? I think I'm going to be sick.

"Is there anything else I can do for you?"

"No," I whisper. "Thank you."

I stare vacantly at my office wall for several more minutes as I mentally try to make sense of the horrible news. "Well," I say out loud, a moment before my emotional levees bust, "I guess that settles it — Nathan isn't flying to California with me . . ."

CHAPTER EIGHT

Ty

Everything that has a beginning has an end.

I heard those words from my father when I was six, right before we flushed my fish, Clowny, down the toilet. It's one thing for a boy to accept the mortality of a ten-cent guppy, but quite another for a son to comprehend the passing of his hero in the prime of his life. In the tragic wake of Dad's death, I can honestly say that I hate those words — hate that I still remember them; hate that his abbreviated life confirms their awful truth.

For the last few days, since learning of the fatal crash, it's felt oddly like the entire family died along with Dad, and given Mom's endless moaning and weeping, I'm guessing we've been banished to hell. Emptiness abounds at home; lethargy defines our existence.

People keep stopping by the house saying

what a great man Dad was, and that we should take solace knowing that he lived a life of honor and distinction, and that he touched so many lives for good over the years that he will not be forgotten. And they're right, I suppose. But on the flip side, remembering the kind of life he lived and the type of man he was only amplifies the pain of having to continue on without him, making us miss him all the more.

On Monday morning a representative from the hospital calls to say that we are welcome to pick up the personal belongings Dad had on him at the time of the accident.

"I definitely don't want the clothes," I hear my mom say into the phone. "Did he have anything else?" A few seconds later she says, "All I want are the wallet and the rocks. Everything else can be thrown out."

Mom's emotional state seems to be deteriorating with each new day. She's in no shape to drive, so I volunteer to take her and Alice to the hospital. As I expected, when the red stones are given to her, Mom cups them in her hands like they're precious diamonds. She closes her eyes and tightens her fingers around them, feeling them more with her soul than with her skin. Then her shoulders slump forward as she begins to whimper, then cry, then howl, all in a mat-

71

ter of seconds. The two hospital staff who are with us pretend not to notice that Mom is having a breakdown. Alice and I both put an arm around her to make sure she doesn't melt into a puddle on the floor.

Once she's calmed down a bit, Mom insists on taking an arrangement of flowers to the man Dad was helping on the side of the highway, and who happens to be in a room up on the third floor awaiting heart surgery. We're told his name is Jesus Ramirez.

Figures. Dad helped Jesus.

Mr. Ramirez's entire family is in the room with him when we enter. I don't catch all of their names, but there are eight of them, including the boy who was with him when Dad died. The wife, Maria, speaks the best English, so she does all the talking for the family.

"My husband so sad for your husband died," she says. Then she motions to the rest of the family. "We all very sad."

Mom nods and tries to smile, then hands her one of her signature bouquets. "Tell him we hope his heart heals quickly."

Maria translates, then says, "My husband say he hope your heart heal too." She pats her chest lightly with the palm of her hand.

Alice has been pretty quiet since Friday

night, but she takes a step toward Maria and asks for any details about the accident. The reports Mom got from the hospital on the day of the accident were pretty sketchy, so I'm glad my sister has the nerve to ask.

Maria and Jesus speak in Spanish for a minute or two, then Maria turns back to us. "Okay, I tell. My husband and son — Paul — he's eight. They were driving, and Jesus, he having pain in his chest. He say it hurts so bad he worried about crashing, so they stop, waiting for it to go. But the pain it keeps coming, he think he can't drive no more. Not safe. He worried he's going to die in the car, but then Mr. Nathan, your father, he pull up behind him and comes to the window. Jesus didn't have no cell phone in the car, but Mr. Nathan, he calls the ambulance." She pauses and asks a question of her husband and son in Spanish. They both reply briefly, then she continues. Her voice is now much softer. "It was raining. Too much rain for October. After he calls the ambulance, another car slipped on the rain. The other car hit our van, and it went into the wall. Your father . . . your husband . . . he was trapped next to the wall. Had no wheres to go."

The room goes completely quiet.

So that's it, then. Dad was crushed be-

73

tween a car and a concrete wall along the highway.

I can tell Mom is about to lose it. Before she does, I thank the Ramirezes for their time, and escort her from the room.

On the way home, Mom is very quiet. For the first time since my football game she doesn't have that perpetually sad look about her. If anything, she looks mad.

Out of the blue Alice says, "Mom, you look like one of Dad's rocks."

"What's that supposed to mean?" she snaps back.

With one eye still on the road, I glance to my right. Mom's face is all contorted and turning red. Alice is right — *just like Dad's rocks.*

"Stone-faced," my little sister replies. "Are you angry at someone?"

Mom turns slightly to lock eyes with Alice in the backseat. "Maybe," she says.

"How are you *maybe* mad?" I ask.

"Because I haven't decided yet," she growls. "Anger is a choice, after all." She takes a moment to think, then says. "Okay, I've made up my mind. I'm officially mad now. But I know I shouldn't be, which makes me mad at myself too."

"Who are you mad at?" Alice asks, before

delicately venturing a guess. "The driver? The one who crashed into Dad?"

"No, of course not," Mom protests. "It was an accident. It wouldn't be right to hold feelings against him."

"But Mr. Ramirez didn't do anything either," I point out. "Except have a heart attack, but you can't be mad at him over that."

Mom's bottom lip begins to quiver. Out of the corner of my eye I see the familiar signs of sadness settling back into her countenance. "You're right," she mumbles. "He did nothing wrong . . . which is why I don't blame him either." She sniffles twice, staring blankly out the window at the passing landscape. "But your father . . ."

"Dad?" Alice gasps.

I'm equally dismayed. "How can you be mad at him?"

A small fire ignites for a moment in Mom's eyes, but is quickly extinguished by a new burst of tears. "Because he should have known better!" she bellows as the water trickles down her cheeks. "Without thinking of you, or you, or me, he put himself in harm's way to help complete strangers. I know people will say he was a hero — and he was — but can't I also be a little mad at his selfishness? He was always so concerned about helping everyone. But

75

what about his own family? We're the ones who have to go on without a father and husband. We're the ones left to pay for his generosity."

Nobody says anything else for the rest of the ride. I don't know if that's because Alice and I don't want to argue with Mom when she's obviously hurting, or because we know there's some truth to what she said.

As fragile as Mom seemed at the hospital, and as upset as she was on the ride home, the worst is yet to come. On Wednesday night, after sending us to bed, she locks herself in the master bathroom and wails uncontrollably for what feels like hours. When the noise eventually stops, I call through the door to make sure she's okay. She doesn't respond, so I call again, louder, but still nothing. I've watched enough movies and read enough books to know what people — even sane people like my mom — can do to themselves when they're depressed, so I quickly dismantle the handle with a screwdriver to let myself in.

Alice is urging me to hurry up, while simultaneously rattling off everything she knows about lifesaving techniques and how long the brain can go without oxygen and not have lasting brain damage.

I'm so nervous about what I might find when I get the door open that I can taste vomit in the back of my throat, lurking there, waiting to come all the way up should my worst fear be realized.

Alice and I gasp at the same time when we finally get in. Mom is lying prone on the bath mat. I run to her side and shake her. She opens her eyes with a jolt. At first she's confused. Then very embarrassed. "Sorry, guys," she says groggily. "I guess I cried myself to sleep."

No pills, no booze, just a tired widow who surpassed her emotional limits and crashed on the floor. We help her to bed, cover her with the duvet, then I head to my room and cry myself to sleep too.

Is it too much to ask to sleep in when you're mourning your father's death? Yes.

At nine thirty the next day I wake up to the sound of my mom yelling down the hallway that she wants to have a "heart-to-heart" in five minutes. Ten minutes later I drag myself out of bed and make my way to her bedroom. She is sitting on the edge of her and Dad's bed in her pajamas, still looking emotionally thin, but with a new calm about her.

Alice is in the room too, cuddled up with

Dad's pillow.

When Mom sees me, she clears her throat and starts right in. "Last night was . . . bad. I know that. From the looks of the disassembled door, you thought it might have been even worse. I'm *so* sorry. I didn't mean to give you guys a scare. It's just . . . this has been really hard."

"We know," I mumble. "It's fine."

"Yeah, Mom, it's fine," echoes Alice.

Choking up for the millionth time in seven days, Mom continues. "I just want you to know that no matter what, we're going to be okay. It's not easy, but we'll get through this, one way or another." The way she says it, I wonder if she's mostly trying to convince herself. "Yes, Dad is gone. But I'm here, and I'm not going anywhere. You can count on that. Okay?"

Alice nods, but I groan aloud. "Stop trying to convince us that we're all okay, when you're in worse shape than all of us. I don't want another pep talk. I just want to go back to bed."

"This isn't a pep talk, Ty," she says, undeterred. "There's something I'd like you to see." The vaguest hint of a smile plays at the corner of her mouth — the first sign of joy I've seen in a week. She crosses to the desk in the corner of the room where Dad's laptop from work is plugged in and running. "One of your father's partners at the firm called on Tuesday to pay his respects. He gave me the password to his computer, just in case we want to remove any of his personal files before they take it back."

Alice follows her across the room. "He's gone less than a week, and they're already asking for his computer?"

"It's a courtesy that they're giving us access to it at all, so I'm not complaining." She types to log in, then quickly clicks open a web browser. Mom isn't computer savvy by any stretch of the imagination, but for a woman in her forties who has no formal training, she does all right. Somehow she's learned to manage her store's web page, pays most of the bills online, and even has a blog with a growing contingent of followers who love her periodic tips on floral arrangements. But her greatest computer skill, by far, is connecting with people, especially on Facebook. It seems like everyone she's ever talked to in her life is now her Facebook friend. It's a little embarrassing actually; she has like three times as many friends as me. Needless to say, I'm not at all surprised when she jumps straight to her Facebook profile. "I was having a bad dream this morning," she continues once the page is fully loaded, "so I woke up super early and didn't want to go back to sleep. With nothing else to do, I thought I'd poke around on your father's laptop, but before I got into any of his personal files, I logged in to my Facebook account just to see what's been going on." For the first time since my football game, there is a subtle excitement in her voice. She doesn't sound giddy, and maybe not even happy, but neither does her tone have the familiar weepy melancholy of the past few days. "Anyway, I had lots of invitations from people I don't even know to a new fan page that someone created." She clicks another link and the page springs to life.

Alice is the first to read the title near the top. "The One Good Thing." Below that is a picture of Dad flashing his infectious smile.

Scanning down the left-hand column, I silently read a brief introduction, written by the site's anonymous creator.

In memory of Nathan Steen, who gave his all helping others. He quietly, freely, unselfishly served his fellow man, expecting nothing in return. Once, when I asked why he bothered, he said simply, "Because one good thing leads to another." Nathan has done countless "one good thing(s)" for me, yet I know I am not the lone beneficiary of his kindness. This site is for friends — or fans — of Nathan Steen to document the many good things he did for you. We love and miss you Nathan . . . rest in peace.

For a moment, we're all quiet. Then Alice starts crying openly, which triggers tears from Mom again as well. These, I suspect, are the first happy tears either of them have shed in a long time.

I watch my mom's face for a moment longer as she goes back to reading the screen. It's nice that she doesn't still seem upset at my dad. Hopefully this is a turn for the best, because I can't have Mom mad at Dad when I'm still coping with the fact that he's gone.

I take control of the optical mouse and scroll down farther. The site is less than three days old, yet it already has more than five hundred fans, who've posted nearly two thousand comments. Some of the things people wrote about are big, overt tokens of kindness, such as Christmas presents for families he knew were struggling, or helping a friend land a job after being laid off. Others were much simpler acts that could just as easily have gone unnoticed, but were obviously appreciated by the recipients — things like waiting to hold the door open for someone on a rainy day or taking time to listen when a friend needed to vent.

The most recent post is from David Brennerman, one of Dad's partners at the law firm, who wrote, "The One Good Thing Nathan did for me happened just this past week. My wife has been ill; Nathan picked up Chinese food for us on his way home from work so Theresa wouldn't have to endure another night of my cooking. What a pleasant surprise! We'd have survived on leftovers, but he made that night something special for us. The best part was simply knowing someone cared. That's the way Nathan was. He cared about people."

I remember that night, because Dad picked up an order of Chinese food for us too. It was Thursday, the night before the football game — the final meal we ate together as a family.

The last supper.

Another entry reads, "When we were in college, N.S. skipped a test so I wouldn't have to be alone right after learning that my parents were splitting up. That wasn't the only good thing he ever did for me, but it was certainly one I'll never forget."

A former client wrote, "Mr. Steen was a

man of principle, and that's saying a lot for a defense lawyer. Not only did I benefit from his honesty and integrity, but also from his generosity. When I needed a break, he came to my defense. Literally, he defended me in court, knowing full well I couldn't pay him unless my innocence was proven. Who does that??? Nathan Steen, that's who. God bless him."

Much farther down the page, a woman who apparently knew Dad as a kid wrote a flurry of things all in a row: "I could list a thousand different ways that Nathan touched my life, going all the way back to third grade. I'll just list a few of the highlights. Even if they sound trivial, they were HUGE to me: On the day we met, he apologized to me. Later, he held my hand. He sat with me. He wrote a poem for me. He believed in me. He danced with me. He sacrificed for me. And ultimately . . . he saved my life."

I read the entry again, this time taking note of the author's name. Even in the silence of my thoughts it's a mouthful. *Madeline Zuckerman.*

I move the cursor until it's hovering over the woman's comments. "Did you see this one, Mom?"

She nods. "I read it earlier this morning.

Probably some girl who had a crush on your father way back when."

"Yeah, but . . . 'saved my life'? What do you suppose that means?"

"Saved her from making a bad choice? Saved her from heartache or embarrassment? Could be anything really. But that was the thing about your father, the thing that really set him apart. He had such a knack for seeing people's needs and finding a way to help, no matter what it was." She pauses, glancing at me, then at Alice, and back to me. "You're a lot like him in that regard. You, too, Alice. Aside from how you sometimes treat each other, you're both kindhearted and caring."

I quickly dismiss the comparison. "No one cares like Dad did. Just look at all the people he helped." I point to the computer screen. "He was like Superman, for crying out loud."

For several seconds nobody speaks. Then Alice, her throat raspy with emotion, points out the folly of my comment. "Yeah . . . except Superman wouldn't have died in the accident. In the end, Dad was able to help everyone but himself."

And on that depressing note, the conversation abruptly ends.

CHAPTER NINE

Alice

If you've ever had a loved one die, you may know a thing or two about frozen dinners. I had no idea, until recently. I've dubbed them MRRs — meals ready to be reheated — and they have been stacking up in our freezer like crazy. Mom says the food from our friends is a tremendous blessing. I've tasted a few of them, and I'm not so sure.

After showing us the Facebook page about Dad, Mom is spending most of the rest of the day either resting in her room or taking care of the final details for the funeral tomorrow. I don't know what Ty is up to — sleeping probably. I bide my time reading through old blog entries, remembering the good old days of last week when the only thing I had to worry about was getting made fun of.

At six o'clock in the evening I'm parked on the sofa with my laptop. Mom comes downstairs and throws one of the frozen dinners in the oven, then gathers me and Ty to the formal dining table. Though the food has been pouring in all week, this is the first time we've eaten a meal together. "So," she says once we are all seated with food on our plates, "another casserole. This looks . . . good."

"The food looks fine," remarks Ty. "But this just feels . . ."

"Like someone is missing," I say.

All of our eyes zero in on the vacant seat at the table.

I shouldn't have said it. When I look up, Mom is teetering again on the edge of another meltdown. Her face is flushed and she is trembling slightly.

She takes a few long breaths to steady herself. "Yes," she finally says, pushing the word out against its will. "Someone *is* missing. But we're still a family. You, you, and me," she says, pointing at us each in turn, "we're all still here — *together* — and we . . . we need to get back into a routine. This dinner is a good start. So let's just eat and enjoy the food and pretend that . . ."

The resolve on Mom's face is slipping. I know what that means. It's only a matter of time before she'll be a blubbering heap of tears on the kitchen table.

86

"Maybe you should go lie down," I suggest. "You don't look so good."

"I'm really not in the mood to eat," says Ty, shoving his plate to the center of the table.

The combination of our comments is enough to push my mom over the brink . . . again. She crosses her arms and lays her head down on top of them, right between her plate and the casserole dish. In an instant she is gasping and heaving and moaning things like "Why?" and "It's not fair!" and "He should have thought about us before he went and got himself killed in the rain!" and "Please, God, I need my husband back!"

Ty shoots me one of his nasty looks. "Now look what you did!"

I love my brother, but sometimes I really hate him. "Me? You're the one who's not in a mood to eat."

"So? You're the one this morning who said Superman wouldn't die."

Now I put my hands on my hips and give him "the stare" — the one I've perfected at school over the past year when I don't like what people say. "Whatever. You're still the jerk who hurts people's feelings by only caring about yourself and thinking you're so cool."

In the middle of our bickering, the doorbell rings.

"I'll get it!" we say in unison as we make a break for the front of the house.

Mom remains at the table, trying in vain to pull herself together.

"Uh . . . Mom," I say a minute later as I come back into the dining room. "We have visitors."

"I'm not in the mood," she replies with her face still tucked in her arms. "Tell them it's a bad time."

"We already know that much," says my grandpa Steen, who has followed us in. "It's a bad time for all of us. But I hope you won't send us away just yet."

His voice sounds eerily like Dad's, which is enough to get Mom to lift her head above her elbows.

"Hello, Halley," Grandpa continues. "I'm sorry we showed up unannounced. We weren't sure exactly when we'd get in, but we came straight here as soon as our plane landed. Haven't even checked into our hotel yet, because we wanted to see how you and the kids were doing first."

Mom wipes at her face, suddenly embarrassed by how she must appear. "Oh," she says, "I'm so glad you came, Tim. And you, Colleen. But please don't stay at a hotel.

Stay here. We want you here with us."

Grandma and Grandpa share a quick glance. Grandma Steen steps closer and pats Mom on the back. "We don't want to be an imposition, dear. You've got enough to worry about right now without us getting in the way."

Mom wipes at more tears and sits up straight in her chair. "Have you paid for the room yet?"

"No," Grandpa replies. "Just a reservation."

"Then it's settled," Mom states emphatically. "You're staying here. You're family, and right now we need all the family we can get."

Christy Love Barker
October 22
About 6 & 1/2 years ago, when we still lived in Texas, I was pregnant with my second child. I was severely ill, my husband did not have a job, and I was trying to help our family by working. I was driving to work on a stormy day, hit a rough patch of road, crossed into oncoming traffic, drove into the ditch, and rolled my car. There I lay, upside down in the ditch . . . Stunned. My friend's husband happened to be coming the other way, and even

though he wasn't the first car to pull over, he was the first one to get out of his car to help. The "good thing" he did was stop, but the GREAT thing he did was to give me his coat and ask if he could pray with me. We prayed that my baby would be okay. Shortly thereafter the police pulled me from the car. Nathan Steen was my angel that day.

Like • Comment • Share

CHAPTER TEN

Alice

MY OWN LITTLE WONDERLAND:
October 26th

Dear Blog, it's me, Alice.
It's late at night, and I'm not really sure where to begin, so I guess I'll just say . . . life goes on.

For some of us, anyway.

Right now, though, life seems to be going much slower than the last time I wrote. Slower and drearier. Is that a word? Drearier? Whatever. Whether I use real words or not, no words can really describe what I'm going through right now.

Honestly, I'm a little hesitant to write at all, which is why I haven't posted anything this week. I doubt anybody reads this blog but me, so I don't know why I'm so scared to put my thoughts and feelings into words, but I am. Maybe I'm afraid of what I'll say. Or maybe I'm just afraid of facing reality.

Well, here's the reality . . .

October 19th was officially the worst day ever. Maybe not for everyone, but definitely for me. For starters, I thought maybe because it was a Friday that kids at school would be thinking about their plans for the weekend, and that maybe they'd forget about me and leave me alone for a while.

Didn't happen.

I wasn't in the school five minutes before Lisa Dillender stopped me in the hall and told me she thought my outfit was really cute, which totally shocked me that she would say something nice. Of course then she asked if I got it at Baby Gap.

I wanted to laugh at her for being so immature. I also wanted to punch her. But

I just forced a smile and walked away. As I left, I could hear the laughs from all of her friends.

Why do they have to be so mean?

The book on bullying that I checked out last month from the Dallas County Library says there are several key risk factors. For instance, if kids lack supervision at home, if their parents bully them, if they don't feel enough love, or if they have friends who are bullies — all of these things make it more likely that they'll bully others. Sometimes it's just a matter of having low self-esteem, and picking on others makes them feel better about themselves.

Since reading the book, I've been trying to imagine the motives for my tormentors. For example, I have to believe with Lisa it's a lack of self-esteem. I mean, sure she's pretty and popular, but somewhere deep down she has to know she's as dumb as a doorknob, and I bet that really hurts. The fact that I'm smarter than just about everyone probably makes her want to bring me down to her level.

Oh man, I'm getting way off topic here. Maybe I'm deliberately trying to avoid writing about the rest of my day on October 19th.

Back to reality . . .

In third period Mike Smits, who has this weird birthmark thing on his arm that grows hair as thick as fur, waited until the teacher was busy helping someone at the back of the class, then he said, "Hey Alice, do you like shrimp?"

As soon as I said yes, he and his buddies started laughing, then he told me I should try eating myself.

I'm guessing that Mike doesn't get a lot of love at home.

Then during lunch one girl "accidentally" bumped another girl, who then "accidentally" dumped a blob of green Jell-O on my lap. They both giggled wildly, along with everyone else in the cafeteria who saw it. Before they skipped away, the first girl smiled obnoxiously and said, "Keep the Jell-O, Alice. My mom says it's a safe food for little kids to eat."

Really? I think both of those girls need more parental supervision.

But you know what? I don't care about any of that stuff. Well, I do a little, or I wouldn't write about it. But ultimately, whatever those kids do to me doesn't matter at all. If they think they can hurt me or make me sad, they're wrong. And here's why . . .

Later that night I learned what real hurt feels like. I learned exactly what it means to be so sad that it feels like the world is ending.

Later that night I learned that my dad died.

Killed actually. Not intentional or murder or anything like that, just some stupid accident. So he's gone now . . . and I miss him.

When Mom first told me about it I totally thought she was joking. Not that she looked like she was joking, because she didn't at all. She was a total wreck (she still is, btw). I think I even laughed, because I didn't know what else to do. It was like, you better chuckle or something, Alice, because then maybe you can believe for another moment or two that she is playing some horrible joke on you. After all, how could she be serious? How could she just walk in the house and tell me that a car lost control on the highway and that my dad happened to be standing in the wrong place at the wrong time? How could that be anything other than a huge fabrication?

Only it wasn't.

Everything she said was true. I knew it even when I laughed. I could see it in her eyes. It was written all over her face and in her posture and in the way she flopped on the couch next to me.

She'd already gone to identify Dad's remains and spent the better part of two hours dealing with police and hospital stuff. As distraught as she was, I'm surprised they let her drive herself home. But they did, and she came straight into the house and broke the news.

Hearing it almost killed me, too.

After an hour of holding each other and crying, we went to the football game to tell Ty. I stayed in the car, though . . . the last thing I need is for one of those stupid girls from school to see me crying and make a big deal about it.

Why is all this happening to me? Why are kids so mean? Why did my dad have to die?

Whatever. Like I said, life goes on.

Not much has happened since Dad's accident. Ty and me are staying home from school this week. The funeral is tomorrow, but I'm not looking forward to it.

I don't want to see his dead body in the casket.

Then again, at least going to the funeral is an excuse to get out of the house. We've been holed up all week, living off food that other people keep bringing by the house. About the only thing we do to pass the time is read all the stuff people are writing on Facebook about what Dad did for them. It's actually quite amazing. People from all over the country have posted comments — even a few from overseas. He always encouraged us to find ways to serve or help people, but I never realized just how many people he touched.

And on that note, let me add a quick final comment, on the off chance that anyone ever reads this. I want you to know the last thing my dad said to me before school last Friday, and therefore the last words he spoke to anyone in our family before he died: "Remember who you are."

Well, I know who I am and I'll never forget it. I won't let other people forget it either . . .

I am Nathan Steen's daughter.

Travis Naef
October 23
I had a big project installing hardwood floors and tile in my house. Nathan found out I was installing it myself, so he came over for several days to lend a hand. I'm not saying he's real handy, but the extra

hands and tools were a huge help.

Like • Comment • Share

Rob and Jenni Kelley
October 23
Last year Nathan randomly texted me that he had food left over from a business luncheon, and wanted to know if he could drop it by our house. He had no idea that Jenni had been sick all day or that I was stressing about what to feed the kids for dinner. His text was a godsend. One good thing; one good meal; one great man.

Like • Comment • Share

CHAPTER ELEVEN

Ty

It's Friday, four thirty in the morning. I know why I'm awake, but have no idea why anyone else would be up at this ungodly hour. I sit perfectly still in the kitchen and listen as footsteps come down the stairs in the hallway.

"Yes, Miss May," I hear someone say. It's definitely Grandpa, but he's trying hard to whisper. "I'm still here. What can I do for you."

The sound of his footsteps stop before he enters the kitchen, so he still doesn't know I'm here.

"Oh, I'm so sorry to hear that," Grandpa says after a sizable pause. Then, "If I was in town, I'd come right over." More silence. "That's right, I'm in Texas." Silence again, but only briefly. "No, I don't think the coyotes are any bigger out here." He talks off and on for another minute or two, and then he finally says, "Of course, May. Feel free to call again, no matter the time. Bye now."

A cell phone snaps shut, then Grandpa appears in the kitchen doorway.

"Oh, hello, Ty," he says as he enters. "I thought for sure I was the only one up."

"Nope. I've been up a couple hours already." I wait for Grandpa to sit down next to me, then ask, "You get a lot of calls at this time of day?"

"Oh, that was just my girlfriend checkin' up on me." He says it so straight-faced that I'd almost believe him, but my dad had that same dry sense of humor, so I'm conditioned not to bite.

"Cool," I say, just as straight-faced. "Does Grandma know?"

He chuckles at my response, then explains, "That was old Miss May, an eighty-eight-year-old, white-haired angel in my congregation. She's got a bit of a memory problem, you might say — usually can't remember her own children, sometimes can't remember the day of the week. But for whatever reason, she never forgets me. Whenever she has a problem, I'm the first one she calls."

"So what's today's problem?"

"The cat," he responds dryly.

"The cat?"

"Yep. Princess. In her own words, 'Princess got et last night by them coyotes.' "

"Wow. That sucks."

"Yeah, it kinda does. The only thing is, it didn't happen. Well, not last night anyway. Poor Miss May's cat got eaten three or four years ago, but periodically she remembers it like it just happened, and then I end up getting a call. This is the seventh or eighth time already." He pauses, then says, "Good thing cats have nine lives."

That's totally something my dad would have said. It's uncanny how much the two are alike. Which is why I never understood why they didn't get along better. As similar as they were, you'd think they'd be real close. Instead, there was always this unspoken "thing" between them; a gulf of some sort. Everyone in the family noticed it, even if it was subtle. It's not like they weren't civil toward each other, but you can only have so many awkward pauses or funny looks before you know something isn't quite right. I asked about it on several different occasions, and Dad usually said not to read too much into it. But one time he admitted that not everything was as good with his father as he wished it was. Then he added, almost under his breath, "Just always be honest with me, and we'll never end up like that."

He didn't explain it any more than that. Was he accusing his own father of lying to him? Had that caused the great divide between them?

I guess I'll never know.

Grandpa watches me for a second and his smile starts to fade. It's like he's reading me or something. "So," he says, glancing at his watch, "what's been on your mind all this time?"

"Just . . . stuff," I reply. "My mind wouldn't turn off, you know?"

"It's hereditary," he says. "Your dad was the same way. You got it from him and he got it from me, so blame me if you like."

"I can usually crash on demand, but last night was different. I just couldn't stop thinking about . . ."

He lets a long time pass before he takes a guess at my unfinished thought. "About your dad?"

"Yeah," I say so faintly that I can barely hear it myself. "And other stuff."

"Care to share?"

"Not really."

He raises his eyebrows questioningly, and then smiles. "Fair enough. Have you eaten breakfast?"

"At this hour? No."

"Well, my stomach is saying it's time to fill up. Mind if I cook us up a little something? I bet a strapping young man like you could eat round the clock."

Come to think of it, I'm starving. "Sure, I guess I could eat. What do you have in mind?"

"Oh, I'll have to see what there is to work with. But I was thinking bacon and eggs, hash, and maybe some flapjacks with syrup."

"You mean pancakes?"

"No, I mean flapjacks. Almost identical to pancakes, but with a much snazzier name. You any good with a flipper?"

I shrug. "I guess."

Grandpa Steen pats me on the back of the shoulder. "Well, let's find out."

For the next thirty minutes we work side-by-side in the kitchen preparing a meal that could feed my entire football team. The whole time we keep going back and forth, sharing bits and pieces of information about ourselves. To my surprise, the conversation flows as smooth as Mrs. Butterworth's from a brand-new bottle. It's sad, really, that I don't know him better than I do. He and Grandma live so far away that we don't get to see them all that often. They usually make it out to Texas once a year, but never for more than a few days, and some years they aren't able to come at all. Maybe if there weren't that awkwardness with my dad they would have made an effort more often. Anyway, now that it's just him and me alone and we're talking and cooking, it's almost like I know him without really knowing him, if that makes any sense.

Then we sit down to eat, and the conversation doubles back to where we started. "So, you gonna tell me now what's on your mind?" asks Grandpa.

I stick my fork in a stack of pancakes — er, flapjacks. "Tell you what, I'll answer that if you answer a question first."

"Deal," he responds without blinking an eye. "Fire away."

"Um, okay." How do I phrase this without sounding as nosey as Mom? "Well, I guess I've always sort of wondered why you and my dad didn't . . . you know, get along better?"

His eyebrows jut straight up. Not like he's surprised by the question; more like he's surprised that I noticed. "Did he tell you we didn't get along?"

"No. I just sort of figured. Even when you'd come to visit, you guys hardly talked. And when you did, there was always this weird vibe."

"Ty, I loved your father very much. He was a good man — raised a good family. Had an honorable job. He did very well for himself."

"I know. But that doesn't really answer my question, does it."

Grandpa's shoulders sag forward, and for a moment he doesn't speak. Then he says, "You picked about the hardest question I can think of. To be honest, I'm not even sure I know anymore." He takes a measured breath. "Have you ever stuck a pebble in front of a trickle of water on the street? Even the tiniest little stone can split that water into two separate streams. Sometimes it joins back up on the other side, but other times the two streams head off in their own directions. I guess with me and Nathan it was kind of like that — a little rock got in our way, formed a wedge, and we never fully found our way back together." He punctures a sausage with his fork and bites off a chunk. "I'm to blame, though. For a long while I thought I'd raised the prodigal son, and I was just waiting for him to return. But sooner or later — well, later — it dawned on me that maybe I was the prodigal father. I did what I could to mend fences, and that helped to some extent, but there was always a little gap between us that we never could quite close."

"What was the wedge?"

He tries to smile. "That's ancient history, Ty. Or dirty laundry, or whatever you want to call it. But it's not even worth mentioning. Besides, you've used up your one question." He gives me a big wink and says, "I've shared mine, so it's your turn. What's had you up all night?"

Here goes nothing . . .

"Football."

His eyebrows jut up again, but not quite so far as before. "Oh? What about football?"

"Nothing. Just that I quit yesterday. I texted my coach last night before I went to bed to let him know."

"Why on earth would you do that?"

Does he mean why would I quit, or why would I text the coach? Probably the former. "I'm not a hundred percent sure. That's why I was up, trying to sort it out."

"I thought you really liked playing."

"Love it."

"Then why quit?"

Though I'd like to convince myself otherwise, the truth is that I know exactly why. Or at least I've narrowed it down to what prompted it, even if I can't fully form it into a single, coherent reason that would make sense to anyone but myself.

"It's complicated," I mumble. Yeah, and the sun is hot.

"Because your dad's gone?"

It would take a shrink to fully unravel what's going on in my head, so I don't even try. Instead I nod once, and then offer up the best half-truth I can think of. "He was my biggest fan. He got me into the game as a kid, and I just don't have the motivation anymore now that he can't be there to cheer me on."

I look down at my food, and realize that I'm no longer hungry. I'm waiting for Grandpa to object, or to tell me I should reconsider, or simply to see through my lame excuse. Instead he drops a funeral-day bomb. "Like father like son, I guess."

"Huh?"

"Well, I just mean that he didn't finish his senior year of football either."

I'm suddenly at a loss for high-school-level words. "Nuh-uh."

Grandpa puts down his utensils and furrows his brow up tight. "You didn't know that?"

No, I'm joking. And my heart is racing for the fun of it. "I always thought he was a three-year starter on varsity."

"Yeah, freshman through junior year."

"He *started* as a freshman?"

"Sorry, Ty. I thought you knew."

"Why did he quit?" After all, it's not like his father died unexpectedly.

He hesitates for a second, giving me the impression that he's trying to wordsmith his answer. "Well," Grandpa drawls, "I guess it all boils down to choices. Sometimes we make choices, and we have to live with the consequences. In Nathan's case, he chose to give up something he loved."

I stir a pat of butter on my plate. "Did he regret it?"

"I don't know, Ty. I just don't know."

Arlene Trani
October 23

I was trying to mail a package to my son, who was stationed in Iraq. I was told I had to get that box out ASAP, as mail service was going to be cut off. The weight and size of the package totaled $70, and I only had $40. Nathan was behind me in line, and he pulled out some cash and paid the difference. I was in tears. Such a generous act!

Like • Comment • Share

CHAPTER TWELVE

Halley

" 'After all the cheers have died down and the stadium is empty, after the headlines have been written, and after you are back in the quiet of your room and the championship ring has been placed on the dresser and after all the pomp and fanfare have faded, the enduring thing that is left is the dedication to doing with our lives the very best we can to make the world a better place in which to live.' " I'm staring at the paper, but not reading it. I don't need the paper today; I've read my little speech so many times in the past twenty-four hours that I could recite it backward in my sleep.

Not that I'm sleeping much these days.

We're at the cemetery. I'm standing beside the open grave. The crowds from the funeral have gone, and now it's just a private burial for family and close friends. I didn't want to speak at the church, but I thought I should at least give a thought or two here — to say good-bye one last time, to honor the man I loved. If nothing else, I want to hold my head high for the kids and show them that I'm going to be okay.

"That was Nathan's favorite quote," I continue. "Football legend Vince Lombardi may have said it, but my husband exemplified it day in and day out, as best as he knew how. To the bitter end, Nathan kept trying to make the world a better place, one kind deed at a time. And he did it in such an unassuming way that it came off as effortless, even though it wasn't easy. It was his labor of love — a burden that blessed so many lives."

Listen to me. I sound just like those people at the funeral today who talked about Nathan like all he ever did with his life was serve others, like it was his full-time job or something. Maybe to outside observers it seemed that way, but I knew better, and so did he. Six good things per day — that was his goal. Some days he managed to squeeze in a few extra, but other days he fell short. And not to trivialize what he did — because I absolutely adore him for it — but most of the time his little acts of kindness took hardly any time at all. How many seconds does it take to hold a door for someone in the rain, or to let another car take the good parking spot even though you were there first? Sure, some things ended up taking longer, but those were the exceptions, not the rule.

Nathan once estimated that he spent, on average, only eight minutes a day doing things to help others, and that's accounting for those times when he'd be gone half a day helping a buddy move or taking an hour after work to visit someone in the hospital. *Eight minutes.* That's half of one percent of an entire day. It doesn't sound like a lot, but now that I don't have him around, I find myself wishing I could have every last one of those minutes back, all for myself.

Compared with what I have now, a single second would feel like a lifetime, and eight whole minutes an eternity.

Focus, Halley! People are watching!

I drop the paper to my side. Not only because I don't need it, but because I no longer want it. There are other things that aren't spelled out on the page, which are written in my heart, and they need to be said too. Looking up, I find Ty and Alice watching me from the other side of the grave. "But," I say softly, going off script and fighting off tears, "the man lying here wouldn't want to be remembered for the outward ways in which he improved the world. He never sought honor or recognition that way. Maybe that's how the world will remember him . . . but to me he was much more than that. I'll remember a gentle man, one who laughed easily and spoke with sincerity, who was trustworthy and honorable, and yet who had the audacity to steal my heart, even though I'd have gladly handed it over without much persuasion. I'll remember a father who loved his children more than life itself. And when I look into the eyes of those children — especially in moments like these, when I'm not altogether sure I can carry on without my best friend — I'll remember that he lives still . . . in them. They are Nathan's greatest legacy, and I'm the greatest beneficiary of his time on earth, because not only was I allowed to live and love and laugh with him for nearly twenty years, but he gave me two wonderful pieces of himself in Ty and Alice."

I didn't want to cry again, but I find myself wiping at my face. Only . . . I don't feel so sad anymore. The hurt is still there, but I can feel a part of my beleaguered soul is starting to heal. I let the paper slip from my hands. It floats down into the earth beside the casket. "I love you, Nathan. We all do. Mr. Lombardi was right — the cheers and fanfare may have faded, but the thing that will last is what you've done to change the world. And Nathan . . . you've changed *me.*"

I said the graveside service was just for family and close friends. That's not one hundred percent correct. Randy Rawlins, Ty's football coach, was there too. I invited him because I thought it would be good for Ty, who this morning announced that he quit the team. Unfortunately, the two didn't get to talk much at the cemetery, so afterward I also invited him to a family gathering that Colleen is putting on at our house a little later in the day.

To be honest, I never got the full scoop from Nathan on what happened between him and Randy when they were kids. "Just high school drama," he'd said. But the fact that Randy apparently still held a grudge didn't stop Nathan from working some behind-the-scenes magic to get him an interview for the vacant head coaching position in our town when my husband heard that his onetime friend was out of work.

"You sure that's a good idea?" I asked him at the time. "If he really hates you, what makes you think he'll give your son a fair shot on the team when Ty comes up through the program?"

"Ty will have to earn his spot like everyone else," he said. "And I think he'll be a really good coach. If not for a blown knee in college, he'd likely have gone pro, so he definitely knows a thing or two about the game."

When Randy shows up at three thirty, he is still wearing the navy-blue suit he had on earlier. We chitchat in the entryway for a minute, and then I take him around and introduce him to a few people in the living room before pulling him off to the side to speak in private. "I take it you heard about Ty's decision?" We're not standing particularly close, but even from this distance I have to crane my neck to look up at him.

"About the team? Yep. I can't say as I'm real thrilled about it."

"Me neither. I think he needs football right now, to help him refocus after all this."

Randy nods. "That why you invited me here? To try to change his mind?"

The way he says it suggests he thinks it's a bad idea. "I was hoping."

He shrugs. "I can try, I guess. But teenage boys aren't always the most rational human beings. Once they get something in their head, it's hard to sway them. Unless you happen to be a teenage girl." He pauses. "Where is he?"

I smile, and then point behind him through the window. "He must be thinking about something. That's his thinking bin."

I lead Coach Rawlins to the kitchen, where there's a door to the back. It's drizzling, but I follow him quietly onto the deck and watch as Ty throws footballs through a tire swing in the backyard. With his back to us, he picks up the next ball in his giant practice bin and throws it as hard as he can. It sails through the center of the hole in a perfect spiral, striking the fence on the other side with a loud *thwap.*

"Nineteen for twenty," Ty drones, then reaches for another ball.

"Looks like a week away from practice hasn't spoiled your throwing motion," Randy says. "That's good."

Ty spins around, shrugging mightily when he sees me standing behind his coach. I suddenly wish I'd left the two alone for a man-to-man conversation — *dang my nosiness.*

"The motion doesn't mean squat when the man who taught it to me isn't around." He cocks his arm and whips another one through the tire. "Twenty for twenty-one."

Randy shoves his hands into his suit pockets. "Any chance that you tossing balls out here means you've changed your mind about finishing the season? Assuming we win tonight, the first play-off game is in fourteen days, and the guys would love to have you leading them."

"Any chance my dad will be there to watch?" Ty asks calmly.

"Ty, you've got a right to feel like throwing in the towel." Randy's words come out with way more compassion than I'd expect from a man his size. "But quitting right now would be giving up a lot, don't you think? A possible state championship, the pride of giving this team everything you've got. It's your senior year, man, and it's almost over — let's finish this thing." He pauses. "Heck, I say stick with it just to take your mind off all this other stuff for a few hours a day. Isn't that what your dad would've wanted for you?"

Ty's face turns a little red. "Oh please," he says, "don't pretend like you're only thinking of my best interest. Admit it, you need my services on the field."

"I guess you don't know me as well as I thought."

"Oh yeah? And I guess you didn't know my father very well either. Why would he care if I finished my senior year or not? My grandpa told me this morning that Dad didn't play *any* of his senior year of high school."

This isn't going as I'd hoped. Is this how men grieve? By getting pouty and grumbling at each other?

Randy's color is now even brighter than Ty's. "Oh he did, did he? Well, back then Nathan was my best friend, Ty, and I promise you, your old man would have given his right arm to play that year. Problem was, he didn't know when to —." He cuts himself short, his eyes glowering. After a few seconds he mumbles, "Your dad was a good man. And I truly believe he'd want you to finish what you started. Think about it."

Before I or Ty can say anything else, Randy slips back inside the house, then out the front door.

Donna Cullen
October 23
Wow! Such great stories from everyone. I don't have anything better, but I'll add my "one good thing" anyway. My car was out of commission and my hubby was talking to Nathan, our neighbor, about how I was going to get around while my daughter was having surgery. He said anytime you need to borrow one of his cars, just let him know. We could use it for as long as needed.

Like • Comment • Share

CHAPTER THIRTEEN

Ty

I've heard people say that my dad got Rawlins the head coaching job in Mesquite.

It's actually not true.

Yes, they were best friends once upon a time. And yes, my dad hooked him up with the hiring committee. But after that it was all Rawlins's doing. He was the one in the interview getting grilled, not my dad. Rawlins had to show them he had what it takes to win, and he did that all on his own.

Unfortunately for me, rumors spread. The same people who think my dad pulled a favor also believe that Coach took it easy on me because of it, so I had to double my effort every time I stepped onto the field. The last thing I wanted was anyone saying I didn't earn my spot on the depth chart just like everyone else.

Although they used to be friends, I don't think I ever saw Dad and Rawlins talk, even at team meetings and such. Maybe that's just what happens as you get older, your childhood friends go in different directions and the friendships fizzle.

Is that going to happen to me and Dillon? Graduate from high school, and then . . . what? We see each other twenty years from now and we're not even on speaking terms? I can't imagine that happening.

I wish I knew what Coach meant when he said Dad would have given his right arm to play his senior year. Grandpa made it sound like it was Dad's decision, but Rawlins's version didn't sound like there was much of a choice at all. Of course, Coach is probably twisting the truth to lure me back into action.

No matter. It won't work. I love football, but I'm done. No Dad, no football . . . no pressure.

I cock my arm and let another ball fly. It nicks the inside lip of the tire and bounces out. "Twenty for twenty-two."

After forty throws — and thirty-seven makes — I go back inside.

Alice is sitting by herself at the kitchen counter, staring at the fine print on the back of a Dr Pepper can. I doubt very much that she is just casually perusing it for interest's sake. More likely, she's trying to learn a

120

ridiculously obscure piece of information. That's just how she is — loves to learn. And honestly, she's really good at it. I just . . . I guess I wish sometimes that she were a little more normal. You know, just so I could have friends over without her saying something random about the Ming Dynasty or reciting the alphabet backward in pig Latin. Everybody I know thinks she's a complete goof.

"Mind if I join you?" I ask as I grab the stool to her right and sit down.

"It's a free country," she replies without taking her eyes off the Dr Pepper.

"You sure about that? With all these people here, I'm starting to feel like a prisoner in my own home. Don't you wish they'd just leave us alone?"

She doesn't say anything.

"Alice, why are you so interested in that soda?"

Now she pulls her gaze up to meet mine, and then runs a hand through her cropped hair and tousles it around. "I swear, it feels softer now than it did just a few months ago. I've had pop dumped on me a couple times at school, but the more it happens the silkier it gets. Crazy, right? Last night while I was in Mom's tub, I memorized the ingredients in a bottle of conditioner, and I was just checking the can to see if any of them match. Do you think I could market Dr Pepper as a hair softener?"

"You memorized the conditioner bottle?"

"Yep, in order of volume from most to least. Is that weird?"

Typical Alice. "Yes! It's completely weird. But it's also kinda cool having a sister who can memorize random information on a whim. We should put you on *Jeopardy!* We'd make a killing."

"Kinda cool?" she asks. " 'Kinda's' not even a word. And I'm sure 'kinda cool' still isn't cool enough for you to be seen with me in public."

Here we go again. This is what I get for trying to pay her a compliment. "Al, how many times do I have to say I'm sorry? I know you're still mad at me about the hot-dog thing. I don't blame you. But there's nothing I can do about it now. It's over."

"Not for me. Every day I have to go back to school and face those kids who think I'm this complete freak. If you'd stood up for me . . . who knows? Maybe it would have fixed things."

I'm sure it wouldn't have fixed things, but I get her point. "I'll say it again. *I'm sorry.* If I had to do it over, I'd help you out. My bad. Now can we please call a truce?"

Her eyes perk up a bit. "Really? You'd stick

up for me?"

"Well . . . yeah. I guess."

I guess? What kind of lame answer is that? Obviously not a convincing one, because she slumps forward again and mumbles, "Yeah, right. Like King Cool would be caught dead mingling with the peasants."

I give up. "Fine. You're right. Don't come crying to me the next time someone dumps a soda on your head."

"And don't come crying to me," she counters, "when I discover a new conditioner and you're dumping soda on your own head!"

I'm trying to figure out what that even means when two elderly women that I don't recognize approach from the dining room. One puts a hand on my shoulder and the other puts an arm around Alice. "How are you two holding up?" the first one asks.

We both nod politely and say we're doing fine, just as we've been saying all day. Then, without even telling us how we're related, the two old ladies leave to mingle with Aunt Patricia. When they're gone, Alice says, "You're right, this is a prison. I'd much rather be up writing my blog."

Like Mom, Alice has become quite a proficient blogger. Her blog is called *My Own Little Wonderland*. Last year she spent so much time writing posts that Mom and Dad eventually invested in a small laptop for her to use so that the rest of us could get some time on the family computer.

"Hang in there," I tell her. "Eventually they'll leave."

And eventually they do.

By eight thirty the only guests still in the house are Grandma and Grandpa Steen. Alice sneaks off upstairs to her room, but I figure I'd better at least make half an effort to be hospitable to my dad's parents while they're here. Especially Grandpa, who's been really quiet today. Like vow-of-silence quiet. I don't know if it's the whole funeral thing that's got him down, or something else, but I'm sure something's eating at him. Since our early-morning conversation about Dad and football, he's hardly said two words to me. Now that everyone's gone, I want to ask him why he and Coach Rawlins's version of the past don't quite jive, but he's nowhere to be found. Grandma, on the other hand, is sitting perfectly still on the living room sofa. Her sad eyes are fixed on her own lap.

"Can I sit?"

She looks up slowly, trying to smile. "Need you ask?"

Usually I'm very capable when it comes

to talking to adults, but as I take a seat, I find I'm unable to come up with anything interesting to say. I could go with the typical Grandma topics — school, grades, future college plans, Metamucil — but none of them seem appropriate at the moment. Instead, I decide to lead off with the one question I've been answering all day. "So, how are you holding up?"

She dabs at her eyes with a white hanky. "Not good. Not good at all. And you?"

"About the same. How about Grandpa? He seemed kinda . . . umm, distant today. At least since breakfast."

"Oh? Did you two have breakfast together?"

"He didn't tell you? It was pretty early, I guess. Everyone else was still sleeping."

"Well, don't take it personally that he's not real talkative. He's been a little moody all week. He's just heartbroken over your dad's passing, that's all."

"My mom mentioned that you're going to stay with us for a while."

"I hope that's okay. Tim can only stay a week because he's got to get back to keep the church going, but I thought maybe you all could use an extra hand around here while things settle down."

"Yeah, of course."

Grandma tries smiling again, but it turns into a wrinkled old frown, and then she's dabbing once more at her eyes. "You're so much like your father. Has anyone ever told you that?"

"Most people say I look more like my mom."

"Looks, oh yes, you definitely take after Halley. But personality? Demeanor? You're Nathan's boy through and through."

"Thanks. I mean, I hope so. Someday I want to be just like him." It's true, I'd love nothing more than to be just like my dad someday. The only problem is — and I'd never tell Grandma this — I don't think I have it in me. Dad and I had the same size feet, but I know his shoes are too big to fill.

I smile at Grandma, and she smiles back. It's a nice moment — maybe the nicest one we've ever shared. Then my mother comes into the room carrying Dad's laptop from work, and the moment is lost.

Mom is trembling again, and sobbing, and I know instantly that something is terribly wrong. What happened to the woman who stood beside the grave and said such amazing things? I thought she'd turned a corner. I guess not.

As she crosses the room, I get the distinct feeling that this isn't just ongoing mourning

126

of a husband. It's more than that. In ways that I can't put a finger on, she somehow seems more broken now than the night she learned of Dad's awful fate.

At first Mom looks at me like she isn't sure if she wants me here, but then she focuses on Grandma Steen. In a move that makes Grandma jump, Mom tosses the computer next to her on the couch. "Please tell me," she says between tight, tearful gasps, "that you don't . . . already . . . know about this."

For a second or two Grandma's eyes dance back and forth, like a scared squirrel just before it becomes roadkill. Then somehow she regains her composure, picks up the computer, and gives a long stare at whatever is on the screen. Finally she looks back up, but her face is hard to read. Conflicted? Embarrassed? Dubious? Indifferent? I can't tell. She takes a long breath, and then calmly states, "Had Nathan wanted you to know, I'm sure he would have told you."

"So it's true." Mom crumples into a ball in the chair next to me. "*It's true.* All these years and he never told me!" She groans, rubbing at her temples with both index fingers.

Grandma seems to be debating what else

— if anything — she should say. Finally she speaks, though the brevity of her words does little to comfort. "For what it's worth, I know he loved you more." Then she stands and smooths out her long black dress. Almost apologetically she adds, "It's been a long day, and I should probably go check on Tim. If you don't mind, I'd like to go up to our room. We'll likely just turn in for the night."

Mom dismisses her with a curt wave and a sideways glance, the combination of which carries an obvious message: Just go away!

For several minutes I sit silently watching my mother bawl. Occasionally she stops to catch her breath, but then she starts right up sobbing again. I want to console her, but without knowing what's going on I'm not sure how to do that. Based on what my mother said, and my grandmother's comments, part of me doesn't even want to know, for fear that such knowledge will jeopardize my memory of the man who was ripped away from me a week ago.

But I have to know.

Slowly, like a mouse that senses danger but can't resist the smell of the cheese, I creep over to the couch and pick up the computer.

On the screen is an e-mail, sent to my

dad's work account. The sender's familiar name is the first thing that jumps out at me: Madeline Zuckerman, the same woman who'd said all of those things on Facebook. My heart was already pounding, but now it really starts thumping against my rib cage. This was a kid from Dad's youth. A childhood crush, right? Why is she sending him e-mails at work?

The note was sent just eight days ago, one day before Dad died. The subject line reads, "Re: Your Daughter."

Why, I wonder, was Dad swapping e-mails with this woman about Alice?

The message itself is very brief. Then again, it only takes a tiny little bomb to blow up the world around you.

Hey Nathan! Here's a picture of Zoe and her fiancé to brighten your day. I still can't believe our little girl is getting married. Listen, I know I hinted at this before, but now I'm going to come right out and ask. Would you mind flying out to California with me for her wedding? Just come meet her, so she can have some small knowledge of her dad as she starts her own family. I know it's a lot to ask, but it would mean the world to her . . . and to me. Let me know.

Love ya lots!
Madeline

The woman in the picture is gorgeous. She looks like she's maybe just out of college, but I've never been good at guessing ages. The guy with his arm draped around her is about the same age.

A wave of shock and anger surges up inside me.

My dad had another kid? Did he cheat on my mom? Was he having an affair for their entire marriage? How was that possible?

Before peeking at the computer, all I'd wanted to do was console my mom, but suddenly I need consoling too. Losing a father was painful enough, but losing the bright memory of a father? That is as crushing to me as the blow that stole his life.

I place my hand on Mom's back for a few seconds, just to let her know I'm there — as if that'll do any good. Then I follow Grandma's path upstairs. This is all too much to handle . . . I just want to be alone.

Jenn O'Brien

October 24

Nathan did a big-time favor for me earlier this year, and because of his example I've been on the lookout for ways to help others. About a month ago, an opportunity finally presented itself! I was pulling into the parking lot of my apartment complex. I was coming around the corner by the trash containers and there was a woman leaning on the hood of her car waving at me. I thought there was an animal in the road or something she wanted to warn me about. I unrolled my window and she asked for help. Immediately, I thought she was having a heart attack or something. I jumped out of my car to see what she needed. In the garbage area, someone had left rolled-up carpeting on the ground; she was throwing away her trash and slipped on the carpeting. She had been in the trash "cubicle" for about 20 minutes before pulling herself to the car bumper hoping someone would come along. It turned out that I was that someone! I then drove over to her apartment, went inside to find her cell phone, and then drove her to urgent care. They were closed, so I drove her 20 minutes away to a hospital emergency room. An attendant and I got her unloaded and wheeled inside. I parked my car and went inside to see if she was okay. It turned out that hospital wasn't covered by her insurance, but the hospital 2 blocks down was. We loaded her back into my car and drove her to the second hospital. Once again, an attendant and I got her unloaded and then I went to park. I went inside and stayed in the waiting area until a nurse came out and said that this woman's friends were on the way and I could go home. I know this is my experience, not Nathan's, but I wanted to share it because it proves that he was right: one good thing really does lead to more good things! Without his example, I might have been less willing to help out. It wasn't convenient to drive that woman around, but because of Nathan's "good thing" for me, I was glad to lend a hand to someone else.

Like • Comment • Share

CHAPTER FOURTEEN

Halley

Have you ever been at the bottom of a deep pool and felt like you might not make it back up to the surface? Your lungs are burning, and the fear of death turns to panic? In my dream, I am drowning . . .

I wake with a start, punctuated by a gasp, like I'm coming up for air. I touch a palm to my face; it's still as wet as when I drifted off to sleep on the couch two hours ago. To be honest, I'd hoped that the blackness of slumber would quell my tears, but I wasn't that lucky. Instead, my rest was haunted by the words of a stranger named Madeline Zuckerman and by the face of her daughter, Zoe, the twenty-something beauty who was fathered by my late husband.

I sit up and look around. The living room is dim, but there is enough borrowed light from the hallway to make out my surroundings. I scan from left to right, taking in every shadowy detail: the empty lounge chair where Nathan and I would sometimes snuggle while watching a late-night movie; the silk Ficus tree he surprised me with on our ninth anniversary; the cherry woodwork surrounding the fireplace that Nathan and Ty worked so hard on; the white figurine on the mantel depicting a father with his arm around a daughter, which Alice gave to Nathan on Father's Day a few years back. Centered above the mantel is an antiqued wooden plaque that reads, *All because two people fell in love.* Directly above that, the most recent family photo.

In the darkness from where I sit I can only make out four fuzzy shapes in the picture, but I know which is his.

"How could you!" I yell as I wrap both arms tightly around my waist, my stomach knotting up for the umpteenth time. "I don't get it. *How?* How could you keep this from me all these years? How could you lie to me? How could you have this other woman and child in your life, and make me believe you only ever loved *me*?" I take a long, tearful breath, then whisper, "Were you ever going to tell me . . . or was it always your plan to take this to the grave?"

With great effort I pick myself off the couch and approach the family picture to get a closer look. I stare at Nathan's friendly, innocent-looking eyes, searching for any hint of deceit that I might have overlooked when he was still alive, but there is none to find. "I would have eventually gotten over your death, Nathan," I tell him. "But I will never get over this."

My husband's computer is still sitting on the coffee table. I retrieve it before heading upstairs and crawling into bed, though sleep is not my aim. No matter how tired I am, there are too many thoughts swimming around in my head; questions that need answers. With a large pillow propped behind my back I flip open the laptop's screen. When it flickers to life, the picture of the woman is still there, smiling sweetly back at me.

A few taps of the mouse opens up a search box in the e-mail client. I type two words, *Madeline Zuckerman,* and then click "Find."

The cursor loops for several seconds as the computer queries old records for a match. Then the screen begins filling up with results. When it is done, there are hundreds of exchanges, dating all the way back to 1998.

I scroll down to the oldest one on the list and begin to read.

Nathan! It was SO good to see you at the reunion. Thanks for encouraging me to go. Given how high school ended for us, I was worried it might be weird, but I'm really glad I went. Just seeing you again and knowing that you are doing well made everything we went through together worth it.

Given the situation, I'm not surprised we lost contact so quickly after going our separate ways. But I often wondered if you had any lingering interest in knowing how our little girl was doing, or if you still thought about us from time to time. I'm so glad to learn that you did!

I've attached a recent picture so you can see for yourself. I also included a few pictures of Zoe from the past ten years so you can see what a cutie she is. Isn't she precious!? My favorite is the one in the tiara. She likes to call herself a princess, and says one day she'll marry her prince. I don't want to be the one to burst her bubble, but experience says that fairy tales don't always have a happy ending. Then again, the reunion has me thinking about the past. I know it's a long shot, but who knows? Maybe someday I can still get my prince back . . .

Anyway, I hope you enjoy the pictures — the fruits of your labors, so to speak. I know she came into this world under difficult circumstances, but every time I look at her, I'm just thankful that she had the opportunity to come at all . . . and I have you alone to thank for that.

If you don't mind, I'd like to e-mail you from time to time to keep you up on things. We really need to stay in touch more.

All my love,
Madeline

I take a long breath, recalling the night Nathan attended his ten-year high school reunion. They gathered at his alma mater in Rockwall, just a couple towns over from our home in Mesquite. I'd wanted to go with him so I could meet all of his old friends, but Nathan was adamant that it would be boring, so I stayed home with Ty. Big mistake, obviously. When he returned home sometime after midnight, he claimed to be too tired to go into any great detail about how the evening went. The most I could get out of him was, "There were people there I never thought I'd see again. It was really good seeing how their lives are turning out."

"I should have gone with him," I mutter angrily as I open up the next e-mail.

Hi Nathan. Me again. Thanks for your quick reply. I really appreciate the pictures you sent of your family. Your little boy is a doll, and your wife is cute as a button.

The photo from Halloween is the best. Was it your idea to dress your son as Clark Kent? Like father like son, I guess . . . you always were my Superman. :-)

You still are.

Love ya,
M.

I continue going through old e-mails until my eyes are blurry with fatigue. Reading them is like a drug addiction: I know it's killing me, but I can't stop. Most of the notes are short and relatively benign updates about Zoe. Many of them, at least the incoming ones from Madeline, have pictures attached: Zoe at dance recital, Zoe's class photo, Zoe blowing out candles, Zoe's first dance, Zoe in the school musical, Zoe playing basketball, Zoe at the homecoming dance her freshman year, Zoe at homecoming her sophomore year, and on and on. By four in the morning I know everything there is to know about Zoe Zuckerman from birth to high school graduate, and there are still many e-mails to go.

I skip ahead to one marked urgent, sent less than two months ago.

Nathan, I have some news that I'm absolutely dying to tell you about: Our little girl is getting married! Zoe met a man during her final year of college, and they've been dating very seriously ever since (I think I sent you a picture of them hiking in the Redwoods about five months back). You'll be glad to know that he also played football in high school (not a quarterback, though, sorry). He's got one year left of law school out in California. They're looking at either April or May for the wedding; I'll let you know when the date is firm. You deserve to be there too, to see the result of our final year in high school. I won't be mad if you say no, but at least consider it.

Love,
Maddy

"Why did you keep this from me?" I ask aloud, speaking to Nathan as if he's lying there with me as he had for nearly twenty years. In a fit of anger I slam the computer lid shut and shove it away so that it lands on the floor. Then I curl deeper into the covers. Staring at the empty pillow beside me, I whisper, "You should have told me right from the start."

I sink deep into my pillow, keeping my eyes open long enough for a brief glimpse of Nathan's face in our wedding photo on the nightstand. "You're not the man I married," I tell him groggily. Then the world disappears into nothing.

Nancy May
October 25
I recently had hip replacement surgery and only work part-time, so I have no benefits from my job. Nathan and his dear family helped me out in so many ways. They put money into my checking account without me knowing. They gave me gas and grocery cards. They cooked meals for me. They visited me in the hospital and at

home. I don't know how I would have made it through without their help. I am so grateful.

Like • Comment • Share

CHAPTER FIFTEEN

Ty

Adults are naturally grumpy creatures.

This is the first thing that pops into my head as my grandfather marches down the stairs at ten in the morning, wearing a purposeful frown on his face. Grandma has been sullen this morning as well, and Mom's about as unpleasant as I've ever seen. Then again, I've got a bit of a chip on my shoulder today too, so who am I to judge?

The only person in the family who isn't in a bad mood is Alice. She's also the only one who doesn't know about dad's little secret, and Mom made me swear as soon as I woke up that I'd keep my mouth shut.

When Grandpa finally stops on the stairwell's landing, I can almost see Mom's thoughts, willing him to keep quiet about Dad. But sure enough, he clears his throat loudly and says, "Listen, I'm tired of hiding the truth about Nathan's past, so if you'd like, I'm happy to answer any questions you may have."

Mom and I are both on the opposite side of the great room; she's writing in her journal, while I'm catching up on school-work. Alice is nearest the stairwell, lying on the floor trying to decide which is the best chess move to make against herself, while Grandma is rinsing dishes in the sink.

For a moment, everyone stops what they are doing and the whole place goes quiet.

Then Grandma blurts out, "What the devil is wrong with you? Didn't I say not to talk about it unless asked?"

"Well," he replies, "there's a ten-ton elephant in the room, dear, and I thought I should just tackle it head-on."

Alice sets down a pawn and addresses Grandpa. "What truth? And would that be an Asian elephant metaphor, or African? Probably African, because the Asians only grow to about six tons."

Grandma crosses her arms and shoots her husband a look. "Yes, dear . . . what kind of elephant would that be?"

Tim's eyes dart around the room, stopping briefly on every incredulous stare. "You mean she doesn't . . . ? I figured everyone knew."

"Not quite everyone," Mom huffs in

frustration. She closes her journal and tosses it on the coffee table. "I'd hoped to shoo the elephant under the carpet, but now you've shined the circus lights right on it." She pauses, then sourly adds, *"Thanks."*

Another fiery silence erupts, which Alice finally extinguishes with a muffled burp. "Excuse me," she says as she picks herself up off the floor and moves to a spot where she has a better view of everyone. "So, I guess I'm the only clueless one here. That's unusual. Would someone please tell me what we're talking about?"

With a beckoning wave, Mom summons Alice to the couch. "Have a seat, sweetie."

"I'm really sorry," Grandpa says. "I just thought —."

Grandma shoots him another look, warning him to keep quiet.

When Alice is seated, Mom puts an arm around her and gives a long squeeze. "Alice . . . ," she starts, searching for the right way to break the news. "We . . . I . . . was going through your father's e-mails last night. The ones from work. And I discovered something."

Alice pulls back a bit. "It sounds bad."

"It's not great."

"And this something . . . it's about Dad?"

The wrinkles in Mom's face seem to have

doubled overnight. She's obviously hurting, and I feel her pain. No person should have to go through so much heartache in one week. "Yes, honey. About Dad. It's . . . I don't even know how to say this. It's so surreal, I don't know where to begin."

"Mom, I'm thirteen. That's old enough to understand almost everything." She gives me a little smirk and adds, "If Ty understands, then I definitely will."

Before I can get my own jab in, Mom raises her hand, warning me to stay quiet. Then she takes a deep breath, the kind to ward off unwanted emotions. "You're right. You're old enough to know. I just thought that you, of all people, should be sheltered from this, because . . . well, because you were Daddy's little girl." She hesitates. "But . . ."

"What?" Alice nudges.

"Well, the thing is . . . It turns out you weren't the only one."

Alice stares at Mom like she's a lunatic. "What's that supposed to mean?"

Now little drops of water begin to pool up at the corners of Mom's eyes. "It means that before you came along, before Ty, even before me, your father had another little girl. With another woman."

Alice's eyes bulge, and she is momentarily

speechless. "You mean, like, he was married before? And you didn't know?"

"No, sweetheart. He wasn't married. He was Ty's age, in high school."

I see a look pass between my grandparents. I'm not fluent in old-people body language, but if I had to venture a guess, I'd say Grandpa is gently urging Grandma to speak up. When their nonverbal conversation ends, they both join us around the coffee table, taking a seat in the plush chairs opposite the couch.

"Umm . . . can I say something?" asks Grandma. "In the interest of full disclosure."

"Of course," replies Mom.

"Well, you're mostly right, Halley. They weren't married when Maddy got pregnant. But once they found out she was expecting, well, they decided it was best that baby Zoe not be born to single parents."

Mom just stares at her for a moment. "You mean to tell me," she says finally, choosing her words correctly, "that not only did your son have a child that he didn't tell me about, but that I was not the first Mrs. Nathan Steen?"

"They wanted to take responsibility for their actions," says Grandpa. "We agreed to it, though I sometimes wish we hadn't."

"So they got married *in high school*?" I ask.

My grandparents' heads nod in unison.

Meanwhile, the wheels in Alice's head are obviously spinning, but it's tough to tell which direction.

Mom's head looks like it might explode at any second. After taking a moment to simmer down, she rubs Alice's arm and says, "It's okay to be mad, pumpkin."

"Are you mad, Mom?" Alice asks immediately.

"You mean you can't tell? I'm so mad I could scream. In fact, I screamed a lot last night, while you were sleeping. I'm not mad that he had another child per se. But I'm absolutely furious that he hid it from me. Here was this huge piece of his life that I knew nothing about. And now to learn that I wasn't even his first wife? And on top of that, for the last fourteen years he's been communicating with this other woman in secret, right under my nose? More than anything, I feel betrayed."

Alice looks around at everyone in the room. "Well, I'm upset too. I'm mad that any of you believe this."

Oh boy, here we go — Alice is finally acting her age.

I put down my textbook, dropping it on

the table a little more forcefully than intended. "What's that you were saying about being old enough to understand? I saw the e-mails, Al. Mom's not making this stuff up."

She brushes me off like I'm not even there, then turns to our grandparents. "You think it's true, too?"

Grandpa leans forward to say something, but Grandma beats him to it. "Alice, I don't know why your father didn't tell your mom about this a long time ago. It wasn't right to keep secrets from her, I'll admit that. But that doesn't take anything away from the love he had for all of you. Yes, he made some mistakes in the past, but he was a good man. You know that. And I know for a fact he loved you like nobody's business."

"And you, Grandpa?" Alice asks.

"I, umm . . . ," he mumbles. "I think your grandmother summed it up nicely."

While Grandpa is speaking, my mind suddenly puts two and two together: *This is why Dad quit football!* I'd wager this thing with Madeline Zuckerman is also what caused a rift between Dad and Grandpa. She was the pebble, as he described it, that sent their little streams on divergent paths.

Before I can think it through any further, Alice pulls out of Mom's reach and stands up, taking another disappointed look around the circle. "You're all going to say I'm stupid, that I'm just a dumb little girl. Well, I'm neither of those things. What I am is the only person who really knew Dad. You all only thought you did."

"Alice," my mom chides, reaching out for her. "Sit down and let's —"

"No!" Alice shouts back, turning a deep shade of red. "I don't want to hear you talk about him like this. You think you know everything because of some stupid e-mails, but you don't. You don't know him! He told me all the time that I was special because I was his only daughter. And you know what? I believe him! So think whatever you want, but Dad wasn't the guy you're trying to make him out to be. He just wasn't."

Grandpa leans forward again to speak. "Alice, dear, it's not just the e-mails. Remember, your grandmother and I were there. It's not a matter of whether he did or didn't. *He did.* Now, I know it's not what you want to hear right now. And we all understand how hurt you must feel, sweetheart. We really do."

"Don't call me sweetheart!"

"C'mon, Al," I chime in, "it's okay to be upset. But don't take this out on us. We didn't do anything wrong."

The way she whips around and stares at me, eyes blazing, I expect she's really going to let me have it. But instead she takes another second to think, then she crosses her arms and quietly asks, "So you really saw the e-mails?"

"One of them."

"And?"

"And what?" I respond with a shrug. "What do you want me to say? That I don't have an older half sister wandering around somewhere in the world? That Dad wasn't hiding things from all of us? I'm sorry, but I can't do that."

Alice scrunches up her face while she contemplates what to say next. Finally she turns back to Mom. "I want to see for myself. Will you send me one of the e-mails?"

"Do I have to?" she replies. "I was hoping to never have to look at them again."

"Well, I won't believe you until I see it with my own eyes." With that she spins back around and heads for the stairs, stopping when she is halfway up. "I'll be in my room . . . waiting for one of those e-mails."

Jeehye Kim
October 25
Oh . . . That's so sad. i'm short at English..

150

but i'll try it!! I am so grateful.

Like • Comment • Share

Jeehye Kim
October 25
My boyfried, Jihoon, he loves me very much (and so do i). When I was in sadness, his American boss, Mr. Steen, help him fly to see me.

Like • Comment • Share

Jeehye Kim
October 25
he try makes me happy. i fell in painful love before, but after then i met real love.(oh . . . is it right?) I am so grateful for Jihoon to visit, and for Nathan Steen for to allow it and help pay.

Like • Comment • Share

Jeehye Kim
October 25
to someone, my story is may be common. but is so special to me.

Like • Comment • Share

CHAPTER SIXTEEN

Halley

We just sit there staring at each other long after the slam of Alice's door reverberates through the house.

Tim eventually breaks the silence. "I just wanted to be straight with everyone," he says dejectedly. "I'm so sorry, Halley. You welcomed us into your home, and this is how we thank you."

I *so* want to be mad at Tim for saying anything in front of Alice. Clearly she is not ready to handle something like this. I'd really like to stay upset at Colleen too, for not ever having told me about this part of her son's life before. But is it fair to blame them for something that my husband is ultimately responsible for? I'm plenty upset, but not so much at them. "Forget it." I sigh. "It's not your fault."

"But if I hadn't opened my big mouth," Tim continues, "Alice might have avoided all this."

"That was my plan. But in retrospect, I don't think that would've been right either. She deserves to know. And given how she reacted, it wouldn't have mattered how we broke the news. She'd have put up walls no matter what."

"Can you say *denial*?" Ty quips beneath his breath.

"I'd much prefer to blame Tim," says Colleen. I can't tell if she's being serious or not. "But I think you're right, Halley. No matter how much lipstick we put on it, Alice wasn't ever going to like this pig."

As Colleen is talking, a look passes between her and Tim, like a lifetime's conversation in a single second. It reminds me of something that I was thinking about all night. "Tim, I always got a sense that things weren't quite right between Nathan and you — like there was always something unspoken in the way you two interacted. He always dismissed it, but I wasn't wrong, was I?"

Now Tim exchanges a look with Ty. "I asked the same thing yesterday," Ty states.

"No," Tim says. "You weren't wrong."

"And did this have anything to do with it?"

Another quick glance between Tim and

153

Colleen is all I need for an answer, but Tim confirms it with a nod.

Colleen adds, "What happened back then . . . well, it came as a bit of a shock to us. Nathan was always such a good boy. I know he didn't intend it, but getting that girl pregnant had some unexpected ramifications on our family, and we probably didn't react as well as we could have."

Tim shakes his head. "You did fine, honey. It was me who acted poorly." He turns to look at me. "Actually, in the beginning I thought I handled myself very well. I'll readily admit I was disappointed, but I still loved him, and I did whatever I could to help him through it. I even offered to have them stay in our home until the baby was born so they could get through high school. But those kids were bound and determined to go it alone. I didn't like the choices they made, but I accepted them, right up until they decided to get divorced. Call me old-fashioned, but marriages are supposed to last. So after everything they'd put us through, when they told me they were calling it quits, I blew up at him over the phone. We didn't talk for a whole year after that. Eventually I realized my mistake and apologized, but our relationship never got back to what it once was."

"And the pregnancy?" Ty asks. "That's why he quit football?"

Tim nods once, and then folds his hands on his lap. He and Colleen both sit there waiting to see if we have more questions.

I do. Just one. "Why didn't he tell me any of this?"

"We don't know," says Colleen.

"What we do know," Tim adds, "is that while the two of you were dating, he specifically asked us that we never bring the topic up again. He said he was tired of discussing it with us, and he just wanted to move on." Tim rubs his chin thoughtfully. "I've thought about this a lot over the years, especially when I've had to counsel people who either did bad things or had things done to them. How much information are we required to share about our past?"

"All of it," Ty says. "You've got to be honest, at least with the people you love."

"Really? Even the stuff you've put behind you?"

"Sure. It's part of what defines who you are."

"Only if you let it define you," Tim counters. "Ty, have you ever made a mistake?"

"Sure. All the time."

"Name one."

155

"Uh . . ." Ty looks at me guiltily. "I exceeded the speed limit . . . once."

Tim chuckles. "No, I meant something that you really feel bad about. I know you're a good kid, but you must've done something in these past seventeen years that you wished you hadn't."

I'm not really in the mood for humor, but it's amusing seeing Ty squirm. He looks at me again, then turns away in shame. "Yeah," he mumbles very softly. "I did something I'm not proud of. But you're all going to hate me if I say it."

As a mother, now I have to jump in. "You don't have to say it, Ty. But we won't think any less of you if you share. I promise."

He hems and haws for a few more seconds, then reluctantly admits, "I did one of the worst things you can do. *I did nothing.* I saw Alice getting bullied. Some kids were shoving a soggy, half-eaten hot dog in the hood of her sweatshirt . . . and I just walked by. Completely ignored it, when I could have stopped it."

"Oh, Ty . . ." I say, but I don't know what to say next.

"I'm sorry, Mom," he whispers back.

"I know you are."

After a moment of quiet, Tim pipes back up. "Thank you for sharing. Now I want you to imagine yourself five, ten years from now, when you meet some pretty gal that you're over the moon for. Are you going to start out that relationship by telling her, 'I should warn you, I'm the kind of guy who lets little girls get bullied? In fact, I once watched my sister be humiliated, and I did nothing about it'?"

"I don't think I'd tell her that," concedes Ty.

"I think that was Nathan's thinking too. He'd moved on. He'd done all he could, and he was ready to bury the past."

I feel my pulse quicken. "I agree with you, Tim — to a point. We all have things we've done wrong. Once they're buried, there's no sense digging them up again. What I take issue with is the lying. Nathan was under no obligation to tell me of his teenage exploits." Saying exploits, in this context, with Ty in the room, suddenly makes me a little uncomfortable. I point a finger at him. "Close your ears for a second, Son." I shift back to Tim and Colleen. "But your son proudly declared that I was the only woman . . . er . . . the only one he'd been with. That wasn't a requirement I forced on him, but it was something special that we shared — or at least I thought we did — that we'd saved ourselves for each other. In retrospect, everything we had feels so cheap now. Soiled. So maybe he didn't have to reveal all of his transgressions to me, but he sure as heck had no right to lie to me the way he did."

Both Tim and Colleen are very quiet. It must be hard hearing this about their son, having to relive all this stuff from the past. Eventually Tim says, "Halley, I'm so sorry for all of this. I don't know what else to say. But if you have more questions, I'll gladly answer them."

"No," I tell him, shaking my head. "I'm all questioned out. Questioned out, cried out, burned out — you name it. I don't want to think about it any more. At least not right now."

Tim and Colleen head to their room upstairs, leaving me and Ty alone in the living room. Once they're gone, I close my eyes and lean back into the cushions. A catnap never sounded so inviting as it does this very moment. I hear Ty pick up his book and flip through some pages. After a minute he asks, "Are you really making us go back to school tomorrow?"

I open one eye and squint out. "It's been an entire week. Sorry, but it's time."

He lets a little more time pass before asking another question, but the way he asks it sounds like he's afraid of what my answer will be. "Mom? Do you still love Dad?"

Now I open both eyes, slowly, staring off into space as I analyze my own feelings. "I want to," I tell him. "But I'm finding it hard to right now. I'm still struggling to process all of this."

"Me too. It's so weird to think that when he was my age, he had a kid. He always talked about the benefits of waiting until marriage, and all that. Now it seems so hypocritical."

I turn my head to look directly at him. "Or," I say slowly, "the voice of experience. Don't take this the wrong way, Ty, or as a license for you to go off and do something stupid, but you know as well as anyone that teenagers do occasionally make mistakes. Sometimes big ones. That doesn't have to be the end of happiness for them, though. Like anyone, they have to deal with the consequences and try their best to learn from their mistakes."

"You're defending him now?"

"No. I'm just trying to separate what happened when he was a teenager from who he was as an adult. Remember, I fell in love with the man that you and I both knew, not the boy your grandfather remembers. He was a good man — or at least I thought he was — so I never would have judged him for the mistakes of his youth."

"So you're saying that you still love him?"

"I'm saying . . . I don't know. Finding out that he'd been hiding his past from me, and knowing that he was carrying on some sort of secret relationship with that woman for years and years? It's tainted so much of what I loved. The man I knew had nothing to hide, no secrets. I thought we shared everything. Now it turns out some of the biggest parts of his life had nothing to do with me at all, and that hurts. It makes me wonder what else he was up to that I didn't know about." I stop to lie out lengthwise on the couch, stuffing a silky red throw pillow under my head. "Maybe he was doing more than just e-mailing that woman. I hope not, but I'll never know."

"You could contact her and ask her yourself."

I want to laugh, but the sound that comes out is withered with remorse. "Can you imagine the humiliation? *'Hi, I just found out you're my husband's first wife and the mother of his first child. Care to tell me the extent of your secret relationship for the past decade?'* No, I don't want to have anything to do with her. No good could come of it."

Ty remains quiet for a long time. Then he

leans back and mumbles, "I wanted to be just like him." He sounds confused, and rightfully so. "I never really believed I could, but I at least wanted to try."

Seeing the disappointment on my son's face sends a new wave of emotion flooding over me. "I know you did," I whisper. Ty probably wants me to say something more than that, but I'm at a loss for words. I watch him close his eyes on the other couch. Then, sensing that the conversation is at an end, I curl up and close mine again too.

Sandy Betza Valentine
October 26

A couple weeks before Christmas a knock came at the door, and because my husband is disabled, they knew they had time to run before we opened the door. What they didn't know was that I was watching the whole thing from the kitchen window. Nathan Steen and his two beautiful kids left a card with money. How much is not important, but it was so wonderful to know that someone thought about and cared for us.

Like • Comment • Share

CHAPTER SEVENTEEN

Ty

What is normal? Is there a clinical definition? Who chooses which thoughts or feelings make someone normal rather than abnormal? I ask only because since the accident I haven't felt that at all. Normal, I mean. I feel out of place, like the world isn't quite right. But the world hasn't changed. I have. And it's not hard to figure out why.

Simply put, ten days ago I had a father — someone to look out for me and look up to — and now I don't. My whole life I had this great man who I idolized. Now that he's dead, and the image of him tarnished, I'm floundering. It's almost as though the uncertainty over who he was makes me wonder who I am.

Does that make any sense? Does it sound abnormal?

All things considered, though, Monday morning is a good start toward the center of the normalcy curve. Mom is finally going back to work at her flower shop, Alice is returning to her life as a seventh-grade target, and I'm heading to high school to lose myself in the drone of teachers' voices and the chime of hourly bells. Other than the presence of my grandparents, this has all the makings of the first seminormal day in more than a week.

"Can you ride the bus today?" I ask Alice as I sit down for breakfast. "I want to get to school early."

She swallows a spoonful of Froot Loops. "I want to go early too. I'm ready whenever you are."

"But —." Ah, man. "Mom! Do I have to take Alice today?"

"You don't have to shout," she says as she walks through the kitchen, digging through her purse. "I'm right here."

"Well, do I have to?"

She stops and thinks, then says, "What would your father say, Ty?"

Given everything that we've learned about my dad in the last forty-eight hours, I'm genuinely surprised to hear her say that. I wouldn't think she'd still be pointing to his example for anything. Whatever — I don't have time for a debate. "Fine," I tell Alice. "But I'm leaving in two minutes. If you're not ready when I am, you're on your own." I shove half a piece of toast in my mouth and chase it down quickly with a large swig of milk. Then I inhale the other half of my toast and drain my cup, all in a matter of seconds. "Make that one minute."

Alice is determined to not be left behind. She scarfs down two more bites of cereal as fast as she can, tosses her bowl in the sink, grabs her backpack from the entryway closet, and is standing on the front porch a full fifteen seconds before me.

Mom also beats me to the porch. "Did either of you brush your teeth?" she asks.

Alice and I look at each other, then sprint to the bathroom, jockeying for position at the sink. When we're through, Mom is still waiting for us at the front door. She opens her arms and hugs us both at the same time.

"Are you leaving now too?" I ask when I spot the car keys dangling from the hand that has me bound.

"I have a lot of catch-up to do this morning. The gal I had running things last week is good with bouquets, but I don't pay her to keep the books." She gives an extra squeeze and then lets go. "You guys have a terrific time at school, okay? Just forget about these last few days. Today is a brand-new day, so let's make it a good one."

"I will," says Alice.

"I'll try," I say.

Before we climb into my old Charger, Mom calls after us. "I almost forgot. Remember who you are!"

Alice again says she will, but I just nod. The phrase doesn't sound the same coming from Mom, and now that Dad's true character is exposed, the saying has lost its luster. Who am I anyway? Nathan Steen's kid? A chip off the old block? The son of a liar and a cheater? Is that my new normal?

Five minutes later we pull up in front of the middle school. "Stay out of trouble," I tell Alice before she jumps out of the car.

A few minutes after that I arrive at the high school. Some of the teachers are still showing up. Mr. Davis, the calculus teacher, sees me and waves. Mrs. Howard, my English teacher from last year, is just a few steps behind me as I walk through the front door.

"Hello, Ty," she says. "You're in early."

"Yeah."

She picks up her pace to catch up. In a few steps she's walking right beside me through the main hallway. "I was very sorry to hear what happened."

"Yeah," I say again. "Me too."

"How are you holding up?"

Ah, that question again. "Okay, I guess. Just taking one day at a time. Waiting for things to feel normal again."

When we reach the staff lounge, she stops me. "Ty, I know things must be hard for you right now. If you feel like you need to talk, my door is always open."

I appreciate the gesture, but she's not the teacher I'm interested in talking to right now. "Maybe I will."

I continue down the hallway for another twenty yards, cut through the cafeteria, then down a short set of concrete stairs to the main gym. On the opposite corner is the entrance to the boys' locker room, where I'm guessing I'll find three male PE teachers huddled around a table behind a glass window, sipping their coffees while rehashing yesterday's NFL games.

True to form, there they are — Mr. Bryson, Mr. Smith, and the giant, Coach Rawlins, vigorously recapping their favorite plays. Rawlins is leaning back in his old wooden desk chair like it's a plush recliner. When he sees me, he wipes the smile off his face. He'd had his feet on the table, but they drop instantly to the tile floor with a tremendous *thwump.*

The other teachers stop talking too and look back over their shoulders.

"Hey," Rawlins says tepidly. "Welcome back."

"Hey, Coach."

"It's good to see you."

"Thanks. Got a minute?"

"For you," he says, standing to full height, "I got as many minutes as you want."

Coach Rawlins has a separate office just around the corner, aptly named "the war room," which is reserved for him and his coaching staff. We enter and close the door behind us.

"What's up?" he asks as he takes a seat in another hardwood chair. "You give any more thought to coming back to practice? Big game this week. You know we could use you."

I smile, but with only half my mouth. "I thought you'd say that. But no, I haven't changed my mind. I think I'm really done."

Rawlins grimaces, but at least he says the right words. "I'll support you, whatever you choose."

There are several empty chairs surrounding the war room's table. In the evenings, the assistant coaches sit there to strategize for the next gridiron assault. I pull out the nearest chair and sit down. "So, on Friday, after the funeral, in my backyard, you said some things about my dad and his senior

167

year of football."

"Yeah, about that, I'm really sorry. I should have just kept my mouth shut."

"No. It's fine. I'm actually glad you did. There was something you started to say but didn't quite finish. Something about the problem being that he didn't know when to . . . When to what?"

I've never seen Rawlins so stonelike. For a good five seconds he doesn't flinch one iota. Then he scratches thoughtfully at the scruff on his face and says, "Ya know, I don't really remember where I was going with that. Just rambling, I guess."

"You're lying," I say flatly.

"Excuse me?"

Coach Rawlins always demands the utmost respect from his players, especially from the team captains. That's the natural order of things on the football team — the freshmen take their cues from the upperclassmen, JV takes direction from varsity, the varsity players fall in line with the team captains, and the captains hang on every word that comes out of the coach's mouth. For a football player to talk back to the head coach is unheard of. I might as well have stood up and kicked him in the groin. But I'm not a football player anymore, so I press on. "I said, you're lying. I know you are, so don't say you're not."

Rawlins has that fair sort of skin that turns red easily. I notice it a lot when he's winded from jogging or yelling at the team, but I've never seen him like this. His forehead and cheeks are the same deep maroon as the Crimson Tide pennant hanging above his desk. "You're calling me a liar?" he pants. *"To my face?"*

"Look," I tell him, softening my tone a bit, "I know you're not a liar. I didn't mean it like that. I'm just . . . I need answers, that's all. I do know you're hiding something, and I'm sure you have your reasons, but right now I need you to be straight with me."

"What's going on, Ty? This isn't like you."

"Let's just say that after the funeral, later that night after you left, things got a little weird at home. Mom found . . . well, she stumbled on something that all of us wish she hadn't."

"And you think it's related to your dad giving up football?"

"Pretty sure."

"But not one hundred percent?"

"No, I'm positive. But there are some pieces of information that I'm missing, and I was hoping you could fill in the blanks."

"Such as?"

"Such as why Dad never told us."

Rawlins hesitates before asking, "Can you be more specific about what you think he didn't tell you?"

I sit up in my chair and rest my forearms on the table. "Okay. How's this? *Madeline Zuckerman.*"

I'm expecting a big reaction, but almost immediately — and sounding completely genuine — the giant says, "Never heard of her. Who is she?"

"Madeline Zuckerman," I repeat. "You know, my half sister's mother."

Coach Rawlins doesn't move a muscle. He doesn't speak. Doesn't so much as breathe for the longest time. And then, in a sure sign of defeat, he exhales slowly. "At least you didn't hear it from me."

"So you do know her!"

"Oh, I knew her all right. Better than most, in fact. But back then she went by Maddy. Maddy McFadden. Or McFatty, as she was more commonly known. She was a real piece of work, to put it mildly. Certainly not the kind of girl anyone thought your dad would go for." He pauses just for a second. "I'm sorry I was evasive before, Ty. I didn't know how much you knew, and I didn't want to stick my nose in that mess again."

"Well, my mom feels like she's been totally played. Do you happen to know why it was so important to him to hide all of this from her?"

"Not a clue. Look, Ty, I've always thought the world of you. You know that, right? But your dad and I — well, let's just say that our friendship didn't end on the best of terms, so I'm the last guy to be asking about how or why he did anything that he did, especially as it relates to Maddy."

"Then can you at least answer my original question? Dad didn't know when to what?"

By his expression, it is perfectly clear that Coach Rawlins still doesn't want to finish the sentence, but he finally relents. "Even though I wasn't on good terms with your father, I know full well that he did a lot of good for a lot of people. Even back in high school he was always looking out for kids on the fringe. But when it came to Maddy, he didn't seem to know when enough was enough. The way he went out of his way to help her, it was . . . over the top, I suppose is the right way to say it. So to answer your question, in my view, your dad didn't know when to draw the line, and I think that was his downfall." He pauses briefly to scratch his knee, then says, "He used to tell me that one good thing leads to another. Kind of like a chain reaction — you know, a pay-it-forward type of thing. You ever hear him say that?"

"More times than I can count."

"Well, in this case, one thing led to another, all right, but it wasn't necessarily a good thing. Not for her, and certainly not for him. One day he's being nice to a loner in the hallway, and the next thing you know they're getting married and expecting a baby."

"Did they kick him off the team for that?"

"No, I don't think so, although I'm sure a lot of people would have frowned at the starting quarterback being a dad-to-be. You know, image of the school and all that. But he felt obligated to get a job to help pay for the pregnancy, so he stopped playing and started working after school. They got an apartment, and I hardly saw him after that, except when we passed each other in the hallway. He tried to convince people he had no regrets about football, but I knew better. It killed him." He waits a moment for the school's first bell to ring. "Does that clear things up at all?"

I nod. "It's so weird to think of him as married in high school. What did people say?"

He raises his eyebrows. "A lot. It was all

172

the buzz around town for several months. The pastor's son — the All-American boy and model citizen — moving in with his pregnant wife before graduating. It tore your grandparents up, I'm sure. It wasn't long after that they left town." He pauses and gives me a funny look. "You okay?"

"Just processing. But . . . I still don't understand why, if my dad owned up to everything back then, why he was so secretive about it later on?"

In one giant motion Coach Rawlins stands, steps around the table, and places a hand on my shoulder. "If I knew, I'd tell you, Ty. But there's only one person who might be able to answer that question."

I stare down at the wood grain of the tabletop and whisper, "And that person is dead."

Coach furrows his brow. "No. I was going to say Maddy McFatty."

Kelly Hunsaker
October 26
Okay, so this isn't about Nathan directly. But his son and my son are friends, and they had a sleepover last year after a late football game. The next morning, those two boys cleaned my entire house and let me sleep in! Crazy nice!! Just reading

173

what everyone else has posted, I'm sure Nathan's selflessness has rubbed off on his son, and now it's rubbing off on my son too! Couldn't be more sad to hear he passed away, but thanks to everyone for sharing your memories of him.

Like • Comment • Share

CHAPTER EIGHTEEN

Madeline

Monday-morning lectures should be banned.

This is my final thought before I stand up to address the fourteen students who have managed to pull themselves out of bed for the seven o'clock session. I don't blame the five students whose desks are still empty for not coming — if I had a choice, I wouldn't be here either. "Good morning. How are we all doing today?"

There are a couple of enthusiastic responses, but mostly just garbled grunts and yawns.

Usually I'm a morning person. Usually, but not today. Not on the first day back to work since finding out about Nathan. Not after slipping into the very back row at his funeral on Friday and seeing his casket up front and then spending the rest of the weekend crying.

"I assume all of you did your reading over

the weekend." Most of the heads bob at least once. "Good. So someone please enlighten us. Last year, approximately how many cases of head and neck squamous cell carcinoma were diagnosed worldwide?" Several hands go up as I take another sip of tea. I pick a student at the rear whose hands are busy texting, just to keep things lively. "Miss Peterson?"

"Oh. Sorry. What was that?" She quickly drops the phone in her bag.

I smile, though I'm not feeling very smiley. This young lady is a very capable student, if she'd just apply herself a little more. "Head and neck squamous cell carcinoma. How many cases last year?"

"In the United States or the world?"

"How about both."

"Um, okay. About forty thousand here, and another five hundred thousand worldwide."

So she did read the packet. "Very good. Half a million people. It's a big number. And of those, how many deaths were related to the disease? Mr. Jarvis?"

"Fifteen thousand?"

"Close. Twelve thousand. That's twelve thousand too many, but it suggests that there are at least treatments with some degree of efficacy. And Mr. Talbot, would you be so kind as to tell us what those treatments are?"

Vincent Talbot sits in the second row. I know he'll know the answer. He's one of those kids who always has the answers — kind of reminds me of Nathan in that regard. I'm looking at him, watching his mouth move, but I'm not hearing what he's saying. I shouldn't have asked about the death rate for HNSCC. Anything associated with death is liable to trigger thoughts of Nathan right now.

"Thank you," I say when I see his mouth stop moving.

My mind is suddenly blank. What was I going to ask next? Could I compare HNSCC with the mortality rate from car accidents on the highway? No . . . cars have nothing to do with targeted molecular therapy. They are dangerous, though. And they do kill. Much quicker than cancer.

A hand at the rear of the room goes up slowly. Miss Peterson doesn't wait for me to call on her. "Uh . . . Professor Zuckerman? Are you crying?"

Am I? Is that what I felt trickling down my face?

Yeah, Monday-morning lectures should be banned.

"I'm sorry," I manage to say, feeling very

177

embarrassed. "I think maybe it's best if I cancel class today. I apologize. But if you would please read the next chapter in your syllabus before our Wednesday class, I think I can catch us up rather quickly." With that, I grab my things and go.

My office is in the next building over. It takes me three minutes to walk there. I take care to pull the door closed behind me. "I should have taken another vacation day," I say aloud as I park myself in the reclining desk chair, leaning back as far as it will go.

Maybe it's silly to be reacting like this. After all, it's not like I haven't experienced loss before. So why does losing Nathan hurt so bad? *Because it was Nathan* — the one person I always knew I could count on. His love carried me through the darkest moments of my life, and now that love is just . . . *gone.*

I hate to think of his poor wife and kids, how heartsick they must be right now. I wish he'd have just told Halley about me. That would have made things so much easier.

There is a knock at the door. Without waiting for me to respond, Amy, the new administrative assistant, pops her head in. "Hey, Professor. You doing okay? I heard you canceled class."

Word travels fast. "I'm fine. Thanks for asking."

"You sure?"

Not really — I'm not sure about anything right now. I feel like a boat adrift on the sea. Nathan was always my rudder. "Yes," I tell her. "I'm just . . . I lost a very good friend last week, and I'm still working through the emotions. But I'll be fine."

"I'm so sorry to hear that. Is that why you were out last week?"

"Yes."

"Well, let me know if there's anything I can do."

"Maybe hold my calls for a while?" I suggest. "I really just need some more time alone. To think."

With a sympathetic smile she says, "Totally understand. If anyone calls for you, I'll just take messages. Sorry to interrupt you." Her head disappears as she pulls the door closed.

It's funny, in a very sad and pathetic sort of way, that I should need more time to think about Nathan. He's been on my mind nonstop since I spoke to his secretary last week. I've thought about him, dreamed about him, and even read and posted about him on Facebook. Over and over again, I've rehearsed the details of our lives, like a play

179

in the theater of my mind. Reliving the special moments we shared — and the secrets we bore — is my way of keeping him alive, if only in my heart.

I know most people, including his wife and kids, probably remember him as this incredible guy who was always trying to help people. And he was; and he did. He was a beautiful human being in every sense of the word. But that's who he grew into, not who he always was. I had the privilege — if that's what you want to call it — of knowing him long before any of that. Back when he was still just a bratty little boy.

Before he changed.

Before he changed me . . .

■ ■ ■ ■

PART II
THE TRUE STORY OF
MADDY MCFATTY

■ ■ ■ ■

Madeline Zuckerman

October 27

I could list a thousand different ways that Nathan touched my life, going all the way back to third grade. I'll just list a few of the highlights. Even if they sound trivial, they were HUGE to me: On the day we met, he apologized to me. Later, he held my hand. He sat with me. He wrote a poem for me. He believed in me. He danced with me. He sacrificed for me. And ultimately . . . he saved my Life.

Like • Comment • Share

CHAPTER NINETEEN

Madeline

I hated being the new kid, but it's all I knew.

The move to Rockwall, Texas, in the middle of third grade was my fourth relocation in just under two years, and it was getting old fast. I started elementary school in Plano, but my mom, Stacy Zuckerman, lost her bank job during a layoff, which triggered a series of moves in quick succession. First we landed in Grand Prairie, then Fort Worth, both temporary contract positions as a financial adviser. From there Mom dragged me to Richardson, just north of Dallas, to manage the books at a car dealership. It was there that a mutual friend introduced her to a high school teacher from Rockwall named Grant McFadden.

Having never known my real father on account of a defect in his heart that went undetected until it was too late, the idea of having a father figure around greatly appealed to me, even if I found this particular one a bit too perfect for my liking. He was young — several years younger than my mother — with pristine hair and a flashy smile. I assumed, correctly I think, that growing up he'd been one of the popular kids; you know, the kind who either ignored or made fun of kids with a brain like me. But he was friendly, good-looking, and he had a stable job. All things considered, Mom could have done much worse.

Mom agreed.

After dating for half a year, she and Grant were married at a park along the shore of Grapevine Lake. The following Saturday we moved into Grant's apartment over in Rockwall.

The very next day, before we even finished unpacking boxes, Grant called us into the kitchen for the first-ever McFadden family council. "I've been thinking," he told us, "that I really want to start our lives together on the right foot. We're a family now, and I'd like us to be the best family we can possibly be. And so, drumroll please . . ." He stopped talking for a moment and tapped his fingers on the table like drumsticks on a snare. "Since it's Sunday, I think we should all go to church. What do you say, Stacy?"

"I don't know," my mom replied skeptically. "I've never really done much church-going. Have you?"

"Heck, yeah. All the time . . . when I was a kid."

"But not since?"

"Not really, no."

"So why start again now?"

I was listening with great interest. "I don't want to go," I interjected. "I already have to meet new kids at school tomorrow. I'd rather not meet kids at church too."

Mom and Grant both acknowledged my comment with a blank stare, then continued their conversation.

"I dunno," Grant told her. "Isn't that what good parents do on Sunday? Take their kids to worship God and all that? I've never had kids before, so I guess I don't know."

"Some of them do, I suppose. Though I'm not sure if they go to church because they are good parents, or if they are good parents because they go to church. And I'm sure a heckuva lot of lousy parents go to church too."

"To get better, right? Isn't it worth a try?"

"It's your call," she told him. "If this is what you want, I suppose it can't hurt."

I spoke up again. "I don't want to go, if anyone cares."

Grant waved off my comment like I must

be joking. "You're gonna love it, kiddo. Go find something nice to wear."

Kiddo. That's the only thing Grant ever called me. Never Maddy or Madeline, or something more endearing like Munchkin or Sweet-cheeks. Just kiddo. I sometimes wondered if he knew my name at all.

There were lots of churches in Rockwall, so we weren't short on options. Within a five-minute drive we had a smorgasbord that included Presbyterian, Methodist, Mormon, Anglican, Catholic, Baptist, and Lutheran, plus a smattering of others with no particular affiliation. But Grant didn't have much interest in orthodoxy or doctrine; for him it was more a social endeavor, so it didn't make much difference where we went. As a result, an hour after our family council we found ourselves at a nearby intersection with a choice to make: the big church on the left or the even bigger one on the right. Grant flipped a coin — *tails* — then pulled into the one on the right, a massive, three-story nondenominational with stained-glass images above all the doors.

Looking back, I've often wondered what my life — and especially my childhood — would have been like if Grant's quarter had come up heads. Would it have changed things for the better? Could it have gone any worse?

Crazy, isn't it, what a difference twenty-five cents can make?

A guy named Pastor Stevens, whose suit was the same gray color as his hair, was already in the middle of his sermon when we came through the chapel doors. I ignored what he was saying, choosing instead to memorize new words in my pocket dictionary.

At the conclusion of Pastor Stevens's remarks, a younger man named Pastor Steen offered a benediction on the meeting. As soon as I heard him say amen, I slammed my dictionary shut and stood up. "Amen and hallelujah, it's over. Can we go now?"

Mom chuckled at my enthusiasm. "Yes, sweetheart. Let's go."

Grant, however, wasn't quite ready for the church experience to be over. "Whoa, hold your horses. What about Sunday School? The bulletin says Pastor Steen runs a Sunday School. He has a meeting just for the kids for one more hour."

"An hour?" I groaned.

"An hour?" echoed Mom. "What do parents do in the meantime?"

"I think they serve doughnuts and coffee in the foyer. Why don't you go socialize a bit? Chat with the ladies and get a bite to eat. I'll take her to meet the pastor and the kids."

I fervently prayed that my mom would say no. Unfortunately, she was in the mood for a doughnut. That's how churches get you, you know — *through the stomach.* "I suppose I could stay," she said. "I hope they have a nice Bavarian cream."

Grant smiled broadly and turned to me. "C'mon, kiddo. Let's go meet the gang."

"Gang" turned out to be an eerily accurate description of the Sunday School bunch. Pastor Steen may have been the ecclesiastical leader, but the fifty or so kids who'd gathered in the large assembly room were obviously running the show. When Grant and I entered, some of them were literally climbing up the walls, or at least trying to. Others were playing tag. And a brown-haired boy about my age was leaning back in his chair while shooting paper spit wads through a straw at unsuspecting targets.

Grant was unsuspecting.

A gooey ball of paper came flying at him as he stood surveying the scene in the doorway. It splatted on his neck, just above the collar. To my amazement, he didn't even blink, but just brushed it aside like he'd hardly noticed. Of course, he was a high school teacher, so he was probably used to disgusting objects being hurled or spat at him. A few seconds later he took me by the hand and marched to the front of the room, where Pastor Steen was trying in vain to get the kids to quiet down so he could start his lesson.

"Pastor," Grant said, "I'm Grant McFadden. This is . . ." He hesitated just a second. I figured he was going to say something like "my stepchild," or "my wife's kid," or maybe even "my new legal obligation." Instead he started the sentence over and proudly stated, "This is my new daughter."

I liked the sound of that. A lot. "Maddy," I added, smiling.

"We're new in the area," Grant continued. "Or at least some of us are. We're interested in trying out the whole church thing, so we just dropped in. Hope that's okay."

"Of course! Welcome. We're glad you came," the pastor said. He had to speak up to be heard above the noise of the children. "We don't have tryouts at church, though. Around here everyone makes the team." He snickered at his own comment. "Sorry for all the ruckus right now. Sometimes it takes a while for them to get their energy out after sitting through the first hour's sermon." He looked around the room and snickered again. "And by 'sometimes' I mean every Sunday for the whole second hour. They pretty much never calm down."

"I see," said Grant thoughtfully. A moment later he asked, "Have you had any formal training working with children?"

"Afraid not, unless struggling with my own child counts. I'm the junior pastor here, so this is sort of a trial-by-fire experience. The youth ministry is my very first assignment. I'm learning on the fly."

"How long you been here?"

"Just long enough to get my feet wet," the pastor replied. "This will be week six. I left a corporate job to come work for the church; just felt like I wanted to do something different with my life. It doesn't pay as well, but I'm told the eternal benefits are to die for." Once again he laughed at his own joke.

Grant smiled pleasantly. "So is one of these children yours?"

"Yes," he said, pointing to the brown-haired spit-wad shooter. "Right back there. His name is Nathan."

Grant seemed to forget that just a minute earlier he'd been on the receiving end of Nathan's blowgun. "I'm sure you're very lucky." He paused, then his voice became more serious. "Pastor, do you accept volunteers here? I'm a high school teacher, so I know how to handle large groups of young people. You can say no, of course, but I'd love to try to help you out."

Pastor Steen scanned the chaos in the room, then looked at Grant like he must be joking. "Don't kid a kidder, or I might just take you up on that."

"I'm totally serious. You look like you could use an extra hand . . . or ten. There are some pretty easy tricks I've learned to help focus kids' attention. I bet after a few weeks I can have them in their seats listening to you. Once you know the tricks, you should be good to fly solo. Honestly, it'd be no problem at all."

The Pastor stuck out his hand. "Then I'd be delighted to have you, Grant. You're hired. Zero dollars an hour, of course. Half that amount for overtime."

Grant shook his hand with a wide grin. "Perfect. And will I qualify for those eternal benefits you mentioned?"

"Tell you what, if you can get these kids to listen to me when we all know they'd rather be goofing off or eating goodies with their parents, I'll personally vouch for you at the Pearly Gates. How's that for benefits?"

I let out another small groan. "Does this mean we have to come every week?"

"*Get to,* kiddo." Grant said happily. "It'll be fun. Trust me."

"But Sunday is my encyclopedia day," I whined.

Pastor Steen cocked his head quizzically. "Encyclopedia day?"

Grant spoke up before I could explain it on my own. "Oh, yeah, you should see it. Her mother picked up a complete set somewhere and she reads the volumes straight through like novels." He seemed proud when he looked down at me. "What are you on now, 'E'?"

I pushed my thick-rimmed glasses up higher on my nose. "Almost through 'G.' I would probably be on 'H' already if we didn't have to get ready for the wedding last weekend."

Grant turned back to the pastor. "See? It's actually kind of impressive. She soaks up facts like a sponge. But I'm sure coming here will be really good for her. Broaden her horizons a bit, help her make new friends."

"I'm sure you'll fit right in, Maddy," said Pastor Steen. "Since you're here, how would you like to take a seat, so we can get started? Before our time runs out today, I'm very interested to see if we can get an actual lesson in for once."

I took a long look around the room. "Where should I sit?"

"Hmm. There's an empty one back there beside my son. Maybe your good example will rub off on him."

"He spits things through straws," I replied flatly.

The Pastor laughed like I'd said something very funny. "One of these days he's going to grow up . . . I hope. But in the meantime, I promise you, he's never shot at a girl. I think you're safe."

I stared back at him momentarily, then at Nathan, then again at Pastor Steen, and finally up at Grant.

"Go on," Grant prodded, motioning with his head. "It'll be fine."

Against my better judgment, I squared my shoulders and strode slowly toward the back of the large room, my gaze fixed on the empty chair next to the pastor's son. When I was ten feet away I heard Grant loudly addressing the group, his voice filled with an element of authority I hadn't heard before. I looked up for just a second to see how the other kids were responding to his directions, but that was enough.

A spit wad came flying out of nowhere, smacking me square in the middle of the forehead, just above the rim of my glasses.

The Pastor's son stood up and shouted, "Bull's-eye! Did you guys see that? I hit the four-eyed giraffe dead on!"

Giraffe. That was a new one, but not without merit. Tall, clumsy, knock-knees, buck teeth, high forehead. Yeah, basically a giraffe. My mom blamed my awkwardness on my biological father. "He was tall and gangly as a kid too," she used to tell me, "but he grew out of it . . . eventually."

The whole room erupted in a chorus of laughter.

I froze, remembering how calm and collected Grant had been when he got hit in the doorway. I wanted to be brave like that, but quickly decided that it was beyond me. In a panic, accompanied by a burst of tears, I swatted at the sticky paper on my forehead until it came loose, then made a beeline for the exit.

"Madeline!" shouted Grant from the front of the room. "Wait!"

It wasn't his command to wait that stopped me in my tracks, but his use of my name. A few minutes earlier he'd introduced me as his daughter, and now, for the first time, he'd called me something other than kiddo.

"Don't go," Grant continued. I stayed put, but didn't turn around to face the crowd. A newfound quiet settled over the group, and I knew all eyes were on me. I could hear footsteps approaching from behind. A second later Grant put his arm around me. He leaned in and whispered so only I could hear. "I'm so sorry that happened. But if you leave now, it's all over. None of these kids will ever respect you. Trust me, the best thing you can do is turn around, march over to that empty seat, and sit right next to that awful kid. It'll catch him off guard. Can you do that? I'm going to talk to Pastor Steen, and I think I have an idea that can fix this so you don't have to be embarrassed at all."

I wanted nothing more than to run away and never show my face in public again. But at the same time, I wanted to believe that Grant knew what he was talking about. "Are you sure?" I whispered back.

He smiled affectionately and patted me on the back. "I'm your new dad, kiddo. You can trust me."

With a long breath, I slowly turned around and forced my legs to walk over to the empty seat.

Before I sat down, Nathan smiled wickedly as he popped a small piece of paper into his mouth and started chewing. "Hey," he whispered. "From this close I bet I can get the next one in your ear."

"Just try it," I hissed back without making eye contact. My gaze was fixed firmly on Grant, who was again standing at the front of the room talking with Nathan's father.

The Pastor kept nodding and looking up intermittently at his son and me. When they were done talking, Grant sat down at the end of the first row, and Pastor Steen stepped to the center of the room. "Well, at least that little interruption quieted you all down," he joked. "Welcome to Sunday School. As you can see, we have a couple of new friends with us today." He briefly introduced me, and in the same breath said, "And Grant is her father. He's volunteered to join us for a while to help make sure the hour we have together is a positive experience for everyone. Now then, let's go ahead and get started with our discussion." He paused and scanned the room, making sure all eyes were still on him. "Believe it or not, our new friend Maddy was part of my lesson today. My son, Nathan, too."

"I was?" Nathan and I said almost in unison.

The Pastor waved at us like we were kidding. "Maddy and Nathan, why don't you come up here next to me so everyone can see you without turning around." We exchanged puzzled looks, then reluctantly went forward. Pastor Steen waited for us. When we were close enough, he took one of us under each arm so that we were all standing side by side. "Now then, let me ask you all a question. When Nathan hit Maddy with that spit wad, how do you think it made her feel?" He waited, but no one spoke. "Anyone?"

Then a few hands came up.

"Sad," said the first.

"No, mad," said another almost immediately. "Mad Maddy."

A few kids laughed at that, but the pastor quickly quieted them down.

One of the older girls in the room took a guess. "Well, she was crying, so probably sad. But also embarrassed. I know I would be. I felt really bad for her, like I wanted to cry too."

The Pastor nodded. "Excellent answers, all of you. I'm sure she was feeling all of those things. By a show of hands, after it happened did any of you wonder what you would do if it were you getting a zinger like that in front of a bunch of people you didn't know?"

A few hands shot up immediately, then almost everyone followed suit.

"And also by a show of hands, would any of you like to be the one in that situation?"

Everyone dropped their hands.

He lowered his voice. "I won't ask for a show of hands this time, but how many of you were laughing at what happened?" He let the question settle on their consciences. "And finally, raise your hand if you think it would be cool to be the one on the straw end of that spit wad, the one who was making another person feel that way, essentially humiliating another child of God?"

Again, no hands.

"I'm so glad to hear that. Because today our lesson is on the Golden Rule. 'Do unto others as you would have others do unto you.' You could also flip it around and say, '*Don't* do unto others what you wouldn't want done unto you.' " He paused again. "Now, why don't you all give Nathan and Maddy a generous round of applause for their Oscar-worthy performance."

Everyone just stared at him without clapping.

The older girl who'd spoken before said, "You mean they were just acting?"

"Do you think I'd let that sort of thing go on in my Sunday School class unless it was planned? Ask yourself, if it happened to you, would you turn around and go sit next to the kid who just spit in your face? Probably not, unless you were secretly friends putting on a show. We really had you going, didn't we? I'm sure you all figured that Nathan was just being . . . well, Nathan. But he wasn't. Not this time, were you, Nathan?"

"No?" Nathan ventured.

Nathan's dad smiled approvingly. "No. Not my Nathan. He wouldn't do such a hurtful thing, because he knows if he did, I'd send him straight to Pastor Stevens's office for a little heart-to-heart, and then he'd be grounded for *at least* a month." He squeezed his son very tight, like he was trying to emphasize the point. "And how about Maddy turning on those tears like a regular faucet? Real top-notch. Have you been practicing that at home, Maddy?"

I stared briefly at the pastor, unsure what to say, and then glanced toward the end of the front row. Grant was all smiles. He nodded his head almost imperceptibly. "I guess so," I said.

Pastor Steen looked back up at the crowd of youth. "See? Now, seriously, you guys, let's give these two a round of applause before they head back to their seats." The Pastor started clapping first, then everyone else joined in.

As the clapping died down, Nathan and I trudged to the back row and sat down again. Neither of us spoke for the rest of the hour, though we did glance at each other once or twice. I paid close attention to the lesson; I could tell Pastor Steen was new at this, but I still enjoyed what he had to say about being kind to others. To my surprise, the kids who'd been rowdy and obnoxious when I first came in were eating it up too. On the few occasions where attentiveness in the room began to wane, Pastor Steen would calmly turn to Grant and say something like, "And now I'll turn it over to Mr. McFadden for a few minutes," at which point my stepdad would stand up and work his magic to corral their attention. Usually all it took was a well-phrased question to whoever was causing the disturbance. One time he invited a freckly redhead to the front to share a personal experience that related to the discussion, and, just like that, everyone was quiet again. I don't know if it was because they were genuinely interested in the boy's comments, or because they didn't want to be the next one to go up front, but it worked.

As the hour was winding down, out of the corner of my eye I saw Nathan Steen unraveling another small piece of paper, and I immediately assumed he'd grown tired of his dad's lesson and was preparing another saliva assault for me. But then he pulled a pencil from his pocket and started scribbling. When the class was over, before I had a chance to stand up, he slapped the note down on my lap. He didn't say anything, but just stared at me like he wanted me to read it, so I picked it up.

My dad was right. That wasn't very nice of me. We probly won't ever be friends, but I want to say sorry. For give me? Circle YES or NO.

I looked up to find Nathan nervously holding out his pencil. I took it, made a quick circle, then handed both items back.

Nathan glanced briefly at the note, nodded, and then scampered off without saying a word.

Just then Grant was there. "What was that all about?"

I shrugged. "He said he was sorry."

"Wow. Maybe he's not so bad after all. What did you say?"

I shrugged again. "Nothing. I just circled yes."

CHAPTER TWENTY

The next day was the first at my new school. It wasn't the worst day of my life, though it definitely wasn't good. The low point came during lunch when a boy and girl approached and told me I had to move down because that end of the table was saved for the cool kids. I made the mistake of informing them that I was cool too. "Honest," I stammered. "At my last school everyone liked me." That wasn't really the truth, but I thought a well-crafted lie might score some points.

They both laughed, then the boy made sure everyone else nearby could hear what was going on. "You?" he shouted. "Have you seen your glasses? They look like my grandma's, only about a million times dorkier. You're probably the biggest nerd on the whole planet."

It wasn't the first time I had been called nerdy.

Factually speaking, I was exceptionally smart. On top of that, I had exceptionally thick glasses, and I was exceptionally tall for my age. But did that make me a nerd? In my mind, it made me exceptional! I stood up, towering at least six inches over the boy, and swiped the thick plastic frames from off my nose. "Is that better? Just because I have glasses doesn't mean I'm any different than anybody else. Maybe you're just too blind to see that."

My mom always said I was a pretty girl, with cheekbones inherited from her and gigantic blue eyes inherited from my dad. I believed in my heart that I was beautiful, but I knew the bifocals masked it. Sadly, I couldn't see without them.

When I squinted at the boy and girl, they only laughed harder.

"Still a nerd," the girl hooted. "Now, move so we have room for people we actually like."

The only semipositive part of that day was that, for the first time in all my childhood moves, I actually recognized someone in my class. *The pastor's kid.* Though Nathan didn't say a single word to me all day, I kept a steady eye on him from across the room. Surprisingly, in the classroom setting he was much better behaved than he'd been the previous day, which made me wonder which boy was the real Nathan Steen? The one who acted like an angel at school, or the one who acted like the devil at church?

Mrs. Vasser, the teacher, assigned me a desk near the window beside a girl named Stephanie, who was cute as a button, but dumb as a brick. During math time I caught her cheating off of me during a pretest, so I promptly raised my hand and told the teacher. Stephanie landed in the principal's office. When she returned a while later, she had a note folded up that she slid across the desk when no one was looking. I hoped it was another apology, like the one the day before from Nathan.

It wasn't.

All it said was, *I hat your guts!*

Can anyone really fault me for laughing out loud? Unfortunately for Stephanie, my outburst got the attention of Mrs. Vasser. "Is there something you'd like to share, Madeline?" she asked.

"Not really," I replied, still giggling.

Mrs. Vasser approached anyway. "C'mon. Out with it."

I didn't want to get Stephanie in trouble again, but it's not like she didn't bring it on herself. I handed the note to the teacher and said, "Stephanie just gave this to me. I guess she really *hats* my guts." I let out another little snicker.

Stephanie took another trip to the principal's office, only this time she was gone for the rest of the day.

The next morning Mrs. Vasser found a new place for me to sit — right next to Nathan Steen. We still didn't talk to each other for most of the day. During a quiet reading period late in the afternoon the teacher called both of us to her desk at the back of the room.

"Maddy," Mrs. Vasser began, "I had a chance this morning to look at your test scores from your last school. You're quite a little academic dynamo, aren't you?"

"Yes, ma'am," I said candidly. I'd already been invited to move up to the next grade on multiple occasions, and the only reason I hadn't was because we'd moved around so much.

"Then I've got you at the right desk. Nathan is my top student. You two can push each other, helping and challenging each other to go beyond what you might otherwise."

The timing may have been awkward, but I finally broke the silence between me and Nathan. "You're smart?" I asked.

"Smarter than you," he answered.

I rolled my eyes dramatically. "As if."

"Whoa, it's not a competition, guys," the teacher warned. "I just want you to nudge each other toward more challenging work. Raise the bar, if you will. I'll probably be giving you both some special assignments to work on so you don't get bored. Can I count on you to work well together?"

Nathan stared blankly at me for a moment, then nodded reluctantly.

I waited to see his response, and then I nodded too.

"And hopefully," she continued, "you both can be leaders with your peers by helping them along in some of the things that might come easier to you. Do you think you can do that?"

"Yes," we both told her in turn, eyeing the other suspiciously.

Mrs. Vasser may not have intended to start an intellectual competition between me and Nathan, but she did anyway. From that day on, both of us did all we could to prove that we were the smartest. It was a close race, to say the least.

Close, but not inconclusive. Over time a definite leader emerged.

Nathan may have been popular, he may have been liked by everyone, he may have been athletic and outgoing and funny, but time and time again he fell just a hair short when it came to school. He never said so, but I knew it bugged him, which was a major victory for me. Sometimes, though, when I was playing by myself at recess, or sitting alone at lunch, or walking by myself after school, there were moments when I wished I were just a little more cool and a little less smart.

A little more like Nathan.

We stayed desk partners through the remainder of third grade, but we never became anything more than academic foes. Outside of school, the only real social activity I had was going to his father's Sunday School class, accompanied by Grant. In that setting, Nathan continued to act like a complete brat. Within the confines of "God's house," the only time he bothered acknowledging my presence was when he wanted to flaunt the fact that he knew more about the Scriptures than I did.

"It's just the Bible," I told him once when he was gloating over answering a question that I knew nothing about. Something about the parable of the pearl of great price, as I recall.

"The Bible is history," he replied smugly. "And don't tell me you don't like history."

Okay, so he had me there. But his pompous gloating was just the sort of carrot I needed to make me want to learn more. To help close the gap in our religious education, I had my mother pick up some Bible study manuals, plus I read the New Testament from cover to cover. God and I both know I wasn't really interested in learning all that stuff, I just didn't want that know-it-all Steen kid to know more about it than me.

The summer between third and fourth grade was a memorable one for the McFaddens. First, Grant officially adopted me, so I was now a McFadden just like him and my mom. Next, we moved out of our apartment and into a house. Then, once we were settled in, Mom broke the news that she was pregnant. Before summer's end we found out that the new baby was going to be a girl, which thrilled me to no end. The other thing about that summer that I will never forget is that a new boy moved into the area, just a couple blocks from my new home.

His name? Randall Theodore Rawlins. Randy.

The first thing I noticed about Randy was that he was tall. Not just taller than me, but taller than any student at our elementary school, including the fifth-graders. The next thing I noticed was his hair, which he left kind of shaggy, with a part down the middle. He could run his hands through that mane and it would all fall like feathers right back into place — so cool. He did that one day as I sauntered past his house while he was playing in the yard, and it triggered a thought I'd never previously had about any boy: *he's cute.* And thus began my first childhood crush. Of course the fourth-grader in me was too giggly to tell him that he had an admirer, but I hoped he'd figure it out by the way I smiled and waved at him every time he walked by.

Once school started, it took Randy a few weeks to find his niche, but by virtue of playing together on the same Pop Warner football team, he and Nathan managed to start a friendship. By the end of the football season they were almost inseparable.

For the first half of the year, I didn't mind that Randy had befriended my academic archrival. It was nice that they hung out together, because it meant that I could watch both of them at the same time. But following the Christmas break, Randy did something that completely ruined my entire year: he told a fellow student, in strict confidence, that he had a crush on me. *Me!*

The giraffe with glasses!

Naturally, the informant went right out and leaked the news to the entire world.

On one hand, being noticed by a boy — especially by Randy — for something other than my test scores or bean-pole legs was a nice change. On the other hand . . . no actually, there was no other hand. It was just really nice.

Unfortunately, it lasted all of two days.

When it got back to Randy that his secret was spreading like wildfire throughout the school, he tried to downplay it. But when he realized that his own social status was taking a major hit for crushing on the brainiac, he violently denied the accusations. I was sitting close enough in the lunchroom to hear him getting grilled by his buddies. In a panic, he told them, "I heard Maddy has lice! Why would I like her? Lice is even more contagious than cooties, and I heard she has that too!"

That did it. Suddenly everyone was sure that Madeline McFadden had lice. Even though I didn't. And despite cooties being more of a second-grade phenomenon, the fourth-graders bought into that little piece of fiction as well. Almost overnight I went from the tall girl nobody liked because I was way too smart for them, to the tall girl nobody liked because I was way too smart for them *and* whose level of contagiousness was so high that simply breathing the same air as me put you at risk of infection. I became "McCootie," or "Lice Girl," depending on who you asked. Nobody wanted to be around me then. Nobody dared, even after Randy admitted to making it up. The teachers caught wind of what was going on, but even they couldn't end the faux pandemic, because it had taken on a life of its own.

At night I would cry in my room. Mom and Grant knew what was going on, but they didn't know how to help.

"I went through similar things as a kid," Grant told me one night when he and Mom were tucking me into bed. "You just have to keep your chin up and carry on. Sooner or later, it will go away."

"You sure?" I asked, wiping my wet face on the covers.

He ruffled my hair. "Trust me, kiddo. Eventually, something will happen to make them forget all about it. And then life will get back to normal. Isn't that right, hon?"

"Absolutely," Mom said. "You just hang in there, sweetie." She leaned in and kissed me on the forehead. "And don't forget, Grant and I love you, and that's all that matters. Whatever bad things happen at school, at least you have a safe home to return to every day."

I hugged her, then looked back up at Grant. "What did kids say about you when you were my age?"

He thought about that for a second. "Honestly? They called me fat. Or other less kind ways to describe my weight."

"You were fat?" Mom asked.

Grant chuckled and poked at her very pregnant belly. "Well, I didn't have a gut like that, if that's what you're asking. I like to think I was husky. But you know what, because of the way people treated me, I became stronger. I was determined to shed the pounds so they couldn't hold that over me anymore." He ruffled my hair again and laughed. "So all you need to do is shed the lice and cooties, and you'll be all set."

I frowned. "How do I get rid of something I never even had?"

"You can't. But if you just keep smiling, something will happen to show everyone else that you either didn't have them to begin with or you're no longer contagious, and then this will all go away."

Two weeks later the baby was born, which was a welcome distraction. My parents named her Eliza. I held my new baby sister every chance I got. Sometimes, when no one else could hear, I'd confide in her, telling her how mean some kids can be. "I'm not going to let people pick on you like they pick on me," I'd say softly as I cradled the infant in my arms. "That's what big sisters are for. To always stand up for you. To always love you. Big sis will always look out for you, Eliza. I promise."

For the next couple of months I waited patiently for that mysterious "something" to occur that Grant had promised would magically dispel the rumors. In the meantime, the nightmare at school continued day in and day out.

By April I had almost given up hope that public opinion would ever return me to a disease-free life. I was just trying to look ahead to the summer, hoping that a few months off might be enough time for my peers to dream up something else to occupy their time so they could leave me alone. I was tired of having kids run away when I approached the playground, or having them hold their breath whenever I walked by, or pretend to put on invisible protective suits when they were forced to sit within a ten-foot radius of me in class.

In May, an announcement was made that the fourth grade's incredible behavior had earned us all a day at a rollerskating rink for the final field trip of the school year. Given the way everyone treated me, I couldn't understand how the teachers could possibly call anyone's behavior incredible, unless they meant incredibly mean, but I was still excited to go rollerskating. Outside of learning, it was one of the few things I was really good at. My mother had given me a pair of skates when I was six, and I hardly took them off my feet until I could roll like a pro. This, I thought, was my chance to impress.

The big day came on a Friday. Immediately after morning announcements the fourth-graders were herded onto busses and shuttled across town to Skate World, where we had the whole rink to ourselves. I was one of the last students in line to get my tan-and-orange rentals, so by the time I had my skates laced up, most of the other kids we already out wheeling around beneath the disco ball. To my disappointment, some of them were better skaters than I was. One or two of them were even going backward. A few were very shaky, but most kids were at least able to navigate the oval floor without falling. "So what if I'm not the absolute best one," I told myself. "I bet I'm at least in the top ten."

I hadn't noticed, but Randy was within earshot when I said that, shuffling along the rink's carpeted half wall, clinging for dear life. It was the least cool he had ever looked. He was a fish out of water on rollerskates. His wobbly legs kept wanting to buckle beneath his weight. "Are you talking to yourself, Maddy?" he asked. "You know, there are people here to talk to."

He didn't say it meanly, per se. In fact he may have been suggesting that I talk to him. But I was too embarrassed to think, so I went on the defensive. "Are you rollerskating, Randy? You know, they do have a kiddy section over there, if you need extra help."

It took about half a second for his face to turn bright red. "Let's see you do any better, four-eyes!"

That was the first time he had ever said something blatantly mean to my face. Even though he'd inadvertently started the whole Lice Girl revolution, he'd never actually played along with the nonsense, and even tried to put a stop to it once he realized what he'd done.

Hearing Randy call me a name stung way worse than all the ridicule I'd endured from other kids. I cocked my head to the side, letting all my hair cascade onto one shoulder. "Fine. I will." With that, I veered out through the gap in the wall and sailed onto the rink. I was fluid, gliding in and out of others with ease. As I finished my first lap, I looked over my shoulder to make sure Randy was still watching, and I was glad to see his face was even redder than before. Clearly, it bothered him that I was showing him up. When I came around on my next pass, I saw that his expression had changed. The glare was gone, replaced by a smile. Only, it wasn't a good smile. It was the sort of wry smirk that spelled certain doom.

As I got closer, he lifted one hand off the rail and pointed at me. Then, in a voice so loud that everyone could hear, even above the sound of the music, he screamed, "Watch out for Lice Girl! She's shaking bugs all over you!"

I kept skating, though I was vitally aware that all eyes were now on me. I made some nice cuts to the inside, then banked to the right and cruised along the outside wall, strutting my stuff for the onlookers. But by the time I'd gone halfway around again, I began to see that Randy's warning was having its desired effect. The other kids were no longer out there skating just for the fun of it, they were skating with a purpose: *to avoid me at all costs.* I felt like a shark in a pool of salmon. If I bobbed one way, they'd bob the other. I'd bank left, and they'd bank right. I'd weave here and they'd weave there. Wherever I went, there was a safety bubble between me and everyone else.

After five laps of that, I couldn't take it anymore. I went to the side and sat by myself on a bench, reeling from the hurt, but unwilling to cry in front of my classmates.

While I was sitting there, I happened to spot my teacher waving down Nathan, who was playing tag with some guys and girls in the middle of the rink. He was a pretty decent skater, which didn't surprise me, because he was good at everything. I watched as he left the group and went to the side to have a chat. He nodded a few times as the teacher spoke, and once, he even looked up and glanced at me, which caught me off guard. I quickly diverted my gaze, pretending not to notice.

Ten minutes later the DJ announced he was slowing the music down for couples to skate together, which sent a shock wave through the entire fourth grade. *Couples? Boys and girls holding hands? Voluntarily?* This was exciting new ground, and everyone wanted to see who would be first to cross the great gender divide. The DJ's voice boomed again over the loudspeaker. "This is couples skate only, please! Couples skate only. Everyone else, please clear the floor. Boys, now is your chance to ask that special girl!"

In a matter of seconds the rink looked like an empty parking lot. Then, slowly, a few brave souls rolled onto the floor hand in hand, while the rest of the kids pointed and whispered. The first ones to break the ice were Andrew and Gretchen, who were also dance partners outside of school, so they'd obviously held hands before. Next came Paul, a boy with long wavy hair, locking fingers with a girl named Amanda, who was visibly blushing. The third pair was Aaron and Erin, neither of whom could skate a lick, but they looked like they were having fun working together to keep on their feet.

I was parked on a bench near the snack bar, watching the couples and longing for the field trip to be over, so I didn't notice Nathan approaching from behind.

"Maddy, you want to skate?"

I jumped when he said my name, nearly falling off my seat. Once I regained my balance, I looked him over suspiciously. "Why? So you can get Randy and your other friends to laugh at me?"

"No. I just want to skate with someone who won't trip. I saw you before. You're pretty good."

I glanced around, correctly sensing that others were watching. "What about everybody else? Don't you care what they say?"

He just shrugged. "I won't force you. Do you want to skate or not?"

Scanning the onlookers again, I made up my mind. How could I turn down the opportunity to skate with Nathan Steen? "Fine," I said, playing it cool. "But if you're just being mean, your dad will hear about it."

Nathan shrugged again and extended his hand.

There were audible gasps from all around.

"He's touching McCootie!" kids shouted.

"Doesn't he care about lice?"

"Maybe he's already infected!"

Holding hands with Nathan, in front of the entire fourth grade, didn't atone for months of public torment, but I had to admit, it felt good. For a full minute we skated without saying a word, neither of us taking our eyes off the floor directly ahead. I wanted to sneak a peek at the crowds who'd gathered on the other side of the half wall to watch, but I didn't dare. Finally, with my eyes still straight ahead, I said, "Mrs. Abernathy made you do this, didn't she?"

"No. She didn't make me."

"But I saw you talking to her."

"Yeah. She asked me if I would. And I said yes."

I processed that for a second, then asked, "Why? Aren't you afraid of . . . you know, my lice and cooties?"

"That's stupid. I know you never had those things."

I felt a small smile creeping onto my face. "Really?"

"Yeah. Everyone knows that. They just like to keep it going. Randy shouldn't have started it in the first place. He just didn't want to admit that he liked you."

For the first time while skating, I thought I might fall to the ground. I even started to stumble, but Nathan held firm and kept me upright. "He *what?* I thought he just thought I was . . . you know, nice or something."

"Right. Which means he liked you. I think he still does."

My smile spread farther. I didn't want to spoil the moment with more words, so I stopped asking questions until the song was over. Once the music died, I let go of Nathan's hand and wiped my sweaty palm on my stretch pants. There were lots of things I wanted to say, but the thing that felt most appropriate was a simple, "Thank you."

"You're a good skater," Nathan said sheepishly, then he skated off to rejoin his friends.

I stayed on the floor as ZZ Top began to play. The fourth-graders who hadn't participated in the couples skate flooded the rink again, and I braced myself for the renewed catcalls and kids swerving to avoid me.

Only it didn't happen.

One song with Nathan changed everything. Even if he hadn't done it on his own, he'd done it. Now instead of jeers or taunting, the kids just skated by, minding their own business. A few of them even smiled at me. And that was that — no more Lice Girl.

Randy had to stick to the outside wall, but a little while later he called me over and apologized for everything he'd said. Then he asked me if I would help him learn to skate.

The next slow song was ladies' choice, and Randy agreed to hold my hand as we inched around the wall. To a fourth-grade girl with a crush, it was magic.

Later that night, after Mom and Grant were home from work, I shared the good news. "Today was a really good day. And you were right, Grant," I said, beaming.

"Something finally happened that showed everyone how silly those rumors were."

"What was it?"

I didn't want to go into details about the boys, because that would have been too embarrassing. As I thought of how to respond, I remembered a story Pastor Steen had told us on Sunday about Jesus healing a leper with the touch of his hand, and then I knew just how to describe what had happened. "Oh, nothing much . . . just a miracle."

CHAPTER TWENTY-ONE

As with prior years, the first Wednesday of September was Back-to-School Night, a chance for students to introduce their parents to their new teachers and an opportunity for teachers to shed light on the curriculum and expectations for the year ahead. Since Grant had his own Back-to-School Night at the high school, Mom and I took baby Eliza and made it a ladies' night out. First, there was a trip to the library to check out enough books and magazines to satiate my mind for at least a month. Then we had dinner at Sunshine Pizza. And lastly, a tour of the fifth-grade wing at my school.

Nathan and his parents were leaving the school just as we were coming in.

Pastor Steen was as blithe as ever. "Stacy! Maddy! How are my two favorite McFaddens this evening?" He glanced at the bundle on my mom's shoulder. "Oh, make that my three favorite McFaddens. It's

Eliza, right?"

I loved how friendly Pastor Steen was with everyone. I wished his son would talk to me that way.

We'd only seen the Steens twice over the summer, once at the grocery store and another time at the local pool. Nathan didn't say a word either time. In fact, he hadn't said anything to me since we skated together, but I'd read in an encyclopedia about how prepubescent boys can be awkward around girls, so I figured that was just him being a boy. "Hi, Pastor," I responded. "We're quite well, thank you."

"Always so polite, aren't you," commented Mrs. Steen.

"We've missed you guys at church," the pastor said. "Sunday School just isn't the same without Grant there to play warden."

I knew he was kidding about needing Grant, but it was cool of him to say so. Early on, there's no doubt that Grant was a huge help. Within a couple months of us showing up he'd turned the place from a three-ring circus into a legitimate Sunday School. By the fourth or fifth month he'd shared enough group-management tricks that the pastor could effectively run the whole thing by himself with great success.

"Now he's trying to play warden at the

high school," my mom said proudly.

Mrs. Steen's eyes lit up. "That's right. I heard he's got some sort of a promotion."

"Yes and no. He's been given more work, but it's not necessarily a promotion. Not yet anyway. They've named him the interim vice-principal, so he's doing that while still teaching math. It's very hectic right now, but it's a great opportunity for him to show them what he can do as an administrator. He's really putting his whole heart and soul into it. With any luck they'll name him the permanent vice-principal before the year is through."

It warmed my heart to hear my mother talk about Grant like that. Back when they said their I-do's, I'd wondered if the marriage would last. After all, there had been so many years of watching her date guys who didn't pan out that I'd begun to doubt there was anyone out there who could make her happy. Then Grant came along, and with their second anniversary just a couple months away, and with a new baby in the home, everything seemed to be working out perfectly.

"I'm sure they'll give it to him," Mrs. Steen said. "He's so good with kids, he'll do great."

Pastor Steen nodded his head in agreement. "Absolutely. Grant is perfect for the job. Tell him we said so, and give him a great big 'howdy' from all of us." He paused just a second, then added, "And hopefully we'll see you all at church one of these weeks."

"Oh, not to worry," Mom told him. "Now that we're finally getting into the swing of things with the baby, I'll definitely get the family to church very soon. You can count on it."

I'll never forget those words or that night.

One week later, Mom made good on her promise, though not in the way she'd intended.

They seated family in the very front row for the service. I could hear the voice at the pulpit, but I lacked the will to look up to see who was speaking. It sounded like Pastor Stevens.

"Our hearts go out to the McFadden family," the voice was saying. "We know what a difficult time this is for you. We grieve with you. Stacy was taken from us far too soon. Today we honor her, and celebrate her life . . ."

I tried so hard to tune everything out. I didn't want to hear anyone talking about my mother from the pulpit; didn't want any of this to be real. I just wanted the world to go back to the way it was before Back-to-School Night. I tilted my head to the side and looked up at Grant, who was seated right beside me. He'd hardly talked to me since that night. His jaw was clenched tight and his eyes were open, but he didn't seem to be looking at anything in particular. He was just staring off into space. Not only did he lose his wife, but on account of the unexpected tragedy, the high school principal decided it was in his and the students best interest if he focused solely on teaching for a while, so the vice-principal duties were yanked away from him too.

If that weren't enough, now he was stuck with two kids to raise all by himself.

Eliza was being tended by a friend during the funeral. I wished I could hold her and talk to her. I wanted to put her on my shoulder and tell her all about the mother she would never know.

The voice at the pulpit was still talking, saying things that were supposed to bring healing, but I continued to block it out. In my head, I rehearsed the events of that night over and over, trying to figure out what I could have done differently to change the outcome.

It all happened following the school open house. We'd spent longer than expected talking to my new teacher about how exciting the big fifth-grade science fair would be, so it was already close to my bedtime when we got home. As we pulled into the driveway, Mom remembered she still needed a few things at the grocery store for breakfast. She sent me inside to brush my teeth and put on my pajamas so she could tuck me into bed as soon as she returned.

"What about Eliza?" I asked.

"She's asleep anyway. I'll just take her with me."

"You'll hurry back, won't you?"

She promised that she would, and then drove off.

The store was only a two-minute drive, so I knew it wouldn't take long. Only, it did. I kept waiting and waiting and she didn't come. Then, while I was lying in bed, expecting her to show up and say prayers with me, the summer breeze carried the sound of distant sirens through my open window. When the sirens faded, I drifted to sleep.

Maybe I should have thought to pray on my own. God knows, Mom could've used those prayers.

The next day I woke up and Grant was a complete mess. Nobody wanted to tell me exactly what happened; all Grant would say was there was an accident. But the next morning, while he was still sound asleep in bed, I read about the whole thing on the front page of the paper, under a headline that included the words "homicide" and "carjacking."

According to the newspaper article, an eyewitness caught the tail end of a struggle near Mom's car in the grocer's parking lot. The "assailant" was yelling for the car keys while Mom was screaming about a baby in the backseat. When she wouldn't let him have the keys, he pulled out a knife, jabbed it in her neck, and then ran off.

A couple days later the police traced the prints on the knife to a college kid downtown named Jake Spitz. Turns out he'd been on drugs; at the time of the attack he was hallucinating that someone was after him. The police told us later that he was shocked to learn that the stabbing wasn't part of the hallucination.

Not that any of that mattered. Mom was still dead.

". . . and we'd like to thank everyone for coming today. Pastor Steen will now offer a benediction, after which we invite the pallbearers to please come forward."

I looked up when I realized the funeral

was coming to a close. Grant was still staring at nothing. After the closing prayer he and the other pallbearers stood up and went to the casket. He seemed almost oblivious to what he was doing. I watched as he and a handful of other men carried my mom out of the chapel. I knew I was supposed to follow, but I couldn't get my legs to move, so I just sat there, crying, wondering why this had happened and whether my prayers that night could have prevented it.

Pastor Steen walked by and told me not to hurry, that I could stay there as long as I wanted. Within a few minutes the rest of the chapel was empty, which was fitting, because without Mom I felt completely alone anyway. I looked up at the pulpit again and prayed, in my head, that I wouldn't always feel so lonely.

Right then I heard the sound of feet shuffling along the carpeted chapel floor. When I turned to the sound, Nathan Steen was walking slowly up one of the side aisles, dressed in a white shirt and blue tie. He saw me looking at him, but he didn't stop walking. When he reached the front pew, he turned to his left and continued straight toward me. Without saying a word, he sat down on my right, exactly where Grant had been. He was so close that our shoulders rubbed.

I tried smiling at him, but then looked away and continued to cry. He let me sob until I was done.

Nathan never said a single word to me that day. He didn't need to. Just having him near me told me that I was not alone. And that was enough.

CHAPTER TWENTY-TWO

People are funny. Creatures of habit, I guess. I showed up at school on Monday following the funeral, not knowing fully how the other kids would treat me, but sort of expecting that things would be different. And it was . . . for a brief moment. When I walked into my classroom, a group of girls who'd never given me the time of day came right up and welcomed me, asked how I was doing, made me feel like one of the gang. It was so nice. Foreign, but nice. It's like they all forgot that they didn't really like me. I knew that they were just pampering me because of what happened to my mom, and probably because they'd been given explicit directions from their parents to do so, but I didn't mind.

By that afternoon, though, I could tell that the coddling was already wearing on the coddlers. And by the next day? *Done.* No more "nice to see you Maddy" or "do you want to join our group?" Not so much as a halfhearted "hello." Everyone seemed to have forgotten that maybe they should try to be a little nicer to me, and just like that I went right back to being the tall, nerdy girl with thick glasses who sat alone at lunch.

Sad to say, but even Randy and Nathan kind of left me alone. I don't think they knew quite what to say. Randy tried to strike up a conversation once, but it didn't go very far. "Hey," he said, "what's new?"

How was I supposed to respond to that? *Gosh Randy, I don't know. Oh yeah, my mom was brutally murdered. What's new with you?* "Nothing," I said, and that was the end of it.

By day number three everything was back to status quo in the social world of fifth grade. The cool kids were at their lunch table, the not-so-cool kids were at theirs, and I was an island. Life goes on as normal. School life, anyway.

Home life was another story.

Once Grant got over the initial shock of everything, he sort of bottled up his grief and pretended like everything could go on as normal. Not unlike the kids at school, I guess. Only with Grant, everything wasn't just like it had always been. He was continually on edge. And it became obvious that

the gregarious teacher with the can-do attitude who could tackle anything that came
his way was quickly reaching his wits' end.
For one thing, money was tight, because on
top of paying for a funeral with all the trim-
mings, we'd traded Mom's part-time in-
come for Eliza's full-time child care. But
Grant's irritableness wasn't just about the
money. It was everything — all the stuff he
either hadn't done before or hadn't planned
to do all by his lonesome. Like late nights
with a crying baby, grocery shopping, cooking balanced meals, and tending sick kids.
On top of that, there was never any time for
himself, because there was always something
that needed to be done — dishes, laundry,
and bills, for example, all of which kept pil-
ing up.

"It never ends," I'd hear him grumble occasionally. Once, when I got the stomach
flu and made a mess all over the bathroom
floor, he looked heavenward and pro-
claimed, "Just kill me now." The way he said
it, I wondered if he wished he really could
just die and be done with the misery of
single-parenthood. When I asked if he was
serious, he said, "No, kiddo, it's just an
expression. I'm only trying to get God's attention, that's all."

In a strange way, his answer made me feel

better. At least he hadn't given up on God. When I was over the flu, I suggested to him that maybe we should start going back to church. Surely that'd get God's attention. "You've got friends there," I told him. "And did you hear about old Pastor Stevens? He retired, and they made Pastor Steen the new head pastor. I bet he'd be glad to see us."

"Oh sure," he mumbled sarcastically. "He'd welcome our donations with open arms."

Okay, maybe Grant wasn't ready for church. What he was ready for, though, was something to take his mind off his new spouseless life. You know, just a little something to take the edge off, to make his burdens light. "Liquid gold," he called it. "Medicine for the man's soul." At first I didn't mind his newfound friendship with beer, but I did start to worry when he'd head straight for the refrigerator after work to grab a six-pack.

All things considered, though, Grant did a good job keeping it all together. He may have been tired and grumpy, but he kept going day after day, putting all his time into making sure our little family's needs were met. That is, until we got through the Christmas break.

Once the new year started, Grant finally

hit a wall. Looking back, I'm sure he was depressed, still struggling with all that pent-up grief. I don't know what he was like at school with his students, but at home he exuded sadness. About the only thing that made him smile was Eliza. Sometimes he'd hold her, kiss her forehead, play with her, make her giggle, and for a short while he'd be his old self, but then he'd put her down and slip right back. I certainly never got those same reactions out of him. Not that I expected to. I knew he loved me, if only for my mom's sake, yet I also accepted the fact that he loved Eliza more.

No biggie, it's just how it was. Nothing I could do about it anyway. Just like there was nothing I could do to get Grant out of the rut he fell into. If I'd wanted, I could have set my watch by his daily routine: get up, take Eliza to the sitter, go to work, pick Eliza up, play with Eliza, put Eliza to bed, drink beer and watch television, then fall asleep and do it all again the next day.

I remember one night, near the end of January, after Grant laid Eliza down for the night, I stopped him before he turned on a show. "Um, Grant . . . we're out of clean clothes."

"*We* are?" he asked skeptically. "Or *you* are?"

"Me, I guess."

With a big yawn he checked his watch. "It's late, kiddo. And it's Thursday. You can get by tomorrow, then on Saturday I'll teach you how to do it yourself. That'd be good for you to take over anyway."

The next day at school I wore the one clean outfit I had left, which happened to be the same outfit I wore the day before. It's funny how kids don't seem to notice you for weeks on end, until you wear the same shirt twice in a row.

"Did you sleep in those clothes, Mc-Stinky?" asked one boy in my class while we were in line to go to morning recess.

Great, a new nickname. That whole day it was McStinky this and McSmelly that. Boys were constantly sniffing the air when I walked by, and girls who hadn't talked to me in months suddenly bothered to "compliment" me on my hair, only to point out that it looked like I hadn't washed or brushed it in a week.

Sadly, I couldn't argue with them. My hair was thick and unruly, so even though I brushed it every day, it often looked like a rat's nest. Grant didn't know how to do a girl's hair, and my attempts at braids and ponytails failed more often than not, no matter how many books I read on the subject.

Sometimes at night I'd cry myself to sleep, wishing my mother could do those things for me. *How many of those mean girls at school could do their own hair or wash their own clothes?* I wondered. *How many of them would look even worse than me if they were in my shoes?*

But clothes and hair weren't the only things suffering. As the year progressed, so did my waistline. Maybe it was the start of puberty, or perhaps I was just overeating as a means of coping with the stresses in my life, but by spring my shape was definitely expanding.

One evening after putting on my pajamas, Grant walked by while I was looking at myself in the upright mirror. "Have I gotten bigger?" I asked him straight out.

He sized me up and down, then said, "I wouldn't worry about it, kiddo."

"So . . . no?"

"I didn't say that," he replied before continuing toward the privacy of his bedroom. "I just wouldn't worry about it, that's all. There's nothing you can do about it. Some people are just heavier."

That gave me something new to cry about at night.

It wasn't long before kids at school started noticing that my clothes — last year's clothes, to be exact, since we hadn't gone clothes shopping since the previous summer with Mom — were getting snug around the middle, which is how, right before the end of fifth grade, I earned the nickname that would finally stick for the remainder of my youth: *Maddy McFatty.* It had a nice ring, I'll admit, but I can't say it didn't hurt.

I'd always loved school, but summer couldn't come soon enough that year.

As soon as school let out in June, I became Eliza's full-time caregiver, because Grant and a teacher friend spent the long summer days painting houses to earn extra money. Taking care of my little sister was one of the best things I ever did. I'd put her in a stroller and walk her to the park, play with her on the grass, let her devour Oreos in her high chair, and then give her a bubble bath to clean up. And through it all, I'd tell her everything I remembered about Mom.

"If you're going to be like her," I'd find myself saying, "you've got to know the things she loved. Let's see . . . clean sheets, yellow roses, thunderstorms, and rhubarb pie. Oh, and chocolate-peanut-butter ice cream, she could eat a carton all by herself. I bet you'll love it too. And campfires and s'mores — we'd go camping at least once a year. Watching birds in the birdbath always made her smile." Then I'd smile, the way Mom used to smile at me. "And *me,*" I'd tell her. "She loved me and you most of all."

That was easily the best summer of my life. I had Eliza, she had me, and there was nobody around to tell me I was too fat or too tall or too smart or too anything else that I wasn't.

But like all summers do, eventually it ended. With one day running into the next, I'd lost track of time, until one afternoon a form letter came in the mail reminding me about Back-to-School Night. I was moving up to the middle school that year, and I wanted to find my locker before the first day, so naturally I wanted to go.

"You busy?" I asked Grant late at night, once he'd had a while to settle in after work.

"What does it look like?"

It looked to me like he was sitting in his jeans, working on his fifth Corona, and watching a rerun of *The Love Boat.* But it was a commercial, so I ignored the question and pressed forward. "Well, next week is Back-to-School Night, and I was wondering —"

"No," he said flatly before I could finish.

"But my locker, and the different classrooms, and there are all these teachers that I've never met before. Plus, I need to figure out . . ."

Grant stood up while I was talking and stared at me until I shut up. His face was so dark and angry. "I said no, and that's final. We're not doing anything on that day. Period."

That's when it hit me. "Oh, this is about Mom, isn't it? Because that's the anniversary of —"

"We don't talk about that night!" he barked. And that's when he hit me. With the back of the hand, right in the mouth. The impact knocked me to the floor. It was so sudden, I felt more shock than pain. My lip was already swollen and bleeding as I got up. Then my instincts must have taken over, because as soon as I was on my feet, I ran to the safety of my room.

"Wait!" he yelled. "I'm sorry!" He chased after me and practically knocked my door down when he came in. "Maddy," he panted, using my name for the first time in forever, "Oh my gosh! I'm so sorry! I don't . . . I don't know what came over me."

I was too scared to reply, so I just kept crying.

"You have to know, sweetie, I would *never* hurt you. That wasn't me . . . I don't know what that was. I just . . . I had an awful day, that's all. I didn't get paid from one of my painting jobs, the mortgage is due in a week, and I probably had too much to drink on an empty stomach. And then you mentioned Back-to-School Night and I just — I'm *so* sorry." He knelt down beside my bed and put his arms around me and gave me a big hug, like he used to do when he tucked me in before Mom died. "It won't happen again, kiddo, I promise. And I'm going to make it up to you. You'll see." He pulled back. "In fact, we're going to make sure you make it to your new school for Back-to-School Night." He became more cautious when he stopped to examine the fatness of my lip. "Of course, it's just a week away but . . . well, I'm sure the swelling will be gone by then. If anyone asks, though, you've got to say you fell off your bike or something. You understand?"

He waited for me to nod.

"Good girl. Because even though this was an accident, and it's never going to happen again, not everyone would understand. Some might even want to take you away from me for a while, and we don't want that, right? We need to stick together. We're a family."

His voice was so loving and sincere that I

actually felt grateful for having been hit, because it was like it woke up the old Grant that was hibernating inside of him. He even started to tear up when he ruffled my hair before tucking me in. "I'm going to do better. You'll see."

And he did. The next morning, when I woke up, Grant was in the kitchen cooking pancakes, which he hadn't done in six months. There was a smile on his face as big as Texas. "I'm not working today," he announced. "It's our family day."

"But what about the bills?"

"We'll be fine. Families have other needs besides money, and today our family needs to stay at home in our pajamas and watch movies all day long. What do you say?"

It didn't occur to me until much later that he probably wanted us all to stay home to make sure no one saw my fat lip, but that doesn't diminish the fun we had. We popped popcorn, watched *Star Wars,* pretended we were in the movie — I was Princess Leia, Eliza was Yoda, and Grant was Darth Vader — and had our first really good time together in an entire year.

I didn't know it, but that day turned out to be a real blessing. Sort of like a camel filling its humps before going into the desert, the memory of those happy mo-

CHAPTER TWENTY-THREE

As promised, Grant took me to the Back-to-School Night at the middle school, foregoing the one at the high school where he worked, which he said hardly anyone attended anyway. The swelling in my lip was almost completely gone, so thankfully no one asked about it. Actually, I don't think anyone even noticed me other than Randy and Nathan, who politely waved at me as I walked by.

"You friends with the Steen boy?" Grant asked when he saw the gesture.

"I'm not really friends with anyone."

And it was true. As if to prove me right, even Lorna Green, a girl who could barely read and who wore a brace on her shoulders to straighten her spine, shuddered when she found out she was assigned to be my locker partner. "I can't start off middle school with Maddy McFatty," she said as if I wasn't standing right there, "or no one will ever like me."

"That's what they call you?" Grant asked after Lorna went off begging for someone — *anyone* — to let her double up with them.

I nodded. "Doesn't matter. They're just words." Yeah, just words. Whoever said that only sticks and stones could hurt was delusional.

"Good attitude," he said, patting me on the shoulder. "That's being the bigger person. Besides, if she finds another locker, it just means you'll have more space for your encyclopedias and whatnot."

Once classes got going, I hoped to just blend in, sort of fly beneath the radar. But no matter where I sat in my classrooms, or how close to the walls I walked in the hallways, or how many people I avoided making eye contact with, the teasing still found me. Usually it was jokes about my hair or clothes or weight. Once or twice I even heard them say off-color things about my mom. Individually, none of the comments were too much to bear. But collectively? Well, there are only so many times you can hear what an awful person you are before you start to believe it. They all started to blend together — just because kids are cruel doesn't make them original. But there was one that I will always remember.

It was near the end of the first semester, during math class, right before the lunch bell. Several popular boys — including Nathan — were talking about what they wanted to eat for lunch. One of them caught me listening. "How about you, Maddy, what are you going to eat? I bet you're starving."

Another boy piped up, "She looks like she could eat a horse."

"No, I got it," another said. "She's gonna have a super-sized McFatty meal with extra-large thighs!"

That brought the whole group to tears they were laughing so hard. Even Nathan was laughing.

I didn't cry. I was used to it, sort of numb. This wasn't any worse than what I experienced on a daily basis. But still, right then I could feel something inside of me sort of . . . crumble, I guess. Or burst. Or evaporate. I think it was my will. From that moment on, I stopped caring. About anything. After hearing how awful I was so many times, I concluded that everyone else must be right.

I'm a loser? Fine, being a loser requires no effort at all — I can do that.

I'm fat? Fantastic, hand me a box of

doughnuts and let's make it official.

I smell like last week's laundry? My hair is greasy? I'm too tall to talk to face-to-face? I have Coke-bottle glasses and knobby knees? Gosh, I sound like a circus sideshow. But hey, who doesn't like a good circus? Step right up, kids, and have a peek at the girl who'll prove just how lucky you are to be you! As long as you're nothing like her, you must be pretty darn special!

By the end of that first semester I was pulling straight Cs. The only one who wasn't overjoyed by my academic demise was Nathan. He didn't come right out and say it, but I think it bothered him that he no longer had any real competition. He'd always gone out of his way to find out how I did on big tests and projects, as a way to benchmark his own success. Without me in the mix, I think the joy of scoring a hundred percent on a final exam was gone, because he knew without asking that no one else would even come close.

On the home front, things seemed to be going better. Grant's edginess was more sporadic than the previous year. So was his drinking. Only now if he needed something to settle down his nerves, he rarely settled for beer. "It's medicinal," I would remind myself while cleaning up bottles of vodka after a weekend binge.

Eliza turned two at the start of second semester, and she definitely kept us on our toes. She also gave me and Grant a common purpose. Funny that a little child, who only cared about food, milk, toys, and sleep could be so important to a family, but she was literally the glue that held us together. She craved our attention constantly, and as we focused on her needs, it allowed us — or at least me — to forget everything that was bad in my life. Even if it was only for an hour or two at a time, it helped.

Toward the end of sixth grade — maybe April or so — Grant got word that Jake Spitz, the man who murdered Mom, was finally going to trial. It seemed to all of us like it should have been a slam dunk, but the state took their sweet time making sure they had all of their ducks in a row. As the lead prosecutor explained to Grant early on in the process, "It's much better to do a very thorough job up front, than to miss something obvious and have the case overturned later on a technicality. Besides, Jake's being held until the trial, so he's not going anywhere. We've got all the time in the world to get this right for your wife."

After all was said and done, it turned out to be as cut-and-dried as we predicted —

the whole thing took a little more than a week. Grant was invited to attend the trial, but he chose not to, since anything less than a guilty verdict was a foregone conclusion. He did, however, agree to go for the sentencing a few weeks later, and he invited me to tag along, saying I deserved to see the man at least once with my own eyes before they locked him up and threw away the key.

I didn't know that Grant had prepared a statement until the judge, who reminded me of Boss Hogg from *The Dukes of Hazzard,* called him up. "Mr. McFadden, before we proceed, I believe you'd like to say a few words to the defendant. Come forward, please."

"Thank you, Your Honor." Grant pulled a paper from his suit coat and settled in behind the microphone on the witness stand. "Four hundred ninety-three," he started, staring directly into the other man's eyes. "Do you know what that number is?"

Jake stared back, but didn't respond.

"Four hundred ninety-three," Grant repeated. "It's *my* number. It's the number of consecutive days that I've missed my wife since you took her life. I'm a math teacher, Mr. Spitz, so I like numbers. Here's another one for you. Seven hundred fifty-four. That's my youngest daughter's number. It's how old she is, in days. If you subtract one from the other, then we can deduce that Eliza was exactly two hundred sixty-one days old when you callously murdered her mother, making her too young to ever remember the woman who brought her into this world. I also have a stepdaughter, Madeline, who is here today. She's seated right over there." Grant pointed in my direction. "Her number? One thousand. Rounded down considerably, that's the number of tears she's cried at night, wishing she still had a mom around to teach her and love her." He paused again, briefly, then asked, "I wonder, Mr. Spitz — *Jake* — did you know your mother growing up? I'm told you did. In fact, I'm told that she's pleaded for leniency on your behalf — for mercy — suggesting that you shouldn't be held wholly accountable for your actions because you were hallucinating at the time of the attack. Well, you know what number I have to say to your mother? *One hundred twenty-eight million, six hundred seventy-three thousand.* That's what you get when you multiply my number by each of my daughter's numbers. It's a lot, to be sure. Yet it's exactly the number of *minutes* I hope you rot in jail. In case you can't do the math, that works out to almost two hundred forty-five years."

Grant stopped for a second, staring first at Jake Spitz, then at me, and then at his paper. Before resuming, he folded his notes and tucked them away, apparently choosing to wing it. "A couple of my friends at work suggested to me that I should come in here and tell you that I've forgiven you, that even though my family has been destroyed, that we're okay. They wanted me to do you a courtesy, to wish you well as you head off to begin your new life behind bars. Well, I can't do that. I can't lie. It is my sincere hope that this court sees fit to punish you to the full extent of the law. If my understanding of the law is correct, that would leave you behind bars until the end of your miserable life — when *your number* is up."

The courtroom was absolutely silent as Grant walked slowly back to his seat beside me. We listened to a few more procedural things, then the judge recessed to his chambers.

Several hours later, Boss Hogg gathered everyone back in the courtroom and announced that a decision had been made. With a hush settling over the crowd, he cleared his throat and said, *"Twenty-five years, with possible parole after fifteen."*

It wasn't the decision Grant was looking for. With eyes burning, he shot up out of his seat and went on a minute-long tirade about the injustice of the legal system that caters to criminals. During the rant, an officer escorted Jake from the courtroom, just in case things got out of hand.

The judge had to wait for Grant to calm down before explaining the ruling. "Keep in mind that Mr. Spitz had no prior criminal record. Other than recreational drug use, what we have here is a young man with a lot of potential. It's also important to note that he's been nothing but remorseful from day one, which shows character, and at twenty years old he is still young enough to contribute positively to society at some point in the future. But most important, what he did, vile as it was, was not premeditated, nor was there an express intent to kill. As the defense and prosecution both pointed out during deliberations, he was not acting of his own accord at the time of the incident, but was experiencing an unfortunate, yet uncommon side effect of drug use. I've taken all of these factors into consideration, weighed them against the state's sentencing statutes and guidelines, and find the sentence to be appropriate." He paused momentarily, folding his arms together on top of the bench. "Mr. McFadden, I am truly sorry for your loss. Earlier, on the stand, you suggested that no mercy be shown to Mr. Spitz. In my position, I have an obligation to uphold justice to the full extent of the law. It's been my experience that justice is often merciful. However, rest assured that mercy can never rob justice. Not in my courtroom. In this case, I believe that justice has been served."

In retrospect, I can't necessarily disagree with what the judge said that day. He'd clearly weighed lots of factors before making his decision. In the end, I think the only thing he didn't take into consideration was how the ruling would affect Grant.

Or the fact that anything affecting Grant . . . affected me.

CHAPTER TWENTY-FOUR

"These dishes have been here for three days, Maddy! Get in here and make yourself useful!"

It was Saturday night, and Grant was in one of his moods again. The Spitz trial sent him tailspinning right back down to where he was after Mom died, which meant more booze. He made a conscious effort to stay sober during the weekdays, but Friday night through Sunday was always a bit touch and go.

"Can I finish this chapter first?" I asked.

He came and ripped the textbook out of my hand and tossed it across the room. *"Can I finish this chapter first?"* he mimicked in a whiny voice that sounded nothing like me. "You sound like my students — give 'em one little thing to do and they gripe about it. *Can I turn my homework in late, Mr. McFadden? Can I do this on my calculator instead? Mr. McFadden, can't we just have a few extra days to study before the test?* No, you can't!"

"I'm sorry."

"Oh, you're sorry now?" He took a swig from the bottle in his hand. "Sorry and lazy — a great combination. Do you know how hard I work to put food on the table every day, Maddy? Every single day I work my tail off so you and Eliza can be taken care of. And what do I get for my efforts? Nothin'. No respect. All I get is an ungrateful little twelve-year-old who can't get off her big fat butt to do the dishes."

I knew arguing wouldn't do me any good, so I went to the sink and started washing, which thankfully shut him up. When I was almost finished, Eliza woke up crying and came running out of her bedroom. Grant tried shooing her back to her room for a minute or two, but she wouldn't stop screaming.

I finished putting the last few dishes in the washer and went to console her.

"Just shut up already!" Grant finally yelled at Eliza right as I was picking her up. "I can't take it anymore!"

"Don't yell at her!" I blurted out. "She's just scared."

That little outburst earned me my second bloody lip in two years. "Don't talk back to me!" he barked as I covered my mouth with my hand to quell the pain. "I deserve a little respect around here."

It was summer by then, so no one saw the swelling in my face. Or the black eye I got a month later.

I don't know exactly why he was taking his frustrations out on me, but he was. It only ever happened when he was drunk. Afterward he'd beg and plead for forgiveness, and promise never to do it again, then he'd hug me and tell me he was going to be a better dad, and recount how stressful everything was between work and the house and the bills and the kids.

When seventh grade started he sat me down and explained how he just had too much on his plate. "I know you don't want to hear this," he said, "But I really need you to step up. To help out more. I need you to take on a bigger role around here. You're nearly thirteen, which is plenty old enough to be doing more of the things your mother used to do, and I think me having a little less to do will really help keep me from getting so upset all the time, which will be good for all of us. Can I count on you?"

Of course I said that he could. What else was I going to say? *Gosh, sorry Grant, but here — take a swing at me if it'll make you*

257

feel better.

The "bigger role" that Grant was talking about turned out to be almost everything. Cooking, cleaning, laundry, bathing Eliza, you name it. It didn't seem to matter to him that I had school to think about, but that was okay, because I didn't give school much thought anyway. I was coasting — listening in class, but doing very little in the way of homework or studying. At home, though, I was doing all I could to keep Grant happy.

Unfortunately, Grant didn't hold up his end of the bargain. Sure, he was less stressed because I was doing everything except buying groceries, but his drunken fits continued. Twice during the first semester I had to wear long-sleeved shirts when it was over eighty degrees outside just to cover up the bruises on my arms, and once during second semester I missed eight straight days of school because no amount of makeup could cover up my shiner. That time Grant had to call and tell the vice-principal that I had pneumonia.

I remember sitting at home during those eight days, staring at myself in the mirror, running my fingers over the puffy blackness that surrounded my eye. By then I was plenty old enough to realize that Grant had a problem, and that it probably wasn't going to get any better. I felt sorry for him, though. I knew he was trying. When he wasn't drunk, he was just as good as any dad out there. I mean, he loved us, I knew that much, but that love only confused things when I ended up on the receiving end of his temper.

As I saw the swollen version of me staring back at me, I weighed my options. The obvious thing to do was to talk to someone at school, either the counselor or one of my teachers. But would any of them believe me? Everyone in the school district knew Grant; they'd worked with him for years. Would they believe me over him? It would be hard to dismiss if I showed them the bruise, but what if Grant said I was lying? What if they believed one of his stories of me falling off my bike? What if they all bought in to the idea that this is just my way of acting out because I hadn't fully dealt with the trauma of losing my mother? Then what? *Then Grant would be mad, that's what.* Then maybe he'd be *really* upset with me the next time he got drunk. I decided the risk was too great.

Another option was to run away. I'd heard of kids trying that before, fending for themselves on the streets downtown. Frankly, the thought terrified me. At least with Grant I knew what to expect. On the street, who knows what kind of creepy men I might run into in the middle of the night? Would that be any safer? And eventually the police would probably find me, and then Grant would be irate. But the biggest reason why I couldn't run away was my three-year-old sister. Who would take care of her if I was gone? Who would protect her?

In my adolescent mind, that left me with only one path forward: *stick it out.* Suck it up, don't talk back, keep my head down, stay out of his way, do everything I could to keep him happy. I figured when I turned eighteen I could leave, report the abuse to the authorities, and then apply for custody of Eliza as an adult.

It wasn't a perfect plan, but as I touched my swollen eye once more in the mirror, it was the best I could come up with.

In early May of that year, we were focusing on creative writing in English class. The teacher wanted us to really put our hearts and souls into a poem. She said it could be about anything, as long as it was something that made us feel something. A crush, a special friend, a fear, a personal loss, whatever. She said we didn't have to put our names on the paper, so I honestly thought it was just going to be a classroom exercise to get the creative juices flowing, not something that we would have to turn in. But at the end of the period Miss Thayer asked us to pass our papers to the front of the row. Before I even realized what she was saying, Mark Rigby swiped mine from my desk and passed it forward.

I could have killed him.

The next day in class, once we were all seated, the teacher began handing the papers back out. "I haven't read any of these," she said, "and none of us has any idea who wrote what. If you get your own poem back, let me know and we'll swap some around."

"Why are we doing this?" asked a kid up front.

I was near the back of the room, fidgeting with my long sleeves, freaking out about who was going to get mine. I tried to watch for my handwriting as she handed them out, but it was useless.

"Why indeed," Miss Thayer said. "I like to think of creative writing, and especially poetry, as a window into the mind of the author. A good poem should give you insights into their hopes and dreams, or maybe their struggles and disappointments. So as you get a poem, I want you to start by simply reading it through several times. No talking, so everyone can focus. Then read it again, but as if you were the author. I want you to try to get inside his or her head. Pretend like you're reading it through someone else's eyes. As you do so, and as you think about what the poem might mean to the person who wrote it, I promise you'll get a lot more out of it. Then see if you can guess who the author is."

She handed me a poem that was only three stanzas long about a pet rat that died. I read it once before deciding I didn't care about some stupid rodent. I just wanted to know who was reading mine.

After ten minutes the teacher stood back up. "Okay, now I'd like a few of you to share the poem you've been reading. As you read it aloud, try to do so in a manner that you think its author would want it read to best convey the meaning."

I wanted to throw up.

Angie Rowe was called on first. She got up and read a poem about ovarian cancer. It was actually pretty good, but would have been better if the boys in the room didn't snicker every time she said the word "ovaries"; I don't think most of them even knew what ovaries are.

Next, a boy named Marcus was called

forward. The page in his hand looked a lot like mine. I slid lower in my seat and wiped my sweaty palms on my jeans, praying that it wasn't. It turned out to be a sweet little sonnet about wanting to get a first kiss. Following the teacher's instructions to read it in the voice of the author, Marcus did his best impression of a dreamy-eyed girl, which had everyone but me and Randy rolling in the aisles. It was assumed, but never confirmed, that Randy penned the poem.

"Nathan Steen," the teacher said as soon as Marcus sat down. "I'd like to hear from you next."

He looked up at her nervously. "No thank you."

"Really?" she asked with a chuckle. "I had no idea this was optional. Probably because it isn't. I'd like you to read the poem, please, Nathan. The fact that you don't want to has me all the more intrigued."

When Nathan stood up, I caught him glancing back at me, and I knew I was dead. He had my poem, and he was about to read it in front of God, Mrs. Thayer, and a classroom full of kids who hated my guts. He went to the front of the room, dragging his feet the whole way. When he got there, he stared at the paper for a few seconds, looked up at the teacher, and then he scanned over the rest of the students. As his eyes moved across the room, he seemed to pause for a split second on me. Then he cleared his throat and started reading in a voice so serious and forlorn that you'd think he was giving a eulogy.

Probably my funeral, I thought.

"Roses are red . . . and violets are blue . . . I don't like English . . . and neither should you. Daisies are yellow . . . and carnations pink . . . at least math is fun . . . but English class stinks. Violets are purple . . . and lilies are white . . . Miss Thayer is evil . . . you know that I'm right. So many flowers . . . and colors in bloom . . . oh please, oh please . . . let me out of this room."

At first there was nothing but silence, then a few flurries of nervous laughter. Many of the kids didn't know what to do or say, so they just sat there waiting to see how Miss Thayer would react.

Nathan slunk back to his desk. While he walked, he stealthily folded up the paper and slid it in his pocket.

I couldn't believe it. I'd dodged a bullet! I let out a long sigh of relief as the teacher got up from her desk with an awkward smile on her face. "Well," she said, with just a hint of laughter in her voice, "while I think that poem lacks substance, it certainly is a window into the mind of its author, wouldn't you say? But bravo to Mr. Steen for reading it with such eloquence. And thank you, Nathan, for trying to spare me. Next, how about we invite Amy . . ."

I didn't hear what she said after that. My head was too lost in thought to process anything from the outside world. How did Nathan pull that off? And why did he do it?

After school, as I was passing through the south soccer field, just beyond the parking lot, Nathan caught up with me. He reached in his pocket and pulled out a folded piece of paper. "You got a minute?" he asked.

"Maybe."

"Can we go sit down? I want to talk to you."

I didn't want to talk to him, but he'd pulled off a miracle in English class, so giving him a few minutes was the least I could do.

He unfolded the paper as we sat down under a giant hackberry tree at the edge of the field. "It's yours, isn't it?"

I kept my eyes low, focusing on a green leaf on the ground near my knee. "Pretty sure."

"It's really good. Sad, but good."

I looked up into Nathan's somber face. "Why didn't you read it to the class?"

"I just . . . I saw you in your chair and —. I didn't think you wanted it read. Besides, everyone would have known it was yours, and I'm not sure it would have helped you any. For your sake, I thought it best to wing it."

"So you came up with the flower poem on the fly?"

"Pretty much." He tossed the paper on my lap. "Will you read it to me?"

"Why?"

"Because Miss Thayer said we'd get more out of it if we tried imagining how the author would say it. I've read this over and over in my head, and now I want to hear how it's really supposed to sound."

I picked up the paper and unfolded it, staring at the words for several seconds. I wished they weren't my own, but I couldn't deny that they'd come from my head, the fruit of my troubled existence. Honestly, I don't know why I went along with his request, because I thought for sure he'd run straight to the principal if he learned about Grant's physical abuse. But I read it anyway. Maybe it was my way of calling out for help. Nervous as I was, I cleared my throat and started in, reciting the penciled words exactly as I felt them in my heart.

Bully Ache

Laughing, mocking, scorn, and jeers,
Preying on my lonesome fears;
It seems some people love to hate me,
Cruelly curse at and berate me.

Every day I walk in silence
Through a life of verbal violence;
Think those words will not sink in?
Oh fool . . . think again, think again.

Grab a dart and throw it true,
Any piercing phrase will do:
Fatty, four-eyes, geek, or loser,
Come one, come all and let's abuse her!

Last week I woke up blue-and-black
With hatred bruised upon my back;
And what, you ask, was the doctor's take?
"Poor girl . . . she has a bully ache."

Shattered is the life I lead,
At home and school I hurt, I bleed
A thousand tears, then thousands more,
Like endless waves upon the shore.

Does God above not hear my pleas?
I beg for help on bended knee
That this will end, and soon! I pray.
Or else, God, just take me away.

For I can't bear to live like this —
No friends, no love, no life, no bliss,
No hope, no help, no happy day,
Please God . . . take the ache away.

When I finally peeked up from the page, Nathan looked like he was going to cry, which was weird. I'd never seen him like that. Even at my mom's funeral he hadn't been really emotional, but I could tell he was feeling something there under that tree. "I'm so sorry," he whispered.

"Why?"

"For allowing you to feel that way. For letting people make fun of you."

By what he said, I realized he didn't fully understand my poem. He got the part about school, but seemed to completely miss the word "home." I wasn't sure whether to be relieved or disappointed that he didn't learn my secret, but decided anew it was best for Eliza if nobody found out. "Compared to some people, Nathan, you're a saint."

He shrugged. "Not really. Just because I'm not mean to you doesn't mean that I'm nice. I've watched and heard what people say to you, and I haven't done anything to stop it."

"Nathan, you've been —"

"A jerk. When I read your poem, I knew it

268

was yours. And you know what I thought?"
Now he did start to tear up, and he didn't
even try to hide it. "I thought about the first
day we met, when I shot that spit wad at
you, and my dad said something like, 'My
son would never do that to another child of
God.' And then I wrote that note and asked
you to forgive me, and you actually did! Yet
here I am, four years later, and I haven't
learned a dang thing! Maybe I haven't been
the one pointing the straw at you lately, but
I've still been one of the faces in the crowd
who sees what's going on and does nothing.
Or worse, laughs." He takes a long, deep
breath and wipes at his face. "I'm so sorry,
Maddy."

I looked around to see if anyone was
watching. For Nathan's sake, I hoped they
weren't. For my sake too — I didn't need
any more bad publicity. "Thanks. That
means a lot. But . . ."

"What?"

"Well, don't take this the wrong way, but
is anything really going to change just
because you suddenly feel sorry for me? I
kind of doubt it."

"Yeah, of course it will," he shot back, getting all defensive. "I'm going to change it.
You'll see."

"Really? I mean, you're obviously emotional about it today. But what about tomorrow? And the day after that, and the day after that? It's one thing to feel sorrow, and another to actually do something about it. I heard your dad say that once."

"I *will* do something," he insisted. "Just you wait and see."

"Yeah," I said with a shrug of my own. "I'll wait and see."

Then he got this mischievous, determined look in his eyes, the kind he used to get back in fourth grade when he was gearing up to beat me on a school project or a trivia game. "You really don't think I can do anything to help you, do you?"

"At this point, my life is pretty hopeless. So, no, I don't."

Nathan paused for another moment to think. Then he stood up as a confident smile spread across his face. "I accept the challenge," he said, and then he started to walk away. "I'll see you tomorrow, Maddy."

I sat there on the ground beneath the tree for several more minutes, watching Nathan disappear into the neighborhood. I still doubted that he'd carry through on whatever he thought he was going to do to help me. In fact, at that point in my life I doubted that I was even worthy of such help.

But true to his word, when I saw Nathan

the following Monday, he went out of his way to make sure I was noticed. He'd say hi and wave as he passed by in the hall, or if there was time he'd stop at my locker to see how I was doing. It was almost over-the-top for the first week or so, and I think he got a lot of flak for it from his friends, who thought he was out of his mind for being kind to a lowlife like myself.

In the second week he started sitting with me occasionally at lunch and introducing me to kids I didn't know. None of them were very interested in getting to know me, but the cool thing was that Nathan wasn't embarrassed by me, or if he was, he didn't let on. There were also a couple days when he'd walk me home and we'd talk, and once he even had me and Randy over at his house and we played video games together. It was nice having someone my age to talk to. And Randy was so sweet, he even let me beat him at Super Mario.

For Memorial Day, Nathan's parents took him to spend the weekend on Galveston Island. When he came back, he was so excited, saying he'd found something at the beach that was going to change both of our lives. I told him he'd already done plenty for me, and he didn't have to keep it up if he didn't want to. He said not only did he want to, but that he had a plan to make sure he didn't forget to. He insisted that he had lots of making up to do for all the times he'd ignored me or let others be mean to me, and he was going to make it up to me at least seven times a day.

When I asked about his plan, he pulled seven small, red stones from his pocket.

"Rocks?"

"Yes, rocks," he said, obviously disappointed that I didn't sound more excited. "But not just any rocks. *Serving stones.* That's what I'm going to call them. But you can't tell anyone about them. They'd think I'm nuts."

"But why rocks?"

"I don't know. I saw them on the beach and it just seemed like a good idea. My dad has a rock tumbler at home, and we sometimes go hunting for stones to smooth up in the tumbler. I thought it would be fun to keep these little guys in my pocket and see how long it takes for them to get smooth too. And if they're in my pocket every day, they'll help remind me to look out for . . . you know, you, or anyone else who might be having a bad day."

"So what are you going to do with them?"

A quick look of frustration crossed his face, like I wasn't getting it fast enough.

272

"*Nothing.* That's the point. They're just going to stay in my pockets every day. When I do something nice, I'll move one stone to the other pocket. But that's it. They'll just sit there, out of sight, until I do something good for someone else."

"For how long?" I asked.

He stuffed the rocks back in his pocket and shrugged. "I don't know. However long it takes." He patted the outside of his jeans. "This is my tumbler. I guess they'll stay there until they're smooth, or the day I die. Whichever comes first."

"You *are* nuts," I said with a chuckle.

"Maybe so." He laughed. "But if it's all the same to you, can I carry your bag?"

Chapter Twenty-Five

With the onset of another summer, I fully expected Nathan to forget about me for the next three months, but I severely underestimated his determination. He rode his bike over to my house nearly every day to check on me. Some days it was a quick visit to say hello, other times he'd bring a book that he thought I'd like to read, or sometimes we'd just sit on the grass in front of my house and talk while Eliza ran around picking dandelions. The best days, though, were when he brought Randy. The three of us would make cookies or drink lemonade or just shoot the breeze until they had to go.

Eighth grade turned out much better than seventh grade, and it was all because of Nathan. The guy just didn't give up. What was really impressive, though, was that he started branching out. I saw, through very simple acts of kindness, that he was trying to be a friend to everyone. During that year

274

he really established himself as the "nice kid." Everyone seemed to think he was their best friend — the jocks, the cheerleaders, the band geeks, the drama club, the nerds, the shy kids, the fat kids, and of course the nerdy-shy-fat kids like me.

Interestingly — and thankfully — the more overt kindness that Nathan showed to me, the less other kids made fun of me. And if he or Randy happened to hear someone teasing me or joking about me, all they had to do was tell them to give it a rest, and they did!

My grades were still in the tank, and I still looked like a mess, and my life still really sucked, but it sucked a lot less knowing there were at least one or two people at school who cared about me.

On the last day of the school year, Nathan received awards for Citizen of the Year *and* Student of the Year, both of them well deserved. Afterward, the teachers handed out yearbooks, and all the kids were going around getting them signed. Nathan found me in the crowd and wrote something very sweet about how bright I was and that I needed to shine. The only other person who wrote anything was Randy, and I think his comment was "Stay cool." Anyway, after signing my yearbook Nathan informed me that he had got a job at a youth camp, so he probably wouldn't be able to see me as much during the summer.

"Oh," I said. "Bummer."

"Yeah, I need the money. Dad says it's time to start saving for college." Then came the best part of that year: he leaned forward and gave me a hug. A long one. I don't think I'd ever been hugged by a boy before, except maybe by my cousin when I was little. And to have him do it with so many people watching? I was on cloud nine. That hug was all I needed to get through the summer, with or without his regular visits. It wasn't even a romantic thing; I knew he didn't like me that way. It was just . . . medicine for my soul.

The next school year was even more of a turning point for me, and not just because I was a freshman. Even though I tested off the charts in terms of intellectual ability, I'd been moved down to more remedial classes on account of terrible grades. Due to that, I saw less of Nathan at school, which was disappointing, to say the least. After we got our first-quarter grades, he stopped by my house to see how I'd done.

"I'd rather not show you," I told him.

"I'll show you mine."

"*Pfft.* Like I don't already know you got all As"

"Oh, c'mon, Maddy. Just show me your grades already."

Reluctantly, I produced the report card from my backpack. "There. Read it and weep. That's what I did when I saw it."

He scanned it over for a second or two, then diplomatically said, "Could be worse."

"How can you say that with a straight face? I got all Cs and Ds. I probably should have flunked PE, but Mr. Carr is one of Grant's buddies." That was the other thing that was weird about that year: Grant was a teacher at the high school, so I saw him all the time in the halls and at assemblies. I never talked to him or anything, and I never had him as a teacher, but he was there. All of the kids seemed to love him, which I didn't understand at all. The teachers loved him too, especially the single ones. I, however, chose to keep my distance.

"Well, look at it this way," Nathan said. "These grades just leave that much more room for improvement. I bet with some extra credit, you could turn those Cs into As by the time the final-semester grades come out."

"Impossible. That would require me to do something other than go to class."

"Why don't you do more? It's not like you're not capable."

"Well, I'm busy, for one thing, around the house. But also . . . it's just easier being average. I mean, it's hard to be a nerd with Cs and Ds, right?"

"Right," he said, but the way he said it didn't sound like he agreed with me.

The next day Nathan showed up at my locker with an old photo that our teacher had snapped of the two of us from fourth grade while we were working on a science project together. To be honest, I hardly recognized the fourth-grade version of myself. My clothes matched, my hair was done up in curls, I was smiling, I was skinny, and I was obviously enjoying whatever it was we were working on. "I was thinking about you last night," Nathan said, "when I came across this old picture in my scrapbook."

"Oooh," I teased, "thinking about me at night? Don't tell the other girls, they'll all be jealous."

"Oh please."

"Didn't you have late basketball practice last night?"

"Yeah. So?"

"So how late was it? That you were thinking about me, I mean."

He rolled his eyes. "Keep dreaming. So anyway, I stumbled across this picture, and it reminded me of your report card."

"Huh?"

"Yeah . . . it reminded me that you've given up."

"That's a nice thing to say . . . Not." Everybody said "not" back then. It was the cool thing to say, I guess. Not.

"Just calling it as I see it. You've given up, and I think you need to give up giving up."

"Is that a double negative?"

He rolled his eyes again, which made me laugh. "Can you just hear me out? I'm trying to be serious here. Do you, or don't you, recognize the girl in the picture?"

I looked at the photo once more. "Yes . . . vaguely."

"Me too . . . vaguely. But guess what? The girl in this picture just happens to be the smartest girl I've ever met. She's probably the smartest kid this school has ever seen, and nobody knows it because she gave up trying. Back when I knew this girl, she was brilliant, and she wasn't afraid to let everyone know it. She was ten years old and already trying to decide which Ivy League college she was going to attend."

"The smartest one at school, eh?" I asked sarcastically. "Even smarter than that Steen

279

kid. I hear he's a genius."

"Maddy, I hate to admit it, but I've always known you're smarter than me. Which is why it's so stupid that I could end up valedictorian, and you're on a path to-ward . . . what? Flunking out?"

"Something like that."

"Don't joke. I know you've had a tough few years, but you can do better than you've been doing. You owe it to yourself."

I felt a little hint of anger creeping in. "You don't even know how tough I've had it, Nathan. So who are you to judge?"

"What's that supposed to mean?"

"Forget it. Just . . . you don't know everything, so maybe you're wrong. Maybe Cs and Ds is the best I can do right now."

He shrugged. "Maybe. But I don't believe it." He handed me the picture. "It's yours to keep. Maybe it will motivate you to get back to the student you were before." He hesitated for a second, then, with even more intensity, said, "We don't have many years left before college, Maddy, so if you're still planning on going to one of those great schools you used to talk about, it's probably time to get on the stick."

I didn't want to be mad at him, but I kind of was. I wasn't used to being challenged like that. For the past few years everyone

280

had just sort of let me do my own thing. Even Grant didn't seem to care that I'd let my grades fall into the toilet. "Maybe I will," I barked.

"Good," he fired back as he turned to go. "Maybe you should." Then he relaxed and winked at me. "I could use a little competition. If you think you're up to it."

That night it was me staying up late, thinking about Nathan. I was still mad at him for what he'd said. His life was so perfect — a happy little family, great parents, all the friends he could ask for, a starting position in every sport he played, and on and on. And my life? He didn't know what it was like to be me. How dare he judge me for slacking off? Yet somehow, I knew that he was right. Yes, my life sucked. But was sitting in remedial classes and getting mediocre grades going to make it suck any less? Not in the long run.

That night I made up my mind to not only compete with Nathan academically, but to beat him.

The next day I went to my guidance counselor and asked to be moved up to the advanced classes. Unfortunately, though not surprisingly, she said no. "Not a chance," I think, were her exact words. Something about needing to show proficiency by completing my current coursework.

"What if I tested out?" I asked.

"What do you mean?"

"Well, what if I had the teachers give me all the tests for the whole year and I did well on them? Could you move me up then?"

"I . . . well, yes, I suppose we could look into that."

That weekend and for the next two weeks I spent every waking moment reading ahead in every subject, absorbing as much information as I could cram in. The dishes and laundry piled up during that time, but I didn't care. The week after that I sat for three straight days in the library with a proctor taking every test they threw at me.

I aced them all.

By the start of the next week I had a brand-new schedule, back in with the "advanced" kids. The guidance counselor worked out a deal with the teachers that they would base my semester grade on how I did in the second quarter only, kind of like a transfer student from another school. It was a fresh start, with no Ds to weigh me down.

Nathan couldn't believe it when I showed up in half of his classes, but he was excited for me.

"You've got three and a half years to beat me to the valedictorian podium," I told him during Algebra II.

He rubbed his hands together like he was savoring the challenge. "You're on!"

The next couple of years were hard work, to say the least. Not only was the schoolwork increasingly difficult, but I still had to deal with everything at home. Grant was learning to control his temper, but whenever he was drinking, I made sure to avoid him. Somehow or another, I maintained straight As throughout my freshman and sophomore years.

Then came junior year, which, as everyone knows, is a really important time in terms of college preparation. That's the big year for admission tests, AP tests, college visits, and all that. It's also a big year for a less spectacular reason: junior prom. I swear, after the holiday break, that's all the girls talked about. *Who's going to ask me? What color dress should I wear? How can I tell him yes in a really creative way? What if the wrong guy asks me? Do you think he'll rent a limousine?*

Ugh.

I wanted to puke every time I heard them mention it in the hallways. Not that anyone was talking to me about it. After all, in many people's eyes I was still Maddy McFatty, the nerdy girl who'd blown up like a balloon in seventh grade. Still, to be fair, I'd slimmed down considerably since then, to the point that I almost liked how I looked. I even traded in my Coke bottles for a pair of sleek, Guess glasses. It didn't matter to most people, though — the stigma of being a nerdy fat girl remained.

Nathan was a busy guy that year too. He'd had a stellar season as quarterback on the football team, he led the basketball team into the play-offs, and he was right in the middle of baseball season when prom rolled around. With his busy athletic schedule we didn't have as much time to talk after school as we used to, but we'd catch up here and there during class or occasionally at lunch. It never ceased to amaze me that he had the guts to chew the fat with me, when half of the popular kids he hung out with either disliked me or didn't even know my name.

During one of our lunchtime conversations in early April I poked around about prom. You know, just curious to find out what Nathan was planning. "So, which lucky lady have you asked? A cheerleader, I bet."

"To prom?"

"Yeah. Or can pastor's kids not dance?"

"Oh *puh-lease,*" he said. "You should see me bust a move."

"I bet," I snickered. "So, have you asked someone?"

"Not yet. I have someone in mind, though. I'm just waiting for the right moment."

"Who? C'mon, you know you can trust me with your secrets."

Just then a beautiful girl named Abby came over and sat down. She'd moved to Rockwall from California just a couple months earlier, and it took her all of a week to establish herself as one of the popular kids. I didn't know much about her, other than she was always chewing gum. "Hey, Nathan," she said. "What'cha up to?"

"Just talking with one of my friends."

I loved it when he said that to people. It was like he wanted to make sure that everyone knew we were buds, in case there was any doubt. He wasn't just chatting with a stranger and he wasn't just talking about schoolwork. He was with a friend.

Abby kind of smiled at me. Or sneered; it was hard to tell which. "Hey," she said absently, then turned back to Nathan. "So I was just over talking to Erika, and . . . well, she'd kill me if she knew I was telling you this, but she would totally say yes if you asked her to prom."

285

I wanted to gag. Like Erika wasn't the one who sent this girl over to talk. "Ooh," I said, teasing. "Is that who you were alluding to, Nathan? *Erika?*"

Abby's head snapped back to me. "He was talking to you about prom?"

"Yep. Apparently he has someone in mind, but he won't say who."

She looked me up and down again, like she was determining what size my clothes were. I don't think she knew if I was being serious or yanking her chain. After a moment more of brushing my hair with her eyes, she turned back to Nathan. "Is it her? I totally won't tell her if it is."

"Sorry, Abby," Nathan replied. "It'll be my secret until I finally ask her."

" 'Her' who?" Abby nudged.

"Whoever she is, she'll be the first to know."

Abby stood up. "Fine. But seriously, Nathan, the dance is like three and a half weeks away. Erika can't wait much longer. You're lucky someone hasn't already asked her. And if you want, we could double-date."

"Oh, who are you going with?" I asked.

Staring down her nose at me, she said, "No one you would know. Or at least no one who would know you. His name is

Randy Rawlins, and he's like super popular. He's even got a scholarship offer to play football at Alabama after we graduate."

I laughed. "Well, Randy has great taste."

The way Abby smiled made me want to gag again. She was so incredibly full of herself. "Wow, thank you. That's so nice."

"Yeah," I continued, "he had a crush on me in fourth grade."

Instantly, Abby's vanity grin turned to a piercing glower. When Nathan laughed, she stormed off without looking back.

"Is that true about Randy?" I ask once she was gone. "Did an offer finally come?"

"Just yesterday. Not many people know yet. I'm sure he was going to tell you soon."

I didn't mind that I wasn't the first to know. Nathan was right, Randy would have told me in due time. That's just sort of the relationship we had. I still had a thing for him, and I think he knew it, but he was thick with the popular group, so he was careful not to let our friendship become too visible, which was fine. I completely understood. Periodically we'd run into each other in a quiet moment, when there weren't a lot of judging eyes, and then we'd catch up. Now that I was thin again, or average anyway, I even caught him checking me out a couple times, which was encouraging, but I didn't force myself upon him in any way. I just let him come to me whenever he was ready to talk, and then it was like old times again, like we were still the little kids in fourth grade who were too embarrassed to admit we liked each other.

"So what about you?" I asked Nathan. "Any football scholarships on the horizon?"

"Nothing firm yet. I think a couple of the smaller Texas schools are going to offer, but we'll see. Most of them want to make sure I have a good senior year before they finalize their scholarship plans for the quarterback position. Unfortunately, I lack the size that Randy has. He's the sort of specimen that schools go after. I mean, the guy is a beast. But I'm sure I'll land somewhere. It's just a matter of time."

"Any school would be lucky to have you," I told him.

Two days later, on Friday before school, I ran into Abby again, only this time she wasn't alone, and Nathan wasn't anywhere near. I had come in early that day to make up an oral test with the French teacher from the week before, when I had to miss a couple days of school because Eliza had the flu and couldn't stay home alone. Abby and Erika were there for early-morning cheer practice. When they spotted me coming out of the language lab, they made a beeline, each of them taking up a post on either side of me, effectively hemming me in against the wall in an empty hallway.

"Okay," Abby said, "spill. Is Nathan going to ask Erika to the prom or not?"

"How should I know?"

Abby had two hands on her skinny little hips, and was chewing gum like mad. "Because everyone knows that you and Nathan have some weird little thing going on. No one knows why — and no one really cares why — but he has this strange fascination with you. So we know you know."

"Trust me, girls, I have no idea who he's going to ask. Nor do I care."

Erika cocked her head to the side and crossed her arms. "I bet you're just dying for him to ask you, aren't you?"

I smiled back at her. "That's the pot calling the kettle black, don't you think?"

Abby and Erika traded confused glances, followed by a joint, "Huh?"

"It means . . ." I tried to think of how best to explain it, then decided it wasn't worth it. "Never mind. I just meant, *no,* Nathan and I are just friends, and I could care less about some stupid dance."

Erika looked appalled, like my indiffer-

289

ence toward prom was a personal affront. She glared at me for a moment, then her eyes lit up unexpectedly. "Maddy, didn't your mom die when you were younger?"

"Yeah," I said hesitantly. "So what?"

"So you know what your problem is?"

"I have a problem?"

"Makeup! You didn't have a mom around to teach you how to spruce yourself up. Honestly, boys like Nathan Steen would be much more interested in you if you just added a touch of color once in a while. Trust me."

Abby seemed to get what Erika was up to. "Oh yeah, totally. A little lipstick and eye shadow, and you'd have the boys lining up." She quickly searched her backpack and pulled out bright red lipstick and a palette of eye shadows.

Erika grabbed the lipstick from her friend's hand. "Just hold still, Maddy, and we'll do you up right." Before I could resist, she had the lipstick pressed against my mouth and was smearing it from side to side.

I wanted to fight back; I might have even struggled a little bit. But something in me said I shouldn't. No, this wasn't Grant landing the back of his hand on my face, but the emotions were exactly the same. I wanted those girls to pay, but I was accustomed to suffering. I was conditioned to accept it. I'd learned through experience just to wait it out — to put up with abuse, move on, and live to see another day.

By the time their makeover started, some of the early busses had arrived, so we were no longer alone in the hallway. A handful of students stopped to see what was going on. Girls giggled as Erika continued to smear and smudge until my lips, and everything nearby, were caked in red. I wanted to yell and scream, but these girls weren't worth it. I'd endured worse, so I just let them have their fun. During the ordeal I heard one female spectator say, sarcastically, "Ooh, very pretty!" A boy yelled, "Houston, we have a hottie!"

I could feel myself sweating.

When Erika was done with the lipstick, Abby took off my glasses and began working on my eyes. She picked the darkest shade of orange in her compact and swiped on a thick arc with her brush, then she did the same over the other eye. "I think your eyes would match every color I have," she said wryly. "So we should probably go with a rainbow." She dabbed her brush in a bright purple and added another wide swath.

My line of sight was mostly blocked by Erika and Abby's hands in my face, so I couldn't tell why the crowd suddenly got quiet. My makeup artists sensed the change too. They both turned around at the same time and gasped.

Even without my glasses on I could see that Nathan was standing there in a dress shirt and tie, holding a single long-stemmed rose. His face was as red as the petals. "Erika? What are you doing?"

Erika turned multiple shades of red too. "I was . . . I mean . . . you know . . . just teaching Maddy how to put on makeup. She doesn't have a mom, you know, to help her look pretty."

"Yeah," Abby added with a snicker, "we're *helping.*"

"Why are you all dressed up, Nathan?" Erika asked.

Now he looked past the two cheerleaders and stared at my face. I looked away, embarrassed to be seen by him like that. "I wanted to look nice today," he muttered, "when I ask someone to prom."

Erika was suddenly all smiles. "Well, I must say, you already look the part of a prom king to me. All you need is a beautiful queen to go with you."

"You're right, Erika," he said, his face

softening. "That's exactly what I need." Then he held up the rose and walked slowly toward her. "And you're about as beautiful as they come." Abby was giddy with excitement. Erika puffed up her chest, her eyes quickly scanning her audience as she proudly awaited the magical words that were about to come from his mouth. When he was standing face-to-face with her, he leaned in slightly, as though he might kiss her on the cheek, then he dropped his voice even further and said, "At least on the outside."

The look on Erika's face was priceless. As her jaw dropped to her deflated chest, he turned to me and asked me if I would go to prom with him.

There were more gasps from the crowd, but none greater than the yelp that came from Erika's mouth.

It was a perfect moment. I'm sure some people thought he was joking, but I knew Nathan wouldn't joke about something like that. Not to me. It was so surreal. I mean, he was my friend, so it wasn't weird for me, but looking at it from everyone else's perspective, it must have seemed beyond insane. Maybe it's a little sappy, in hindsight — the school's geekiest geek being asked to the biggest social event of the year by Mr.

Everything. I knew, when he handed me the rose, that I wasn't his first choice. He was doing it to save me from the humiliation of my public "makeover," and probably also to teach those awful girls a lesson. Nathan never told me who he'd intended to ask, though I suspect it really was Erika.

"Are you sure?" I asked. "I mean, I'm fine not going."

"I want to," he insisted. "C'mon, say yes. We'll have fun together. And like Erika said, I need a queen."

My cheeks were on fire, and I'm telling you, I could have kissed him right there. But I maintained my composure and happily said, "Then it's a yes."

CHAPTER TWENTY-SIX

Word about Nathan's heroics spread like wildfire that day at school. Some people — the entire cheer squad, for example — were horrified by the turn of events, but most seemed at least a little impressed by Nathan's convictions, even if they felt sorry for him being stuck with me for prom. For his part, Nathan acted like it was no big deal.

Over lunch I asked him if we were going to go to prom with anyone else.

"Like who?"

"I don't know. I'm not sure how these things work. Do we just go together, or is it better in groups?"

"A group would be a lot of fun," he admitted, "but Randy's going with Abby, and I don't want to be stuck all night with her." Then he got that look he always got when he was feeling inspired. "You know what, let me ask around. I have a really good idea."

I don't know how he did it, but by the

end of the next day there were three other girls in the school who, like me, would have never planned on going to prom, walking around the halls with balloons and roses. Somehow Nathan had talked a few of his football buddies, who he knew were on-the-fence about prom, into asking these girls to come with us.

"Is this charity work for you guys?" I asked him somewhat indignantly when he told me we had a group of four couples.

"Would you give me a little credit?" he replied, looking genuinely hurt. "This isn't to stroke our egos. We're doing it because everyone deserves a chance to go to prom. Aren't you glad you're going? Because I sure am."

"Yeah, I'm excited."

"Good. And I think those other girls are pretty excited too. And remember, one good thing leads to another, Maddy, and I think this will be a really good thing. Not just for you or those girls, but also for me and my friends. I think some of the guys were afraid of getting rejected, so they hadn't asked anyone. And I guarantee we'll have a better time than if we went with someone like Erika, who's only worried about herself."

"You had me at 'egos,' " I said with a chuckle. "You're right. We're going to have a great time."

And we did.

When prom night finally came, there's no way to put into words what it felt like to be me. I'd always been the outcast, yet there I was, arm in arm with Nathan Steen, wearing a beautiful dress I'd found on sale — it was made of blue taffeta that looked green when the light changed — eating at a fancy restaurant, driving all over town in a limo with a group of kids who just wanted to have a fun time. It was truly a beautiful experience, one of the best of my life. Strictly speaking, I was still a taller-than-average geek, but when I was with Nathan, it didn't matter. We were just us, if that makes sense.

I was grateful to Nathan for what he was doing. He was so kind and funny and sweet, and he didn't act at all like he was doing me a favor. I just loved being with him, loved that he made me feel important. During dinner I leaned in and whispered, "I owe you big-time."

"For what?"

I looked around at the restaurant, at the beautiful table, at the rest of our group laughing and enjoying themselves. "For this. For everything."

"No," he said. "I owe you. For making me

a better person. I might be very different today if I hadn't read that poem of yours."

This is love, I thought. Not a romantic love — because I still had a crush on Randy — but a love that made me just want to wrap my arms around him and hold him forever. Nathan was safe. He cared. He would never hurt me. "I still owe you," I said, "and I promise, I'm going to repay you."

The first thing I saw when we got to the dance was Abby dragging Randy around by the cummerbund — first to the punch bowl, then to the DJ, then to the snack table, then back to the punch bowl. Between each stop she'd wave dramatically at anyone she thought might be looking at her. Oh, that girl was so annoying. And if I'm honest, she didn't even look all that great. Randy, on the other hand, was stunning in his tuxedo. I think he thought he was being sneaky, because I caught him taking periodic peeks at me and Nathan as we moved through the crowd.

About halfway through the night, when I went to get a drink, Randy slipped away from Abby for a couple of minutes to have a chat with Nathan. When I joined them, Randy smiled at me, maybe even blushed a little, and then scurried off.

"What was that about?" I asked Nathan.

"It was about fourth grade, as near as I can tell."

"Huh?"

He chuckled. "You know, fourth grade. When Randy liked you? Well . . . I think he still does."

I tried to play it down, but inside I was doing somersaults. "Really? You think?"

"Oh, don't tell me you're disappointed. I've seen how you look at him when he's around. But hey, do me a favor and don't let him know I mentioned it. I think he's hoping to make a big splash."

"What was he saying to you?"

"Just that he's having a terrible time with Abby, and he wished he'd asked someone else. I told him he should just come hang with us. You'd dance with him, right? I think he'd really like to."

"You wouldn't mind?"

"Me? Heck no. I've been telling him all year that he should ask you out. Now that I've broken the ice, I think he might just do it."

Right then, shouting on the other side of the dance hall interrupted our conversation. When we turned to look, Abby had a finger pointed up at Randy and was yelling at him at the top of her lungs. "You can't just cancel our date now! This is prom! They haven't even named me queen yet!"

Randy said something in return that we couldn't hear from where we stood, but whatever it was, it only incited her more.

She looked back over her shoulder until she spotted me, Nathan, and the other kids who'd come with us. "Fine! Go join the charity cases!" she yelled. "You're pathetic!" In a move that was so quick and skilled that it almost looked rehearsed, she reached up and ripped the boutonniere from Randy's suit, threw it on the floor, then squashed it with her heel. When she was satisfied that the flower was dead, she slipped the matching corsage from her wrist and threw it in Randy's face.

Personally, I felt sorry for Abby. I don't think she realized just how badly she was embarrassing herself. As she stormed off, trailed by a flock of snotty popular girls who acted like their lives had just been ruined, the DJ's voice came over the PA system. "Hey, like I always say, it's not a memorable prom without some good ol' teenage drama! What do you say we pick things up a bit with some Def Leppard? Everyone that's been dying to let loose, now is the time to hit the floor, and see if you can't 'Pour Some Sugar on Me.' "

A small cheer went up as dozens of kids

headed for the center of the dance floor. Nathan was asking me if I liked Def Leppard when Randy approached from behind and tapped me on the shoulder. It was the most nervous I'd ever seen him. "Maddy . . . I know you're here with Nathan, but . . . would you like to dance?"

I glanced at Nathan just long enough to see that he was grinning from ear to ear. "Yes," I said. "I'd like that."

Randy took me by the hand and led me to the middle of the floor, where people were jumping and thrashing around to the beat, many of them singing along or playing air guitar. Without saying anything, Randy grabbed my other hand and pulled me close, then wrapped one massive arm around my waist and began slow-dancing.

"What are you doing?" I asked.

"Dancing," he said. "I don't fast-dance."

Not that I minded being held close, but I could already tell that kids were watching and pointing at us. "Oh. But . . . don't you care what other people are thinking?"

He smiled sheepishly. "I used to. Right now, though, I just want to dance." He hesitated. "With you." We didn't say another word for the rest of that song. Maybe he was waiting for me to strike up a conversation, but I kept my mouth shut to avoid spoiling the moment.

The song right after that was an actual slow song — Bryan Adams, "Heaven" — and lo and behold, we kept right on dancing. It wasn't until halfway through that song that Randy finally spoke again. "Ya know, Abby was too short for me," he said, chuckling. "I really need to be with someone taller."

That sent a welcome tingle down my spine. "And smarter," I agreed.

He let out another little laugh. "And don't forget 'glassier.' "

" 'Glassier'?"

"Yeah, you know . . . with glasses."

I leaned in and hugged him closer. "Yeah, you definitely need someone glassier." Another minute went by, during which time I built up the nerve to ask a question that I hoped wouldn't be too forward. "Why now, Randy?"

"Why now what?"

"Why are you . . . um . . . you know, being all nice to me?"

"I'm always nice to you," he shot back.

"Okay, yeah, but why are you, like . . . showing a sudden interest? Or am I misreading this?"

He stopped dancing and pulled back just a bit so he could look at me. "What are you talking about? I talk to you all the time."

"Yes, but only when nobody's watching, except maybe Nathan. Not when other kids are around."

There was an instant look of guilt in his eyes. "I've never been like Nathan," he lamented. "I guess I've cared too much about being cool. I'm sorry for that. Nathan's always saying I should forget what other people think, and just do what I want to do. Well, right now, dancing with you, this is me doing what I want to do."

I was glad to hear it, but still not fully convinced. "So tomorrow, or Monday at school, when people are talking about how you ditched Abby to dance with me, you're not going to be embarrassed?"

"Let them talk," he replied with a sudden confidence as he took hold of me again and started swaying to the beat.

"And what if some of them think we're like . . . an item or something?" Now I was pushing the envelope, but I didn't care — better to take a chance while I've got it, than to let the opportunity pass.

Randy smiled. "What if? Would you mind?"

I thought about that for about a nanosecond. "Um . . . no. Would you?"

Now his smile morphed to a mischievous

grin. "Actually, I'd just as soon have them thinking those things right now."

There was an unfamiliar look in his eyes that caught me by surprise. I could feel my stomach turning in knots, as though it somehow knew that something unexpected was about to happen. Whatever it was, I *wanted* it to happen. My throat went so dry I could hardly speak, but I managed to say, "Why . . . er . . . how could we get them to think that . . . now?"

"I have an idea," Randy whispered. The look on his face made my heart skip. Slowly, purposefully, he leaned in and kissed me! Not a kiss on the cheek, like the ones Eliza sometimes planted on me, or one on the forehead, like Grant used to give when he tucked me in. This was *it,* the real deal, right there on the lips. I don't even know how long it lasted. Probably not as long as it felt, but long enough that I was transported, like magic, to some other place that I didn't know existed.

After the kiss, we made our way on wobbly knees to the side of the dance floor. Nathan and some of the kids he was with began clapping and hooting as we approached.

"Sorry, dude," said Randy, blushing again.

"No worries," Nathan replied, punching

Randy playfully in the side. "At least one of us got a kiss tonight."

I could feel my own cheeks heating up too, and the rush of it was thrilling beyond compare. It was so surreal that I had to keep asking myself if I'd somehow landed in a fairy tale.

For the rest of the night Randy and I split time between slow-dancing on the floor — whether it was a slow song or not — and hanging with Nathan near the punch bowl and munchies. When we were alone on the dance floor, we talked to each other like we'd been going steady for years, which was totally cheesy, but we didn't care — it was all part of the charm of the evening.

At eleven thirty they announced the final song of the night, which Randy insisted I dance with Nathan as a way to say thanks for sharing me. After the song we lingered for a while, until the adults finally shooed us out of the building. Randy had driven his mom's Ford Probe, and I would have loved to have him take me home, but I'd come with Nathan in the limo, and it only seemed proper that I return with him as well. Besides, trying to explain to Grant why I was coming home with a different guy would have been awkward.

Before we parted, Randy pulled me off to

the side and very sweetly gave me a kiss good night.

My arms lingered around him for a few extra seconds, not wanting the moment to end. Then I placed my hand on his chest, where his boutonniere should have been. "Did I mention how good you look in a tux?" I asked. "All you're missing is a flower."

He laughed. "We could go try to salvage the one that Abby murdered."

"No," I told him, "that one was red. I think white would look better with your complexion."

"Nah. I'd want a bight blue one, to match your eyes."

My heart swelled a little more. "Sadly, roses don't grow in blue."

Randy raised his eyebrows questioningly. "And you know this because . . . ?"

"Read it in an encyclopedia once. They lack the gene to produce a true blue color."

"Really?"

"Pretty sure. Then again, three weeks ago I was sure I'd be sitting at home tonight reading a book by myself. And three hours ago I was sure you were on a date with Abby, so maybe not everything is always as sure as I think."

"But the fact that we're standing here talking like this, or that we kissed, means that anything is possible. Even blue roses." Before I could say anything else he leaned in and gave me a final kiss, which sent my stomach fluttering again.

A few minutes later Randy drove off by himself in the Probe, while the rest of us climbed into the stretch limousine. The sequence of drop-offs was such that Nathan and I were the last ones alone in the car. When we reached my house, he opened my car door, took my arm in his, and walked me to the door like a proper gentleman. I told him he didn't have to, but he insisted. Then, standing there on the dimly lit porch, he gave me a long hug, thanking me for a wonderful time.

"Randy's really lucky," he said. "You're so much more than people give you credit for."

If the evening had ended right then, I dare say it would have been the best night of my entire life — a perfect memory to cling to in future times of need.

But perfect memories are like friends — or moms. Just because you want one or need one doesn't mean you get one. Personal trials, however, are much less elusive. They stalk you, waiting to steal your happiness, lurking like a thief around every corner.

CHAPTER TWENTY-SEVEN

When one door closes, another one opens. That's what they say, and maybe it's true. But sometimes, you just wish the door would stay shut.

While Nathan and I embraced to say good night, the porch light flipped on and the front door flew wide open. Grant was standing there, barefoot, with a bottle in his hand. I knew right off that this was going to be bad. He had that glossy look in his eyes that I knew so well. I immediately told Nathan to leave.

"No, no, no . . . not quite yet," Grant said, waving a finger back and forth. "The preacher's boy have a good time with my little girl?"

"Yes, sir," Nathan told him. "It was fun."

"Please," I begged, "just go. He's a little drunk, see, and . . . you need to go. *Now.*"

Grant just laughed. "A little? Kiddo, I'm a lot drunk. Let's call a spade a spade." He shoved the nose of the bottle up under Nathan's throat. Nathan didn't flinch one bit as Grant then went on a verbal tirade, slurring half the words. "And being thus ineb-er-riated, I have no problem letting you know . . . *I never liked you.* You or your holy old man! Too dang good for the rest of us! And what kind of father lets his son get away with shooting spit wads at strangers in church?" He curled the fingers on his free hand into a fist and cocked his arm like he was about to strike. "I should have taught you a lesson that day on being humble and submissive. Maybe I oughta teach it to you right now."

I was afraid he was actually going to take a swing, so I pushed Nathan out of the way and screamed at him to leave. With Nathan out of reach, Grant dropped both arms to his side and relaxed a little. I told Nathan again it would be much better for everyone if he left. Reluctantly, he backpedaled to the limousine, with Grant shouting profanities at him the whole way. I stayed on the porch long enough to watch the limo drive away, then I ran up to my room.

Worried that Grant might still be wanting to punch something, I stayed under my covers, still in my prom dress, for what seemed like forever, just waiting to get smacked around. But it never happened. After an hour, maybe more, I snuck downstairs to see what Grant was up to. He was sitting in the living room in the dark, with his back to me, alternating between swigs of alcohol and puffs on a joint. A bottle of pills lay tipped over on the ground near his feet. With that much junk in his system, it was only a matter of time before he passed out. Relieved, I crept back up the stairs, checked that Eliza was sleeping, then began getting ready for bed, thinking I was safe for the night.

Only I wasn't.

I don't know if he heard me in my room, or if the squeak of a stair caught his attention, but while I was undressing, the bedroom door swung open, and there he was, still gripping a bottle.

For several long moments he just stared at me. It made my skin crawl. Then, as he approached, he went into this rant about how I shouldn't be allowed to go on dates with kids like Nathan Steen, and how I wasn't worthy of their attention. "How could the starting quarterback have any interest in someone like you?" he slurred. He stopped, cocked his head to the side, and squinted at me. "Then again . . . you are starting to look a lot like your mother.

Yeah, maybe he's not such a saint after all."

"Get out," I told him, trying to cover myself with my dress. "Please."

That's the last thing I said before . . . *smack!* He caught me in the side of the head with his clenched fist, sending me flying back. The whole world went cold after that. All I could think was, *This isn't happening, this isn't happening!* It was so incredibly sickening. I don't even really remember anything after that because I blocked everything out.

The next morning, when I woke up, I tried to convince myself it was just a horrible dream. *Grant's a decent guy,* I told myself. *My stepdad. He cares for me. He wouldn't hurt me like that. Right?*

I took a shower, and didn't realize how long I stood under the water until I noticed it had turned cold. After getting dressed, I went downstairs to find him passed out in his recliner, the pills and pot scattered around on the floor. Eliza was sprawled on the sofa watching cartoons on TV and eating cereal out of the box. He woke up sometime after midday complaining of the world's worst hangover. Whether real or a show, he acted like he didn't remember a single thing about the night before. He even asked me how prom went. When I truthfully told him it was the most awful night of my life, he looked genuinely sad and said maybe my senior prom would be better.

"How about you?" I asked nervously, looking for any signs of deceit in his response. "How was your night?"

"Tough to say," Grant replied, sounding embarrassed. "After I put Eliza down, it's all a big blur. I remember watching a high-speed chase on *COPS,* and then . . ." He paused to look around at the mess on the floor. "Then I guess I had a little too much to drink."

"Yeah," I said quietly. "Looks like it."

I spent the rest of the afternoon alone in my room, splitting time between consoling myself and hatching a plan of escape, all while struggling with overwhelming feelings of embarrassment, shame, guilt, self-doubt, and fear. Every few minutes I'd go to the window, trying to muster the courage to open it, slip through, and run and never come back. Then I'd panic and back away, finding all sorts of reasons why running wasn't possible.

What if everyone at school finds out why you ran? What if Randy finds out? What if you go to the police and nobody believes you? What if you file a report and they open up some humiliating investigation, and then they conclude that you dreamed the whole thing up? You think that will go over well with Grant? What will happen to Eliza if you're gone . . . ?

If not for Eliza, I would have done it, I'm sure. But I had a plan — the same plan I'd had since he started hitting me. And a plan, I told myself, is only good if you see it through to the end. *You're almost eighteen, Madeline. Less than a year, then everything changes. Then you can go to the authorities. Then they won't take your sister and put her in some foster home. They won't split you up. She needs you to protect her. She needs you . . . she needs her mother.*

I took a deep breath to fight the panic. "You can do this," I told myself. "You have to." With another long breath I went downstairs and pretended like everything was perfectly fine. The fact that Grant remembered nothing from the previous night helped make the illusion real.

After dinner the doorbell rang. Grant was closest, so he answered it. "Maddy," he called merrily, "there's someone here to see you."

My mind was on other things, so I didn't even bother trying to guess who it was until I came around the corner of the entryway. "Randy," I gasped.

"Don't sound so surprised."

"I'll leave you two alone," Grant said. Then under his breath, but so that everyone could hear, "Two different guys, two nights in a row. Not bad, kiddo. Not bad at all."

"Oh. Yeah," I said absently.

"Go for a walk?" Randy asked.

"Uh . . . yeah. Let me grab some shoes."

We only walked for about five minutes, then spent the better part of an hour talking on the swings at the park. He was so cute, going on and on about how free he felt now that the pressure of always trying to please the cool kids was gone. "We can be our own kind of cool," he stated proudly.

"Any kind of cool will be a change of pace for me," I told him.

"You seem a little distracted," he observed at one point. "Is everything okay?"

I shrugged. "I didn't sleep much last night," I said, trying to be as honest as possible.

"Me neither," he replied. "I couldn't stop thinking about what an amazing time we had."

Sometimes honesty is hard. "Me too," I lied.

The next week at school, Nathan and Randy both noticed that I was on edge about something, but I just told them I was stressing about upcoming finals, and they bought it.

True to his word, though, Randy was a changed man, no longer beholden to what other people thought, which meant we started hanging out. A lot. Spending time with him was therapeutic — the more we were together, the less time I had to dwell on things that I desperately wanted to forget.

I wish I could say that my budding relationship with Randy somehow elevated my social status, but just the opposite was true: Randy's standing with the social elites dropped like a meteor. I guess I should have seen that coming. I mean, I'd been openly hanging with Nathan for several years, which had garnered little more than contempt and jealousy from those who wanted him all to themselves. In Nathan's case, though, he was known to float in lots of different circles — he'd been nice to everyone for as long as anyone could remember, so his befriending me was just viewed as "Steen being Steen." Randy, however, was a different story. He'd been categorized more as a popular elitist, only willing to mingle with the cool crowd. So him choosing me over Abby, and doing it in such a public way at prom? It shook the very foundation

315

of the high school social hierarchy, and he paid dearly for it. Jokes, teasing, laughing, name-calling, slander — you name it, he endured it.

Amazingly, though, he stuck with me. He even defended my honor — and his — when guys occasionally said that the only reason he'd want to be with me is because maybe I was "friendlier" than other girls. Usually when he heard an offhand remark, he'd let it slide, but when it came to suggestions of impropriety or loss of virtue, he'd stand to full height, and all six-seven of him would dare the accuser to try and say that again.

To my knowledge, no one ever took the dare.

A few weeks passed, finals concluded, and then summer began. That's when my relationship with Randy really blossomed. He had a part-time job in the mornings doing landscape maintenance around Rockwall, but afterward he'd come hang out with me and Eliza while Grant was away painting houses. It seemed like the three of us, or four when Nathan was free, did everything together that summer — swimming at the lake, walks to the park, movies, or just hanging out in the backyard picking blades of grass. It didn't matter so much what we were doing, as long as we were together.

As often as he could, Randy would take my hand in his and interlock our fingers. "It's a good fit," he'd say.

"The best," I'd reply.

"Stop holding hands," Eliza would chirp. "That's gross."

Sometime in early July Randy took me and Eliza to see a matinee showing of *La Bamba*. Thinking we were clever, we got my little sister her own popcorn and drink, then sat her down in the row in front of us so we could be "alone" in the half-empty theater. But partway through the showing, in a very quiet moment, Eliza turned around and shouted, "Yuck! Stop kissing! I'm telling Dad!"

"Busted," I said with a sigh as people around us laughed.

"Yeah," said Randy. "I'll go get her some more popcorn."

As the summer rolled on, I continued distancing myself from the thoughts of what had happened to me on prom night. Not that I accepted it, only that life with Randy was so good that I didn't want to believe in something so bad. *Just ignore the truth,* I reminded myself periodically, *until you're eighteen. Then everything changes. But for now, don't let it spoil what you've got with Randy.*

It really was a perfect summer, full of perfect moments and perfect memories. At least until football season started in early August.

Randy's mom didn't have a lot of money, so he knew football would be his only ticket to college. But that meant investing his whole soul into being the absolute best player he could be, which required a lot of work and time.

Nathan was focused on football too, though not so much for the scholarships. He lacked the prototypical size of a collegiate quarterback, so he knew schools would be pickier about handing him a full ride. Besides, like me, Nathan had all-star grades and SAT test scores that were bound to get him an academic scholarship somewhere, so there was less pressure on him to dazzle scouts and recruiters on the field.

For most of August I only saw the two of them on weekends, and even then their time was limited.

During that same month I began to notice I was putting on extra weight again, especially around the middle. I couldn't remember the last time I'd had a period, but I wasn't regular anyway, so that was no great cause for alarm. It wasn't until I began vomiting, on the last Sunday before we were to return to school, that I started to worry. To put my mind at ease, I took a morning walk to the pharmacy and picked up a pregnancy test.

Part of me felt foolish for even bothering. That was the same part of me that was still clinging to false hope that maybe the incident with Grant was all in my head. As I made my way from the checkout counter to the bathroom stall, I even tried talking myself out of taking the test, by reason that only one virgin in the history of the world had ever conceived a child, and such a feat wasn't likely to happen again.

Ultimately, I convinced myself to take the test. When I saw the results, I literally wanted to die.

The horror of prom night came flooding back all at once. I left the drugstore in a daze, trying to sort out a trillion awful thoughts, but there was really only one thing on my mind: *escape.* This was too much. Just when I was so close to having survived it all, to reaching eighteen and freedom . . . Just when I thought I could have a normal, regular life. But I wouldn't . . . ever. I wanted, in the worst way, to bolt from everything and just be done with all the misery and heartache.

I started walking, frantically, to a place I

thought could bring me peace. As I was turning onto a street that passed over the highway, a car slowed and pulled up beside me.

"What are you doing?" Nathan asked from behind the steering wheel. "Whoa, are you crying? Did something happen with Randy?"

"No, just . . . out for a walk."

"Well, something's up. Where you headed?"

Not far, I thought, shrugging.

"I'm on my way to church," he said. "I'm running a little late, but I can give you a lift if you need to get somewhere." He paused. "Or you could come with me. I know my dad would love to see you there. It might cheer you up."

"I doubt it," I mumbled. I didn't want to, but I got in the car and consented to go to church with him.

When we walked into the chapel, Pastor Steen was already up at the pulpit starting his sermon. I tuned him out and sank deeper into the abyss of my own thoughts. Part of me was still desperate to get where I was going before Nathan stopped me.

Nathan let me sit in silence for ten minutes or so, then he leaned over and whispered, "So are you going to tell me what's really going on?"

"I can't," I said, my voice cracking under the weight of my self-loathing. "Not here."

"Then at least tell me where you were going."

How do you tell your friend something like that? How do you explain your darkest intentions to one who never had a dark thought in his whole life? How on earth do you confide to the pastor's son, during the middle of his father's sermon, that instead of listening to a message about God, you'd rather be taking steps to meet your maker?

I couldn't form the words, so I just started bawling.

Sensing that this was no ordinary bad day for me, Nathan grabbed my hand, yanked me from the pew, then led me back outside to his car. "C'mon," he demanded, "spill."

"I can't tell you!" I cried, hiding my face in my hands. "You'll hate me."

"You know I won't. I just want to help you. Seriously. Or, if you prefer, we could go talk to my dad. He's pretty good at —."

"No! Nobody can know!"

"Know what? Just tell me what's going on, Maddy. Where were you going earlier?"

Still crying, I looked up into his eyes and saw nothing but earnest compassion, maybe the most genuine concern I've ever felt from anyone. It triggered something inside me. Almost as if to test the depths of that compassion, to see if he'd still look the same if he knew the truth, I consented to tell. "You really want to know? Fine! Here it is. I was going to the highway overpass . . . *to jump.*" Before he could react, I added, through sudden sobs, "I just want to die, Nathan. I'm so done! I just want a Mack truck to knock the life right out of me. I just . . . want to be with my mom again."

"Why?" he gasped. "How can you say that?"

Turning away out of embarrassment, I whispered, "Because I'm pregnant." I kept my gaze out the side window while awaiting a response. His next question was no big surprise.

"Have you told Randy?"

"I can't," I said hopelessly. "It wasn't him." Explaining the truth right then to Nathan might very well have been the hardest thing I've ever done. I started with, "Remember how drunk Grant was on prom night?" and ended with, ". . . which is why I just want to die." The harsh reality, though, was that I was as good as dead anyway once Grant found out.

Nathan, however, saw it differently. When I was done bearing my soul, he started his car and peeled out of the church parking lot. He wouldn't say where we were going, but I had a pretty good guess.

I warned him that confronting Grant was a dangerous mistake. "It's suicide," I said. "He has a bad temper." But there was no stopping Nathan. When we got to my house, he parked out front by the curb, warning me to stay in the car. I rolled down my window so I could hear what was said. At first there wasn't much of a conversation, because as soon as Grant opened the door, Nathan landed a punch right in his face. Grant fell back into the house, then came running out at him. The two collided on the porch, then rolled onto the lawn near the car. When he had a chance, Nathan struck him again, this time in the gut.

The skirmish ended shortly after that, when Nathan used his knees to pin Grant on the ground. There was a trickle of blood coming from my stepfather's mouth. Swearwords too. He cursed Nathan up and down, telling him he'd be going to jail for assault and battery.

"The only one going to jail is you, Mr. McFadden," Nathan spat back.

I'm sure Grant figured I'd finally gathered the courage to tell someone that he'd been physically hurting me for years. "Why? What lies has Maddy told you?"

"You're sick," Nathan said. "You know that? She's pregnant, and when we leave here, we're going straight to the police to let them know."

"Maddy's pregnant?" Now Grant looked genuinely confused. "I guess she and Randy should have been more careful. But hey, she's almost eighteen, so it's not like I could stop them from —" When Nathan just glared back at him, he got the message. "Wait. You think it was me? Whatever she told you, I never . . . Hey, I've been a crappy dad to her, but never that."

I couldn't stand to look at the man, especially with another round of tears coming on.

"Prom night," Nathan told him bluntly. "You were drunk. Stoned too. But I don't think a jury will sympathize."

Grant groaned. "I don't . . . I don't remember anything from that night. How could I . . . ?"

In a weird way, for a moment I felt a sliver of sympathy for him. I'd suspected from day one that he didn't know what he'd done, and I know he wouldn't have ever done something like that were it not for the booze and drugs. But when he started wriggling and cursing again, and trying to get Nathan off of him, my sympathy vanished.

"It's not true!" Grant barked defiantly. "I could never!" He was a wounded animal, a predator, backed into a corner, and he was not giving up without a fight. "You want to run to the police? Go ahead. But who are they going to believe, me or her?"

"Tests will prove who's telling the truth," Nathan snapped, still pinning him down.

"Fine. What if I did? I'll say she came on to me! It was consensual!"

"Doesn't matter. She's underage."

Grant was fishing for something, anything, to get the upper hand in the situation. "Then . . . then . . ." And then a new expression formed on his face, one that caught me by surprise. *Remorse.* I couldn't tell if he was sorry for what he'd done to me, or sorry that he couldn't think of a way out of it, but he definitely looked defeated. "Fine," he said. "Just get off me. Let's go inside and talk this out."

Nathan gave me a quick glance over his shoulder, then slowly got up. Just in time, too, because one of the neighbors was coming down the sidewalk, walking a yipping little dog.

"Everything okay, Grant?" the neighbor called as the two stood up and dusted themselves off.

"Fine, Steve," Grant chimed back. "Just a little lesson in the art of wrestling."

Once inside, Grant sequestered us where Eliza couldn't hear. "Listen," he began, "Maddy, you know me. You know I wouldn't intentionally hurt you like that. I was out of my mind that night. I've never once even thought about . . . I mean, you're my stepdaughter. I've done nothing but love you and take care of you all these years."

"And hit me," I pointed out.

"He hits you?" asked Nathan, appalled.

"Not for a while I haven't," countered Grant quickly. "And that was only when I was drunk." He plopped down on a chair, briefly burying his face in his hands. When he looked up again, he said, "I'm *weak,* Maddy. You know that. I've been weak ever since I lost your mom. But I'm not a bad man. If you go to the police, and what you say is true, they're going to lock me in jail and throw away the key. After all I've done for you, is that what you think I deserve? For something I don't even remember?" He looked at me like I should say something, but I couldn't think of anything.

When he saw that sympathy wasn't working, he tried again from a different angle. "Listen, there has to be something we can do to fix this. I made a mistake, if that's what you want to call it, but it doesn't have to ruin our lives. You can't go to the police, Maddy. Think about it — we can't tell *anyone.* Do you know what will happen if we do? It will get out. Even if they're supposed to protect your identity, someone will let it slip. There will be police asking questions, and reporters trying to get the scoop. It'll be everywhere. Everyone will know, Maddy. Kids at school, Randy, Eliza — they'll all find out. For the rest of your life, everyone will know." He paused, trying to read my reaction. Maybe he could see my worry, because he went right back at it, appealing to my sense of reason. "Is that what you want? Do you want your sister to know about this? She doesn't have to! We can make this go away. I'll take you to a clinic, they'll get rid of it. No one has to know. You can have a normal life, Maddy. We all can. And I'll get treatment, I promise. No more alcohol. No more drugs. *None.* I promise. I know I have a problem. I know that now, and I'm so sorry. It should have never come to this. Never in a million years."

"But it did," remarked Nathan.

"And I'm sorry!" Grant shot back. "How many times do I have to say that? I screwed up, kiddo. But let's not throw our lives down the drain over one mistake. And forget about me — take me out of the equation. Just think about *you.* Do you deserve the public humiliation? Does Eliza deserve to be taken away from her father and be sent to some orphanage or foster home? Maddy, you're smarter than that. Think this through. I'm a teacher, for cripes' sake. If the media finds out a teacher did this, they'll crucify our whole family. It'll be on every news channel and paper from here to New York. You want your face plastered on The *Today* Show, or *60 Minutes*? Everyone in the world will know, Maddy. *Everyone.* Is that really what you want?"

The more he talked, the more I knew he was right, and the more I felt like I just wanted to escape. Run away, hide, never be seen again. The panic settling in my chest made it hard to breathe. "I . . . I need some air," I said. "Nathan, please, let's go outside."

Nathan nodded. "You stay right here," he told Grant. "We'll be back."

By the time we reached the privacy of the backyard, I thought I might hyperventilate. I laid out flat on my back on the grass, trying to calm myself down. "He's right," I said. "He's absolutely right. This is why it would've been better if you hadn't shown up in your car."

"Don't say that, Maddy."

"It's true! Don't you see? I can't live with everyone knowing what he did to me! What he *took* from me. The fact that he's a teacher and I'm a student at his school — *and his stepdaughter!* — the media will eat it up. And you know as well as me how people around here will talk. I bet some will say this is all somehow my fault, as if I threw myself at him or something. No, I can't do this, Nathan. There's no way out of this for me. I just have to . . . go away."

Nathan pulled a clover from the grass and studied it. He was silent for a long time. Finally he asked, "So why not take him up on his offer? He said he'd take you to a clinic. No one would have to know."

"*I* would know! And I'd never forgive myself."

"But given the circumstances, maybe it's okay."

"Maybe. But not for me."

"You wouldn't do that, but you'd throw yourself off a bridge?"

"At least then I wouldn't have to live with the guilt." Did I really mean that? "Why?" I asked. "Do you think I should let him 'take care of it' that way?"

"No. I'm just trying to help you sort through the options, that's all."

329

I grabbed a fistful of grass and sifted it through my fingers. "Did you know my mom got pregnant in college, before she was married?"

It was meant to be a rhetorical question, because I knew I'd never told him or anyone else about that, but he answered anyway. "No."

"In third grade I did the math between when I was born and when she and my dad got married, and it was considerably less than nine months. When I asked her about it, she was very open. She said she hadn't been sure if she was ready to be a mom, and that she'd considered an abortion, like Grant suggested." I had to stop to find the right words to express what I was feeling. "Don't you see? If she'd gone through with it, *I* wouldn't exist. So I know what's growing inside me, Nathan. It's a little me, and no matter how it got there, I don't think I can just get rid of it."

The compassion returned to his eyes. "I get it. But you don't want this going public, you won't get an abortion, and I won't let you kill yourself. What's left?"

"Nothing! That's what I'm saying. I'm trapped. I've been trapped my whole life, and now the cage just keeps getting smaller and smaller."

He plucked another clover. "There's another option I can think of. Maybe this baby just needs a father."

I wasn't following. "Huh?"

"Someone other than Grant, of course. Let's face it, you're not going to be able to hide the fact that you're pregnant forever. So don't. Maybe you just need a cover story. You accidentally got pregnant, and now you're dealing with it. You wouldn't be the first teenage girl to be in this situation. Not even the first at our school."

"No way," I replied immediately. "I couldn't ask Randy to do that. Then I'd have to tell him what really happened. And even if I he'd go along with it, what would that do to his football season? And college?"

Swallowing, Nathan replied, "Maddy, Randy wasn't the one who took you home on prom night. He wasn't the last one alone with you."

"You mean *you*?"

"It's not a perfect solution, but I think it would work."

I was floored. Nathan had already done so much for me in my life, how could he possibly tackle this too? "But . . . *why*?" I asked.

"Because you can't do this alone. No one could. And I can't stand by and watch you suffocate. Not when I can help." He paused, guarding his emotions. "And what if . . . I mean . . . just say word got out, and everyone knew what really happened, and suddenly your picture is all over the TV. Are you going to make it through that, Maddy?"

"I don't know," I whispered.

"Tell me honestly," he said. "If I hadn't driven by earlier, would you still be alive?"

I couldn't admit the truth with words, so I just shook my head and cried.

"Which is why I have to help."

Still crying, I asked, "What about Grant?"

"What about him? He needs to pay for what he did, and he will — in time. Once you've had the baby and are out of high school. For now, though, he's right — you and Eliza don't deserve to suffer more for what he did. If I'm the father of this baby, I can protect you from all of that, and still make sure Grant gets what he deserves."

"And Randy? He's going to take it hard thinking you and I . . ."

"Yeah," Nathan said. "But you're right about him. If you tell him the truth, and if you asked him to help you, he'd do it in a heartbeat. But that might spell the end of his college dreams. Better to have him mad at us than to risk all that."

Feeling like I could finally breathe again, I sat up. "You're the best friend there ever was. But I can't ask you to do this, Nathan."

"You're not asking. I am. And let's not forget, I was the one who took you home that night. I should have never driven off with him in that condition, so don't think I don't feel somewhat responsible. Believe me, if there were another way, I'd take it, but I just don't see it."

"What about your parents? Won't they be crushed?"

I could see in his eyes that he hadn't considered that yet. It took him a moment to think through the possible ramifications. His response came as another shock. "We'll have to get married."

"What!"

"For damage control, it's the only way. Having 'the pastor's son' get a girl pregnant will be hard enough for some of my dad's parishioners to swallow. But if we get married, it'll show that at least I'm trying to do the right thing. Hopefully that'll be enough."

"Nathan, I didn't ask how your dad's congregation will react. What about your mom and dad? What will they say?"

He shrugged. "I don't know. They're always talking about forgiveness. I guess this will be their chance to show me what it means. It might be hard on them for a little while, but down the road, once we go to the police, they'll understand."

I took a moment to weigh what he was saying. Nathan was so convincing, but I was an emotional wreck, so maybe I wasn't thinking clearly. "Are we even old enough to get married? I mean, we're both under-age. Wouldn't Grant and your parents have to consent to such a thing?"

"Grant is a no-brainer, because he doesn't want to get caught. And my parents? I'm sure they'd rather have us get married than make you an unwed mother. They'll go along." He glanced over his shoulder at the patio door, then back to me. "So?"

"Are you absolutely sure about this?"

He took a long, deep breath. When he exhaled, his mouth eased into a smile. "No. But for your sake, I'm willing to give it a try."

When we went back into the house, Grant was still planted right where we'd left him. Seeing him again made my stomach lurch. There was panic in his face; he obviously understood that his fate was in our hands. "Do I dare ask what you decided?" he asked nervously.

"We decided you're a pathetic excuse for a human being," Nathan deadpanned. It's not how I expected the conversation to start, but I liked his candor. "*And* . . . we decided that Maddy and Eliza don't deserve the public embarrassment that would come if everyone knew just how much of a scumbag you are."

Grant sighed a breath of relief. "So what's the plan?"

Nathan stepped closer and put his arm around me. "I'm going to be a father," he said. "And me and Maddy are getting married."

"Married?"

"To make it easier on my parents."

"So that's it? You two get married and we move on?"

"Not quite," Nathan said. "You're going into rehab, and Eliza will stay with us until you're completely clean." He glanced over at me. "Maddy, there's another reason to get married — it'll make it easier to get custody of your sister until Grant is straightened out."

Grant looked stricken. "No way. You can't take Eliza! She's my baby girl."

Now I finally found my voice. "We're not 'taking her.' We're watching her while you get help, however long that takes. She's my little sister, and I need to keep her safe."

Seeing that it was useless to argue, Grant mumbled, "So what now?"

Nathan and I looked at each other again.

We really hadn't thought that far ahead. Sure, we had a strategy, but how to implement it? Nathan checked his watch. "Church is almost out. Should we go tell my parents?"

I nodded slowly. "But . . . can we have Randy there too? I'd just as soon only have to say it once."

He nodded back.

"What about me?" asked Grant. "Should I be there too?"

"Absolutely not," I told him. "I don't want you anywhere near there."

"Well, how do I know you're not going to tell them . . . something else?"

"Like the truth?"

"Don't worry," Nathan assured him. "We've got our plan, and we're sticking to it."

"What are you going to tell them about me?" Grant pressed.

"That you're checking yourself into a drug-and-alcohol program. They're going to find that out one way or another."

There was really nothing he could say, so Grant just gave a single nod.

Twenty minutes later I had some clothes packed in a suitcase for Eliza and me and loaded it into Nathan's car. Grant was crying as he hugged Eliza good-bye.

"Sweetie," he told her, "Daddy has to go away for a few weeks. Sissy's going to take care of you while I'm gone, okay?"

"Where are you going?" she asked.

With his lip quivering, he said, "To take some classes on how to be a better daddy. But I promise, I'll see you as soon as I can, and I'll miss you every day."

"I'll miss you too, Daddy."

I didn't bother saying good-bye.

CHAPTER TWENTY-EIGHT

Nathan's parents were still gone when we got to his house. The first thing he did was go in the kitchen and call Randy. I would have called myself, but was afraid I'd break down crying on the phone.

Pastor Steen and Colleen arrived about ten minutes later. Randy pulled into the driveway just as I was shaking hands with them.

"Looks like we have another guest," the pastor said when he heard the car.

"It's Randy, Dad. I invited him."

"You guys have big Sunday plans? 'Cuz I was hoping later this afternoon you could help me polish up some rocks I've got going out in the tumbler. Some of the kids at church reminded me today that it's been a while since I've given my object lesson on rock tumbling, so I was thinking —."

"Dad," Nathan interrupted. "I don't think that's going to happen today."

Right then Randy walked in the front door, and I suddenly wished we could just keep talking about rocks. I remembered the lesson Pastor Steen was talking about. A few months after we started attending church, while Grant was still helping out in Sunday School, Nathan's father gave his first-ever lesson on how each of us are like rocks. The gist of it was that, like rocks in the ground, we all get dirty, and everyone begins life with a few rough edges. Then he explained how our lives — the experiences we have, the people we meet, the choices we make — are meant to help polish us up and turn us into smooth stones before we go back to God. As part of the object lesson, everyone got one of the polished stones he'd had churning in his tumbler for several weeks. They were like glass, lustrous and clean.

I remember in Sunday School thinking I wanted my life to be like that — well-rounded, no jagged edges, spotless. But standing in Nathan's living room with his parents and Randy all wondering what was going on, I felt exceptionally dirty. Worse, I knew I was about to add to my filth by deceiving them all.

"Is everything okay?" asked Mrs. Steen instinctively.

"We just . . . need to talk," Nathan replied. Then he turned to Randy. "All of us."

Pastor Steen sounded concerned. "All right, let's have a seat and find out what's going on."

We sent Eliza into the other room to watch a show on TV so she wouldn't have to witness the drama that was about to unfold.

Randy came and took my hand, trying to give me a hug. I wanted his arms around me so badly, to make me feel safe, but for both our sakes I knew I couldn't do that. Not with what we were about to tell him. I let go of his hand and quickly sat down. A flash of confusion crossed his face as he took a seat next to me. "Maddy," he whispered, "what's up?"

I could already feel my eyes getting wet. "Nothing," I whispered back stiffly. "Just . . . I'll let Nathan explain."

Nathan took a moment to collect his thoughts and then eased into the fabrication. "This is . . . hard," he began. "Hard for me to say, and it's probably going to be even harder for you to hear." I could feel Randy's gaze bouncing back between Nathan and me, but I couldn't bring myself to look at him. "The thing is . . . we made a mistake."

"Who did?" Randy blurted out.

"I did," Nathan asserted. "Just hear me out, Randy. I made a mistake. Me and Maddy, we . . ." Before he even finished the thought, I heard Colleen gasp as she guessed where this conversation was headed. Pastor Steen was as white as a sheet, but otherwise looked calm. "We . . . well, on prom night, after we dropped everyone else off, we were alone for a while, and . . ."

Randy finally guessed what was about to be said too. Shaking his head, he jumped up out of the chair, looking down at me like a rattlesnake. "No!" he shouted. "No way. Don't say what I think you're going to say."

Now the tears started flowing freely down my face. Nathan's mother was tearing up too. Randy turned every shade of red, and Pastor Steen turned even whiter. "We didn't mean to, Randy," I gushed. "I swear. It just . . . happened."

"I'm sorry, Randy," Nathan added soberly. "You're my best friend, and I didn't mean to hurt you like this."

Randy began pacing around. "My *friend*? No 'friend' would do this, Nathan." He turned to me again, his eyes ablaze. "And you! Acting all pure and innocent this whole time, telling me how we should wait until we get married. I actually thought that we would!" He paused, panting slightly. "So why the guilt all of a sudden? Why bother telling me now?"

There was an awkward moment of silence, then Pastor Steen astutely said, "Because, I don't think the story is quite over." He glanced back and forth between me and his son to see if his intuition was correct.

"No," Nathan confirmed, his voice wavering. "There's more. This morning . . . Maddy found out that she's pregnant."

"What!" Randy bellowed. "You knocked her up! You sorry piece of — !" But rather than curse at us — which I thought was well within his right to do — he cut himself off, taking a deep breath as he stared dejectedly at me and his "friend." His gaze burned my soul. "I hate you both," he said finally. The cold way it came out of his mouth hurt worse than anything else that day, because I knew he really meant it. "Stay out of my life." He turned his back on us and walked out the front door.

Part of me desperately wanted to call after him, to tell him the truth, but I knew doing so would bring about other consequences — repercussions that I felt unable to endure. *It's better for him if he doesn't know,* I told myself again. *It's better for all of us . . . isn't it?*

Once Randy was gone, I mostly just sat and listened as Nathan carefully tied a bow for his parents around our "predicament." It was actually quite a marvel how good he was at pulling lies right out of thin air.

"You know what bothers me the most about this, Nathan," his mom remarked at one point, "is that we've always trusted you to behave maturely and to think things through. Clearly, that trust was misplaced."

"I know," Nathan said remorsefully. "And I'm sorry."

"And what about all the kids who look up to you at church and in the community? How are their parents going to explain this to them?"

"I know," Nathan repeated. "I feel terrible about that too."

Mrs. Steen turned for a moment to her husband. "Tim, how is the congregation going to react when they find out?"

"I don't know," he replied with a shrug. "I hope they'll all understand that no one is infallible. I'm sure most of them will get over it, but there'll also be some who will be sorely disappointed that their pastor can't keep a better handle on his own son."

Nathan's parents shared a long, questioning look, then Pastor Steen turned his attention back to Nathan and me. He was very stern, but there was also compassion in his eyes. "I'm sorry," he said. "We shouldn't have mentioned the church or anyone else. This is none of their business, though I'm sure they'll try making it their business. This is about the two of you. Near as I can tell, you both seem to recognize that you've made a mistake — and in the spectrum of mistakes, this one ranks up there as a real doozy. But guess what? *Everyone* makes mistakes. The question is, what do you do when you mess up? Some people cower from the consequences, while others accept their wrongdoing, own it, and try to learn from it." He paused, taking another moment to look at each of us individually, letting his words marinate. "I'm sure we could spend the rest of the afternoon expressing regret over the situation or rehashing all the things you could have done differently to avoid this. But what I'm really interested in is where we go from here. How are the two of you going to respond to this situation? Have you figured out what you're going to do now?"

"Yes," I blurted out, wanting him to feel reassured that I was not the cowering type. "And we're going to take full responsibility for everything. Whatever consequences there are, we're ready to face them." The twisted irony, of course, was that we were ready to face consequences of something we didn't do, in order to avoid facing consequences of something else we didn't do. I wasn't sure if that made us brave or weak.

"That's right," added Nathan. "We've made up our minds. We're going through with the pregnancy."

"Oh my," Mrs. Steen mumbled to herself, "I'm going to be a thirty-nine-year-old *grandma.*"

"And we're getting married," Nathan slipped in.

"And a *mother-in-law!*" his mom added.

Pastor Steen's brow furrowed sharply. "You're awfully young. Marriage is a big responsibility."

"Dad, we got ourselves into this, and we're going to behave like adults and get ourselves out. Like you said, we're going to own it."

"But there are other ways, you know. For example, lots of married couples out there can't have children of their own. Have you considered adoption?"

Nathan sat up, looking confused. "I thought you'd be glad we're getting married."

Tim leaned forward. "Do you love each other?"

Love? What did that have to do with any-thing? I quickly turned to Nathan, wondering what he'd say. He turned to me, too. This clearly wasn't going as he'd expected. He looked me up and down, and then he pursed his lips and turned back to his father. "Yes. Of course we do."

"I can't make you do anything," Tim continued, "but if you really love each other, I'd counsel you to wait. Give the other a chance to grow up and experience the world a little bit. At least get out of high school, for Pete's sake. Then, if things are meant to be — if you really do love each other — it will all work out."

Nathan was turning red, and I understood why. If his parents didn't go along with a marriage, then where did that leave me and Eliza? Our plan would crumble. There's no way the pastor would let his teenage son live with me if we weren't married, so what would we do? Go on living with Grant? Fat chance. "Why are you being like this?" Nathan asked defiantly. "We're doing exactly what we thought you'd want."

Pastor Steen sighed. "Think for a second, Nathan. There are other consequences in play here — other people that your actions will affect. Most importantly, the baby. I've spent a lot of time counseling split families, consoling wives and children whose husbands have run out on them. Given what I've seen, I have to believe that the best situation for little kids is to be reared by a father and a mother who can provide for them and who are committed one hundred percent to making things work. So first, ask yourself if you're going to be able to provide for this child. And if you think you can do that, then you two need to be pretty darn sure you're going to stick it out and raise that baby together. Because I honestly believe it would be much better for the child to be reared by loving adoptive parents than to end up in a broken home with parents who were in over their heads."

Right then Eliza came prancing back into the room. "My show's over," she said. "Can we go now?"

"Not yet, Sissy," I said. "See if you can find something else to watch. We're almost done talking. I'll come get you when we're through."

Nathan cleared his throat as Eliza left the room. "So you're saying you won't let us get married? Because Maddy's father said he'd give consent."

"Stepfather," I corrected.

Pastor Steen shook his head slightly. "I didn't say I wouldn't. I just . . . I want you to be sure, that's all. Remember, this is my grandchild we're talking about, so don't think I take any of this lightly. I just want the best for that little kid. If you feel ready to take on that responsibility, and you're fully ready to commit to it — *to each other* — then I'll support your decision. But if there's any concern that your marriage might not last, then I'd suggest waiting until you know what you really want."

Nathan held his head high. "Then it's settled. We're getting married."

"Maddy?" asked Pastor Steen.

In the second before answering, I thought about Grant and the awful picture he'd painted of our lives if everyone knew what he'd done to me. I thought about how hard it would be for Eliza to grow up with the knowledge of what her father did to her sister. I thought of the embarrassment and scorn I'd face from my peers at school. How people would think I must have brought it on myself because I didn't tell anyone it happened. I imagined how revolted Randy would be to know the truth. I wondered where I'd go if I *didn't* marry Nathan — would I be forced to live under the same roof as Grant, while carrying his child in my womb, or would I eventually find my way back to the overpass? And finally, I considered Nathan and his parents, and what this would mean to their family. It didn't seem fair that Nathan was willing to save me like this. But he was. And given the alternative, I wasn't about to get in his way. "Yes, sir," I said without flinching. "I love your son. And we think the best thing for us is to get married and have this baby."

Chapter Twenty-Nine

After we delicately explained Grant's growing dependency on alcohol and drugs to Nathan's parents, they graciously offered to let me and Eliza stay at their house as long as we needed.

"Just until we find our own apartment," Nathan told his parents. "We'd like to be settled in somewhere pretty quickly."

"Why the rush?" his mom asked him. "Our house is plenty big for a couple of extra."

"So you don't think we can do it on our own?"

"I didn't say that. I just want to understand, that's all. We're your parents, we want to help."

"Well, for one thing," Nathan replied defensively, "there's Eliza. We don't know how long Grant is going to be in treatment, and we'd like her to have some stability, you know. Staying here would feel too much like being a guest. Plus, as I already told you, we're taking responsibility for the situation, which includes putting a roof over our own heads."

"Just seems like a lot to take on during your last year of high school, that's all."

"We'll manage just fine. You'll see."

Watching the exchange between mother and son, I caught a rare glimpse into a side of Nathan I hadn't really noticed before. *Pride,* and not the good kind. I'd always known him to be confident and self-assured, but this felt like something more than that. In hindsight, I realized I had witnessed a similar reaction at least once before — when he read my poem in seventh grade, after which he became obsessed with proving that he could permanently change how he treated me.

Personally, I'd have had no problem mooching off the Steens for a few months while preparing to have the baby, but Nathan had it in his head that he was going to show them he could do it all on his own, and there was no swaying him.

Or slowing him down.

The very next day, on Monday morning, he went to the courthouse all on his own to gather the necessary paperwork for a marriage license. On the way home he stopped by my house, woke up Grant, and dragged him to a notary-public for signatures. Upon his return, the rest of us were dragged to the same notary to finish the rest of the documentation.

That afternoon Nathan and I drove by ourselves to the courthouse to seal the deal.

School started two days later. The first day back was ugly. Word about our situation had obviously gotten around, because I sensed a newfound disdain in the eyes of those who bothered to look at me. Nathan didn't have it any easier. In addition to the flippant — and sometimes outright disgusting — remarks in the hallway, he had to spend the entire lunch hour getting chewed out by the head football coach for his "lack of self-control." At the end of their conversation the coach warned him that boosters might be unwilling to contribute financially to a team led by a soon-to-be father and that he'd have to consider splitting reps with an underclassman.

"I don't want the team to suffer on my account," Nathan told him. "So let me do you a favor and turn in my helmet and pads right now. Besides, I've got a wife and kid to provide for, so who has time for sports."

When he told me about it, I could see how much it hurt to give up football. But realistically, it would have been very hard for him to be on the field or in a huddle with Randy, especially with what happened later that afternoon.

Nathan was helping me get my books at my locker after school when Randy and several other boys approached. "Is it true?" Randy demanded.

"What?" Nathan asked.

"You know what. Did you guys really get *married*?"

"So what if we did?"

Randy didn't need to hear any more. He cocked his arm and punched Nathan in the side of the ribs, then once more in the center of the gut. "There's your wedding present."

Nathan was doubled over in pain, coughing, trying to catch his breath. I watched briefly as Randy and the rest of them walked away. I wanted to cry. "We don't have to do this," I told Nathan, putting an arm around him. "Maybe it's not worth it."

He coughed a few more times, then stood up. *"It,"* he said, breathing hard, "is *you*. And you're worth it."

That afternoon we found a cheap, semi-furnished, two-bedroom apartment within walking distance of Eliza's school, and on Saturday we moved in. The following Monday Nathan started a part-time job detailing cars at an auto-body shop, while I took on several middle-school kids as a private tutor. Between the two of us we made just enough money to cover our expenses — provided we ate ramen noodles at least three times a week.

Grant taught the first two weeks of school before finally checking himself into a rehab clinic like he'd promised. He checked himself out after three days, saying he'd try again in another month, "when the timing was better."

He never went back.

By the time fall gave way to winter, Nathan and I were wearing thin from the combined pressures of school, work, and caring for Eliza. Plus, there was the baby inside me, whose regular nightly kicks were cutting into my sleep. In early December I was seriously considering throwing in the towel. "This is harder than I thought it would be," I confessed one night after Eliza had gone to bed.

Nathan was working on a homework assignment for AP Physics, which I'd completed earlier in the day. "The pregnancy?" he asked.

"No. I'll survive that. It's all the other stuff. The cover-up."

He nodded. "It's hard. But the alternative is harder."

"I don't know about that. When I see Grant walking around at school, teaching students when he should be in jail? Makes me wonder if we did the right thing."

"He hasn't gotten away with anything yet. His fate is just delayed a little while, until we graduate. Then we can take our baby, get a paternity test, and let the authorities know. We'll go off to college somewhere together, and it'll all be behind us."

I nodded. Not because I agreed, but because I didn't want to interrupt his homework anymore.

When Nathan finally closed his textbook, I asked him to join me on the giant beanbag we used for a couch. "Were you able to solve the one about vacuum permeability?" I asked. "It hung me up for a while."

"You don't look like you want to talk about Physics, Maddy."

"How about Chemistry, then?"

He gave me a sideways glance, and a well-deserved "Huh?"

"Listen," I said, "I've been thinking. A lot. About the future, and what's going to happen in a couple months when this baby finally pops out."

"This sounds more like Biology," he

quipped. "Or Anatomy."

"Forget science, Nathan. Just . . . I need to tell you what I'm thinking and feeling. So . . . Psychology, maybe."

For the past several months we'd occasionally hinted at what might transpire in the future, but had never really come to any definite conclusions. The more time we spent together, though, the more apparent it became that Nathan had a clear plan: raise Eliza as our own, raise our new baby, and prove to himself — and especially to his parents — that we could do it all by ourselves.

I wasn't so sure.

"Okay," he said tentatively. "But is that a true science?"

"Just listen," I told him. Then I took a deep breath. "I'm just . . . I've given this a lot of thought, and I think your dad was right."

He rolled his eyes. "Of course. My dad is always right. *Mr. Perfect-Pastor.* What's he right about this time?"

"Don't be mad, Nathan. But . . . I'm not ready to be a mom. I've decided I want to give the baby up for adoption."

His face went white, just like his father's did when Nathan told him I was pregnant. "But what about *us*?"

"I know," I said weakly. "That's the hardest part." And it was. The hardest part of the whole mess we'd gotten ourselves into was that somewhere along the line, Nathan may have actually begun believing we were in love. But as much as I loved him for what he'd sacrificed for me, I didn't love him like that. "At some point, we need to be thinking about our own futures. I don't want to hold you back, Nathan. I know you'd do anything for me — you always do the right thing. But I don't want to be a tether anymore."

"You don't hold me back," he protested. "You make me better."

"You make *the world* better, Nathan, and you can't waste all of your effort on me. Not forever."

He paused, then asked the question that really hurt, though he already knew the answer. "So you don't love me?"

"I do!" I said quickly. "Just . . . not like that."

"Oh, I see," he said quietly. "*Chemistry.* You're saying you don't love me like you did Randy."

I didn't respond, but then he didn't say it as a question. Nathan knew the answer as well as me.

There was a long silence, then acceptance

seemed to settle in. Eventually he let out a little chuckle. "So what? Are we, like, getting divorced?"

The comment made me laugh too. "If that's what you want to call it." I reached over and gave him the tightest hug I could possibly give. "I can never thank you for everything you've done for me, Nathan. No matter what happens in the future, you'll always be my dearest friend. You've saved my life over and over again."

That made him smile, but it only lasted for a second. "But we're still going to see this through a little longer, right? Until the baby is born and we're out of high school?"

"I'm going to start looking for adoption services right away, so the new parents can have the baby right after birth. But yes, you and I need to stay together until the end of the school year, if that's okay. It would be better for Eliza if we keep up the charade as long as possible."

"What about Grant?"

"We just need to be sure to get a paternity test done when the baby is born. We'll keep it until the timing is right to go to the police."

He nodded, then placed a hand on my stomach. "What's it like, having a life growing inside you?"

"Weird, I guess."

Right then the baby kicked his hand and he flinched. "Yeah," he agreed. "Weird."

Two weeks later we were at the Steens' house for Christmas supper, but it wasn't the merry occasion we were hoping for. Once we were through eating and Eliza had run off to play with the new doll she got from "Grandma Steen," Pastor Steen ran through his usual questions, and I gave my typical answers.

How are you feeling, Maddy? Fine.

Are you guys keeping up with your schoolwork? Still straight As.

Is Grant making any progress? Not as far as I know — he still won't get the treatment he needs.

Then Nathan jumped into the conversation. "What about you, Dad? Things going okay at church?"

A concerned look passed between Pastor Steen and his wife.

Since coming forward about the pregnancy, Nathan and I decided maybe it was best not to attend his dad's church, so as not to cause a stir. Out of sight, out of mind, so to speak — or at least we hoped.

"It's fine, I guess," Pastor Steen finally said.

"It doesn't sound fine," I said.

"Dad, what's going on?"

His father looked at his mom again, his eyes seeking her approval. "We might as well tell them, honey. They're bound to find out soon enough anyway."

Mrs. Steen gave her blessing with a slow nod.

"We didn't want you guys to worry," continued Pastor Steen. "With our grandchild growing there in your tummy, Maddy, plus the struggles of your stepfather, and caring for Eliza, the two of you already have more than enough on your plates. But before anything is made official, you need to know that I'll likely be released from my duties at church. The board is meeting tomorrow morning to make a decision."

"Oh my gosh," I blurted out.

"Why?" asked Nathan. Then this horrified look swept across his face. *Because of us?*

Another quick glance confirmed it, but Pastor Steen tried to downplay it. "It was probably time for me to move on anyway. And it's not you guys' fault. I should have done a better job teaching them about forgiveness and judging. Frankly, I'm disappointed in how they've reacted."

For the next several minutes Nathan's parents explained how some people — not all, but a vocal few — were put off when they heard about "the pastor's boy" getting me pregnant. Others were offended that their pastor had allowed us to get married so young and move out on our own. Gossip had been escalating right from the start, but had recently reached a point where some folks were publicly calling for his resignation. The most vocal of the bunch was a man in his late thirties who had been trying, unsuccessfully, to get his wife pregnant for the past ten years. He'd come right out and said that the pastor was being selfish and irresponsible for letting us keep it — as if it was his decision.

"Why don't they mind their own business?" Nathan asked. "Or go find another church if it bothers them so much. It's not like there aren't plenty to choose from."

"That's the problem," his mom lamented. "Some of them — even longtime members — have already gone elsewhere. From September to now, attendance has dropped like one of your father's famous rocks. And even among the people who still come regularly, donations are way down. Your father took a sizable, voluntary pay cut last month to help right the ship, but it may not be enough."

"And the Board of Elders?" asked Nathan.

"What's their take?"

The pastor shrugged. "Their concern is the spiritual and financial success of the church. Right now, I can't honestly say that we're seeing the kinds of returns they expect in either of those areas. As one of the board members told me candidly, sometimes before you can stop the bleeding, you have to remove the arrow from the wound. And right now, the church's cash reserves are bleeding bright red."

"And I'm the arrow," muttered Nathan.

"No," his dad corrected, "*I'm* the arrow."

"Then I'm the bow."

Nathan's words hung in the air for too long. When the silence became uncomfortable, I asked, "So what will you guys do if you lose your job?"

His mom gave one of those remorseful chuckles that people sometimes give when something is so not funny that you just have to laugh. "Well, we can't stay around here, that's for sure. The virus has already spread, by word of mouth. Even if there were openings, it's very doubtful that any of the local churches would take your father on right now. Leastwise not as a head pastor."

Pastor Steen perked up a bit. "I've put some feelers out there, and there are a couple jobs out of state that seem promising. We'll just have to see what happens. Whatever it is, I'm sure it will be for the best."

When his parents left to clear the kitchen table, I quietly suggested to Nathan that we should just tell them the truth. "It's so unfair to put them through this."

"No! Don't you dare say a thing."

The way he snapped startled me. "Chill, Nathan. I'm just thinking out loud."

He was momentarily quiet. Then he said, "Well, don't think about *that*. We can't tell them, Maddy, and you know it. Dad would be obligated to report a rape, which would set off another huge firestorm right when we're trying to get the baby adopted. You think anybody is going to adopt it if it's at the center of a huge, public legal mess? We're too far along to go back now. We just have to stick to the plan. You heard my dad — whatever happens, it will be for the best."

I sensed that he had developed new reasons for not wanting his parents to know about our giant lie, but I didn't figure he was ready to share, so I didn't press it. "Fine," I whispered as I stood to go help with the dishes. "You're right. I'll keep my mouth shut." As I walked away, I had the strange feeling that I was now protecting him as much as he was protecting me.

CHAPTER THIRTY

The decision on December 26th was unanimous: Pastor Steen was relieved of his duties.

"Not to fret, though," I heard him say on New Year's Eve. "God has a plan for me, just as he does for all of us."

I thought about that comment late into the night, long after Nathan and Eliza had gone to bed. Given how messed up my life had been, how could God have a plan? Or if he did, could it possibly involve me deceiving everyone I know by hiding what happened to me? No, God doesn't work through human lies. Besides, if there was some divinely instituted plan out there, wouldn't it include me being happy? Why wouldn't his plan somehow involve a better outcome for me and Randy? And what about Grant? Was it part of God's plan for him to beat me up as a kid? Abuse me? Impregnate me? And get away with it?

It had been a while since I'd allowed myself to cry, but that night I didn't fight it. Eventually the weeping lulled me to sleep.

By the middle of the week we got a call from Mrs. Steen saying that Pastor Steen had an interview with a large church in North Carolina whose pastor was seeking early retirement following quadruple bypass surgery. The following week he got a job offer, and by the beginning of February they were packing up a U-Haul. Who knows, maybe God had a plan after all. At least for pastors.

Nathan's parents felt awful about the timing of their departure, what with the baby almost due and their son still not graduated from high school. "But you've both shown that you really can make it on your own," his mom said. "If we didn't know you'd be all right, and that you've got each other for support, we wouldn't go."

Although I'd already selected an adoptive couple — way out in California — we still hadn't found the right time to tell Nathan's parents that we were giving the baby up for adoption. What made it harder was that they seemed to have really warmed up to the idea of being grandparents, even if the circumstances of the pregnancy weren't ideal. We avoided telling them until the bitter end, when we were all standing in their driveway waiting for them to climb into the moving truck.

Pastor Steen wrapped his arms around Nathan, pounding his son's back in a heartfelt man-hug. "Now then, you take care of your sweet bride, okay? And don't let anything happen to our little grandbaby."

"That's right," his mom said, giving me a hug a second later. "You give her lots of kisses from Grandma, until I can make it out here to kiss her on my own."

"Or *him*," remarked Nathan's dad.

"Oh no," she said, placing a hand on my bulging teenage tummy. "And after eighteen years raising a stubborn boy, I need a little girl to dote on." She winked at Nathan playfully.

When Nathan and I looked at each other, we knew the moment had arrived. He stepped to my side and took my hand. Eliza was climbing on the moving truck; she needed to hear this too. "Sissy, come here a sec."

I squeezed Nathan's hand, and he started in. "Listen, I know you're all really excited about this new baby. But Maddy and I have done a lot of thinking lately, and we've come to a decision." Mrs. Steen's face sank before Nathan said another word. "It's just . . . the timing isn't good. Dad, you were right all along. Giving the baby up to parents who can care for her better than a couple of high-schoolers is probably for the best, so we're giving her up for adoption."

Pastor Steen stepped closer to his wife, putting an arm around her. "You're absolutely certain?" he asked. "Both of you?"

"Yes," I told them. "I've already chosen a family for her to go to."

He nodded. "Does this have anything to do with us leaving for Raleigh? I mean, if we stayed and you had more day-to-day support . . . ?"

"No, Dad," replied Nathan. "The decision was made before you even lost your job. We've just been waiting for the right time to tell you."

His mom's eyes were watery. "And this is the right time?"

Eliza took hold of my arm, looking straight up at me. "So I'm not going to be an aunt?" she asked.

"You are, sweetie." *And a sister.* "Just . . . not in the same way, exactly. The baby will have a different mommy and daddy to take care of it."

She frowned ominously and ran off.

"I'm sorry," Nathan told his parents. "We both are. This is just what we feel is the right thing to do."

Nathan's dad let go of his mom and came over to give me a hug, followed by another one for Nathan. "I won't say we're not a little surprised, and somewhat disappointed that we won't get to meet our grandchild. But we're also glad to see you're making tough decisions together. This can't be an easy one, but I will say this: What you're doing — giving your child to someone who you feel can take better care of him than you — is perhaps the most unselfish thing a parent can do, and a huge act of love. I'm proud of you for that. If you always have love like that in your home, you two will be very happy throughout your marriage. I promise you that."

Nathan squeezed my hand hard, which I took as a gentle reminder not to divulge anything more of our future plans.

Mrs. Steen stepped forward and touched my tummy one last time, swatting at tears on her face. "Will you at least send me a picture of her?"

"Of course," I said, choking on my own guilt and tears. "Anything you want."

"Or him," Pastor Steen reminded.

"Yeah, Dad. Or him."

Chapter Thirty-One

The next week at school, Grant stopped me in the hallway when there was no one around. "Your due date is almost here, right?"

It had been a while since we'd talked. He didn't look good at all. There were heavy bags under his eyes, like he hadn't slept in a week. And he had become so skinny that he seemed to be swimming in his own skin. "A week and a half. But I've been having lots of contractions. The doctor says it could come any day now."

"And you still don't know what you're having?"

I shook my head.

"But it's official, you're giving it up for adoption?"

I nodded.

"Good, good. I think that's for the best." He must have seen my scowl, because he quickly added, "Oh, not for me. I just mean, for the baby . . . and for you." He paused. "Look, kiddo, I know I've screwed up. A lot. I wish I'd been a better parent to you. But somehow . . . ?" He seemed to be searching for the right words. "I guess what I'm trying to say, what I want you to know before this baby is born, is that you deserved better. Whatever happens in the future, I just want you to be happy. Eliza too. You both have so much potential, and I want you to reach it, to go for your dreams. Don't let anybody try to knock you down." He paused again, looking around to make sure no one was within earshot. "I'm so sorry for what I did to you. I'm sorry for who I became after your mother died." He reached up, trying to put a hand on my shoulder, but I stepped back, refusing his touch. He grimaced sadly, dropping his hand to his side. "You've been too merciful to me, Madeline," he muttered, obviously making a point to use my full name. I think it was only the second or third time in my whole life I'd heard him say it. As he turned to go, he added something I'd definitely only heard once before, spoken by the judge during the hearing of the man who killed my mom. "But mercy can never rob justice."

I didn't know what he meant by it until later that night when word came that Grant had been killed. His car hit a tree at top speed on a country road outside of town. There was no alcohol involved, but he wasn't wearing a seat belt. It was the lead story on the ten o'clock news. A reporter on the scene showed shots of the mangled car, then they jumped to another reporter outside the high school, who explained that "the victim was a teacher and father who was loved by students and faculty alike." Everyone believed it was an accident, that perhaps he'd caught a tire in the gravel along the shoulder and lost control. But Nathan and I knew better.

Justice was served.

I still cried the entire night. Mostly for Eliza, who had still been looking forward to that day when she could move back in with her father. "Any day now, sweetie," he'd tell her, or "sometime real soon," But I also cried for that part of me that remembered the good times with Grant. As painful as life was when he was drunk, there were also some wonderful memories of the man who loved my mom and who had lovingly guided me through some of the trials of my childhood.

Maybe mercy can't rob justice, but I couldn't help wondering if, in this instance, justice had somehow broken into the bank of mercy and cleaned it out.

The next day Nathan and I stayed at home with Eliza rather than going to school. In the late afternoon we had another discussion about finally telling his parents that he wasn't really the father of my baby. With Grant gone, I no longer saw the reason to keep it from them. It's not like the police or media could do anything about it now.

In no time at all, Nathan got all riled up. "You just don't get it, Maddy! I *can't* tell them. So what if Grant's gone? Has anything really changed?"

"Of course it has. We can keep it private now. There won't be criminal charges or a long, drawn-out trial. I won't have to testify. Everything is different now, Nathan. So why should you continue to carry this on your shoulders?"

"Oh, so now you don't care if people find out?"

"Of course I do. But at least your family deserves to know, after all they've been through."

"What about Randy, are you going to tell him too?"

"He hates me, Nathan. He can never know. None of the school kids can find out. Especially the ones who adored Grant. They'd probably blame his death on me."

He stood staring at me for longer than I liked. "Well, aren't we partially responsible?" he finally asked.

"For Grant's car accident? No."

"Do you think he deserved to die for what he did to you?"

"No," I repeated quickly. "Though I admit, there were times I wished he'd die."

"So if we'd done something different — if we had gone straight to the police at the beginning of all this — would Grant still be alive?"

His question stung. "Yes," I said weakly. "Probably. In jail . . . but alive."

"Don't you see? He died because of *us*!"

"No! He died because he was afraid to live with his guilt. Afraid of the consequences that he must've known were going to catch up with him sooner or later." I paused to read Nathan's body language. "Is this why you don't want to tell your parents? Because you feel responsible for Grant's death?"

"No. Yes . . . I don't know. It's everything, I guess." He paced around the room, nervously running his fingers through his hair. When he stopped, he said, "I'm glad I helped you, Maddy. I'm so happy I was late to church that day, and that I drove by when I did. If you'd taken your life because of this, I'd have had a real hard time getting over it. In that sense, better Grant than you. But look what we did to my parents along the way. Dad lost his dream job. Worse, he lost the trust of his congregation. They had to move from their home state to a place where they have no friends. None of those things were fair, and we didn't know they were going to happen, but they did, because of our choice. How are they going to feel if I call them up and say, 'Guess what, guys, we could have avoided this if I'd only told you the truth at the start. Instead I decided to play hero — the martyr — so I lied to you and everybody else, and now your life has been turned upside down and a man is dead because of it.' " He paused, breathing heavily. "Do you know what my dad drilled into me since before I could walk? 'Honesty is the only policy, Son.' After all our lies have put them through, do you think they'd forgive me . . . for putting you above them?"

"Yeah," I whispered, stung by the way he phrased that. "Eventually."

"Eventually . . . maybe. Honestly, the fact that Grant's gone is a blessing for me, because it means I don't have to explain any of this to them. If he were alive, my parents would figure out we'd lied as soon as we went to the police, right? Now we don't have to tell anyone. The truth dies with him, and no one else has to know! Not my parents, not Randy, not the kids at school. Not even Eliza."

"Wow," I said, "you're really adamant about this, aren't you?" He was whiter than I'd ever seen him. He looked so fragile standing there, like an egg that might suddenly crack. "What's going on? Is there something more that you're not saying?"

Nathan pulled a nearby chair under him and sat, then buried his face in his hands. Within a few seconds his body was heaving up and down. Soon his hands could no longer cover his crying. When he finally looked up, his face was dripping wet. "I killed him, Maddy," he moaned. "It's my fault!"

"Because we didn't turn him in to the police? That's nonsense. You can't think like that."

"No, you don't understand! He came to me. Yesterday, before he talked to you. He pulled me into his classroom during a break."

"What did he say?"

"He begged me to never let anyone know the truth about what he did to you. He said that despite his faults and mistakes, he loved you and Eliza, and he was so ashamed of what he'd done. He said he'd figured out a way to make it up to you, to give you a way to avoid having to deal with this anymore. And he wanted to make sure Eliza never found out. He said he'd already failed her in so many ways that she didn't deserve to be burdened with that knowledge."

"What did you tell him?"

"That I couldn't promise anything."

"Good."

"*No.* He said I didn't understand, but that soon I would. He told me he'd be going away very soon. Not to rehab, but like *gone,* as in for good. I thought he meant he was going to skip town or something to keep from getting caught, so I got all cocky and told him I'd go tell the police right then to make sure he didn't get away. I think he was a little annoyed that I wasn't understanding what he was talking about, because he pounded his fist on the table and said, 'Look, if I were *dead,* would anyone care?' "

I suddenly found it hard to speak. "What did you say?" I whispered.

More tears worked their way from his eyes and swam down his cheeks. "That not only would nobody care . . . but that it'd be the best news all year."

"Oh, Nathan," I said, crouching down so I could put my arms around him.

"It gets worse. Grant immediately asked if we had a deal. He said, 'Great. If I can make sure I'm gone — *permanently* — then you tell nobody about what I did, right? And you make sure that Eliza and Maddy are taken care of.' " Nathan paused to sniffle. "By then I knew what he was saying, but I didn't think he was serious, so I laughed. *I laughed!* And told him I'd happily carry it to my grave if he was in his, but that I didn't think a guy who hit girls had the guts to do something like that."

I started crying then too. "Nathan, I'm so sorry you had to be involved in any of this. But you didn't kill him. You didn't even give him the idea. His mind was made up, Nathan. It wasn't your fault."

We clung to each other for a minute, then he repeated his plea that nobody find out. "Everything has become so complicated," he said. "For you, for me, for my parents, it's just better for all of us if nobody ever knows that Grant got you pregnant." He raised his head to look me squarely in the eyes. "Whether I like it or not, I made a promise to Grant. He held up his end of the bargain, and I intend to hold up mine. Maddy, I don't ever want my parents or anyone else to know."

I hated seeing Nathan like that; hated that

Grant's "accident" with the tree had piled yet another heavy burden on my best friend's back. It wasn't fair. To ease his burden, I slid my hand down his side and reached into his front-left pocket.

"What are you doing?" he asked.

Slowly, I pulled out one of his little red rocks and held it up. "Taking this. For keeps." Before he could object, I shoved it into the front pocket of my maternity jeans.

"Why?"

"As a promise. If you need me to never tell anyone about this, then I won't. I still feel awful for your parents, but if this is what you want, then it'll be my one good thing for you. Nobody will ever know, Nathan. Okay?"

He nodded. Nothing more was ever said about it, because there was nothing left to say. A promise was made; a promise would be kept.

The baby came five days later, on the same day as Grant's funeral. I was glad that they overlapped, because as sad as I was over how his life ended, I don't think I could've handled sitting in a packed church listening to people blathering on about how wonderful he was. Eliza's schoolteacher, who'd known Grant for years, offered to take her to the service while Nathan and I went to the hospital.

Before leaving the house, I called the adoption agency and told them it was time. The agency notified Mr. and Mrs. Schroeder, the adoptive parents in California, who immediately went to the airport. Their flight arrived seven hours later, a full four hours before I delivered.

Mrs. Steen was right — it was a little girl. I got to hold her and nurse her for a full hour before Nathan went and invited the Schroeders to join us.

Even though she was conceived under the worst possible circumstances, I loved that child as much as I could love anything. Handing her into the arms of another woman was the hardest — and best — thing I've ever done. Mrs. Schroeder and I were both in tears. "Have you thought of a name?" I asked as the infant gently cooed in her new mother's arms.

Mr. and Mrs. Schroeder smiled at each other, then at me. "Since this is going to be an open adoption," she replied, "and we really do want you to know her as she grows up, we were hoping you might have a name picked out. After all, you've done so much to get her here, we'd at least like your input."

Now Nathan and I shared a smile. We'd talked about this at length, but didn't dare hope that we'd get a say in it. "Zoe," I replied almost immediately. "It means *life*. In unexpected ways, her life is a miracle to me. And even though you'll raise her and be her parents and give her the things that I can't, I always want to be a part of her life. *Zoe*. That's my vote."

Mrs. Schroeder turned to her husband, beaming. "Dear? Baby Zoe?"

"If the shoe fits . . ." he said.

She looked down into the wide eyes of my — our — baby, and whispered, "Hello there, Zoe. It's so nice to finally meet you."

Two months later, in the middle of March, I received a large envelope in the mail from California. Eliza brought it in from the mailbox after school. Nathan was still at work, but I couldn't wait for him, so I ripped it open.

"What does it say?" she asked, sensing my excitement.

"It says, my little munchkin, that we're going to California!"

When Nathan came home, I was so giddy that I practically jumped into his arms. Then I held up my letter. "It finally came," I gushed. "Full ride, Nathan! I'm going to

Stanford!"

"I'm so happy for you," he said with significantly less enthusiasm than I'd hoped.

"Really?"

"Of course. It's what you wanted — a top school, and close enough to visit Zoe now and then."

"So why the long face?"

He shrugged. "It's just going to be different. We've done everything together this whole year, and soon we'll be heading in opposite directions."

Nathan had already been accepted to a couple different schools, but he hadn't even applied in California.

"We'll still keep in touch," I told him.

With a chuckle, he poked me jokingly in the side. "Don't you know how these things work? Divorced couples don't keep in touch."

"Fine," I said, returning the joke — and the poke. "Then we won't get divorced."

He rolled his eyes. "I still have to tell my parents, you know. Can't wait for that discussion. 'Hey, Dad, remember how you told me to take good care of my "sweet bride"? Yeah, she's leaving me for a guy named Stan. Stan Ford.' "

"Oh stop. It's not that big of a deal. People get divorced all the time."

Actually, it turned out to be a pretty big deal.

In the middle of the summer Nathan called his parents on a Sunday evening to break the news. I was listening silently on the phone in the bedroom. He got them both on the line at the same time and explained how we'd come to the realization that our lives were headed in different directions, and that our brief, but eventful, marriage was over. There was a long, eerie silence, like we'd been hung up on.

When his dad finally spoke, his voice was ice cold. "Let me get this straight. A year ago you got a girl pregnant. At seventeen you married her, because you supposedly loved each other. Then you decided raising a baby together was too much work, so you gave her up for adoption. And now at eighteen you're calling the whole thing quits?" He went mute for another second, then asked, "What's it going to be next, Nathan? You guys could make things work if you wanted to. That poor girl. She has no mother, her stepfather passed away this year, and now you're leaving her alone to raise that little Eliza all by herself? I'm not going to hide it, Nathan — I'm extremely disappointed. This isn't how we raised you."

"It was her decision as much as mine," he

muttered.

"Well, then you've both got it wrong! Marriages have to be worked at. You can't just throw them away when things get tough. You're taking the easy way out!"

"You're wrong," Nathan growled. "Nothing about my relationship with Maddy has been the easy way."

"So that's it? You tried, failed, and now you're giving up? Just like that? I guess I raised a quitter."

I'm sure Nathan was fighting the urge to tell his father where to stick it. Good for him, though, he kept his voice on an even keel. "We're going off to college, Dad. Different schools. It's not going to work."

"Well, good luck with that!" Tim's voice was on fire. "I hope your college experience is better than your high school one. Though I don't see how it could be any worse." He hung up the phone without saying good-bye.

His mom then expressed her disappointment, but at least told Nathan she loved him. She also asked him to pass on her love to me.

I don't know when Nathan spoke to his parents again, but it wasn't that summer.

■ ■ ■ ■

PART III
TUMBLING

■ ■ ■ ■

Lindsay Walker

October 26

A few years ago at our annual "Stuff the Truck" event (for the Michael Grimm and Chelsea Hicks Foundations) Mr. Steen, a father from the opposing team, asked what we were doing. He then said he had a "few" costumes in his truck for us. It took his son's entire football team of 7th- and 8th-grade boys to carry over the "few" new costumes he had to donate to the foundation (between 75 and 100 of them!). What a great show of generosity and sportsman-ship!

Like • Comment • Share

Jay Madaus
October 26
Nathan was a dear friend and colleague, and I will miss him tremendously. A few months back he shipped his favorite chocolate as a gift from Texas . . . just because he knew I liked sweets.

Like • Comment • Share

Chapter Thirty-Two

Alice

My left hand is in my front pocket, fingering six small stones as I walk toward the front door of the middle school. I keep walking in that direction just long enough for Ty to turn the corner and drive out of sight, then I spin around and race back to the sidewalk. A city bus, headed toward Dallas, is coming up the road. If I hurry, I can beat it to the next stop.

Twenty seconds later, fully out of breath, I join a few other people in line, board the bus, drop enough money in the till to cover the fare, then take a seat near the back and settle in for the ride. Normally, going downtown only takes thirty minutes or so, but on a weekday morning on a bus, I'm guessing more like an hour. Once we're out of the suburbs and rolling into the city, I take out the address and map I printed last night. While I'm sorting out which stop will be the closest to my destination, a high-school-age boy sitting two seats over strikes up a conversation.

"Where ya headed? I know the city real good."

I look up and smile nervously. His return smile reveals one front tooth that is cracked diagonally and another that is growing cockeyed in his mouth, but I try not to stare. After all, Dad wouldn't have cared what somebody's teeth looked like, right? "Do you go there a lot?"

"Once a week," he says proudly, "for the past seven months. Five more to go."

"For school?"

"Nah. I gave up school 'bout the time . . . well, 'bout the time they kicked me out." He laughs at himself. "I lived downtown for a while after that. Now I just go to visit my caseworker."

I'm not altogether sure what to say to that, so I just go with a simple "Oh."

"Ain't nothin'. Going to visit a caseworker's way better'n hanging out in juvie, getting busted up all the time."

"Oh," I say again, then sheepishly ask, "What's juvie?"

"Juvenile detention. I spent six months there. 'Course that's better'n where I was 'fore that. Least in juvie I got fed every day."

"Where were you before?"

"In Dallas, like I said. On the street mostly, and shelters sometimes. That's how I know it so good. I can get you anywhere. Where'd you say you was headed?"

"The West Village." I figure that's a vague enough answer for a stranger.

"Ooh, uptown. They got some phat digs up there. You shopping, or going to see someone?"

"Seeing someone."

"Well, if you need a hand getting somewheres, just lemme know. I ain't gonna be but thirty minutes for my appointment. I could show you 'round after that."

I smile again. "I think I know where I'm going. But thanks."

The conversation fizzles after that. I wave good-bye when he gets off the bus on Main Street, in the historic district, right near the old courthouse. My first stop is another twenty blocks, near my dad's favorite doughnut shop.

As usual, there is a small line of people coming out the front door. When it's finally my turn, I step up and give my order. The college kid behind the counter has dreadlocks and a nose ring, but he's friendly. "I need a dozen, please," I tell him. "Two jelly, four fritters . . . um . . . four glazed, and two chocolate frosted."

The man tucks a rope of hair over his shoulder. "Baker's dozen, kid. The thirteenth is free."

"Oh, okay. How about the pink one with sprinkles on it." I hand him fifteen of the fifty dollars I pulled from my babysitting jar before breakfast.

The man makes change, then packs my doughnuts in a pink cake box. "Don't eat 'em all at once."

With a backpack slung over my shoulders and my arms full of doughnuts, I follow a growing line out the door, then continue several blocks east to a highway overpass. My mom would probably flip out if she knew what I was up to, but since she clearly didn't understand or appreciate my father, how can I expect her to understand this? As I near the overpass, I have flashbacks to the last time my dad took me downtown to get doughnuts. It was nearly a year ago, but the experience is still fresh in my mind. I recall telling him there was no need to buy two dozen, that they were so big that one dozen was more than enough for our family. He agreed with me, saying that we'd just have to find someone to help polish off the others. Then, with two boxes of doughnuts in his arms, he led me along the same route to this overpass.

I let the memory fade as I approach the massive concrete columns that support the highway overhead. Beneath the four-lane covering is an old parking lot littered with debris. Tucked in beyond the lot, in the darkest recess where the steel girders meet the earth, is exactly what I hoped to find: *people.* Five or six of them, sprawled out on the ground atop wide swaths of cardboard. Three of them have ragged old sleeping bags, but the others are using newspapers and dirty blankets for insulation against the morning air. I doubt very much that they are the same people I met a year earlier, but I hope their reaction will be the same. With a giant breath I press forward, leaving the safety of the world above.

"Um . . . hello," I say softly once I'm close enough to smell them. "Is anyone awake?"

At first nobody moves. Then one of sleeping bags begins writhing around. Half a second later a little head pops out. A young girl, maybe three or four years old, is staring back at me. Her eyes are as big and brown as an apple fritter. "Mommy," the girl whispers. "Mommy, get up."

The bag's other occupant lazily sits upright. The woman is probably in her twenties, though her general appearance makes it difficult to guess. Her hair is ratty and she has bruises around one of her eyes. Her cheeks are round, but her expression sunken, maybe even a little scared.

"You lost?" the mom asks.

I shake my head.

"Somebody send you here for somethin'?"

Again, I shake my head.

A couple of the other inhabitants begin moving and sitting up to see what's going on. There are two older men, one black and one white, along with two other women, both of them at least forty. None of them look like they've had a decent meal in a while.

The black man is clearly suspicious of me, though what he has to fear from a pint-sized thirteen-year-old girl is beyond me. After sizing me up, he speaks to me in a voice as deep as the ocean. "Wha'chu want? We don't want no trouble, and we ain't here for show, so you best run along."

My hands are starting to shake. I remember being nervous last year too, even with my father by my side. Now that I'm alone, I'm downright petrified. For a moment I forget why I've come at all; my instinct is to turn and run, but as I take another long breath, I remember the stones in my pocket. "I . . . thought you might be hungry, so I brought you some doughnuts. They're fresh. I just bought them a few minutes ago. There's enough for everyone to have two." I take five steps forward, slowly, and set the box on the ground near the little girl. "There's a pink one in there for you," I tell her. "With sprinkles. I hope you like it." By now my voice is almost a whisper. I turn around slowly and head back toward the safety of the main road.

When I'm fifteen paces away, the bellowing voice of the old black man splits the air again. "God bless you, child. God bless you."

I turn and wave briefly to a chorus of humble thank-yous, then I continue walking. Back out on the street, beyond sight of the homeless crowd, I reach a hand into my left pocket, feel around for a single stone, and transfer it to the other side. "One down, and it's not even eight thirty," I say out loud. "Dad's right, this isn't so hard if you set your mind to it. I bet I can move all six stones before anyone at school even realizes I'm not there . . ."

Nancy Tellefsen Greenhouse
October 27
My medical insurance only gave me a few visiting-nurse visits. When it ran out,

CHAPTER THIRTY-THREE

Halley

Monday mornings at Velvet Petals are always crazier than the rest of the week. There's new inventory to deal with, old inventory to evaluate and then either mark down or scrap, general prep for the week ahead, and urgent weekend orders to squeeze in before noon. Today is worse than normal because I haven't set foot in the store in ten days, so there is catching up to do on top of everything else. All of which explains why I don't bother checking my personal e-mail on my smartphone until well after ten a.m.

The first e-mail I see on the list, marked urgent, is from my daughter's middle school.

This message is to inform you that Steen, Alice, is absent from school today. Please call the district's automated attendance hotline to confirm this absence. All other attendance questions concerning Steen, Alice, should be directed to the front desk at the number listed below.

The hotline turns out to be one of the school secretaries. I have her on the phone half a minute later. "There must be some mistake. Alice's brother dropped her off early today, so I know she was there. Is it possible that the attendance record is wrong?"

"If it was just one period, then yes, ma'am," the woman says. I can hear her typing while I'm speaking. "But the system says she's now missed three classes in a row, which is not a data-entry problem. It's an unexcused absence."

I'm dumbfounded. And worried. And mad. "So you're telling me that my seventh-grader, who I know for a fact was dropped off there this morning, and who I trust will be watched out for by responsible adults at the school, has somehow come up missing? She couldn't have just disappeared! Has anyone bothered looking for her?"

"Mrs. Steen, I'm very sorry. But all I have is the attendance record to go by. I do know that if she was just wandering the halls, someone would have shooed her to class by now, in which case she'd already be accounted for. I don't want to alarm you, but it's pretty safe to assume that she is not in the school. Are you absolutely positive she was dropped off?"

As the other woman speaks, I run through everything I remember from before school. *Alice didn't want to ride the bus. Ty wanted to go early, and didn't want to wait for her. Both kids left the house in a hurry . . .*

Through the ear that is listening I hear the woman's question. "Well, . . . no," I reply. "I mean, I wasn't there to see it. But the plan was for her older brother to drop her off."

"How about you let me put you through to the high school? Her brother is Ty, correct?"

"That's right."

"Good. I'll put you through, and they can let you talk with him, just to make sure he dropped her off like you say. That way, before we get too worried about Alice, we're sure we've got all of the information. Does that sound reasonable?"

A sinking feeling settles in my stomach. Call it woman's intuition or a mother's sixth sense, but somehow I know right then in my gut that something is wrong. "Yes. Put

397

me through."

The person who answers at the high school is a student aide; heavy on the "student," light on the "aide." "Who?" she says. "Ty Steen? Oh my gosh, I totally know who Ty is! He's super, super nice. His locker is, like, just down from mine, so I see him all the time . . . Can I get him on the phone? Oh, I'm sorry, ma'am, I don't think I have his number on my cell, but I could totally ask around, 'cuz I'm sure I know someone who has it . . . What? . . . Oh, talk to him now? Like I was trying to say, he's in class and stuff, and they don't really let us talk on the phone during class, but . . . wait, who did you say this is? . . . His mom? Oh, hi Mrs. Steen. So sad about, well, you know. Real bummer with the funeral and everything . . . Um, yeah, I think I can get Ty to come to the office, but it will take a few minutes. Can you hold?"

I want to scream by the time she puts the phone down. The only reason I don't is because a customer is in the store smelling bouquets of roses.

Five minutes later, after the customer is gone, Ty picks up the line. "Mom?"

"Hi, honey. I'm so sorry to pull you out of class. I wouldn't have but . . ."

"You okay? You don't sound good."

"I'm fine. Listen. What happened after you left the house this morning? Was everything okay with Alice?"

"Yeah, sure. I dropped her off at the school. Why?"

The sinking feeling in my stomach spreads like venom throughout the rest of my body, but I do my best to stay composed, for Ty's sake. "She hasn't been to a single class."

"But I dropped her off! I swear I did."

"I know. But did you see her walk through the front doors?"

There is a brief pause, followed by a dubious "No."

I pause too. "I'm scared, Ty. I don't think she ever went inside."

"But why?"

"I don't know. I've got to call the other school back and let them know what's going on. They may have a protocol for such things. Then I'm heading straight home. Can you meet me there?"

"I'll *beat* you there. And I'll look for her along the way. Maybe she ditched and went somewhere else. She's probably curled up under a tree at the park, reading the dictionary or something."

"Well, listen, we're wasting precious time. You get going right away and call me if you find her. Okay?"

"Same here. Love you, Mom."

As soon as I hang up, I dial my in-laws at home. Tim answers. Alice isn't there, so I call the school and give them what little information I have. The secretary says the administrators will immediately start searching bathrooms and discreetly asking kids if they've seen her. They promise to call me back as soon they've run through their standard on-site checks.

"She's small," I warn, "and not well liked. Is there any chance she could be stuck in a bully's locker?"

"Possibly, but unlikely. That usually doesn't last more than fifteen minutes or so, because it's hard to muffle the screaming and kicking. We had one in there for an hour once, but that was a boy who locked himself in and stayed quiet as a mouse. His dad had told him he'd kill him — figuratively, of course — if he came home from school with another F on a math test. The poor boy figured if he could avoid taking the test, there was no risk of an F."

"How sad for him," I remark quickly. "But less sad than losing a daughter." I wait just a second to make sure the other woman heard me, then add, "Please make sure someone calls me the moment they find out anything about Alice. Okay?"

"Of course, Mrs. Steen. The second we know, you'll know."

I hang up the phone, quickly gather my keys and purse, lock up the till, then exit Velvet Petals and lock it up too. A woman in the parking lot is just getting out of her car. "We're closed," I tell her. "Sorry."

"What do you mean you're closed? What am I supposed to do now? My little girl has her first tumbling recital in thirty minutes and I need to get her a bouquet."

I don't like the woman's tone, but I understand the inconvenience. As I hustle to my car, I calmly reply, "*My* little girl has gone missing, and I need to go find her." I consider leaving it at that, but I hate to leave a customer in the lurch. "I suggest the Safeway down the street. Your little girl won't know the difference between theirs and mine anyway. Good day."

Colleen is pacing the living room when I rush into the house. "Did you find her?" she asks.

My heart sinks immediately to my ankles. "I was going to ask the same thing," I reply glumly. "Where's Ty?"

"All three of them are out combing the streets."

"Three?"

"Oh, I guess you didn't hear. Ty mentioned what was going on to Randy, Nathan's old friend, so he came too. Just up and left work right in the middle of the day."

"I see. So they're all just driving around?"

"Ty and Randy had a few places they wanted to check, parks and such. Tim figured three sets of eyes was better than two, so he tagged along." She pauses and clenches a hand over her stomach. "I'd have gone too, but the whole situation has my tummy doing flips, so I opted to man the house instead."

"When did they go?"

"About fifteen minutes ago. Maybe less. Time enough for me to use the bathroom . . . *twice.*"

That's way too much information for me at the moment, but I give her a sympathetic smile anyway before heading upstairs. I want to be out combing the streets for Alice too, but not before checking her room. If her absence from school was intentional, then perhaps she had the good sense to leave some sort of clue about where she was going. Like a whirlwind, I rifle through the loose papers, pictures, and note cards on her desk, then I flip through two stacks of books and magazines, but nothing jumps out as being important. As I scan over the desk a second time for anything I might have missed, my eyes lock onto the mini laptop sitting lid-down right in the middle of the mess I just made.

"What an idiot," I groan.

Colleen exits the bathroom across the hall just as the word "idiot" rolls off my tongue. "Me?" she asks pensively while entering the room. "Did I do something wrong?"

"No, *me*," I say in frustration. "I should have gone online first thing."

"You think she's online? Like a chat room?"

"Her blog. She writes there faithfully." I start clicking away as soon as the computer blinks to life. "In person, sometimes it's hard to get much information out of her. She won't always talk to us about friends or social stuff. But on her blog she's an open book. It's how we first learned that she was getting bullied."

Colleen gasps. "Alice is getting bullied? That's awful! You think that's why she didn't want to go back today?"

Alice's most recent entry pops up on the screen. "I think we're about to find out. Here it is."

MY OWN LITTLE WONDERLAND:
October 28th

Dear Blog, it's me, Alice.
Oh, those stupid, stupid, stupid, stupid adults! That's one stupid for each of them, counting my brother, who isn't technically an adult yet, but he's equally stupid. They think they know everything!

But they don't know my dad.

He would NOT have said I was his only little girl if I wasn't the only one.

He would NEVER have told me that two kids was just the right amount for him if he knew he actually had three!

HE WOULD NOT HAVE LIED TO ME!!

Why am I the only one who sees that? Why am I the only one who will stand up for Dad when he can't stand up for himself? Why am I the only one who trusts that he was exactly the kind of man we all thought he was? Maybe it's because I'm the only one willing to prove them all wrong, or at least the only one not willing to accept it at face value.

If it's true what they say, I have to believe there's something that they don't know. Someone must have more information than them.

Thanks to my mom, I know exactly who that someone is!

Tomorrow I'm going to find out the truth for myself . . .

Colleen finishes first, but I'm just a sentence behind. "Oh my gosh!" I yell, standing up and running both hands through my hair. "I know who she's looking for."
"Who?"
I can't believe Colleen hasn't yet connected the dots, so I ignore the question. "Oh, that sneaky little girl. I thought she really wanted to see the evidence. All she wanted was a little information!"
"Who?" Colleen asks again, sounding frustrated.
"Who do you think? *Madeline Zuckerman.* The mother of your first granddaughter!"

Kelly Hunsaker

October 27

Hi . . . me again! You've all got such wonderful comments! I just wanted to add one more "good thing" that happened to me recently. The truck ahead of me in the fast-food drive-thru paid for my meal. Seriously! Don't know who it was, but wouldn't be shocked to find out it was Mr. Steen.

Like • Comment • Share

CHAPTER THIRTY-FOUR

Madeline

I've been alone in my office for half the morning, reliving my childhood with Nathan all over again in my head. It was such a long time ago, but it feels like yesterday since we said our good-byes at the airport, promised to keep in touch, then hopped on flights to opposite sides of the country to discover our futures. I found my future in molecular therapy and medical genetics. He found his in law and a slender co-ed named after a comet.

I check the clock to make sure I'm not late — an applicant is coming in twenty minutes for an interview to fill an open position on the teaching staff.

I pull out the woman's résumé to go over it once more, but my office door swings open before I can get past the header. "I'm sorry," Amy says. "I know you said you didn't want to be disturbed, but I've got a woman on the phone who says she has to talk to you right away. Says she won't take no for an answer. By the sound of her voice, it's pretty urgent."

"Did she give her name?"

"Yes," she says, checking her scribbled notes. "Halley Steen. She says you'll know who she is."

Hearing that name — knowing that Nathan's wife is seeking me out — sends a paralyzing shiver down my spine. For an instant, the world freezes, and I am alone with the panic of my thoughts. *Why is Halley calling? Where did she get my number? How does she even know I exist?* I've wanted to meet her, to talk with her, for as long as I can remember, but Nathan thought it would complicate things. I gasp for air, then have to exhale before I can speak. "I . . . know the name. Go ahead and patch her through to my office."

"Will do, Professor."

Twenty seconds later the red light on my phone blinks to life just a split a second before it rings. I let it ring. And ring. And ring some more.

With another breath, I finally pick up. "Hello?"

"Is this Madeline Zuckerman?"

"Yes."

"Did the secretary tell you who this is?"

"Yes," I repeat after a momentary hesitation. "Nathan's wife."

There is a brief pause on her end too, then, "I can't believe I'm saying this, because you're the last person in the world I want to talk to right now, but I need your help . . ."

Stephanie Dahl
October 27

A few years ago, my oldest son flew in from Denver to visit me in Mesquite. I had barely started working a new job, my father had passed away a few months earlier, and money was very tight during that time. After picking him up in Dallas, I got home and ran to the store to get a few items for a Christmas Eve dinner. As I was telling the cashier about how happy I was to have all my children home for this time of the year, a gentleman tapped me on the shoulder and asked if the grocery items I had on the belt were all mine. I told him yes, and he said, "Merry Christmas," and handed me a $100 bill!! He walked away and the cashier lady asked if I knew him. I said I had never met him before in my life. She smiled and said, "Well, that's not an uncommon way for people to meet Nathan Steen, especially during the holidays." What a wonderful gift! And what a sad loss . . . my heart broke when I saw the newspaper article about his car accident. My thoughts and prayers are with the Steen family.

Like • Comment • Share

CHAPTER THIRTY-FIVE

Alice

While I was poking around on the Internet last night, planning my trip downtown, I found a website for people to review all of the different Dallas-area neighborhoods. As I approach my destination, the review that sticks out in my mind was from 10Gallon-Joe, who wrote, "The West Village isn't just a place to live, it's a lifestyle — ritzy town homes, pricey art galleries, swanky restaurants, and lots and lots of money to go around. Let's just say there's a reason it's become one of the trendiest urban neighborhoods in Texas."

Amazing, really, that just a few city blocks beyond this gem you could find yourself scraping by on skid row or living under an overpass.

The address I'm looking for turns out to be a tall, shiny building along McKinney Avenue with lots of windows. Unfortunately,

411

it is locked. A tiny sign on the door reads, "Residents only. Solicitors will be prosecuted." Just to the left of the door is a panel of buttons for an intercom system, with names of residents listed beside each button. I scan down the ledger until I find the name I'm looking for.

"This is not a solicitation," I convince myself as I push the button. Nobody answers, so I push it again. Still nothing. I check my watch. Twelve thirty, straight up. If she comes home for lunch, she should be here. I tap it several times in rapid succession for good measure.

Almost instantly a voice pipes through the speaker. "Can I help you?"

Third time's the charm.

"Hello?" I ask, feeling instantly nervous. "Can you hear me? Is there another button I have to push to talk?"

"I hear you fine. Who is this, please?"

"Is this Mrs. Zuckerman?"

"Yes. May I ask who I'm speaking with?"

I wait a moment before answering. "Umm . . . I'd rather tell you that in person. It's really important, though. I promise. And I swear I'm not selling anything."

"Well, you look harmless enough," Mrs. Zuckerman says. "But sometimes looks can be deceiving."

"You can see me?"

"There's a small camera on the panel just in front of you."

I quickly pat at my hair and smile. "Well, do you have a minute? Like I said, it is really important. I've come all the way downtown to talk to you."

"Shouldn't you be in school right now?"

"Well . . . technically, yes. But today I needed to make an exception. Family crises are more important than school."

"Family crisis, huh?"

"Yes, ma'am."

"Can you expound a bit?"

I don't want to play my whole hand, but I realize I'm at least going to have to show a few cards if I have any chance of getting in the door. "Well . . . I think there's someone we both know . . . er, knew . . . that was very special to us. And I'd like to talk to you about him if that's all right. It won't take long, I promise."

"Oh? And who might that be?"

Here's my ace. "Nathan Steen, ma'am."

There is a prolonged pause, then a subdued, "And how do you know Mr. Steen?"

"Because he's my father . . . and my very best friend."

This time the silence lasts much longer. For a moment I fear I've said too much.

Then the voice from upstairs chimes again. "What, exactly, do you want to discuss about Nathan?"

I know the answer to this question could either make or break my chance of talking in person with the mysterious woman from my father's past. Crossing my fingers, I look straight into the camera. "I saw what you wrote on Facebook, and I'd really like to know how he saved your life."

For a long time there is nothing but static over the speaker, then the static goes dead too. "Hello?" I call out. "Mrs. Zuckerman? Are you still there?" I give it a second longer. "Hello?"

After nearly a minute without a response I'm about to give up, when the speaker in front of me springs back to life. "Sorry about that. I had to take a call. What did you say your name was?"

"I'm Alice Steen."

"Well, Alice, as you've obviously gathered, your father was a very dear friend of mine. And I'm delighted to meet you." The tall glass door to my right makes a heavy clicking sound, like the lock has just sprung. "I'm on the eighth floor, apartment seven. I'll be waiting for you in the hall."

With my backpack on my shoulder, I give the door a tug, then hurry inside to the elevator. As soon as I step out of the lift, a friendly voice calls down the hallway. "This way, Alice. To the left."

When I turn, I'm greeted by a woman in high heels, a fancy skirt, and long-sleeved blouse waving at me from halfway down the hallway. As I approach, Mrs. Zuckerman's features come into full focus. My eyes bounce from the flowing hair to the brilliant smile to the perfect cheeks to the slender legs to the painted nails. The only word that comes to mind is *flawless.*

"So you're Nathan's daughter," Mrs. Zuckerman says cheerfully, extending a dainty hand. "What a delight."

Oddly, I feel like I'm shaking hands with a celebrity, and not just because of how the woman looks. It's also the sophisticated, confident way she carries herself. "And you're . . . my dad's friend."

"That I am. Your dad was, without question, the truest friend I ever had." She smiles tenderly and places a hand on my shoulder, above the strap of my backpack. "I'm so sorry about what happened to him. It broke my heart when I heard the news. I literally cried for days, and I have the Kleenex bill to prove it."

"Thanks, Mrs. Zuckerman."

"Madeline," the woman says, correcting

me. "Not even my students call me Mrs. Zuckerman."

"You're a teacher? You don't look like a teacher."

"And what does a teacher look like?"

"I just mean, you're all dressed up. My teachers mostly wear jeans and a polo to school. Where do you teach?"

"At the Medical Center here in Dallas. My focus is research, but I also teach a couple classes in molecular therapy and medical genetics. Very boring stuff, really, unless you're like me and you want to find a viable cure for cancer. Then it's wildly fascinating. But full disclosure: I'm only dressed like this today because I was supposed to be interviewing someone for an open position in my department, but something else came up. On most days I prefer a comfy pair of jeans too." She looks me over once more. "I'm sure you didn't track me down just to hear me ramble on about work and clothes. Would you like to come inside to talk?"

I follow her through a mahogany door to an apartment that is almost as exquisite as Madeline, with beautiful artwork adorning the walls, black granite on the counters, and wall-to-wall marble covering the floor.

"Make yourself at home," she says, pointing to a selection of Victorian chairs in the main room. "I'm going to make some tea, and then we'll chat. Can I get you some? I've got several herbals that are quite good. Mango Tango, Peppermint Peace, Blueberry Bonanza, and maybe a bag or two of Orange-Apple Uproar."

"Umm . . . the blueberry one?"

"Blueberry it is. I'll be back in a wink."

A wink turns out to be nearly ten minutes, but that's perfectly fine by me. It gives me time to rethink how I'm going to broach the subject of the allegations concerning her and my father's past. I've already rehearsed my opening line a hundred times, but another hundred can't hurt.

When Madeline returns, she is carrying a tray with two fancy teacups, two coasters, and a dish of sugar cubes with the tiniest tongs I've ever seen. "Here you go," she says, setting one of the cups on a coaster in front of me. "One Blueberry Bonanza, steamed to perfection. Not hot enough to burn your tongue, but not so cold that you don't have to sip."

"Thank you."

"You're very welcome. There's nothing better than a warm cup of tea to put one at ease. I started drinking it regularly when I studied at Oxford, and now I can't live without it."

My heart thumps delightedly against my chest. "You studied at Oxford?" I don't like to brag, but I doubt there's another seventh-grader in the United States who knows more about the world's top universities than me, since I've been researching their admissions criteria for the better part of a year. The last time I checked, the University of Oxford was sitting at number six on the list. "In London?"

Madeline takes a short sip of tea, sitting up straight in her chair, trying to look very proper. Then, in a decent British accent, she says, "Indeed I did. T'was at Oxford, along the river Thames, where I earned a doctorate degree in Genetics, and I dare say my life is the better for it." She giggles at herself when she is done.

"Wow. You're definitely not like any of my teachers."

"I'll take that as a compliment," she replies with a smile. "Now, back to you, Alice. May I ask how you found my address?"

"Easy. I googled it."

"Oh," she says, as though she was expecting a more complicated answer. "Well then, on to business, I guess. Over the intercom you mentioned something about Facebook that you wanted to know about."

I set my cup down and scoot back in my chair. "Yeah. I mean . . . that's part of it."

"Part of what?"

"Of what I'm trying to figure out."

"I'm listening."

I clear my throat. This isn't how I planned the conversation in my head. I'll have to make it work. "Well . . . there are people saying all sorts of stuff about my dad, like all of the 'one good things' listed on the Facebook page. But there's other stuff too. Things I don't think are true, so I'm trying to sort out what's real and what's not."

"And you thought I could be of assistance?"

I nod.

"Because of what I wrote on Facebook?"

"Yeah. And other things."

Madeline stares at me like she's trying to read my mind. "Such as . . . ?"

"Just things I read."

"Alice, I don't think I can help you unless you're willing to share what you know."

"Well, maybe I'm getting ahead of myself. Can we just stick to the first question for now?"

"Which one was that?"

"About Facebook."

"Okay. What's the question again?"

There. This is where I wanted to start in

the first place. "Did my dad really save your life?"

For a brief instant, Madeline looks like she is going to say something really important. But then she smiles and stands up. "Just a minute." She glides across the room, picks up a tiny wooden box that's sitting on the mantel above the gas fireplace, and returns to her seat. "This is one of my most valuable possessions in the whole world. It was a gift from your father."

She hands it to me. It's small enough to fit in my palm. "Did he make it?"

"Not the box. Look inside."

The box has a small drawer on the front, maybe the size of a finger. I use my pinky-nail to pry it open just a little, then give the pinhead-sized knob a tug with two fingers. Based on what she said, I'm expecting to find a gold ring or diamond earrings or something valuable like that. Instead, inside the drawer, on a bed of black felt, is a small reddish pebble, just like the ones in my own pocket. I pick it up and roll it slowly in my fingers. I can hardly speak. My voice cracks when I try. "When did he give this to you?"

"A long time ago, Alice. To me, this little rock, along with the other ones he carried, attest that Nathan Steen was a true hero. He didn't have to help people. Nobody forced him to, but he did anyway, of his own accord. And, thankfully, out of all the people in the world he could have helped, he helped *me*."

I put the rock back in the drawer. "But *how*? How did he help you?" I don't mean to sound pushy, but seeing the red stone has me suddenly upset, and for good reason. Last year, when Dad took me downtown to help the homeless, we started talking about his funny little rocks, and I asked him if there was any reason why he chose six instead of some other number.

You know what he told me? *"Actually, Alice, there used to be seven, but somewhere along the line I guess I lost one."*

Lost one! That's what he said! Yet there it is, the lost stone sitting right there in little Miss Pretty's stupid little box! I try to stay calm, even though inside I'm seething at the realization that my father lied to me — to all of us — just like Mom said. "What did he do for you that was so great?" I press. "And why on earth did he give you this?

Looking as calm and confident as ever, Madeline takes another long sip of her Mango Tango. "Well, it's complicated. And it was so long ago. Let's just say that your father helped me through a very difficult time."

No, let's not.

I can't take it anymore. I know I was in denial yesterday when Mom and everyone told me about Dad. I didn't want to believe it. I so wanted them all to be wrong, but in the short time I've spent with Madeline, it's become obvious that this wasn't just a girl who had a childhood crush on my father. This was someone who he cared about a lot, of that I'm sure. The evidence has its own little wooden drawer. In a momentary lapse of restraint, I blurt out, "Would that difficult time happen to be the nine months between conception and birth?"

Oh my gosh! Did that really just come out of my mouth? My dad is probably rolling over in his grave!

Madeline nearly chokes on her tea, but quickly composes herself. She crosses one leg over the other, staring right at me, but not really looking at me, if that makes any sense. I can only guess what she's thinking, but before she has a chance to say anything, the doorbell rings.

"Saved by the bell," she mumbles as she heads toward a wall-mounted intercom box near the front door. There is an image on a small screen of several people standing outside the building, but from this distance I can't make out their faces. "You can go ahead and come up," she says as she pushes a button on the box. "Apartment seven, eighth floor."

"I should get going," I tell her. "I probably shouldn't have come anyway."

"No, it's good that you came. I've wanted to meet you since you were born."

I want to say, *why,* but instead go with "No, seriously, I'll get out of your hair."

"First, let me introduce you to my guests."

Half a minute later there is a knock at the door. Madeline opens it just enough to see out, effectively blocking my view of the people in the hallway. They exchange a few muffled words, then the door swings wide and in march five faces that need no introduction: Mom, Ty, Grandma and Grandpa Steen, with Coach Rawlins taking up the rear.

Now I'm in for it . . .

Shelley Boice Ramirez
October 28
While my husband was having brain surgery performed to remove a ventricular tumor, Halley and Nathan showed up out of the blue with my favorite dessert, a gourmet lemon bar. But more importantly, they sat with me while I was waiting during the surgery to comfort me and let me

know they cared.

Like • Comment • Share

CHAPTER THIRTY-SIX

Halley

Figures, the "other woman" is ridiculously pretty. No wonder Nathan was keeping secrets. I hardly have a chance to introduce myself to Mrs. Zuckerman before I hear Randy mumble, "This is a bad idea. I shouldn't have come." He's staring at her like he's just seen a ghost.

"Good to see you again too, Randy," the woman says softly.

Notwithstanding Randy's awkwardness, I have to admit, it's nice having him and the others with me for my first — and hopefully last — face-to-face encounter with the object of my late husband's affection. There is power in numbers. I shake her hand curtly and introduce Ty.

Then I move on to the important stuff. "*Alice Layne Steen!* What in the world were you thinking?" I step past Madeline and storm across the room.

Alice shoots up from one of the matching chairs like a Mexican bottle rocket.

"Mom?" she stammers. "How did you find me?"

It takes about two seconds for me to get close enough that I can look her straight in the eyes. "I'm not an idiot, Al. I read your blog and connected the dots."

"Since when do you read my blog?"

"I'm your mother, Alice, I read it all the time. As soon as I saw your post from last night, I called Mrs. Zuckerman and told her to be on the lookout. She came home for lunch expecting you to show up, then she called me as soon as you buzzed her door."

Alice's eyes dart toward Madeline with a look of betrayal, then back to me. "You had her phone number?"

"I remembered seeing her work number in one of their e-mail exchanges." I turn and purposefully give Madeline an unkind look. Her eyes instantly drop to the floor. "But I'll ask again, Alice. *What on earth were you thinking?* Did you even stop to think about how many people would be looking for you? They've turned your school upside down already, plus the police were put on alert, and the five of us have been pulling our hair out with worry all morning."

"I know, I messed up."

"*You think?* After everything that's gone on during the past week, to find out you've come *here,* of all places? To *her* house? Unbelievable, Al. Truly unbelievable."

Ty is much less emotional than me. "Mom, we all know why she came. But maybe we should go talk about this at home."

"Agreed," says Colleen. "This is Steen family business. We should run along."

"She was a Steen once, too," remarks Randy through clenched teeth.

Madeline looks hurt by the comment. Or embarrassed. Tim sees the pain on her face and steps farther into the room, stopping when he is right in front of her. "Hello, Maddy. I'm so sorry about all of this."

"You feel bad for *her?*" I say, not hiding my displeasure. "She's been carrying on with my husband in secret for years. Let's not misplace our allegiance here, Tim."

"Nathan was keeping the secrets from you, Halley," he calmly responds. "Madeline was simply communicating with her ex-husband." He looks at her again and opens his arms. She smiles at the gesture, accepting his embrace. "How are you doing?"

"I miss him, Tim," she replies, getting tearful. "I can't believe he's gone."

"And I can't believe we're still here. Kids, let's go."

Wiping at her tears, Madeline lets go of Tim and faces me before I can take two steps. "Actually, Halley, I was hoping I could convince you to stay. Just for a little while. I think we should talk."

"What, and swap stories about Nathan? No thanks."

"No. I just feel like there are some things that I need to say — things that you need to hear."

"Haven't you done enough already?"

Madeline appears unfazed by my accusatory tone. She takes a single step closer, as if reducing the physical distance might help bridge the gap between us. "It's unfortunate that we're having to meet like this for the first time. When we spoke earlier, I was very nervous. I've always wanted to meet you and your family, but I never imagined it would be under such unfortunate circumstances." She pauses briefly, glancing first at Randy, then at Alice. "Obviously, when you called, I knew you must have learned *something* about me since Nathan's passing, but I wasn't sure what. Then just before you arrived, Alice got right to the heart of the matter." She glances around at the faces in the room once more, landing finally back on me. "I know you know about my daughter."

"Yes," I say curtly. "I do."

"But if that's all you know about me and Nathan when we were younger, then you deserve to hear more. Alice was asking all the right questions. She wanted to know about the 'one good thing' he did for me, and especially how he saved my life. Without Nathan, I probably wouldn't have made it through high school."

Randy is still standing by the door. "At least not with a baby," he quips under his breath.

The comment makes Madeline cringe.

"Listen," I tell her bluntly, "it's not your high school relationship with Nathan that bothers me. What does bother me is the fact that the old flame somehow rekindled, and that your relationship carried on right under my nose for all these years. And I'm beyond hurt that he never so much as mentioned he'd been previously married. I feel like that's something that should be on the table when two people are starting their lives together. Whatever mistakes the two of you made as teenagers is your business, but his keeping secrets like this from me for our entire marriage is *my* business, and it's inexcusable."

"I understand. But I think if you give me

a chance to explain, it will put the situation in much better light. Nathan was a hero. He saved my life several times over, yet nobody knew how or why but me."

Upon hearing this, Colleen steps closer to the sofa. "Maybe we should hear her out."

"I agree," Alice chirps.

This was supposed to be a quick stop — grab Alice and bolt. I'd still like to, but I know this isn't just about me. "Ty?" I ask. "What do you think?"

He shrugs. "I dunno, maybe Grandma is right. I guess hearing what she has to say can't hurt."

I turn back toward the door. "And you, Tim?"

"I'd like to stay. But I know how hard this must be for you, so whatever you feel is best."

Randy is still staring at Madeline. "I've already been through the McFadden melodrama once," he says sourly, "but if you all want to stay, I can sit and play nice."

I turn reluctantly back to Madeline. "This isn't how I expected this to go, but if you've got something to say, we'll listen."

Madeline seems relieved. "Super. Have a seat. I'll get more tea."

While she's away in the kitchen, I take a minute to call the school and let them know

Alice is safe and sound — and grounded for eternity. When Madeline returns five minutes later, everyone is seated on the chairs and couches in the living room. Madeline is carrying a large ceramic kettle of steaming water, an assortment of cups, and a mixture of green and herbal teas on a large silver serving tray. "Help yourself," she says as she sets the ensemble in the center of the coffee table.

"Madeline," Colleen begins, her voice subdued. "I don't suppose you have any photos?"

Madeline hesitates, then while everyone is choosing their teas, she goes to the bookshelf and retrieves two large photo albums.

"Here," she says, handing one to Tim and the other to Colleen before sitting down gracefully in the vacant chair near Alice. "As I recall, we only sent you one photo of Zoe, from the day she was born."

Colleen's face lights up, even as her lips begin to quiver. Both eyes start filling with water as she reaches quickly into her purse and pulls out her wallet. From a sleeve within the wallet she extracts a small picture of a much younger Madeline in a hospital bed holding an infant, with Nathan beaming at her side. "I've kept it all these years," she says, her emotions wavering. "I look at it all the time. I've always wondered what's become of our little granddaughter."

My mother-in-law's reaction is not what I would have expected, but is nonetheless telling. Amid the devastation of learning about Nathan's secrets, it hasn't occurred to me until right now that all this time she and Tim might have missed their grandchild. Why wouldn't they? Yet I've been so wrapped up in myself, that I've failed to see that the thorn that's been in my side for a couple of days has been festering in their hearts for decades. For me, the pain elicits anger; for them, sadness.

Alice frowns ominously when she sees her father in the photo. She immediately leaves her chair to look over her grandfather's shoulder as he flips from page to page in the album.

"She's beautiful," comments Tim.

"Reminds me of your mother," adds Colleen.

Madeline has a nostalgic sort of look in her eyes. "Thanks," she tells them, then turns to speak to me. "Halley, there's something in that little box on the table — in its drawer — that I want you to see."

I pick up the thing she's pointing at and give the drawer a tug. There is a red rock inside, exactly like the six that Nathan used to carry around. "Where did you get this?" I ask. "Nobody knew about those but me and the kids."

"And me," she replies.

"What is it?" asks Tim.

Madeline and I look at him at the same time, then back at each other. "Can I tell them?" she asks.

I pass the pebble to Tim. "I don't think he'd mind now."

Tim holds it in the palm of his hand for examination. "A rock?"

"Not just any rock," Madeline says. "It was Nathan's special collection. He called them his serving stones. There were seven of them."

"I have the other six right here," says Alice. We all watch as she empties her pockets and shows them to Colleen and Tim.

"Oh, I recognize them now," says Colleen. "Aren't they the ones he found at the beach? The ones he used for his experiment."

"You mean the ones he was tumbling in his pants?" asks Tim. "I warned him it would take hundreds of years for them to get smooth that way. There's not enough friction there to wear them down quickly. But he was determined to prove me wrong."

"He was funny that way," observes Madeline, which earns a quizzical look from Nathan's parents.

Tim is still rolling Madeline's stone in his fingers. "I know he carried them around for quite a while," he says. "Eventually I stopped asking if he was still conducting his experiment. I don't know when he gave up."

There is a long silence, with everyone looking around at everyone else. Eventually I end it. "He didn't," I whisper. "He kept them in his pockets until the day he died."

Tim and Colleen appear equally puzzled. *"Why?"* Colleen asks.

"Because," replies Madeline softly, "the real experiment was never about smoothing the rocks. It was about smoothing himself."

Christy Love Barker
October 28

I know I posted a few days ago, but I keep coming back here reading about all of the lives that have been touched by one man's kindness, and I really want to add another one . . . I hate to admit this, but I am in the middle of a very ugly divorce. Just a few weeks ago I was having a particularly hard day. In the morning one of my best friends dropped off some of my favorite homemade cookies. Then later someone else dropped off a bag of fresh veggies and herbs. And finally, later in the evening, Halley and Nathan dropped off a beautiful bouquet of flowers and one of the nicest notes I have ever received. All of this love shown to me by so many people! The Steens are amazing people, but there are so many good people like them in this community that even though Nathan is gone, I know the love and caring and lifting of others will never die. I, for one, hope to follow their examples by doing as many "good things" as I possibly can.

Like • Comment • Share

Chapter Thirty-Seven

Madeline

I know what I just said is the truth, but I've never really verbalized it like that before. *It was about smoothing himself.* The way Halley is looking at me, I'd say she agrees.

There is continued confusion on the faces of Tim and Colleen. I can't read Randy's expression at all because his face is granite; and because I'm scared to look right at him for fear of the repugnance I'll find in his eyes.

"I don't get it," admits Tim. "So he *wasn't* tumbling them?"

"No, he was. I mean, he loved rocks, just like you, and he was definitely curious to see how many months or years or decades it would take to get them smooth by tumbling them in his pockets. But the primary purpose of the stones was more as a way to tally. Sort of a poor-man's abacus."

"Tally what?" Colleen asks.

I look to Halley, and she answers, "One-good-things."

I give a nod. "Precisely. He wanted to make sure he was doing at least seven good things for others each day."

"That's right," Ty adds. "Dad always started with the stones in his left pocket. By doing an act of service for someone, even if it was something small, he'd move them one at a time to the other pocket. If the right pocket got full, he'd start moving them back in the other direction. At the end of the day he always had a good count of what he'd done."

"What prompted him to do this?" asks Tim. "Was it the object lesson I gave in Sunday School about rocks?"

"I'm sure that played a part," I tell him. "But the driving force was, well . . . *me.*"

"Come again?" says Halley. "He told me he was tired of seeing kids getting picked on, so he concocted this idea in middle school."

"Which is true. But the person he was trying to help the most — at least at first — was me."

"You were picked on in middle school?" asks Alice excitedly.

Before I can give more than a nod, Randy sits up and asks, "Is that why he started be-

437

ing so nice to you all of a sudden at the end of seventh grade?"

I nod at him too, locking eyes with the handsome giant for just a moment. Funny — after all this time, and even though he's now completely bald, he still affects me. I have to look away before he has a chance to read my thoughts. "He read a poem I wrote," I tell everyone. "One that I meant to keep private, which tipped him off about my struggles. I think he felt a little guilty for not having been nicer to me, so, being the fixer that he was, he made up his mind to make me feel noticed. For several weeks Nathan did everything he could to be kind to me. Eventually he realized there might be other people out there who were also falling through the cracks. He worried that without some daily reminder he might overlook them too and they'd end up feeling worthless and alone like me, so he put the little rocks in his pocket as a reminder to be on the lookout." I pause to make sure everyone is following. "Did any of you ever have a prayer rock under your pillow to help remind you to pray as a kid? It was sort of like that. The rocks were his reminders that sometimes people need help, and he was determined to help them, one good thing at a time."

"Well, I'll be danged," says Tim. "My own son discovers what is possibly the world's best use for unpolished pebbles, and I'm the last person to know about it."

"Tied for last," Colleen says.

Halley is being awfully quiet on the other side of the coffee table. Her expression is hard to read. "What are you thinking?" I ask her carefully. "Something's on your mind."

With a long, pouty sigh she says, "Just more of the same. Listening to you for less than five minutes, and I already find myself learning things I thought I knew everything about. Nathan told me about his serving stones back when we were dating, but he never mentioned that they had anything to do with a poem or a girl. It's just one more way in which I didn't know him as well as I thought I did."

Alice is chomping at the bit. "So, back to being picked on. Were you like super smart, and kids teased you because you were light-years ahead of them and they couldn't keep up?"

"Alice," says Halley in a mother's warning tone.

"What?" the younger Steen replies. "I want to know."

"Actually," I tell them both, "being picked

on is directly connected with what I wanted to tell you. It's why I brought up his stones. You see, Nathan went to great lengths to protect me from adolescent bullies because he thought that's what my poem was all about. He didn't learn until much later that the poem was more about my home life than my school life."

That gets everyone's attention, as I knew it would. Randy, Tim, and Colleen, who probably thought they knew everything about my childhood, are particularly focused on me now.

"What are you saying, Maddy?" asks Randy.

I try to smile at him, but I can't. Not when I'm about to shed a small ray of light on the black hole of my past. "I'm saying . . ." There's got to be an easier way to ease into this conversation. I turn to Tim and Colleen. "Do you remember what Grant was struggling with at the time Nathan and I got married? Why we took Eliza in with us?"

They both nod. "Alcohol," says Tim.

"And drugs, as I recall," adds Colleen.

"Mr. McF was an alcoholic?" Randy says, his voice plagued with doubt, and maybe a little disdain.

"He hid it well. It wasn't all the time, either. Usually just weekend binges. He started drinking sometime after my mother was killed, and it escalated over time."

"Your mom was killed?" asks Ty.

"Yes," I reply, "when I was in fifth grade. So I know how hard it must be for you and Alice right now. Losing a parent is awful. When my mother passed, I was left with my stepfather, Grant. All in all, he was a good man who took really good care of us — most of the time. But when he got drunk, well . . . let's just say he had a mean streak. When your father read my poem in seventh grade about getting beat up, he thought I meant by other kids. The kids hurt me with their words." I have to divert my eyes to the floor. "Grant was the only one who used fists."

"Grant?" says Tim instantly, sounding horrified. "*Really?* Oh, I'm so sorry, Maddy. Why didn't you say anything to me about it?"

"Or me?" asks Randy.

"I could have helped," Tim adds.

"I was a kid," I tell them with a shrug. "At the time, I worried that they'd break up our family. After losing my mom, the thought of losing my sister — and even Grant, as weird as that may sound — seemed like a worse fate than enduring it. Of course he always felt terrible after giving me a bruise or a bloody lip, and he'd swear up and down he'd never do it again, and somehow I'd believe him. That just became our pattern."

"That's awful," Colleen blurts out. "Truly awful."

No kidding. And you don't even know the half of it. Trust me, there are "awfuler" things to go through.

Halley has another concerned look on her face. "Madeline," she says, "you said you were going to put the situation between you and Nathan in a new light, that we might better appreciate how he 'saved you' growing up. Is this how? He saved you from being hit?"

Before I respond, the words of my promise to Nathan ring out like a bell in my head, reminding me that I still owe him the courtesy of keeping our secret.

If you need me to never tell anyone about this, then I won't. Nobody will ever know, Nathan. If this is what you want, then it'll be my one good thing for you.

I glance around the room at the faces of these people who so dearly cared for him. Would he want them to know now, or would he prefer that I keep up the charade?

A promise is a promise.

I nod my head twice. "My stepfather was

drunk on prom night, and he was there waiting for us when Nathan dropped me off. I'd never seen him so out of sorts. He took a swipe at me while we were all there on our front porch. Nathan fought back, though, gave him a few good licks and then shoved him back in the house. I was scared to death, so Nathan took me back in the limo and said I couldn't go home until we were sure it was safe."

Randy stands up, running a hand over his smooth head. His face is quickly changing from white, to pink, to red. "Oh, for crying out loud. So instead of going to the police, or coming to me, or telling the Steens, or doing anything even remotely productive, you two geniuses piled back in the limo to wait it out?"

I don't dare point out that our imaginary trip to the limousine, was, in fact, productive. At least in the version they all know about.

"I was scared," I tell him. "You don't know what it was like for me. I didn't want anyone to know that I was his punching bag, Randy. Especially you, because I was afraid if you knew that, you might really want to hurt him."

"And I would have! Anyone who hits kids — especially grown men hitting girls —

deserves to be taught a lesson."

"But I wasn't ready for him to learn that lesson, because I didn't have anyone else to be a parent to me. He's all I had."

"So Nathan agreed to not tell that you were getting beat up at home?" Tim asks. "I'd have thought he had more sense than that."

This isn't going well. They're going to see right through me. I know I've told plenty of lies in the past to hide what Grant did to me, but I'm breaking new ground here. Nathan was more adept at winging it than me . . . I wish he were here to tell me what to say. I wish I could just tell them all what really happened.

But a promise is a promise . . .

"He couldn't," I say. I can hear the panic in my own voice.

"Why the heck not?" demands Randy.

Why indeed? Where does the lie go from here? "Because . . . I . . ." *Think, Madeline! And make it good.* "Because I seduced him!"

Oh, no . . . did I just say that?

The whole room freezes. Mouths are hanging open, eyes are bulging, no one is breathing. Ty and Alice seem particularly shocked. What was I thinking, blurting out something like that in front of Nathan's children?

Too late to take it back now.

"It was so wrong of me, I know. Believe me. But I was scared. So I did the only thing I could think of, which turned out to be the cruelest thing imaginable. I seduced him, in the limo. Then I told him if he ever mentioned anything about Grant's drinking or his punching, that I'd go straight to Pastor Steen and tell him what we did."

"That's not true," protests Alice, which catches me by surprise.

"Sadly," I reply, "it is. To my everlasting shame."

There is more silence. And blank stares. Oh, how I hate lying. Ever since I found out I was pregnant, it's been one story after another. In the beginning, we lied to cover up the fact that I was a victim. Then we lied to cover our lies. And now the deceit has come full circle — instead of the victim, I'm presenting myself as the predator, who willfully took advantage of Nathan so I could manipulate him.

"Well, that certainly sheds new light on the past," says Halley softly.

"Straight from the red-light district," mumbles Randy.

"But it doesn't change the fact that Nathan lied to me," Halley continues, "and kept things from me, our entire marriage.

All it does is point out that he was a poor judge of character when it came to choosing friends."

Can't disagree with that.

Halley picks up her purse in a whirlwind. "C'mon, kids, it's time to go. I've heard more than I wanted. Madeline, thank you for leaving work today and for taking care of Alice until we could get here. We'll let ourselves out."

I take another quick glance around the room. Randy looks the most disgusted. His face is just as I remember it from the first time I put him through something like this. He walks to the door, shaking his head. Tim and Colleen look like they're trying to fit these new pieces of information into a puzzle they thought they'd already solved. They also appear betrayed. I know they've always cared for me like the daughter-in-law I once was to them; now I'm sure they're second-guessing their affections. Ty seems strangely relieved. Then there is Alice. She is the only one still staring at me, her round eyes oozing disappointment.

When I match her gaze, she starts to tear up. "Why?" she asks pointedly. "What are you hiding?"

Her question catches me off guard. How could she know I'm hiding anything?

"C'mon, Al," Halley urges. "Let's go."

Alice remains focused on me, not budging an inch, her voice rising. "Why are you lying?"

"Alice," warns her mother.

"She's lying, Mom."

"Alice! Stop this right now." Halley marches to her daughter's side and begins dragging her by the arm to the door.

My heart is breaking.

"Tell her!" Alice cries as she's being pulled across the room. "Just tell her the truth, Mrs. Zuckerman! *Please.*"

I don't know how a seventh-grader knows I'm lying, but I do know that the look on her face and the sound of her voice is killing me. Is this what Nathan would have wanted? That our lies tear his family to pieces? If he knew they knew the lie, would he want them to know the truth instead? The *real* truth.

Alice reaches into her pocket with her free hand and pulls out all of the red stones. "Here," she pleads, holding them out, "do one good thing for all of us, and tell my family the truth!"

Halley is beyond upset now. "You think you were in trouble for skipping school?" she hisses. "Oh, just you wait, young lady. Your behavior here just *doubled* your punishment."

No. This isn't what Nathan would have wanted. It can't be. The lying has to end now, or it never will. But for promises born of pride and embarrassment, the excuses are all gone.

Grant is gone.

Nathan is gone.

My mind is firing a thousand thoughts a second, but the only one that reaches my mouth comes out as a barely audible whisper. *"How did you know?"*

The front door closes before my words reach their ears.

The Steens are gone, the moment is passed, and the truth remains lodged, however cruelly, in my heart alone.

Sue Cochrun
October 28
When we'd go out for lunch at work, Nathan would often end up paying for us before we even knew it. Never to flaunt, just to be nice.

Like • Comment • Share

Sue Cochrun
October 28
By the way, don't you love it when you

have 5 things in your basket at the grocery store and the person in front of you has a full cart, and they let you go first? Nathan was that sort of a person — always putting people ahead of himself, and never acting inconvenienced by it.

Like • Comment • Share

Sue Cochrun
October 28
Oh, Halley, one thing just for you: If you're reading these posts, please know that our prayers are with you and the kids. I heard someone say recently that God won't protect you from what He can perfect you through. I believe that with all my heart. God loves you enough to let you learn and grow through this trial. I know what you're going through is tough, but we're all here to help you.

Like • Comment • Share

CHAPTER THIRTY-EIGHT

Halley

It's Tuesday morning at Velvet Petals, and things are falling to pieces. In addition to aged petals dropping left and right, I'm late on orders, customers have left nasty messages on the machine wondering why their arrangements didn't get delivered yesterday, my window displays are wilting, and to top it all off, Alice's shenanigans downtown made me miss my weekly delivery of fresh flowers yesterday, so my inventory of sellable product is at an all-time low.

In some ways, though, I'm thankful for the mess at work, because it temporarily takes my thoughts off of everything else that's happened recently. Given how Madeline used my husband, I know I should be a little more forgiving of him, but little things keep cropping up throughout the day, reminding me that my heart still feels betrayed. For instance, just before noon a man calls and orders red roses to be delivered to his wife for their anniversary. It's a benign enough request, but it gets me thinking about Nathan. "Is this your first marriage?" I inquire.

"Sure is."

"Really? Or are you just saying that?"

"Excuse me?"

"Oh . . . never mind."

A little while later a woman orders a bouquet for her daughter who is in the hospital delivering a baby girl. "Her first?" I ask.

"As a matter of fact, it is!" she says. The excitement in her voice makes me think this is a newbie grandmother too. "She and her husband have only been married a little over a year, but they didn't want to wait."

"That's wonderful. Does her husband have any other children?"

"What?"

"Oh, sorry. I meant, is there any chance that your son-in-law has a previous wife or kids that your daughter doesn't know about?"

The next thing I hear is the click of the woman hanging up.

As I set the phone back in its cradle, I tell myself I should laugh at what I just told that lady, but instead I become frustrated.

"I can't do this!" I shout at myself, not realizing a customer has slipped through the front door when I wasn't looking.

"Can't do what, dear?"

I nearly jump out of my skin at the surprise question, until I realize it is just old Mary Lou, one of my regulars, come to purchase her weekly carnation.

I doubt she knows that my husband recently passed; I can't even be sure she knows who Nathan was. The way she's smiling, I figure there's no sense in telling her my bad news. "Sorry, Mary Lou," I say awkwardly. "Just whining, I guess."

She scrunches up her wrinkled nose at me. "Hogwash. I heard what you said on the phone. Sounds to me like you've got man troubles."

"Good guess."

"Oh, we've all been there, dear. Some of us more than others. Sorry for prying, but was it your husband?"

"Yes."

"What did he do?"

He died. "Lied to me."

"A big lie, or a little one?"

"Big enough."

She shrugs her hunched shoulders and says, "Well, he's not the first man to make a mistake. And he won't be the last. Go figure, men are human. Women too, I'm told."

That's not really what I want to hear.

Mary Lou shuffles over to the carnation bucket and pulls out a long pink one. "Back when me and George were first married, he did something that got me so upset I couldn't see straight." She pauses to think. "Huh. It's been so long, I can't even 'member what it was. After sleeping on the couch a couple nights, though, he went out and bought me a carnation as a peace offering. From then on, he bought me a new carnation every week, replacing the old one with the new one — said he was sure he'd make another mistake sooner or later, so he always wanted to have a fresh one handy." She smiles happily as she scoots to the register. "Oh, that George. He never missed a week."

I hate to even ask, but I can't help myself. "Is George . . . deceased?"

Her smile dims slightly. "Not yet, though I think it won't be long. He had a stroke five years back, and his health hasn't been well since. Can't walk. Talks funny. Hardly gets out of bed anymore. But he still wants that carnation there every week, even if I have to get it myself. He says it's my reminder that he loves me, and that I love him back, warts and all." She hands me the flower and pulls out her purse. "That's what you have to ask yourself. *Does he love you?* And if he does, well, then is that enough to forgive him and love him back?"

She's standing there on the other side of the register with her hand out, waiting for me to take her money.

"This one's on me," I say.

Mary Lou winks at me and smiles. "Thank you, dear. See you again next week." She shuffles to the door, but turns back before leaving, pointing to my bucket of long-stemmed carnations near the door. "There's plenty there for a peace offering, if your husband likes flowers." She winks again and then heads out into the afternoon sun.

The rest of the workday passes more slowly. My conversation with Mary Lou keeps circulating through my thoughts. By the time I close up and prepare for my evening deliveries, I'm more conflicted than ever. As I think of Mary Lou and her longtime husband, George, I wonder what would have happened with Nathan and me had he not passed away. Would we have stayed together as long as they have? What if he eventually decided to tell me about his first marriage and his other daughter, Zoe? Would I have forgiven him? Would we have worked it out, or would deceit of that magnitude have put an end to everything we had?

After finishing my deliveries, I drive around town for another thirty minutes, wanting more time alone to sort out my thoughts. Not by coincidence, I eventually end up at the cemetery where Nathan is buried. I don't have a flashlight, but the moon is full, and the path to his gravesite is easy to find.

When I approach, the moonlight illuminates the inscription on his grave marker. I already know what it says, but I whisper the words anyway, weighing their accuracy against the evidence of the past week. "Nathan Steen. Devout husband and loving father. A friend to all. A rock of a man."

In my hand I hold a fistful of pink and red carnations. It's unusually chilly outside, so as I begin to cry, I can feel the warmth of my own tears against my cold skin. "An old woman told me you might like these." I'm staring at the grave, but speaking to the entire universe, hoping Nathan can hear. I wait for a second, thinking maybe I need to give the words time to sink into the dirt. "To her, they mean 'I forgive.' To me . . . I think they mean 'I'm sorry.' "

I try to smile, because I know Nathan

would appreciate it. Then I lay the flowers down against the headstone. "I know what you're thinking. *Why is she sorry?* Well, for starters, I'm sorry I was mad at you for leaving us. I was hurt, thinking you'd somehow put helping others above your own family. Silly, I know. I know deep down it wasn't like that. I'm sure if you thought there was real danger, you'd have done something different. And how can I fault you for helping someone? I would have expected nothing less. And I'm doing my best to trust what you told me the night before you died. *When God says your time is up, your time is up.* It must've been your time."

The wind picks up, rustling the trees around me. In my mind, the whispering breeze is the universe answering back. *I'm sorry, too,* it says. *And I miss you.*

My tears pick up as the wind dies down. "I'm also sorry," I continue, "for doubting your devotion. I never questioned your faithfulness when you were alive, but once you were gone . . . the things I read and heard . . . it was hard not to. But no more. I know in my heart of hearts there was nothing going on between you and Madeline while we were married. Not beyond the e-mails, anyway. I've really struggled to understand why you wouldn't have been more forthcoming about your past, but I believe you must have had your reasons. So while I'm left to wonder, I want you to know I've resigned myself to trust that you knew what you were doing."

I wipe my face on the sleeve of my sweater. "And finally, I'm sorry for how I behaved in front of the kids. I should have been more discrete with the information about Madeline. If I've undermined their love for you in any way, I apologize. You deserved better than that from me."

The evening air is calm for a moment. In the still darkness, I read the bottommost text inscribed on Nathan's grave — his favorite Scripture. " 'And, behold, one came and said unto him, Good Master, what good thing shall I do, that I may have eternal life?' Somewhere along the line, I'm sure you did your good thing, dear. Day after day, week after week, you did your good thing a thousand times over."

The wind picks up again, blowing my hair across my face. I tuck it behind my ear and open up my purse. There's a small drawstring pouch in there, filled with the rocks he carried around in his pocket for so long. I dump them in my hand, and then, one by one, I set them down at the base of the gravestone, spacing them out evenly from left to right. "I think it's only fitting that you continue to carry these."

I wait until the breeze dies down, for fear that it will carry away my parting words before my husband hears them. Wiping away a final flurry of tears, I whisper, "You were always my rock, Nathan . . . and always will be."

"You're home late," Ty says as I walk through the door. "Tough night of deliveries?"

The toughest delivery I've ever had to make. "You could say that." I set my purse down on an end table near where Ty is sitting. He's watching a recorded episode of *Modern Family;* he pauses it when I ask where Alice is.

"Heck if I know. Probably writing on her blog."

"How about Grandma and Grandpa?"

"Grandma's upstairs. I think I heard her taking a bath. Last time I saw Grandpa, he was heading into the garage."

"Will you get them?"

Ty looks at the paused television, then back at me. "Right now?"

"Uh-huh."

"All of them?"

"Yes."

He checks his watch and then tosses the remote on the couch. "Fine."

Three minutes later, everyone is assembled in the living room. Colleen has her hair wrapped in a towel. Alice is in her pajamas. Tim has a smudge of black grease on his forehead, and Ty is wearing a scowl.

"Why are we here?" Ty asks before I can thank them all for gathering.

"To start over," I tell him.

Alice tucks her feet under her rear. "Start what over?"

"Everything," I quip. "We're going to rewind to the day of the funeral and just start fresh. New attitudes, new love in our home, and old memories about Dad that we can make new again too."

Colleen tilts her head and smiles as she grabs hold of her husband's hand.

"Why?" asks Ty.

Excellent question. "Why not?"

He gives me his "duh" look and says, "Because we can't go back in time and magically erase what we already know about Dad."

"So you believe me, Mom?" asks Alice hopefully. "That Mrs. Zuckerman is lying?"

"I'm sorry, Al," I tell her gently. "I would love to believe that, but I have to be honest with myself that there were things about your father that none of us would have expected. Things none of us wanted to be true, even if those things weren't entirely his fault, as we learned yesterday. Regardless, a very wise customer reminded me today that sometimes we need to be forgiven, and other times we need to forgive. Either way, this is one of those times."

"That's a very commendable perspective," says Tim. "I agree completely."

"So what, that's it? We just forget and move on?" Ty is looking around at everyone, but I know his question is for me.

I get up from my seat, taking my purse with me, and sit next to him on the couch. "No, but close. We *forgive* and move on. Forgetting may be more difficult. What I want to remember is the man we all knew and loved, not the stories that had nothing to do with us. Was he perfect? No. Did he do a lot of great things? Of course, and that's what I'll focus on. I don't want to waste more time getting worked up over something that occurred so long ago." I pause, trying to read my kids' faces. Alice seems pleased; Ty is more reserved. "I'm not saying you have to think or feel like me — you don't. You're both old enough to make up your own minds about this. But I at least wanted you all to know how *I* feel, and how I've decided to respond from here on out."

"I always said Nathan married up," whispers Colleen to her husband.

"There's just one more thing," I tell Alice and Ty. "I brought something home for you from my store."

Ty rolls his eyes. "Let me guess. Flowers?"

"Not quite," I reply as I unzip my purse and pull out three small ziplock bags. "Though I do occasionally use these as decorative accents in my bouquets." I hand each child a bag, keeping the third for myself.

"Rocks!" says Alice. "Like Dad's!" The ones I picked out for her are all a common shade of pink. Ty's are a bluish green. Mine are red, like Nathan's.

"I returned your father's serving stones today. But I thought he might like it if we carried on his tradition. There are seven stones for each of you. Again, you don't have to do anything if you don't want to, but I've decided this will be my way to help me remember the best parts of my husband. It'll be my 'one good thing' for him, for the rest of my life."

"I love it!" Alice exclaims. "I'm going to do it too. Even if the kids at school don't like me, I'm going to try to find ways to be

461

kind to them."

I place a hand on Ty's knee. "How about you?"

He's got the plastic bag up near his face, quietly studying the individual pebbles. It takes him a while, but finally he frowns and stands up. "I . . . don't think I can," he mumbles as he heads for the stairs.

Jackie Ward
October 28
After 31 years as a legal assistant, I decided to retire on 12/1/2011. My only regret as the date neared was that Nathan, my boss, and his wife, Halley, who I've grown very fond of since Nathan joined our firm, would not be there for my going-away party, because they were traveling for their anniversary. Without telling anyone, they decided to cut their trip short so they could be there for my life-event. I was incredibly touched by their choosing to do that for me. Everyone says the reason work is fun is the people you meet, and that couldn't be more true of Nathan.

Like • Comment • Share

Chapter Thirty-Nine

Ty

I'm lying on my back on the floor in the center of my room, tossing a football up at the ceiling, when I hear the door knock.

"Anybody home?" It's Grandpa.

"You can come in."

"I'm not disturbing anything important, am I?" he asks as he pokes his head in.

"Just thinking."

He sits down on the chair in front of my desk. "I bet. You've had quite a bit to think about recently."

"Yep."

He doesn't speak for a while, just watches as I continue throwing the ball. Finally he says, "You know, I'm leaving pretty early tomorrow. Flight takes off at seven."

"Yeah, I heard."

"Well, before I go, there was something I wanted to show you downstairs. You got a second?"

When the ball comes down again, I grip it tight, and then toss it to Grandpa with a sigh. "Sure. Why not."

He leads me down to the garage, where a motorized coffee can is doing circles on Dad's work bench.

"What is it?" I ask, even though I already have a good idea.

"A tumbler," he says proudly. "Brand-new. Picked it up while you were at school." He takes a moment to watch it spin. "I guess your mom and I were thinking along the same lines today with the rocks." He chuckles. "Of course, this here'll wear down stone a heckuva lot faster than bouncing it around in your pocket."

"Why'd you get it?"

A mischievous smile splits his face. "What's that you told me last week over flapjacks? Oh, yeah — I'll answer your question if you answer one of mine first."

I'm not sure I really want to, but I reluctantly play along. "Fine. One question."

Grandpa pulls out a stool from beneath the bench and sits down. "Why'd you really quit the team?"

"I already told you. I don't want to play if my dad can't be there to watch."

His response is immediate. "I know that's what you said, but I don't buy it."

464

"Why not?"

"Because since you were a little boy, every time I've come to visit, you've got a football in your hands. And every time I turn around, you're tossing it here or there. You love the game, and losing a father wouldn't change that."

I pull out the other stool. As I sit, I touch a finger to the outside of the can, feeling the metal spin beneath my finger. "It seemed like the easiest way to cut myself free from all of the expectations," I say, still staring at my finger on the can.

"What expectations?"

The question makes me laugh. "*All of them.* No matter what I do, I'm destined to disappoint someone. So why bother?"

To get my attention, he turns off the power to the tumbler. The motor whines to a halt. "Explain."

"There's not much to explain. I'm just never quite as good as everyone wants me to be. I mean, my grades, for example. Sure, they're decent. But not top of my class. Dad and Mom were both straight-A students. Alice, too. I swear that kid's a genius. I've always hated getting report cards, because I knew there'd be a hint of disappointment on my dad's face."

"Did you ever tell him you felt that way?"

"No. What good would it do, other than to make the disappointment official?"

Grandpa has a look of consternation. "What about football? Aren't you the best on the team?"

That makes me chuckle too. "Only when we win. But when we don't, I'm suddenly the guy who wasn't quite good enough — not enough complete passes, not enough heat on the ball, or the one who threw a dumb interception. I hate letting everyone down."

He nods. "Is that all? Grades and football?"

I should probably quit talking. I've already said more than enough, but I seem to be on a roll. I shake my head and then reach into my pocket and pull out the bluish green rocks Mom gave me, still in their baggie. "There's this."

"You just got those today," he says quizzically. "How can there be any expectations there?"

Now, for the first time during our conversation, I look up and meet his gaze head-on. "I'm Nathan Steen's son. Do you know what that means? It means half the people in this town know what a 'swell' guy he was, and they expect me to be exactly like him. For me, it's actually been kind of a relief finding out recently that he isn't — wasn't — perfect. But the whole world still thinks he was this hero-do-gooder. Just look at his Facebook page. It's ridiculous the number of people he helped. And now he's a martyr, too — he saved a guy named Jesus, for crying out loud. How can I live up to that? My whole life I've tried to be like him, because I really did admire him. But sometimes I wondered if I was trying to be nice to people because I wanted to help them, or because I wanted to please him."

"I see."

"Now tonight Mom hands me this bag of rocks, and the writing is on the wall. She expects me to be the same do-gooder that he was. I'm supposed to just step in and fill his shoes. But I don't think I have it in me. I mean, look how I treated Alice after that football game, and that's my own sister!"

Grandpa is quiet for a long time; pondering, watching me. Eventually I get tired of the silence. "So? Why'd you buy the tumbler?"

He immediately reaches into his pocket and pulls out a large, jagged rock. Its size is equal to my seven pebbles combined. "For you," he says as he opens the tumbler lid, tosses the rock inside, and turns the contraption back on. "For this. To see how much work and time it takes to smooth out rough edges."

"Okay?" I say, not really understanding.

"Look, the tumbler is just an accelerator, right? Take that big rock I put in there — eventually natural forces would chip away at its rough spots. Eons from now it would look much different. Smoother. More polished. Its inner beauty might also become more apparent. The tumbler just speeds up that process."

"So why is that important to me?" I ask.

He smiles, casually placing a finger on the turning can, just as I'd done earlier. "Because like it or not, you're being tumbled, so you might as well understand the process — embrace it — if you can. Life is the great tumbler, Ty, and we're the rocks."

"How am I being tumbled?"

He raises his eyebrows as if I should know. "Through trials, mostly. By experiencing things that seem too hard to endure. Sickness, disease, hunger, and natural disasters all come to mind." He pauses. "Or losing a loved father."

"Or losing a son," I point out.

"Yes," he replies with a sigh. "Or losing a son. And those are just the big things. There are also a host of smaller challenges that we face every day. As we work through them, we are further refined — little by little, chiseled into something better."

"Like what challenges?"

"Oh, it's different for everyone," he says. "Tailored to their circumstances. But everyone has them." He pauses again, removing his finger from the can. "If I look at Alice, for example, I think you'd agree she struggles with her height, which no doubt affects self-esteem. And of course, constantly being picked on can't be easy."

"And me?"

He gives me a knowing smile. "I think you already identified your challenges, Ty. From what you said, it sounds like you struggle with expectations, real or perceived."

"Oh they're real, Grandpa. Trust me. And the older I get, the more the expectations grow."

"Okay. So maybe the expectations are there. Can you do anything about them?"

"Yeah, I already did. If I don't play football, there's no way to fail. No expectations." I hold up the bag of rocks from my mom. "And if I don't do anything to help others, nobody will expect me to be like my dad, either."

"What about school? Are you just going to give up on that, too? You can't get perfect grades like your sister, so you're just going to flunk out to remove the pressure?"

"No, that would be stupid. I still want to go to college."

"Exactly. If you withdraw from everything that's hard, it's like you're trying to remove your rock from the tumbler. But even if you thought you could avoid life's refining process, you can't. When we face the challenges head-on, when we embrace them and just do our best, that's when we really start to notice a difference in ourselves. That's when we become smooth quickly. But when we avoid them, all we're doing is slowing down the motor for a while. Natural forces will still wear on us, but in a different way, and perhaps not as much to our benefit."

"Like how?"

"Well, say you really did shy away from doing your best in school and you flunked out. That would prevent you from getting a college education, maybe keep you from a good job, and then the tumbler of life would just start chipping away at you in other ways. It's unavoidable. But that's life. The best we can do is to do our best."

I think about that for a second. "So you think I should rejoin the team?"

"What do you think?"

I give a shrug. "It'd still be weird not having Dad there."

He smiles. "The first play-off game is in a week and a half, right?"

I nod.

"Well then, not to add any pressure, but I was thinking, I haven't spent enough time with you kids over the years, and I'd like to change that. So that day, whether you decide to play or not, I'm going to fly back out here. I know I can't replace your father, but I'd sure love to see you there under the stadium lights."

I can feel the pressure mounting already. "I'll think about it," I say. "But no promises."

Grinning, he says, "Fair enough. And what about those rocks there? You planning on doing anything with them?"

I think back for a moment to all of the kids in school who I know could use a friend. Can I be that person for them? There are so many of them . . . how can I possibly help them all? "I don't know," I reply. "I'm still not sure I can."

"Well, think about that, too. But if you decide you want to carry the torch your dad lit, don't do it because you think that's the expectation. Do it because you want to, at your own pace."

I watch the tumbling can for a moment, listening to the steady thump of the large rock going around and around. "How did he do it?" I ask. "How did he help so many people?"

"The only way you can," comes the gentle reply. "One person at a time."

Lyndsie Beal Burgener
October 28
I had carpal tunnel surgery done on both hands at the same time. My cousin, Nathan, drove over three hours with his family just to cheer me up. He brought treats, his wife made a beautiful flower arrangement, and the kids sat and watched movies with me and made me laugh. That meant the world.

Like • Comment • Share

CHAPTER FORTY

Halley

I've just stuck my little red serving stones in my pocket for the first time. I'm standing in front of the entryway mirror, checking my profile to see if they are noticeable. At the same time I'm wondering how I'm going to help seven different people tomorrow. "It doesn't have to be big," I quietly remind myself. I love helping people anyway. I can do this.

While I'm standing there looking at myself, Ty and Tim come in from the garage. "You look good, Mom," says Ty. "In case you were wondering." He sounds like he means it.

"Wow, an unsolicited compliment from my teenage son. Will wonders never cease?"

"Hey . . . I mean . . . you're looking at yourself," he backpedals, "so I thought you'd want to know."

"No, no, I'll take it. And thank you." I

473

wink at him. "Feel free to pass a pebble to the other pocket."

He rolls his eyes. "No thanks."

Right then, the doorbell rings. I'm standing so close to it that it makes me jump. Tim and Ty both watch as I go to the door and look through the peephole. When I see who it is, my stomach sinks. I quickly turn around and whisper, "It's Madeline Zuckerman! What do I do?"

"Tell her to go away," says Ty.

"No," remarks Tim, "open the door and see what she wants."

"But I don't want to talk to her."

Tim chuckles. "I'm sure she knows we're here. Would you prefer we turn off the lights and hope she goes away?"

"Yes, actually. That'd be fine." But I know I can't do that. I take a deep breath, turn around, and open the door. "Oh, hello, Madeline. What a . . . surprise."

She has tearstains on her cheeks, but is otherwise composed. "I've been driving around your block for half an hour," she says. "I'd convinced myself that nothing more needed to be said. But somehow . . . I can't . . . so I . . . just had to stop by to see Alice."

"Alice? Why?"

Colleen and Alice were in the kitchen, but

must have come to see who rang the bell, because suddenly they are both there.

"Alice!" Madeline says, her cheeks flushed. She looks like she might start crying again. "There you are!" She takes a step inside the door, not minding that I wasn't planning to invite her in. "How did you know? I know you do, but I don't know how. Nobody else in the world knew, so you have to tell me what gave it away?"

A wide grin spreads across my daughter's face. Maybe I can't read her exact thoughts, but I can certainly tell by her expression what she's feeling: *vindication.*

"The baby book you showed us," Alice tells Madeline as the rest of us try to figure out what's going on. "It was right there on page three."

"Gave what away?" I ask.

"The truth," says a very broken Madeline Zuckerman. "About Nathan. Your husband was many wonderful things to me, Halley — a friend, a competitor, a protector, and a confidant. But there is at least one thing he wasn't — *the father of my child.*"

There is a collective gasp in the room, but not from me. Maybe I should be more surprised, but after what she told us yesterday, I'm inclined to view her as a manipulator. And I don't want to be manipulated.

"Are you sure?" I ask skeptically, "Or, is this just a convenient way to play with our emotions?"

"I'm done lying," she replies adamantly. Then, almost to herself, she adds, "I'm tired of lying."

"It's the truth, Mom," says Alice. "And I can prove it."

"Please," continues Madeline, "may I come in for a bit? I have a lot of explaining to do." She looks up at Tim and Colleen, who are completely beside themselves. "To all of you . . ."

Sheryl Mehary
October 28

Nathan and his son, Ty, gave up their Saturday morning to clean my carpets for me. They rented the carpet shampooer, finished the vacuuming I hadn't been able to finish, and helped me move the last few things out of the living room and hallway. I have a heart condition and could never have done it all by myself. It made a huge difference in the appearance of my apartment and gave a great lift to my spirits to have it all finished.

Like • Comment • Share

CHAPTER FORTY-ONE

MY OWN LITTLE WONDERLAND:
October 29th

Dear Blog, it's me, Alice.
Ha, ha, and triple ha! I was right!! My dad is exactly who he said he was. Not a liar, not a cheater, and not anyone's father but mine! Okay, and Ty's . . . but mostly mine.☺

I skipped school yesterday to track down his "first wife" (btw — bad idea skipping school; I'm now grounded until New Year's), because I didn't believe what I was hearing. I know it all could have been true, but it just didn't sound like the dad I knew. Either way, I had to find out for myself.

Anyway, long story short, my whole family eventually showed up while I was

477

visiting with this woman, Madeline. Once they were there she told us this sob story about her past [note: it really was a sob story . . . no laughing matter at all], but still stuck to her claim that my dad was the father of her child (which would make her my older half sister). Yeah, total soap opera. BUT . . . and this is a big but . . . she handed out some scrapbooks of her daughter from when she was a little girl, so my grandparents could see their supposed granddaughter, and that's what tipped me off that she really was lying.

I was looking over my grandpa's shoulder, and on the third page of the album there was a certificate from the hospital that listed her baby's blood type as O. At first I really didn't think anything of it, but as Madeline was telling us her story, something about that O kept tickling my brain. Then right before we left I remembered my genotype project from 6th grade, where I had to map my whole family's blood types back three generations, and I was pretty sure my dad said he had type AB blood. Why is that important? Duh . . . AB *always* masks O! There's no way any of my father's children could have type O blood! So all day yesterday after we got home, and then again today after school, I was trying to find some scrap of evidence around the house to show what blood type Dad had. I even asked his parents but they couldn't remember. Then . . . *voila!* . . . Madeline showed up tonight and confessed to the whole thing!

It's so sad, really. The truth, I mean. It turns out that when she got pregnant she was actually in love with my dad's best friend, Coach Rawlins . . . but he wasn't the baby's father either. I won't go into all the gory details, because it's really just . . . *yuck.* Needless to say, I'm more grateful than ever to have two wonderful parents who love me and would never hurt me, even if one of them is gone now.

After Madeline left tonight, I think Grandma and Grandpa were struggling to wrap their heads around it. Everything they thought was true about their son turned out to be completely false. Dad only took the blame to protect his friend from an awful situation, which is pretty awesome if you ask me. I think Mom and Ty were proud too. Grandma and Grandpa agreed that his motives were noble, they just wish it hadn't taken so long for the truth to come to light.

Madeline admitted that she should have done things differently. Her exact words were, "The lie removed the weight of the situation for a brief moment, but eventually it grew to be much heavier than the original consequences of telling the truth." I get what she means, and I'm sure she's right, but it doesn't change the fact that my dad's intentions were good. He was just doing what he always did — one good thing.

The other cool thing is what Madeline said when Mom asked why Dad never mentioned being married before. "Because," she explained, "we were never married. We got the paperwork signed, but when we went to the courthouse I couldn't go through with it. We pretended to be married for the sake of the situation, but never actually tied the knot. It made it that much simpler when we got 'divorced' — all we had to do was say good-bye at the airport. If he'd told you he had a child and was previously married, that would have been a giant lie too, even though everyone thought it was the truth, and the last thing he wanted to do was lie to his wife. So he decided to say nothing about any of it, and asked his parents not to mention the past either."

The coolest thing of all, though, was that Madeline's Facebook comment was right all along: Without taking any credit for it, he'd quietly saved her Life; her and her daughter Zoe.

I think I'll sleep much easier tonight. Mom will too. Grandma and Grandpa still have a lot to sort through, but I think they are mostly relieved by what they have learned. The last thing Grandpa said as we were heading up to bed was, "He was exactly who we raised him to be."

"No," Grandma said, "he was much more than that."

So that's it. It's getting late so I've got to wrap this up. Until next time, this is Alice Steen . . . Nathan Steen's ONLY daughter, and his youngest rolling stone.

Billy Ray Porter
October 29

Y'all don't know me, but I work at a gas station in Mesquite. I heard word that Nathan Steen passed, and I have to say, I'm real sorry to hear that. There's been all this buzz about his "One Good Things" I keep hearing folks talk about it when they come in to fill up, so I had to check out this Facebook site for myself. Well, dang, you know what? I always figured me and him were pals, because we hit it off real good. He was always as friendly as can be when he came in for gas. How many of you know the first name of the guy at the gas station without looking at the tag on his shirt? Not many, I bet. Well, now I'm wondering if he was nice because he liked me, or if it was him just being nice because that's how he was. Seems like he treated everyone the same way he treated me. I don't know if I should feel disappointed for not being his closest buddy, or if I should feel lucky that I had the chance to cross paths with him at all. Lucky, I suppose. He was a great guy, and I'm gonna miss seeing him at the store. Oh, and hey, he did do a couple good things for me, like tipping me real well now and then — for what I don't even know. The best thing he did, though, was just talking to me like we were equals. I knew he had a big-shot job and all that, but he didn't treat me any less than an equal. Man, I appreciated that.

Like • Comment • Share

CHAPTER FORTY-TWO

Ty

"Got a minute?" I'm standing in the doorway of Coach Rawlins's office. School just let out for the day, so the locker room behind me is starting to fill up with guys getting changed into their football gear.

He looks up from his notepad. "Hey, Ty. Sure, come on in." After the door closes he asks, "This isn't about Monday, is it?"

"Partly."

"Ah. Look, I'm sorry if I made things a little uncomfortable there at Madeline's. What happened with her and your dad has always been a bit of a hot button for me."

I take a seat across the desk from him. "You liked her, didn't you?"

"Did your grandparents tell you that?"

"No." Madeline did, but I don't want him to know that. "But I don't think you'd get so bent out of shape about it unless you really liked her."

With a shrug, he replies, "I thought I did. Once upon a time. But hey, that's ancient history. Is that what you wanted to discuss?"

"Not exactly. I guess I just wanted to apologize, on my dad's behalf, for all that stuff that happened back then. For what it's worth, I really don't think he meant to hurt you."

Rawlins gives me a suspicious look. "Okay . . . I guess. Is that all?"

"The other thing I wanted to know was . . . what are the chances of me rejoining the team?"

His mouth starts to form a smile, but he suppresses it. "Gosh . . . I don't know. Are you sure?"

I think for a second about my conversation last night with my grandpa. "I'm sure."

"Are you willing to put the effort in, and show your teammates that you really want this?"

"Absolutely. Whatever it takes."

He raises one hand to his chin and taps it lightly, trying to look very serious. "What about winning? Can you be ready in a week and a half to give it your all? We can make a pretty decent play-off run if your heart's in it."

"I can't promise we'll win," I tell him honestly, "but I guarantee I'll give everything I've got."

"Well then," he says slowly, "I suppose we can work something out. Of course, the guys are going to want to see that you're putting in your dues. I might have to give you extra laps for the practices you missed, as a show of good faith."

I don't bother to hide my smile. "I'll run as many laps as you want. Can I practice today?"

"Yep. But the clock is ticking. You better go suit up."

"Thanks, Coach!" I get up from my chair and open the door excitedly, wanting to go tell Dillon the good news. I'm halfway gone when I remember the slip of paper in my pocket. "Oh wait. I almost forgot. About what I said about my dad not wanting to hurt you, I think you should check out this website."

"Why? What is it?"

"My sister's blog."

He looks at me cockeyed again. "Alice?"

I smile once more, as big as I can. "Just check it out, Coach. I promise you won't be disappointed. She's a *really* smart kid." I hesitate briefly, then add, "Especially in science. And history."

Carolyn Bostic

October 29

Sheryl, thanks so much for pointing me to this page! I can't believe Nathan is gone, but reading all of these comments makes me realize that he's sort of still here: He lives on not only in our memories, but in all of the good things we do for others as a result of his kindness toward us. For those of you who don't know, I had to quit work more than 4 yrs ago for personal reasons. I worked with Sheryl (posted earlier), and Nathan was our boss. He had a tradition of bringing beautiful candy baskets for people on their birthdays. Even though I stopped working, he hasn't missed a single one of my birthdays since then! I could always count on a basket of candy at my door. Love you Nathan.

Like • Comment • Share

CHAPTER FORTY-THREE

Madeline

Life is so complicated.

It's only six thirty at night, but I'm already in my pajamas, sipping a cup of tea while staring out the window at the lights of the city below. For whatever reason, watching the busyness on the streets is calming to me — gives me the sense that I can stay above the fray, so to speak, elevated beyond the cares of the world. I could sit here for hours watching the cars and pedestrians go about their business.

I wonder if any of their lives are as convoluted as mine.

As I continue to stare, the thoughts and questions that have resurfaced since Nathan's death take center stage in my mind. It's been a full week since emptying my skeleton-riddled closet at the Steens', so there's plenty to think about.

On one hand, I feel freer now than I have

in decades — spilling my guts was the most liberating experience of my life. On the other hand, there are still a few hooks in my conscience that I don't know how to cut free. Eliza, for starters. My sister still has an image in her head of Grant as this wonderful father who tragically died when his car accidentally hit a tree. Yes, there were times when he was that man that she remembers, but does she deserve to know about the other times? Is it my obligation to tell her? She's all grown up, with a child of her own — should I burden her with that knowledge and potentially spoil her happiness? Will knowing the truth help her in any way, or would it only cause her pain? Am I deceiving her if I omit certain things? Would I want to know if I were in her shoes?

Seriously, why is life so complicated?

There's also Zoe to think about. My daughter's parents raised her to believe that the handsome young man they met in Texas was her father. Admittedly, I never corrected that perception. As she got older, she would ask questions about him whenever I visited, and I always did my best to fill in the blanks. Now that she's getting married, though, she's come right out and said she would like to meet him. I tried to dissuade her, of course, but before she starts having a family of her own, she wants to meet the man who gave her life.

What do I say to that?

It was a mistake when I asked Nathan to go with me to California to meet her, but I told her I'd ask. What do I tell her now? It's the same problem with Eliza — does she really need to know the truth? Would she even want to? Or is the merciful thing to continue pretending?

And then there's Randy Rawlins, the boy whose heart I trampled on, not unlike the number Abby did on his flower at prom. I really messed things up, didn't I? If I could turn back the wheel of time, I'd do things differently. But now? He absolutely hates me. I could see it in every inch of him. Do I dare go tell him what I told the Steens? Would he even believe me, or would he think I'm making it all up to get back into his good graces? It doesn't matter, I guess. I can't bear to face him again, not when he looks at me with such hostility.

With my mind preoccupied, I hardly notice the light rapping on the door. When I hear it a second time, I snap to full attention. For a moment I just sit there, listening for the sound again. It doesn't come, but I set down my teacup anyway to go investigate. "Hello?" I call out as I approach the door. "Is someone there?"

The only response is the sound of my own breathing.

I check the peephole. No one is there. Good thing, because visitors are supposed to ring at the street level, not knock on the door.

Still, not wanting to accept that perhaps it was just my imagination trying to rescue me from another lonely night, I crack open the door to be absolutely sure.

I wasn't hallucinating. On the ground in the hallway is a small white box. The logo on the outside reads, "Velvet Petals."

Nervously, I pick it up, checking both directions in the hallway for any signs of the person who left it. Assured that the coast is clear, I close the door, open the box, and *freeze.* Everything in the world just stops, all at once. My heart, my lungs, my thoughts, and even time itself — all as still as can be.

This must be what death feels like. Except . . . suddenly I'm so alive! Heart racing, pulse quickening, barely breathing.

In the box is a rose. A single, solitary rose. *A blue rose,* fashioned into a corsage. I gently lift it out and slide it onto my wrist as the happiest tears I've ever cried begin to fall. There's only one person in the world who would think to send me a blue rose. At the bottom of the box is a folded piece of paper. I carefully pick it up and read the words aloud. "Anything is possible, Maddy. Even a blue rose. I have a matching blue corsage, and would be honored to spend the rest of the evening getting to know you all over again. Are you up for dinner? If so, I'm standing right outside your door."

When one door closes, another one opens. That's what they say, and I suppose it's true. Sometimes you might wish that the door had stayed shut. But other times, like tonight, you just feel lucky for the chance to lift a trembling arm and turn the handle.

■ ■ ■ ■

PART IV
THE EPILOGUE(S)

■ ■ ■ ■

Sunny Side Up
November 8

I had to go to my alter ego to tell this story. Here goes: I e-mailed my son's teacher a while back to ask her for more time for my son to complete his assignment because I had broken the news that his father would be moving out in a few weeks, and he was upset, got a horrid headache, and was not able to complete his homework that evening. She happens to be the wife of a local minister. She replied and stated she typically didn't tell parents this, but every

August as she prepares her classroom for her new students, as she washes each desk she says a prayer for each new student knowing that life sometimes throws each of us something we are not prepared to handle. I thought that was the most beautiful thing. The washing and the praying for each child touched my heart!! Now, to bring this full circle: since Nathan's passing, I learned that my son's teacher's husband (the minister) got the idea twenty years ago from Nathan's father, Tim Steen, who used to be a pastor in Rockwall. He would do a similar thing for all of the children in his youth group at the start of each new year — wash their seats and say a little prayer for whatever things they were going to have to face that year. Amazing, isn't it, how good things seem to last, passing from one person to the next . . . until they end up helping a little boy like my son in his hour of need on something as simple as a homework assignment. God bless the Steens. God bless everyone who takes private moments to help other people in unseen ways.

Like • Comment • Share

Chapter Forty-Four

Ty

Personally, I blame *Glee*. You know, the hit show where the unpopular kids do all that singing and dancing and get made fun of for it. They're the ones who made slushy baths trendy. As the show grew in popularity, dumping ice-cold slushies on so-called "losers" at my high school became the hottest new way to pick on social outcasts. I never did it myself, but I hate to admit, I also never stopped it when I saw it happening to others.

After hearing the lengths that my dad went to to help Maddy, I promised myself to never again let someone get picked on if I have means to stop it.

That includes my sister, Alice, whether she wants my help or not.

Which brings me, in a most unlikely way, to football.

With two minutes left in our play-off

game, we're still ahead by two points, with possession of the ball right around the fifty-yard line. Coach Rawlins's instruction is to run out the clock by running the ball on every down, since throwing it stops the clock too quickly. So far, it seems to be working. We've already gotten two first downs this way. If we get one more, we'll be able to keep possession until the game expires, earning a ticket to next week's quarterfinals.

Which brings me back to Alice.

She hasn't been to a football game since some brat stuck a hot dog in her hoodie (and another brat let it happen), but tonight she decided she can't let other people's meanness dictate where she goes or what she does. Before we left for the game, she kept saying that if Maddy survived what she went through, then a few ketchup stains are hardly worth worrying about. Still, I find it interesting that she chose to stand within ten yards of the football team along the sideline, where I can keep a close eye on her, rather than braving the bleachers with the rest of the seventh-graders.

On third down, with four yards to go for a first down, I hand the football off to our fullback, who only manages to gain three and a half yards. Since we're well beyond the range of our field-goal kicker, Rawlins signals that we're going for it on fourth down. The play he calls? *Quarterback keeper.* On this particular play, I have the option of either running it straight up the middle or rushing around the left end. Either way, the fate of our football season now depends on my ability to gain half a yard.

Eighteen measly inches, and we win for sure!

Of course, Arlington High School's players have a lot riding on this too. They know that if they stop me, they'll get the ball back with enough time on the clock to try to score.

Because the defense is stacked up tight in the middle, I choose to run to the left. As soon as the ball is hiked, I tuck it in my arm and cut hard. I see Dillon out on the end, holding two linebackers at bay. His block is perfectly executed, leaving me all the space in the world to get around. I look up toward the sideline for the first-down marker, just to make sure I've gone far enough.

That's when I see Alice, standing alone behind the player's bench. She's got her eyes fixed on me, watching the action unfold.

Which brings me back to the slushy baths, because what Alice doesn't notice is the girl sneaking up behind her with an open cup.

I can see I've made it past the first-down marker, and there is plenty of field ahead of me to keep going. If I hurry, there's even a possibility of going the full distance for a touchdown, which would make me the hero of the game.

But the girl behind Alice is raising the plastic cup. If I could, I would run to her and intervene, but the distance is too great.

As I continue sprinting, I think of my teammates and how hard they've worked to get to this point in the play-offs. They've worked hard all season long. Would it be fair to let them down now?

Then I think of my dad, and everything he stood for. He didn't care what the consequences were to himself, so long as he did what he felt was right. What would he do in this situation? Would he let his teammates down, or let his sister down?

Finally, I think of a comment I made to Alice several weeks ago, that I'd stand up for her if given the chance.

Here's a chance . . .

Almost instinctively, I focus on the slushy in the girl's hand, cock my arm, and let the football fly.

As soon as it leaves my grip, the entire stadium gasps. Alice gasps too, her eyes bulging when she sees the ball coming like a bullet at her head. It wouldn't have hit her, but she ducks anyway.

A split second later, the nose of the football drills into the slushy at full speed, sending a grape explosion all over the unsuspecting perpetrator.

Somewhere on the field behind me a whistle blows. The crowd immediately groans as the referee throws a penalty marker. Without looking, I know what the flag is for: *Illegal forward pass, beyond the line of scrimmage.* Five-yard penalty . . . and loss of down.

There are thousands of people who are justifiably mortified by what I just did, but the only spectator I care about is the diminutive seventh-grader behind the bench who is standing up to her full height, beaming from ear to ear.

Coach Rawlins is standing fifteen yards away from Alice, staring in disbelief at the girl who is screaming from the shock of getting baptized with her own slushy. He glances back at me, then back at slushy-girl, and then finally zeroes in on Alice's gigantic grin. At that moment he seems to get it. He turns back to me and gives a little nod. Nothing dramatic, just enough to say, "Nice throw."

A minute later, as the game clock is winding down, Arlington's kicker nails a thirty-five-yard field goal for the come-from-behind win.

The season is over, and I'm to blame for a miserable loss. Expectations were high, and I blew it.

Regrets for what I did? Not a chance, because somewhere, up in heaven, I know my dad is smiling.

Afterward, in the locker room, when I'm fully dressed, I reach into my front pocket as nonchalantly as I can and pull out a tiny blue-green stone, and then move it to the other pocket.

A second later, Dillon approaches. Since losing the game, he's about the only person on the team who's talked to me, and even his words have been sparse. But he's smiling now, and I can tell all is forgiven. "So," he says, "why'd you do it?"

"Do what?"

"Don't play dumb, bro. Why'd you huck that ball at your sister?"

For a second I think of my dad, then of Alice, then of the seven pebbles in the front pockets of my jeans. "Because," I tell him, "one good thing leads to another."

Jennifer Pitcher

November 9

About 20 years ago I was housebound for several months. As the mother of a pre-schooler at the time, with no family in the area, I was blessed to have two wonderful neighbors, Nathan and Halley Steen, who rallied the rest of the neighborhood to provide me with unbelievable assistance in so many ways. Halley even came over and not only trimmed my toenails, but also gave me my first pedi! What a gift!! Nathan and Halley, you blessed my life. Halley, I know you must be hurting . . . let me know how I can help you. Now it's your turn to sit and let me wash your feet . . .

Like • Comment • Share

Chapter Forty-Five

MY OWN LITTLE WONDERLAND:
November 11th

Dear Blog, it's me, Alice.
Last Friday, a miracle happened! On the last play of his high school career, Ty effectively forfeited the game by throwing the ball right at Ashley Simmons, just to keep her from dumping a loaded slushy on my head. He hit the cup dead center, making a huge mess all over her!

I've never been more thankful to have a big brother.

Most of the kids at my school were at the game, so they all saw what happened. If they weren't there, they probably still saw what happened, because it was covered all weekend on the local sports news. One of the cameramen caught the whole play from the perfect angle, and they kept showing the clip over and over in slow motion as the cup blew up in her face. One broadcaster dubbed it the "frozen explosion."

HI-LAR-I-OUS!

It's already gotten thousands of hits on YouTube, and I even heard that ESPN played it on their highlight reel!

Suddenly, I'm a celebrity with all the kids. Not just for being on the video, but because I'm the little sister of the guy who threw the ball. Now that the sting of losing the game has worn off, everyone thinks it's really cool what Ty did.

As for Ashley? Well, today at school was rough for her. Everyone she thought were her friends — even those who encouraged her to dump the slushy on me in the first place — have left her high and dry (is that a pun?). Suddenly *no one* wants to be her friend. The new "cool" thing to do in the halls is to mimic her reaction when she was dripping with frozen goo. In truth, the look on her face *was* priceless, but I hated seeing her being made fun of, even if she deserved it.

The teasing, however, wasn't the worst of it. Two eighth-grade boys snuck out over lunch to get extra-large slushies at the gas station up the road. One of their friends had his cell phone handy to record them getting Ashley in the face again when she came down the hallway.

Lucky for me, I was standing right there when it was going down. The first thing I saw was the kid with the cell phone pointed at Ashley, who was walking alone with her head down. Then I saw the two boys coming at her from the other direction with these ugly smiles on their faces. Each of them had their slushy open, ready to fire.

Part of me thought I should just let her get what she had coming.

But then I thought of Maddy. And my dad. There are just some things that nobody deserves to endure.

I should know.

So what did I do? Well, I did the only thing a four-foot, ten-inch seventh-grade girl can do in situations like this: I screamed.

I screamed so loud and hard and high-pitched that even the boys with the slushies stopped dead in their tracks. Then I walked up to Ashley and locked her arm with mine.

"Go ahead!" I shouted at the boys. "If being mean makes you feel cool, go ahead and dump those on us! Give everyone a good laugh at our expense!"

The boys didn't take kindly to me standing up to them, so they walked up and dumped them on us, just like I told them to.

Afterward, while we were still dripping wet, Ashley gave me a big hug and apologized for everything. Then we went straight to the principal's office and told him what happened. Call me a snitch if you want to, but what those guys did was wrong, and they deserved to be punished. The video evidence on the one boy's phone was enough to get all three suspended.

Once we were dry, when nobody was looking, I took one of the small pink pebbles from my left pocket and transferred it to the right side.

There's no way to be sure, but I kind of think my dad would be proud.

Jenelle Christensen
November 11
I call this the "nobody-could-ever-do-anything-nicer-for-me story." I was pregnant with Samantha and had been super busy coaching the high school dance team, and I just didn't have time to get the house in order like I wanted to. A few days before a big dance competition, a Dr. told me that I was measuring small and hadn't grown in several appointments. They were worried the baby wasn't growing and were waiting until the day after the competition to do an ultrasound, and felt they would probably do a C-section then. I was in a panic, not only worried about the baby, but how I was to bring a new baby home to such a disaster. On top of that, I was told to stay on partial bed rest until the ultrasound, so I couldn't really do anything to

improve the state of things around the house. My husband, Todd, was busy that week in court, so he couldn't help either. But Nathan and Halley Steen caught wind of our predicament, and they persuaded Todd to let them in the house while we were getting the ultrasound done (which took the better part of a day). They brought the whole family with them, and by the time we got home, the house was immaculate. They even bought some things to decorate the baby's room, which I hadn't gotten around to yet. When I walked through the front door, I cried such thankful tears. I will never be able to begin to express what that meant to me!

Like • Comment • Share

CHAPTER FORTY-SIX

Madeline

Six months ago, in one of my e-mails to Nathan, I asked him if he'd consider going to my daughter's wedding with me. I knew it was a long shot, but I figured I had to at least ask, and I had promised Zoe I would.

I know, shame on me for encouraging deceit in their marriage. I'm not proud of that, by the way. It was grossly unfair of me to ask him to further perpetuate a fantasy that had already taken a tremendous toll on him. But that was all before Nathan's accident, before my lies came full circle and nearly destroyed his legacy with his own wife and children. Since then, after seeing how covering up the truth hurt so many people, I've decided to tell Zoe who her father really was.

The only problem is figuring out how.

During the past several months leading up to the wedding I must've crafted twenty different letters, each of them breaking the news to her from a slightly different angle. In the end, none of them felt quite right, so they landed in the trash. I called her a few times too, intending to spill the beans over the phone, but once I had her on the line, I could never quite bring myself to do it.

So — and I know on the surface this sounds awful — while Randy is driving me to the airport to fly out for the wedding, I make up my mind once and for all. "I'm going to tell her while I'm out there," I tell him. "In person."

"You're not serious," he says. "That's possibly the worst wedding present ever."

"What is? The truth? I'm not ashamed of it anymore, Randy, and I want her to know that. Zoe's a brilliant young woman, with a wonderful future ahead of her, but as she moves toward that future, I think it's only fair that she fully understand her past."

For a moment or two he doesn't respond. Then, while still looking at the road ahead, he asks, "Would you want to know, if you were her?"

I've asked myself that a thousand times, but haven't yet found the answer, so I don't respond.

A few minutes later we pull up to the curb. Randy steps around the front of the car, opens my door, then grabs my suitcase from the trunk. After setting it down on the curb, he reaches his arms around me and pulls me close. "Don't do it," he says softly, his face close to mine. "Let the past stay in the past, Maddy. It's time to move on. Those of us who needed to know the truth, do. There's no shame in what happened to you, and there's no shame in how Zoe came to be, but let the truth rest in peace."

"That's just it," I tell him. "I'm not sure the truth can rest. Not when she still believes the lie."

"Would you want to know?" he asks, repeating his question from before.

To avoid answering, I lean in and kiss him good-bye.

Ah . . . the magic! I'm not entirely sure how it happened, but somehow, with our ancient past cleared up, Randy and I managed to start over. Officially, we've been dating for the past four months, but I swear, every time we touch it's like we're right back in the middle of the dance floor at prom, kissing for the first time.

"I'd better get going," I say. "They're going to start boarding in thirty minutes."

"Well, have a good flight and enjoy the wedding." He stops to give me another little peck on the lips. "And think about what I said."

"I will, I will, and I'll think about it."

"You'll think about thinking about it?"

I wink at him as I grab my suitcase and head for the terminal. "Uh-huh."

The next day, now just two days before the wedding, I'm sitting in the hotel lobby waiting for Zoe and her fiancé, Greg, to pick me up. They're taking me out to lunch so we can have some alone time before the wedding festivities kick into high gear. As I'm watching people walk through the hotel door, my leg is bouncing nervously. I've given a lot of thought to what Randy said, and I must say, I'm torn. On the one hand, even if I'm only Zoe's biological mother, and not the woman who raised her, I don't want there to be any lies between us. I've seen firsthand what that can do, and it scares me. What if years later she discovers the truth and hates me for being dishonest?

Or, what if telling her now puts an unnecessary wedge in our relationship? Will she resent me for that too? Will knowing why I gave her up as a baby cause her any pain?

I'm fiddling with the beads on my necklace, with all these thoughts going through my head, when I hear Zoe's voice. "Madeline?"

I don't mind that she calls me by my first name. After all, her mother rightfully earned the title of "Mom," not me. I look up to find a tall, slender woman approaching, locked hand-in-hand with an even taller man. They look so cute together I can hardly stand it. "Zoe!" I shout as I jump up and give her a Texas-sized hug. "It's so good to see you again!" I step back, look her over once more from head to toe, and then turn to the gentleman at her side. "And you must be Greg," I say as I embrace him too. "I've heard so much about you."

"Whatever she said, it's not true," he jokes.

"Well, isn't that a shame," I respond. I'm about to add a comment about how smart she made him out to be over the phone, when I hear my name again. Only it doesn't come from Zoe or Greg.

My heart skips a little beat as the voice registers in my brain. Fast as I can, I spin around to find the tallest man in the room standing just three feet behind me. "Randy! What on earth are you doing here?"

In half a stride Randy moves close enough to give me a kiss. "Miss me?"

"Yeah, but . . . you're supposed to be back in Dallas."

Turning, I briefly introduce Randy to Zoe and Greg as my "special friend" from Texas.

Randy smiles at me, but it's not a smile I recognize. "Did you tell them?" he asks, dropping his voice just a hair.

I pretend not to know what he's talking about. "Huh?"

I'm hoping he'll get the hint that I don't want to bring that up right now, but he says, "You know, what we talked about on the way to the airport."

I take a moment to glance back at Zoe and Greg, who are still smiling, but obviously curious about Randy's line of questioning.

Darn him!

I wish he hadn't mentioned anything, at least not right now. Timing is everything in matters such as this, and his timing is downright terrible. "No," I say, hoping my clenched teeth will clue him in to drop it. "Not yet."

"Oh, good," he says, still smiling. "That's why I came; I decided I wanted to be here when you told her the truth."

"The truth?" asks Zoe, now fully intrigued. "About what?"

I turn to Randy and give him a little scowl.

Oh, that man is going to hear about this tonight! He has no right to stick his nose in any of this! If I was going to tell Zoe, it needed to be on *my* terms, when the timing was right, not brought up haphazardly like we're talking about the weather. But now he's backed me into a corner. "Uh, let's talk about it later," I tell her. "After lunch."

"Nah," says Randy. "Let's tell her now. No time like the present to set the record straight."

I give him another sharp look. This one, I hope, sinks through his thick, bald skull: *Stay out of my business!*

Somewhat embarrassed, I turn back to Zoe and Greg. "Well . . . I suppose. Though I hardly think this is the time or the place."

"Sure it is," gushes Randy. "Why wait?"

"Madeline," says Zoe. "Whatever it is, you can tell me."

I take a deep breath. This is so awkward, with people walking by, and with Greg, whom I've only just met, standing right there. I wanted this to be a private discussion, between me and my daughter. Alone. I suppose I could hold my ground and say no, and just defer until later, but after Randy's insistence, not telling her now would seem like I'm hiding something.

"Fine," I say at length, trying to maintain my composure. The last thing I want to do is say this in a way that suggests I'm embarrassed by what happened to me in high school. After all, what happened wasn't my fault. I was victimized, but I'm not willing to play the part of a victim. If she's to know about it, I want her to see me as strong and resilient, and nothing but proud that I was able to bear a daughter as radiant as she is. "Zoe," I start, "I don't know the best way to approach this."

I can see the concern on her face. "Just say it," she gently prods.

I take another gulp of air. "I know how much you've wanted to meet your biological father."

She smiles. "Yes."

"Right. Well, what I need to explain . . . er, what I'd like you to know, which I've been wanting to tell you for several months now, is that the man who conceived you —."

"Was killed in a car accident."

I snap my head to the right, gawking at Randy, who resolutely stares back. I can scarcely believe what I just heard come from his mouth.

"There," he tells me. "Now she knows." Randy turns to my daughter, whose eyes are wide as can be. "I know it's terrible timing for such news. We've gone back and forth about whether to tell you now or after the honeymoon. Finally we decided, since

515

there's obviously no way he can come to your wedding to meet you, you should know why."

"Oh . . . wow," she says, rightfully sounding stunned. "I mean, yeah — better to know now, so I'm not wondering if every stranger I see at the reception is him, right?"

"Right," Greg adds.

"I'm so sorry, Zoe," I say. "I hate to be the bearer of bad news."

With a sad smile she replies, "It's okay. It's not like I knew him."

"But you wanted to know him."

She agrees with a nod. "But I still have my family. I still have everyone who loves me." She straightens her shoulders and wraps an arm around Greg. "I've got too many reasons to be happy, to be sad about losing someone I never had." She hesitates. "Thank you, Madeline, for telling me."

"Of course." I breathe a sigh of relief, feeling grateful to Randy for helping me give Zoe a nugget of truth about her father. If nothing else, it's a good start. *He is dead. Died in a car accident.*

Who knows, maybe that will be all the truth she needs.

I check my watch. "Well, we should probably get going if we want to make our reservation. Do you think they'll have room for Randy?"

"There's always room for one more," Zoe says.

Randy pats his stomach. "Thank goodness. I could eat a horse."

Greg and Zoe lock hands and lead us out to his car. As we walk, I let the nearly-weds get far enough ahead that they can't hear what I tell Randy as I wrap one arm around him and thread a finger through his belt loop. "I'm not saying I don't appreciate it, but what got into you to come all the way out here like that?"

"Just doing one good thing," he says with a chuckle. He pauses, then adds, "I figure if your first husband was so good at helping people, then why not your second husband?"

"You know very well there was never a first —." I have to stop walking so I can replay that last part in my head. "What did you say?"

Randy's sudden nervousness reminds me of the gangly boy in fourth grade who was scared to admit he had a crush on the tall girl with glasses. "I said 'husband,'" he says softly. "If you'll have me."

I could shout for joy, but instead I drape my arms over his tall, broad shoulders, and stand up on my tiptoes to give him my answer in the form of a kiss. "It'll be the one good thing I've ever done."

Gail Rising
November 14
I don't know where I heard this quote from, but I like it: "Today, at this very moment in time, is as far into the future as you can go." To me that means we shouldn't waste time worrying about things that have yet to happen, but instead focus on how we're spending our time at this very instant. I probably didn't know Nathan Steen as well as some of you, but I like to think he was my friend. He was such a great example to me because he really knew how to live in the "now." Just look at all the things he did for others! It would be hard to find a time when he wasn't actively engaged in a good cause. We love and miss you, Nathan. Thanks to you and your family for the ways in which you blessed my life.

Like • Comment • Share

AUTHOR'S NOTE

While working on *The One Good Thing,* I
sent out a request on Facebook for "random
acts of kindness" that people have experienced in their lives (not that any such acts
are ever random). The responses I got were
incredible! The Facebook comments at the
end of the chapters of this book are a
sampling of the real-life experiences shared
by my Facebook friends. Most of them have
been modified slightly to fit the story, but
the basic acts themselves are real — even if
Nathan Steen didn't do all of those things,
someone did. Thanks to everyone for inspiring me! These little Facebook vignettes suc-
cinctly confirm the very thing I hoped to
explore in the novel: that opportunities for
kindness, service, selflessness, and love of
our fellow man abound, so long as we're
willing to open our hearts and lend a hand.

Although the book is done, I would still
love to hear about all of the ways in which

you have either shown or received special acts of kindness over the years. If you would like to share your own "one good things," be they big or small, I invite you to post them directly on my Facebook page. A link to Facebook can be found at www.kevina milne.com.

I look forward to hearing from you!

Kevin Alan Milne

ACKNOWLEDGMENTS

I was listening recently to one of my younger children saying a prayer before going to bed, and I had to chuckle when I heard the phrase "Thank you for dirt." I know, I shouldn't have laughed. Upon further reflection, I realized that my child was actually setting a great example, reminding me of the many little things I have to be grateful for and the importance of expressing that gratitude. With that in mind, there are a number of people I would like to recognize for their help with *The One Good Thing.*

First and foremost, my wife, Rebecca. Without her wisdom, insight, love, support, encouragement, cheerleading, and patience, I could not do this. Period. Thank you, Bec! I love you so much.

My children have contributed to the cause too, if only by allowing me to do what I do when I need to do it. Thank you, Mikayla, Kamry, Mary, Emma, and Kyler for not complaining during those times when I've had to lock the door and say, "Not now . . . I have to write." Your smiles keep me smiling and your laughter keeps me laughing, even through the stress of deadlines. I'm so proud of everything you do.

Thanks to Christina Boys, who has now edited all five of my books (hmmm . . . a glutton for punishment?). She is as insightful as she is professional and I'm so grateful for her efforts on my behalf. Same goes for publisher Rolf Zettersten and his entire team at Hachette/Center Street, who continue to amaze me with their talents.

My mother deserves special props for her willingness to preread and edit on the fly, usually with a very short runway. I don't even mind that her opinions are occasionally partial; her feedback has become an important part of my process. And not to be outdone, my dad has gotten in on the action too, reading the manuscripts just a chapter or two behind my mom. I'm incredibly blessed to have such loving and supportive parents.

Special thanks to the Loop Café in Wilsonville — your free Wi-Fi, soft lounge chairs, and chocolate shakes made lunchtime writing a treat.

To the Metzgers, thank you for drawing

our name last summer in the raffle — what you created as a child's playhouse has become a perfect man-cave for my writing (aka "The Writer's Block").

Jason Wright managed to slip one good thing in *Recovering Charles* several years ago. So thanks, Jason, for beating me to the punch!

I'd like to express my gratitude to all of the international publishers for your wonderful translations and beautiful covers on my previous books — I hope you continue to find value in my work.

Thanks again to everyone who shared their stories with me on Facebook. Keep 'em coming!

And last, but far from least, thanks to all of the readers out there who have chosen to spend a few hours immersed in my words. I love the thrill of putting stories on paper, but without someone to read them it would all be for naught. Of course, if you enjoyed what you read, then let me thank you in advance for telling a friend!

There are probably others I'm forgetting at the moment. If not being mentioned here makes you feel like dirt, don't worry . . . I'm thankful for dirt!

READER'S GUIDE

1. What are the key themes of *The One Good Thing*? Which of those themes is most relevant in your own life?
2. As an adult, Nathan seems to be an amazing man who leads a life of goodness, but as his story unfolds, we see him as a human being with imperfections. What influences Nathan to go from a boy who shoots spit wads at people during church to one who is more concerned with the welfare of others? Do you believe that the change was genuine?
3. What is the most important lesson that Ty learns through the discovery of his father's past?
4. Bullying, in various forms, appears throughout the book. How does Alice's life compare to Madeline's childhood? How are the two experiences similar and how are they different?
5. Have you ever stood up for someone even

though you knew it would be very difficult? Have you ever failed to help someone when you probably should have?

6. In the beginning of the book we learn that Ty failed to protect his sister from the meanness of others. How did learning about his father's past influence his decision to help his sister in the end?

7. Is Nathan's "lie" to his wife and children justified because of whom he was protecting? Do you feel that Nathan was true to his family in keeping a promise of youth?

8. Do you think Halley's anger and feelings of betrayal toward her deceased husband were justified? Have you ever felt anger toward someone without having all the facts?

9. Many think that bullying consists of physical harm. What other forms of bullying are there? What can teenagers do to make a difference in the lives of their classmates?

10. In fiction, a foil is a character who contrasts with another character in order to highlight certain qualities of the other. What "foils" do you recognize in the story?

11. How has reading *The One Good Thing* influenced you as a person?

12. Through the book we learn that sometimes it is the little things that influence

others for good. What can you do in your
everyday life to make a difference in the
lives of those around you?

13. What's the nicest thing that anyone has
ever done for you?

ABOUT THE AUTHOR

Kevin Alan Milne is the author of *The Paper Bag Christmas, The Nine Lessons, Sweet Misfortune,* and *The Final Note.* He earned an MBA at Pennsylvania State University. Born in Portland, Oregon, Milne grew up in the nearby quiet country town of Sherwood, Oregon, where he currently resides with his wife and five children. His website can be found at KevinAMilne.com.